To Jal

Best

Carol M Creasey

2022

EVIL WOMAN

EVIL WOMAN

Carol M. Creasey

UNITED WRITERS
Cornwall

UNITED WRITERS PUBLICATIONS LTD
Ailsa, Castle Gate, Penzance, Cornwall.
www.unitedwriters.co.uk

British Library Cataloguing in Publication Data:
A catalogue record for this book is
available from the British Library.

ISBN 9781852001605

Printed and bound in Great Britain by
United Writers Publications Ltd.,
Cornwall.

This is for Keith, who has
supported me in many ways,
including the publication of this
book, with all his encouragement.

Chapter One

Sadie Morton Brown was born on a day in January. The weather was stormy, the wind howled, and the rain lashed at the windows, as her mother, Isabel, struggled to push her daughter into the world. Sadie's lusty cry of protest confirmed she was strong, and Isabel temporarily forgot her pain when she was able to hold her daughter.

"She's a healthy girl!" said Dr James Martin, exultantly. He was relieved.

Isabel had requested to have her child at home. It was her first, and James had advised a good private hospital. But Isabel was having none of it, and her husband Philip was a close associate of James, which made him anxious to please them, but not to the detriment of the mother or the baby. He had told them that if there were any complications, an ambulance would be called.

Luckily it had all been straightforward. Isabel hadn't wanted a midwife. She had wanted James because he had taken care of her family for years, and he was pleased that all had gone well.

"Well done, she's perfect!" enthused Philip, gazing at his daughter. She had a shock of jet black hair, just like her mother, and he fell for her straight away. He watched as James handed the baby to the nurse to wash her, realising that now their lives would never be the same again.

"She's a feisty little one!" said James, as Sadie continued to protest, even after she had been made comfortable.

"What's wrong?" said Isabel anxiously.

"Nothing at all!" said James. "Her heart and lungs are fine, she'll settle down soon, and you won't even know you've got a baby."

But, sadly for Isabel, this had not been the case. Sadie was a baby who cried and raged her way through her first few years, except when her father held her. She smiled at him, and only he could soothe her. Isabel had lost count of the times she had called Dr Martin. He could never find anything wrong with Sadie, but as she developed, so did her temper, and her stubbornness. Isabel found it hard to love her, and she didn't understand her. She tried to soothe and cuddle her daughter when she was upset, which was frequently, but Sadie rejected her, she only wanted Philip.

Sadie's babyhood passed, and the family settled into an uneasy way of life. Isabel had wanted another child, but Sadie had been so difficult, she had waited. Even taking on a nanny to help her hadn't eased the situation. Sadie had hated all her nannies, and had played up so much, that one by one they had left, shaking their heads and saying they couldn't cope with such a difficult child.

Isabel had taken her to a psychologist; but Sadie was cute. She had a charming side, that only Philip usually saw, so she used it on the psychologist, and Isabel appeared to be the one with a problem: a nervous lady, lacking in confidence, who couldn't cope with her daughter, a bright adventurous girl, growing up, full of spirit. This is the conclusion that the psychologist came to, and he kindly advised Isabel not to take life too seriously, and to enjoy her bright, feisty, and very attractive daughter.

Isabel was aware of Sadie's love for her father, and his tendency to spoil her, and couldn't help feeling jealous of their close relationship. She didn't feel that Philip was backing her as he should, she felt the odd one out, which she knew was ridiculous. Maybe having another baby would be the answer, one for her to be close to, and Sadie would have to learn to share, which would surely do her good.

Philip agreed. He was a man who wanted a peaceful life, and his wife was just as strong-willed as Sadie. He sometimes felt caught in the middle of them.

So when Sadie was ten, Jeremy was born, and he returned Isabel's warmth and love in a way that Sadie never had done. Philip, too, was delighted to have a son, but in consideration of Sadie, he tried very hard not to make too much of Jeremy when she was around.

Sadie resented her brother very much, although she hid it from her father. She didn't see why she should share his love with a spoiled baby who cried to get attention. When she was eleven she was sent to boarding school. Daddy had said it was to give her the very best education, so she could have the best chances in life with her considerable talents, but Sadie believed it was just to get her out of the way. It was bound to have been her mother's idea, Daddy would not have wanted her to go really, and she hated her mother with a renewed passion.

It was whilst she was at home during the summer holidays that an opportunity to change things presented itself to her. Sadie was now thirteen, and Jeremy was three. His nanny was a young woman called Sarah.

On this particular day Sadie had heard Sarah on her mobile phone; she was having man trouble. When Sadie's parents were out, Sarah spent a lot of her time on the phone, and this time Jeremy was playing near the swimming pool. Sadie could see him from behind the bushes, so whilst Sarah's back was turned, she did it, she pushed him into the water, and watched with grim satisfaction as he tried to scream, with water choking his lungs, and held his arms out to her for help.

Eventually his body became lifeless, and by the time Sarah had returned, her mind still on her own troubles, it was too late. The police and the ambulance were called, but nothing could alter the fact that Jeremy was dead, drowned in his own swimming pool, whilst his nanny had been chatting on her mobile phone, not close enough to keep an eye on him.

Sadie had given her evidence, how she had heard him scream from the house, and came running down, but it had been too late, and Sarah had been nowhere around. She had even plunged into the water to save him, but hadn't succeeded, which was confirmed by the paramedics; she was still bringing him out when they arrived, but he was already dead.

Sarah protested that she hadn't heard him scream. She had only been a few yards away and she hadn't heard Sadie come out either, but nobody believed her. Through her carelessness, a three year old child had died, and a devastated Isabel and Philip had pursued her through the courts for child neglect. It didn't bring Jeremy back, but it did stop her from ever working with children again. She was given a suspended sentence, and with her reputation destroyed, was forced, eventually, to go and live abroad.

Sadie had hoped that with Jeremy gone, she would once again be the centre of her father's world. But his death hadn't stopped her parents from caring. To work through their grief, they had formed a support group for bereaved parents, and much of their spare time was spent at meetings and seeing people they felt they could help. Jeremy was still very much alive in their minds.

Sadie was angry. She had achieved nothing. She had tried pretending to Daddy that she missed her brother very much, and although he had taken her in his arms and comforted her, he had then asked her to give her mother some love and support, and even suggested that she could help them in their support group. It was hopeless! She had failed! Her father would never be distracted from this new interest in his life. She had no pity for either of them; Sadie didn't do pity. So at the age of seventeen, after failing miserably at school, she left home to go and live in a squat, with her current, and in the eyes of her parents, totally unsuitable, boyfriend.

Chapter Two

Sadie sat in the little tea shop trying to make her drink last as long as possible. It was cold, wet, and rainy, and she had almost no money left.

One thing she was certain of, she was not going to admit defeat and go home. Even Daddy had no time for her any more. She hardened her heart at the thought of it. Even with Jeremy off the scene, he wasn't like he used to be with her. She felt hatred and jealousy raging away inside her. She didn't regret killing Jeremy, he had been in the way, her only regret was her father's indifference towards her since. After all, it wasn't as if he knew what had happened. It seemed to have been a very tragic accident.

The door opened, bringing with it a strong gust of wind as a reminder of what was in store for her, and she glanced up from her reverie, and watched the man as he came in.

He was about five foot ten, stockily built, with brown hair, which was soaking wet, and he tried to push it back from his face, grimacing as the water dripped down towards his neck. He removed his coat, putting it round the back of a nearby chair, and flopped wearily into it. Then he looked up in an attempt to catch the eye of the waitress, who came over, reluctantly, and before he had a chance to speak, announced, in a bored voice. "Tea only now, we close at five!"

Martin Skinner was fed up. He had been waiting for an hour for a blind date that he had arranged via a chat room, he was wet through, and now this miserable waitress wanted to close the only warm place for miles, just when he needed a cup of tea. He put on his most ingratiating smile, hoping it would work. "I would love a cup of tea, it's so nasty out there."

She did not return his smile, but to his relief, she quickly brought him a cup of tea. Glancing at his watch, he could see why. He only had ten minutes before the dreaded five o'clock.

He noticed the young woman at the next table whilst he was sipping his tea. She looked about eighteen, her face was beautiful, with very dark eyes, her skin cream and flawless, and her long straight hair was black and shiny. He found her fascinating, and to his surprise, she looked directly at him and smiled.

Martin was a very ordinary looking man, and he didn't exactly have adoring women dropping at his feet. At the age of thirty he still lived at home with his mother who was divorced. He worked in an office with computers, and he spent most of his spare time at home on his own computer, hence the idea of entering a chat room to find a date.

He smiled back at her, remarking, "It certainly is wild out there. Trust me to find somewhere that's about to close!" He glanced over at the waitress, who remained unmoved, and he now only had five minutes left.

Sadie could see he was no oil painting, but she was desperate. An ugly man was better than no man at all. She stood, stretching her arms up to display her bare midriff, knowing he could see her slim legs encased in tight jeans. She knew, by the look on his face, that he was impressed, and so he should be! Normally she could do much better than this.

She went in for the kill. "My name is Sadie," she said smiling, although underneath she could feel revulsion towards him. She could act a part when necessary.

Martin took her outstretched hand, which was as soft as he had imagined, looked into those dark eyes, and was absolutely smitten. "Hi, I'm Martin," he said softly, holding her gaze. Never mind the blind date! That paled into insignificance. He was flattered that such a sultry looking beauty had even spoken to him. She had class, too, and breeding, the way she spoke, and moved, graceful like a cat. He wanted to know more about her. He also stood up.

Sadie put on her most forlorn look, making her big eyes mist with tears. It always worked, and she needed to win his sympathy to get money out of him, but with men that was usually quite easy.

They were all fools for a pair of legs and a good time. She'd have to give him that to sweeten him up. Then when the time was right, she could empty his wallet, and be on her way.

She picked up her umbrella, and the hold-all containing the clothes she had with her, then putting on a sad voice, she said softly, "I don't know where I'm going, really. I've just left my boyfriend. He's an alcoholic, and I couldn't take it any more. He kept hitting me, and now I've got nowhere to go." And just to make it all seem real, she allowed a few tears to fall onto her face, which she quickly dabbed with a tissue.

Martin's protective instinct was stirred. What a rat to treat a beautiful girl like that so roughly! Some people didn't know how lucky they were. Mother was always wishing he would get a nice girl. He ignored the little voice inside him that suggested that Mother might think this one was too young. She might be out of his league, but right now she needed a friend, and he was the only person around.

He gently took hold of her arm. "Let me take you somewhere to eat, and then we can work out what's best for you," he suggested. Sadie allowed herself to flash him a smile of gratitude, and without looking back at the waitress, they left the tea shop, dodging the raindrops, and found his car.

Isabel was a strong and determined woman, but right now she felt as if she had the weight of the world on her shoulders. Hadn't it been enough, that her dearly beloved baby Jeremy had been taken from her? Now her husband Philip was falling apart, and all because of Sadie.

Wasn't life cruel? The child she had been so close to was gone, and Sadie, the daughter she had never been able to understand, was left. Maybe it was a wicked thought, but she had frequently wished that it had been the other way round. She had tried really hard to love Sadie, but Sadie hadn't loved her, and Isabel knew it; she had been rejected by her own daughter.

In fact, Sadie had never loved anyone other than Philip. Isabel had felt that Sadie had an unhealthy fixation for her father, and she had even told him not to encourage it as Sadie grew older. They had sent her to boarding school, out of harm's way, and for that brief time Isabel had been at her happiest, having Jeremy, and being able to devote her time to such a loving little son. The all too familiar pain shot through her insides at the thought of his loss.

It may have been five years ago, but to Isabel it was just like yesterday. The only way to keep her sanity had been to form a support group for bereaved families. Helping others might help themselves, and Philip had been a part of it too, but now, since Sadie had left home a few months ago, Philip had lost interest in the support group. He had tried keeping in touch with her by ringing her mobile, but had never been able to get through, so she'd either lost it or changed the number. No surprise there, over the years Sadie had so much money spent on her that she didn't value anything.

Isabel had told Philip that Sadie would be back when she tired of Jake. Well, apparently, six months down the line, it had happened. Jake was back home and penniless. Like all spoiled rich kids; back to enjoy the good life again, but without Sadie. He complained that Sadie had spent all his money, and then left him. Isabel had to admit that sounded just like Sadie, but to Jake's vindictive mother, Rebecca, she had defended Sadie, telling her that she had no doubt that Jake had spent the money too, hence his reason for coming home. That hadn't gone down too well, but Isabel was past caring. She had always been a person to speak her own mind, and the loss of Rebecca's good will towards her was of no consequence.

She glanced over at Philip, once a very handsome man, but the signs of ageing were there. His dark hair was turning grey, although it did make him look distinguished. He was still slim, with long legs and a wiry body, no middle-aged spread there. He ate nothing but organic foods, and although in the past he had exercised well, and played tennis, he no longer did. Since Sadie had left he hadn't eaten properly, didn't shave very often, and had generally let himself go. Isabel was tired of it all: even when she wasn't there, Sadie still managed to take him away from her!

Philip put the handset down wearily. He hadn't been able to sleep since he had heard that Sadie had split up with Jake. Where was she? She was still only a child. If only Isabel could show some concern too.

"It's useless ringing that mobile. You know that!" she snapped accusingly, sick of it all. Their life just seemed to be one big drama.

Philip was a very even-tempered man. Up until five years ago he had been a very contented man with a beautiful wife and daughter, and a bonny young son. Since Jeremy had died, life had been hell. He understood what a loss it had been to Isabel, and it had been to him too, but he knew he would survive as long as he still had Sadie. His stunning daughter, who had worshipped him since the day she was born, and he had been so proud of her. She was so like her mother, this was maybe why they didn't get on, but he was sure that Sadie would grow out of it. After all, children always loved their mother. And Isabel didn't handle her right, so he had been in the middle, placating them both, and although he hadn't wanted it, he had fallen in with Isabel's wish to send her to boarding school. Isabel had been worried that Sadie's fixation for him would get out of hand as she got older, and wanted to discourage it. He had told her quite clearly that he never thought about her in any other way than as a daughter. Isabel had been shocked, but that's what she had thought, they both knew it, so Sadie had to go.

Lately he found a panic setting in. His life just seemed to be going out of control. He found it hard to deal with stress, and when he heard that Jake was back home without Sadie, he thought the worst. Sadie could be in a ditch somewhere, or kidnapped, even murdered, and judging by her attitude, Isabel didn't even care! Something inside him snapped, and a raging voice that seemed to be coming from inside him shouted, "Our daughter has gone, we don't even know if she's alive or dead. Do you even care?"

Isabel looked at him, surprised. So there was still some passion there, but only for his daughter. "I'm as worried as you," she said quietly. "But Sadie will turn up when she wants to. Jake said she's OK. There's nothing we can do. She's eighteen, and legally old enough to leave home."

Philip knew she was right, but she seemed so calm about it. If only Sadie would just let them know she was all right. Then maybe he could sleep at night. "I think I'll go and speak to Jake and his parents. Maybe they know where she is," he told her.

"It's up to you, but Rebecca may be unfriendly. She blames Sadie for spending all of Jake's money," Isabel reminded him.

"I don't care about that. What did he do to make her want to leave him?" said Philip darkly, and Isabel glanced at him again.

Gone was the friendly easy-going man she had married, this desperate and haunted looking man had taken over, but he was still a fool, always believing it was anyone else's fault other than Sadie.

Well, at least she knew for sure he would make an effort to smarten himself up if he was going to see them, so that would be a good thing. If he found out where Sadie was, chances are he would visit her, and if she told him she didn't want to come home, he would accept that, and then maybe they could all get on with their lives. Maybe she should offer to go with him. It was better to present a united front.

"I'll come with you. I can get changed whilst you're shaving and getting yourself ready," said Isabel pointedly, taking control as always.

Philip looked at her gratefully. He liked it that way. Isabel had always been the dominant one. With her beside him, they would find out about Sadie from Jake, and then maybe he could seek her out and persuade her to come home.

Chapter Three

Martin's world had suddenly been ripped apart by an emotion that he had never experienced the like of before. He was in love, so in love, with the crazy and unpredictable Sadie! It had happened with such overwhelming force, that he had no power to stop it, nor did he even want to.

He had stepped out of his safe, but boring world, into Sadie's world. First of all they had eaten well at an Indian restaurant, and then found a pub. He found her excellent company, and so brave, just dismissing the hard times she had suffered with her boyfriend as "Now in the past." She wanted to move on, and with him, it seemed! They had both got really drunk, and then gone onto a night club. It had been great, he had never behaved in such an outrageous fashion before, and the experience was so liberating. To hell with the cost, he didn't care!

Until then, Martin's life had been very quiet. He didn't remember his father, he had been a baby when his parents had parted, and his mother had stopped all contact. He had been told, for as long as he could remember, that his father was no good, and he had grown up knowing how much his mother depended on him. He was gauche, and unsure of himself, so had never had many friends, and once he had learned to drive, that was it, Mother seemed to need him even more to run her about. He didn't resent it, because he needed some sort of company, but he realised, as he was getting older, her company wasn't enough, and he had noticed, that although she told everyone that she hoped he would meet a nice girl one day, whenever he spoke

17

about Ann from the office, or any other female, her face darkened.

He was thirty now, and some people had even hinted he might be gay. He had heard whisperings at work, and it hurt. He had never had sex yet, although this was a closely guarded secret. The only experience had been when he was about thirteen, a quick fumble with his cousin's friend Jenny. She was now married with a couple of children, by all accounts, and had probably forgotten all about it, but Martin had never forgotten how exciting he had found it, touching a woman's intimate parts, so he was sure he wasn't gay, he didn't fancy men!

He had entered the chat room deliberately to find a date, but he hadn't told his mother, she wouldn't have approved. He didn't like lying, but he'd said he was going to help his friend Mark get rid of a computer virus. Mother had not been entirely convinced, so he'd had to wear very casual clothes so as not to make her more suspicious. He tried not to think about how hard it would be when he did have to admit to having a girlfriend. He didn't want to spoil his evening.

They had left the night club at about three in the morning. Martin was full of good will, and his mother seemed a million miles away. It was too late to find somewhere to stay, and he couldn't drive anyway, in that state, so they slept in the car at the side of the road. In the early morning he woke. His mouth was so dry and his head was pounding, it was his first hangover and he found the experience most unpleasant. Usually, if he was unwell, he had Mother to administer to him.

Even through the haze that surrounded his memory of last night, he could still remember what he had promised her. He would take her home to Mother, and she would be looked after. She wouldn't be homeless. He would love her and treasure her for ever.

In the cold light of day, the idea of his mother welcoming Sadie into the family did not seem very likely, but this feeling was just too strong to fight. If necessary he would leave home and find a flat to share with Sadie. If Mother didn't approve, then so be it, Martin had decided, at last, that now he wanted to lead his own life.

"Oh, Sadie, last night was great, but now I'm suffering," he said ruefully. ". . .have you got any headache pills?"

There was no response, and as he glanced up, he noticed that the passenger seat was empty. He turned slowly, wincing at the throbbing pain in his head, expecting to see her curled up in the back seat, asleep. It was empty.

He noticed his wallet on the floor of the car, right where Sadie had been sitting, and he automatically bent down to pick it up. The nausea he was feeling threatened to engulf him, his wallet flapped open and it was empty. He'd come out with £500. My God! He must have spent it all, and where were his credit cards? Panic set in. Martin had always been so careful with money all his life, and last night had been his one lapse. Realisation dawned on him, Sadie had gone, and so had the contents of his wallet, and his credit cards. It was all too much, he covered his face with his hands.

He should have felt rage towards her, she had fooled him and stolen from him, but all he could feel was the pain of knowing he would never see her again. It had been a unique experience, and right now the loss of his money in no way compared with the loss of her. If she had walked back into his life he knew he would forgive her. He was such a fool, and he knew it.

He tossed the wallet wearily back on the floor. His mobile was still in his pocket. He took it out and switched it on, hoping she might have rung him to offer some sort of explanation. There was a message on it, but it was from his mother asking him when he would be home. He remembered that he had switched it off for that very reason; she had a habit of doing this, and he hadn't wanted Sadie to know how dominant his mother was.

Well, he had to come up with something good. He didn't really care right now. He would have to go home and face her, but he would never tell her about Sadie. He had been duped, but he still made excuses for her. She was desperate, that's why she had done it. If only she could have stayed around longer, then she would have known she could have trusted him to take care of her.

He felt for his car keys. They were still in his pocket. He cautiously wound down the window, and the air felt crisp and cold. He would go for a drive to clear his head. Then he would figure out what to tell Mother before he headed home.

*   *   *   *

Sadie was fed up with pretending to like Martin. He was a right bore, but he had money in his pocket, and that had been the only attraction for her.

She had eaten an Indian meal, which was good because she'd been very hungry. If only she could have finished the evening with their Indian waiter. Now he had been sexy, and she had given him some flirtatious looks. Sadly he was at work, so it had to be Martin.

She had watched him get very drunk, but had kept herself in check, if only to get away when she had to. When she had helped him back to the car, he was well gone, and that gave her the opportunity to take his wallet out of his pocket. He was slumped and snoring now. Amazing, this bloke was so stupid, and easy to rob! As if she ever had any intention of going home to live with him and his dearly beloved mother!

Sadie had never slept in a car in her life and wasn't about to start now. There was about £200 in cash left in his pocket too. She decided to get a cab. She was canny enough to realise that the streets were full of undesirables at this time of night, and she had no wish to get mugged or raped, or even murdered. There was only one person she could go to in the middle of the night; she'd done it before. It was Sunita. Sunita would do anything for Sadie; she had no choice because they had so much history. Sadie found her useful at times, and this was definitely one of those times.

Sunita awoke with a jump when she heard the dog from next door barking. Then she heard her doorbell ring. There was only one person who visited her in the middle of the night, but just to be sure she pressed the security button. "Who is it?" she asked, and sure enough, it was Sadie. Her friend since childhood. They shared a love hate relationship, but they knew too much about each other to ever split up. Sunita, as usual, felt a mixture of feelings towards her, annoyance at being disturbed so late, concern that the noise might wake her young baby son Jacob, and quite simply, she'd missed her.

As she pulled on her dressing gown, she peeped into the next bedroom, but Jacob appeared to be sleeping soundly. She heaved a sigh of relief. He had been teething, and her nights had been disturbed a lot this week. He looked so beautiful, laying there,

20

with his dark spiky hair framing the pillow. She felt a warm surge of love towards him. Being a single mother wasn't easy, but he was well worth it!

When she opened the door to Sadie, she put her finger over her lips, and whispered, "Ssh, you must be quiet, Jacob is teething, and I don't want him to wake up!"

Sadie had expected to command her full attention, and she was annoyed that this was not the case. Just because Sunita had been stupid enough to get herself up the duff at seventeen, that was her fault, not Sadie's! All she could talk about was that brat now, that's why she only came round when she needed a temporary place to stay.

She hid her annoyance. Sunita was useful right now. "Poor you," she whispered, inwardly sneering. There was no way she would ever get saddled with a whining brat! "Can I stay? I've just left a bloke who tried to rape me, and it's too late to get a place to stay."

Sunita looked at her without sympathy. Most of what Sadie said wasn't true. She had found this out over the years, but there again, Sunita, herself, had found it necessary to lie at times to get what she wanted in life. When she saw Sadie she was never sure what she wanted in life. Sadie seemed to wreak havoc in hers.

"Can't you go home? Your parents haven't disowned you like mine have," she pointed out. She knew what would happen if Sadie stayed. Her head would be all messed up again. Although living in England all her life, her parents still kept to their Eastern traditions, and her pregnancy had been the last straw. They had thrown her out, she had disgraced the family, and Jacob's father had left her. Not that she was sorry about that. Their relationship just didn't work. She had been lucky to get this dingy little council flat.

Sadie's patience deserted her. "I wouldn't be here now if I had a choice!" she snapped, and then she made an effort to gain her self control, by putting on a look that she knew would win Sunita over. She took her hand, stroking it softly. "Anyway, I've missed you. Have you been keeping your bed warm for me."

Sunita gulped. Why did she allow Sadie to do this to her? She had tried a relationship with a man, Jacob's father, but it had failed miserably. Nothing compared with the way Sadie had made her feel. She had tried so hard not to wear her heart on her sleeve, because she was well aware that Sadie only used her when she had no one else in her life. But it was no good, Sadie always came back to her for more, and Sunita was weak, she couldn't resist her. She had loved her ever since she could remember. Even though she was doomed to a life of jealousy and pain, she still had no power to change it.

Sadie could see it had worked. She'd softened her up. Oh, what power she had, over men and women! They tiptoed hand in hand, like love's young dream, past the washing drying on the radiators. Sadie knew she could only stick this for tonight. The place stank of damp clothes!

"Look, there's Jacob. He's grown since you last saw him," whispered Sunita proudly, as they passed his room. He was her life.

Sadie feigned enthusiasm: "Yes, he's bigger." But couldn't help adding, spitefully, "Did you get a DNA done, to find out who his daddy is?"

"I know who he is, but we're not together anymore!" said Sunita angrily. They had reached her bedroom by now. "Why do you always have to be so nasty?"

Sadie pulled at Sunita's dressing gown. "Take this off, and I'll show you how nice I can be," she said slowly and seductively. She knew Sunita would be like putty in her hands, and she didn't mind whether she slept with men or women, she enjoyed the experience with both.

Sunita's anger vanished as quickly as it had come. She could feel those dizzy thrills running through her, and her heart was pounding fit to burst. Maybe Sadie was jealous of her ex, she did hope so, because if she was, maybe she cared, and Sunita always lived in the hope of that.

Chapter Four

Sadie threw her mobile viciously across the room. She was angry because once again she had no money, and all she got from her mother was grief! Why should she go to work? There was more than enough money in this house to keep her in style. Going back had been a mistake, even her love for her father was not enough to keep her here. She had only gone back because, quite simply, she had no other choice.

Sunita would have willingly let her stay there, but that had never been an option. Sadie had been brought up in a home where money was no object. Her parents had more than they knew what to do with, and plenty of it had been lavished on her all her life. She had no desire to live in Sunita's poky council flat which always smelt of damp washing. The furniture was shabby, and the carpets threadbare.

Sadie wanted the good things in life, but she didn't want to work to get them. Unfortunately for her, even though Philip had persuaded her to return home, her mother reigned supreme, and she was now only allowed what she considered a meagre allowance, and was told repeatedly she needed to get herself a job. Her hatred for her mother knew no bounds, and even her father was no longer the apple of her eye. He had changed towards her. He was weak, just like a puppet in her mother's hands, and Sadie didn't like it. It should be her, Sadie, winding him round her little finger, but she had lost the power.

She had tried to think of a plan to get away, but it all came down to having money. It would be nice to have her own flat.

Maybe she could get Daddy to agree to it if she pretended to take a job. After all, she was nineteen now, and home life was cramping her style. She wanted to come and go as she pleased, and bring home her friends, male mostly, to sleep there whenever she wanted.

Sadie had played her hand very cleverly, being charming in front of Philip, knowing that because he always saw a very different side to her than she showed towards her mother, he would defend her if things got nasty.

With her mother she played mind games, anything to make Isabel think she was losing it. She hid things from her so she was always late for appointments, she messed the place up to make her lose her temper, but the cleverest thing of all was to get at her mother through Jeremy. She had 'accidentally' broken her mother's favourite framed photograph of him. It had the desired effect of upsetting her mother big time, and she had been banished to her room. She had no credit left on her phone, and although she wasn't worried about disobeying her mother's order, and could go out any time she wanted, she stayed put, knowing that when her father found her there, and her mother sobbed out what had happened, he would give Sadie the benefit of the doubt. He would tell Isabel it was an accident, and not to overreact.

She played her music loudly whilst she was waiting for him, if only to block out the sounds of her mother's distress. The woman was crazy! Her brother had been dead and buried for six years now, and still she blubbered for him. She was so pathetic!

Philip could hear the music blaring from the house as soon as he drew up in his car. This didn't bode well. Sadie always played her music loudly when she was banished to her room. Whatever had happened now? He was sick of it all. He knew that her coming home hadn't solved anything. Sadie and Isabel would never get on. He would have to let Sadie grow up and leave home. No matter what Isabel had said about her getting a job, it seemed they would have to set her up in a place of her own. The money wasn't a problem, but as usual, Isabel would say he was spoiling her. Maybe he was, perhaps it had all been his fault, but it was too late now, and he certainly couldn't put up with all this nonsense between them for much longer.

He went wearily into the house, only to find Isabel sobbing over the shattered remains of her photograph of Jeremy. He comforted her, as he had so many times before. It was no use telling her that she had to move on, she couldn't, she was still stuck in the three short years of Jeremy's young life, and the tragedy continued to haunt her.

"She said it was an accident, but she meant it, she loves to hurt me!" said Isabel in a shaky voice. She felt totally drained, there were no more tears left.

"Oh no, you can't think that," said Philip quietly. The thought was abhorrent to him. Maybe Sadie was spoiled and self-willed, but she had suffered too, when Jeremy died, and for her mother to think that it was anything more than a careless accident was unthinkable.

"I'll go and speak to her. I'm sure we can get a new frame," he said gently, trying to sound calm and controlled. Somebody had to be.

When he reached Sadie's room, he tapped briskly on the door. He tried the handle, but it wasn't locked. With the music so loud, she hadn't heard him, so he coughed loudly as he entered. His heart went out to her when he saw her sprawled on the bed. She was pale, she had no make-up on, and her eyes looked huge, and full of melancholy.

He turned off her stereo, grimacing at the noise. "That's better," he commented. "What's been happening whilst I was out?"

"Daddy, I didn't mean to break it. She said I did it on purpose!"

"I know you didn't," said Philip soothingly, as he wrapped her in his arms.

Sadie didn't often cry, but she was now, and he was very moved. This made up his mind. These two were destroying each other. He could see faults on both sides, but he loved them both. This time he was going to make a stand. Whether Isabel liked it or not, they would buy a flat for Sadie and set her up with an allowance. If she wanted more than that, she would have to get a job, but it would be a start in life.

Maybe if they lived apart, one day, when Sadie was married with children of her own, she would get closer to her mother. It was never going to happen whilst they lived in the same house together. If only Isabel had been more patient with her, maybe she

b

would have seen her for what she was, a lovely free spirited girl, who so wanted to be independent. There was good in her. He lived in hope that Isabel would see it one day.

Wrapped inside his arms, Sadie felt very triumphant. She had driven her mother to the limit, and Daddy knew the only way to get peace was to separate them. She wiped away her crocodile tears. As if she cared what her mother thought of her, but it worked a treat on Daddy, it always had.

She said the words that she knew he wanted to hear. "Daddy, I'll try and get a job. I need to try and find somewhere to live. Mother and I just don't get on."

"I know, we need to let you live your own life now. I'll talk to your mother, and I'm sure we can sort things out."

He released her, and then his voice became stern. "Sadie, what you must remember is that you are a very attractive young lady. If you live on your own you have to realise that there are men out there who might see you as a meal ticket, so if we do set you up in a flat, we need to have a say on what goes on there."

"Of course, Daddy," murmured Sadie, inwardly seething. If they thought they could run her life they were very much mistaken. She would have who she wanted, when she wanted, to stay! She would have to play ball at the moment, but no one was going to stop her from leading her own life.

Philip left her, satisfied that she looked much happier now. "Just play your music quietly whilst I talk to your mother," he said gently.

Sadie nodded. She had no desire to go downstairs right now. They would talk about it, argue maybe, who cares, as long as Sadie got what she wanted, she didn't care what happened.

Chapter Five

Sadie sat tight when she heard the buzz of the entry phone. If they thought she was going to let them come in and take all her nice furniture and stereo equipment, they were sadly mistaken! It buzzed impatiently for the next five minutes or so, and she hoped that none of her neighbours were around. Once they got through the main door they could hang about outside her flat, and then she would be really trapped.

After about five minutes, it stopped, but then the telephone started. It was ages since she had taken any calls. They were all abusive, angry, demanding money. She didn't have the money to give them, and even if she had, she didn't see why she had to.

She had been told in a letter that they would be calling to recover goods to the value of her debts incurred. That was a laugh. Daddy had provided her with a few nice pieces, but it didn't amount to £60,000, which was what her credit cards added up to.

Nathan had been a lot of the trouble. He had his finger in a lot of pies, he was a useful person to know, but he was also a drinker and a drug addict. Sadie had partied well with him, and enjoyed the exhilaration of trying out new things, namely drugs, but now she'd tried it she was bored. She wasn't hooked, and she'd rather spend her money on good clothes and shoes, dining out, and generally having a good time, which she did, and her debts grew and grew.

Once again, regretfully, she would have to be on the move. Daddy funded the flat rent, but after a year, she was fed up with

27

his 'check-up visits', as she called them. Luckily, because most of the time during the day Nathan was 'out of it', she'd managed to conceal the fact that he was there, but she didn't really see why she had to. It was her life, she felt, to lead as she wanted to.

Nathan had managed to arrange a fake passport and a new identity for her, so as soon as these bastards went away, she was out of here. Her flight to New York was booked, her hotel was reserved in the name of Marina Virdini. That was good, she thought, just to confuse people: her very English middle class accent, with a name that sounded foreign. She knew, with her dark exotic looks, if she said that she was of European parentage she would be believed.

After she had gone, Daddy might think she had died. She felt no emotion. There had always been a scorn inside her for people who wore their heart on their sleeve. Sadie had always found hating people much more satisfying an emotion. She thrived on discord and unrest to get her adrenalin going. She didn't know why. She recognised those feelings that she'd had for Daddy as stupid childhood infatuation, that she had long since grown out of, and now she felt nothing for him, only contempt that he was still with her mother, who just wasted her life grieving.

The telephone had stopped ringing, and there seemed to be silence at the door. She peeped cautiously from behind the nets, and to her relief she saw them get in their van and go. She needed to go soon, in case they returned and broke the door down.

She called herself a cab, and there was one thing left to do, so she nipped up the stairs to where Nathan lay sleeping. He never got up until the afternoon, and as far as she was concerned, now that he had served his purpose, he was just a waste of space.

She shook the can of petrol around the bedclothes; her bed and her bedclothes they were! She curled her lip sneeringly, she would definitely have the last laugh over this waster. Not only had he sponged off her, but he had kids he'd spawned, all over the place, none of which he took any responsibility for. He wouldn't be missed by anyone.

The first thing he always did when he woke up was to smoke a joint, he couldn't start the day without one. With a bit of luck, and the help of the petrol, he would go up in flames. He wouldn't be around to tell anyone what she'd done, and as the flat was at

28

the top of the building, by the time his body was found, if it was found, the inside would be so bad, they would all think she, too, had perished in the fire.

He stirred in his sleep, his dark hair framing the pillow. He had the looks, but she found his lifestyle boring, and his sex drive didn't match hers, he was too high on drugs most of the time.

"Goodbye Nathan, you won't need any money for fixes where you're going," she said gloatingly. He wouldn't hear her, not in the day, he never did, night-time was his special time, he was the life and soul of the party then.

The cab had arrived. Her one big regret was that she had to leave so many of her clothes and shoes. She would have to find herself somebody quick to provide her with the lifestyle she wanted. But for now she had only one large suitcase on wheels and a hold-all.

She put on the blonde wig and dark glasses she had reserved for this occasion. Hopefully that would help when the police made their inquiries. The cab driver put her luggage in the boot, and she got in, thankfully the coast was clear. She glanced back at the block of flats once more. It had been her meal ticket, but thanks to Nathan she'd lost it. Still, she didn't see why anyone else should have that flat. The fire would take care of that.

"So you're off to Heathrow," said the driver.

"That's right," agreed Sadie. "Terminal three."

He tried to engage her in conversation and find out where she was going, but she was evasive. He didn't know which flat she had come out of, and she'd used yet another name, so she invented a story about meeting her boyfriend off a flight from Australia and then going on to Devon for a holiday.

It was a relief when the journey was over. Once on the plane she felt elated. She was now Marina Virdini, off to America on holiday. After six weeks she would become an illegal immigrant, her visa waiver form finished, but she would have found herself a man by then, and as marriage would be the only way to stay in the country, then that's what she would do.

She only spent a week in the hotel. She had gone through the last of her American dollars on one week's accommodation, so she'd been forced to pick up Rob in a bar and, in return for sex, he'd let her stay at his flat until she got 'sorted out', as he put it when he heard her story about being dumped by her married boyfriend and left to fend for herself in a strange country.

Rob worked for a Real Estate Agents, and whilst he was out during the day, she explored the area. The flat remained untidy and neglected, housework and cooking was something she knew nothing about, and didn't want to. She sensed her time here was limited, he had spoken about family coming to stay next month, and Sadie didn't do families, all that was rubbish. She felt the only person to love was herself, and so she deserved the best life she could have.

She met Mandy quite by chance in the local park. Thanks to her golden retriever Brandy, who ran off with Sadie's glove, they began to chat. Mandy rescued the glove, apologising profusely as she handed it back.

"I'm so sorry, he's still a pup."

"It may be March, but the wind is still cold," commented Sadie, pulling her gloves on to go, but Mandy swept her into conversation once she recognised her accent.

"Oh, you're from England. I've never been there; I just love your accent!"

Mandy was the local gossip, knew everyone, and this was just what Sadie needed. Mandy told her about where she lived, the man she had just dumped when she found out he was married, and Sadie feigned sympathy, repeating her own story about a married boyfriend who had dumped her.

"Wow!" Mandy's big blue eyes mirrored her amazement. "How could anyone dump you, with looks like that? You remind me of Catherine Zeta Jones."

Sadie laughed, but looking at Mandy she noticed how plain she was, apart from her eyes, which were her best feature. She had very mousy brown hair and was short and dumpy, so she wouldn't exactly have her pick of men.

As if reading her thoughts, Mandy said boldly, "He sure was fun to be with, and I hadn't done much dating before."

Whilst they were talking, a tall young man, aged about thirty, appeared from behind the trees, his face looked strained.

"Hi Mandy, how are ya doing?"

Mandy's face broke into a smile. "Hi Ricky, how are the girls? I haven't seen them around."

"They're good." He nodded, but when Sadie looked at him she got the impression that he was just saying the words, he looked very sad, and as if his mind was elsewhere.

"This is Marina from England. She's staying here for a while," Mandy said trying to make conversation.

"How are ya doing, Marina?" there was just a glimmer of a smile.

Sadie liked his face. Although sad, he had a strong jaw, his eyes were brown and very expressive, his blond hair was cut very short and spiky. In spite of being thin, he looked super fit, and his skin was tanned and healthy. He stooped to pat the exuberant puppy.

"No car today?" asked Mandy curiously.

"Sure," said Ricky. "It's parked right over there." He pointed to where a large people carrier was parked. "I saw you talking," he explained, "I was just wondering whether you could stop by for an hour or two and sit with the girls tomorrow. You can bring puppy dog too. You know they love him. As you know, it's parents evening at six o'clock, and Rosina doesn't like to stay late."

Mandy didn't hesitate. "Yes, I'm not on duty. My turn is on Wednesday. Will she stay then, do you think, when it's Brenda's class?" She looked at him sympathetically, his nanny wasn't that obliging. She realised how hard life must be for him trying to juggle his job and his home life, with three children to consider.

"Yes, Wednesday's OK, my sister's available," he said, his eyes showing his relief.

"I'm a teacher," she added to Sadie, by way of an explanation, after Ricky had gone. "I teach his eldest daughter Brenda."

"Where's their mother in all this?" asked Sadie curiously, expecting to hear details of a divorce.

Then it all came out. Mandy, in her usual dramatic way, told her how less than a year ago his wife had been killed in a car crash. They already had three daughters, two of which were in the car with her but thankfully had survived. Brenda had been in the other car with her father, who was taking someone to the airport. Amy, the children's mother, had been killed instantly, also the baby she was carrying, as she was almost seven months pregnant.

Sadie's mind was working overtime when she went back to Mandy's flat to have tea with her. Here was an opportunity; a widower, trying to hold a job down, look after three children, and still not in a fit state of mind to put up too many defences. She must get in there. Life was full of opportunities, and it wouldn't be long before she'd be back on her feet again, with somewhere more permanent to live.

Mandy gave so much information without even realising it. Her apartment, as she called it, was big and spacious, on the ground floor, with a big garden for Brandy. Sadie liked the look of it. She explained that she'd managed to get herself a mortgage by saving her teacher's wages when she lived with her parents. She was now twenty-five, and all she lacked was company.

Sadie made sympathetic noises. She explained to Mandy how she was waiting for some money to come from England, and when it did, if she wanted a lodger, she would be in a position to pay some rent. Mandy liked the idea of having someone to chat to. She told her that she could move in right away, and she needn't worry about the rent until she was back on her feet. She might even be able to help her get some work at the school, because they always needed classroom assistants, and as Mandy had worked there for over four years, if she spoke up for Marina, the school would know they could trust her.

Sadie, or Marina, as she was now known, decided to strike whilst the iron was hot. She lost no time in leaving Rob, and luckily for her he had left a fifty dollar bill lying around. She was able to buy some wine to celebrate with Mandy: the beginning of their friendship, and moving into her new home.

Chapter Six

Ricky Scott turned into the drive of his house after another exhausting day at work. He worked for the FBI, just like his father before him. Once he had flown planes, but was now on the ground. He had gone after this job to realise a dream; but that no longer mattered.

As he got out of the car, he thought ruefully how ironic it was that his life was heavily insured because of his high risk job, but Amy, who had been at home looking after the children until such time as she could return to work, had been the one to go. He felt the all too familiar stab of gut wrenching pain at her loss. At the age of twenty-nine, carrying what should have been their fourth daughter, his beautiful wife was gone. In a blink of an eyelid, her life had been extinguished. It was just over a year, but the pain never went, it lay there inside eating away at him, but for the sake of his girls he had to keep it together. They, too, had suffered so much.

As he opened the door he wondered what would be in store for him tonight, and when he saw Brenda he knew by her face he wouldn't like it. She looked defiant and mutinous, but her mouth softened when she saw him, and she ran towards him.

"Hi Daddy, I'm so glad you're home."

Not to be outdone, Kathy and Maria also ran into his arms, all trying to push each other out of the way in an effort to have his sole attention.

They all reminded him so much of their mother. All three had inherited her blonde straight hair and blue eyes. Brenda had freckles, which she hated, and at the age of eight, knew very much what she wanted in life. Not that he could criticise that, privately Ricky knew that he had also been very self-willed as a child, his father had been very strict, and he had learned self discipline at an early age.

"Daddy, I want to do my homework with you, not Rosina," said Brenda defiantly.

"You were rude to Rosina, and she's leaving," said Kathy, who was five years old. Out of all of them she resembled her mother the most in looks, but generally she had the quieter nature of the three of them. At this moment she knew her words would immediately command her father's attention.

"Oh no! not again, Brenda, what did you say?" He was angry now. They couldn't lose yet another nanny. Rosina was the latest in a whole long line of them, and she had stayed for three months, which was remarkable.

Maria, who was only three years old, chanted, "A bad word Daddy, a bad word."

Kathy continued to look triumphant, and Ricky could feel his heart sinking with despair. He looked grimly at Brenda, who looked suitably chastened, knowing that this time she had gone too far.

"Come into the hall."

He took her away from the others and read her the riot act. It was always the same. She had attached herself so tightly to him after the tragedy, as had the other two also, that she resented anyone else, especially a woman, who told her what to do. He knew it was a combination of her strong will, and also the terrible loss she had suffered, that made her react this way, but he also knew that he couldn't allow her to grow up using her mother's death as an excuse for bad behaviour.

Brenda was crying by the time he had finished, so he sent her to her room to reflect on what she'd done. She didn't want to apologise to Rosina for saying that she didn't want to listen to her 'crap'. After she'd stopped crying, he was going to make sure she did.

Kathy and Maria had gone back into the TV room to watch their programmes, now that the drama appeared to be over, and he turned his attention to finding Rosina.

He made his way towards the kitchen, where he found her

34

loading the dishwasher. He hadn't wanted a live-in nanny because there were too many problems. After the car crash, Kathy had dreadful nightmares, and for months she re-lived the horror, waking up screaming in terror. She had broken her leg and to this day she still bore the scar where she had to have a pin inserted. She had only been four years old and couldn't remember much about it, saying that she had been asleep and only woke up when the car landed in the field. Maria had only been 23 months, too young to remember anything, and luckily, even though sitting next to her mother, had not been hurt, saved by her baby chair. No one knew why Amy had crashed, she hadn't been going fast, and no other car was involved, but Ricky suspected her attention had been distracted. If only he'd been with her, instead of running a friend to the airport. She'd still be here now. His guilt about that was tremendous, and he had wished so many times that he could turn the clock back.

Rosina was short and stocky with dark brown hair. Her parents were Italian, but she had lived in the States all her life. He could see by her body language how angry she was, her movements were fast and aggressive, and he winced, hoping the china would stand up to her assault on it.

"Now you are home, I'm going. I have had it with Brenda!" she said banging the dishwasher shut. "Eight years old, and she won't do anything I ask, and then tells me I talk crap!"

"I'm so sorry," he tried humbly, "she will apologise to you. The children like you really." He wondered if he tried emotional blackmail, would it work? To tell her how much they would miss her if she went was a bit of an exaggeration. The truth was they didn't want anyone except him, and sometimes he found their excessive need of him so stifling.

"No, I'm sorry, Ricky. They are all getting too much. They copy Brenda, they are rude. I don't need this sort of hassle in my life!" said Rosina firmly.

She didn't want to weaken and agree to give it another go. Ricky had his problems with no mother around, but Rosina had been offered another job, with more money, and a new baby to take care of. She much preferred that. Babies couldn't answer back, they slept a lot, and she could have some of her nanny friends round to spend time with her without the risk of anyone telling tales about it.

Ricky could see by her face that she wasn't going to change her mind. There were no ties, she had no affection for the children, and they certainly had none for her. He swallowed painfully when he remembered how loving and demonstratively affectionate their mother had been. They had all adored her. Where was it all going wrong? With a heavy heart he had to admit that his girls were growing up to be rude and difficult.

After she had gone, he tried to telephone his mother. Maybe she would fill the gap for a few days until the agency found him someone. But maybe the agency wouldn't be able to keep on finding someone. He'd been through so many nannies.

His mother sighed when she heard about Rosina. Not that Caroline was surprised by it. Sometimes the girls were rude to her, and demanding, and sad though she had been by their loss, she found it difficult to cope with them, too.

"Well, Ricky, I'll help you out for a while, but only as a stop gap," she told him firmly.

Caroline was sixty years old, a widow, having lost her husband four years ago with a sudden heart attack. She had found his loss tremendous in the beginning, but was now getting used to her single life. She was still very attractive, her skin was unmarked, and her brown hair was cut short with a wispy fringe, which made her look ten years younger.

In an effort to rebuild her life she had joined the local golf club, and now had quite a few good friends. Playing golf kept her fit, there were many social meet-ups, and opportunities for holidays, and she actually found life quite agreeable these days.

She had brought up six children of her own, and had numerous grandchildren, all of whom she loved dearly. However, she found it nice to see them briefly and hand them back. She felt she'd done her stint, but she knew she couldn't be that selfish. Ricky's need was desperate.

"Thanks, Mum. I'll try and fix another nanny up as soon as I can," said Ricky, encouragingly.

"Brenda's the trouble. She upsets them," Caroline reminded him, sharply. "She's been rude to me, too."

Ricky could feel irritation at her words, but hid it. Losing his mother's support would only make things worse. Sometimes he felt she was a little hard towards the girls, but deep down he knew she was right really. Brenda must have some help, maybe some counselling, although he didn't really believe in it, otherwise no one would take the girls on.

He replaced the handset, and sat down wearily on the chair. Someone had scratched the table. When Amy had been alive she had kept that table beautifully polished, and their rented homes had always been lovely, but none of the nannies had done more than watch the girls; if they made a mess, so be it.

Ricky had been so proud when they planned to get a house together. After spending the first eight years of their married life in rented accommodation, they were finally to have a home of their own. His job had taken him all over the place. Originally he had been in the navy, flying planes, and that's how he had met Amy. He was based at the naval Academy in New York State, and one day she had literally jogged into his life.

He was cleaning his car the first time it happened. On campus it was quite normal to see people jogging, it wasn't just the students. The wide roads and pretty setting made it a popular place to exercise away from the busy highways.

He had been with Clint, messing around with their old jalopy, covered in oil, and when he looked up she was there. She was tall and wiry, her legs were strong but very shapely in her white running shorts, and she had a determined expression on her face as she ran. His eyes met hers, and he liked what he saw. Her wavy blonde hair was scragged back in a ponytail, as if she hadn't time to worry about it, but it didn't detract from her looks. She had the biggest and most beautiful blue eyes he had ever seen, almost violet in colour, and her skin had a light golden tan, almost peachy in colour, which was so much more attractive than the deep but ageing tans that everyone seemed intent to go for these days.

Clint had noticed her too, and was quick to say Hi. But Amy hadn't stopped that time. She had smiled briefly, said "Hello" in a very English voice, and jogged on, which to Ricky made her even more intriguing. When he looked back, he had known right from that moment that she was the one, the love of his life.

It took a while to get to know her, but he had made sure that Clint knew the score. Amy came from England, she was very into sport, and at the moment was working as a nanny so that she could live over here and try to get a scholarship. The more he found out about her, the more in love he became. She could run

37

fast, cycle for miles, and was an excellent swimmer. She was so busy with all this that the last thing on her mind was having a boyfriend.

She was missing her family. Her job was caring for a young child of sixteen months. She loved the baby, but she found the family she lived with very cold and distant. She was sticking it out because her dream was to race. She was chatty and bubbly, very competitive in every way, and he soon found out how feisty she was too. Ricky knew he was inclined to be bossy, having had three older sisters he'd had to fight to survive, but Amy was having none of it. She held her own in their discussions, and he admired her so much for it.

They were married a year later, just after her twenty-first birthday, a military wedding at the Naval Academy. He looked up at the photograph on the wall, Amy beautiful and glowing in her white dress which enhanced her tiny waist and shapely shoulders. He was dressed in his white naval uniform. He remembered how proud he'd been. He couldn't bear to look at that photograph, but he couldn't bear to take it down either. Life was meaningless without her!

Amy had never seen this house. The mortgage had been approved, and they were just about to start looking when the accident happened. Initially Ricky and the girls had stayed with his mother. Caroline had encouraged him to pick up the pieces of his life again. Because of the amount of friends they had made during their travels whilst he was in the navy, instead of flowers a trust fund had been set up for the girls, and Ricky had been astounded by everyone's generosity.

There had been enough money to put a substantial deposit down on the house, and he had been so relieved he had that security for the girls' future. When he had left the navy, it was to spend more time with his family, and his job at the FBI started with a very modest wage. He knew it would go up in years to come, but that was before Amy died, when he didn't need a nanny.

The house was small by American standards, but in a very pretty road with a wooded area at the bottom of the garden. It was also a very safe neighbourhood, with respectable families. It had four bedrooms, all with light coloured fitted carpets. He didn't like the mushroom coloured walls, they looked dingy, and he'd been promising himself he would repaint when he got time, but life was so hectic. As well as trying to settle into a new job at the worst time in his life, he also had to learn to care for the girls when the nanny went home. Amy had done virtually everything.

The kitchen door burst open, and three year old Maria toddled in. "Daddy, did you chase any bad guys?" she asked excitedly.

"Not today," said Ricky forcing a smile. She climbed up onto his lap, and he cuddled her, savouring the moment, but it didn't take long for her to wriggle down. Although Maria looked very much like him, she had inherited her mother's feisty but lovable nature, and her laugh was so infectious. Amy, too, had the ability always to see the funny side of everything.

He found himself on the floor tickling her, and they were then joined by Brenda and Kathy in a free for all. Their laughter rang out. His girls were now his life, and they kept him going. His jocular manner returned, which they loved, and they laughed and fooled on the floor until they were exhausted.

Eventually Ricky picked himself up and asked, "Who wants to come out for pizza?" knowing how happy the response would be. The girls squealed with delight, and he sent them off to tidy themselves up whilst he changed out of his office suit into something more casual.

Later, when they were in bed, he sat down. This was the time he hated most of all. The house was so quiet, the need to put on a happy front was gone. He must try and watch a film, and when he finally went to bed, would he be able to sleep? His bedroom was the loneliest place in the world.

Chapter Seven

Sadie was feeling very pleased with the way her life was shaping up. After living only two weeks with Mandy, not only had she found a job where she got paid in cash as a classroom helper, but also Brenda Scott was nursing a school girl infatuation towards her, which she knew she could turn to her advantage.

Greenview Elementary was not only short of staff this spring-time, it also lacked classroom helpers, and she was told she didn't need qualifications, only commitment to children. Mandy was a respected teacher, so Sadie had her way in. She had mentioned to Mandy that her visa ran out in four weeks, which meant she couldn't go on the payroll. She had also told her that the boyfriend who had dumped her had everything in hand, and they should have been married by now, making sure to have tears in her eyes when she said it.

Mandy, having suffered at the hands of a man herself, resolved to help her new friend. She liked having company, and she had felt even more sorry for Marina, as she knew her, when she heard about her parents' death in a car crash, and how she had put all her faith in this man she had met in London, who had asked her to come out to America to marry him.

As soon as Sadie had started helping out she had been a hit with the children. They had all come to her, attracted by her very English middle class accent, her tales of England, and her general exuberance. Sadie soon learned their ways of gushing conversation, saying things you didn't really mean, but that sounded good. Pretending to like the little brats had been easy because they liked her, and although she sometimes felt irritated when Brenda followed her around like a love-sick puppy dog, she never showed it because it was just what she wanted to happen. Ricky had a problem at the moment, his nanny had left, and his mother was only available temporarily to be there after school for the girls. In the mornings Ricky had dropped them off at Mandy's apartment because he had to leave so early for work, and then they had all been brought to school in Mandy's car. This had been Sadie's opportunity to make an impression on them. It had been so easy, particularly with Brenda, who seemed very charmed by her English accent.

It hadn't taken her long to get Mandy to lend her the car. More often than not Mandy had staff meetings or after school activities that made her late, and now the new sports teacher was her newest interest. His name was Calum, he was tall and tanned, with piercing grey eyes, and a lean well toned body which was the result of regular trips to the gym.

He had offered Mandy a lift at any time, as he only lived two blocks away, and from then onwards she had been smitten. Sadie was convinced that he was only being neighbourly, but she let Mandy imagine that he was interested. As if a hunk like that would look at mousy Mandy! Still, it left her car free. Mandy could be taken in by anyone, luckily for Sadie.

Sadie had even contemplated him for herself, but judging by the old jalopy he drove, and the very small apartment which he rented, he didn't seem to have much money. Her original plan to charm her way into the Scott family was still the best, so regretfully she would have to leave hunky Calum alone. From now on, even in her own thoughts, Sadie would become Marina.

Brenda was trying very hard to concentrate on her sums, but the thought that her teacher, as she thought of her, Miss Virdini, was taking her and her sisters home tonight, and staying at their home until Daddy came in, was just so exciting!

After her mother had died, it had been so painful for Brenda. There had been no soft arms to nestle in when she fell over, to make everything all right, no one to cook her burgers in a special way, no one to tell her off when she was fighting with her sisters, only daddy, but as much as she loved him, no one could replace her mother.

41

At the age of seven, she'd learned to form a tough exterior, pretending not to care, that way other children's remarks couldn't harm her. Mothering Sunday meant nothing to her, and she took no notice when the class made cards and gifts of their own handiwork. Her teachers had tried to suggest she did something for Grandma, and Brenda had acted as if she couldn't care less, that way it hid her hurt and pain.

Marina had been her salvation. She had understood that Brenda had no interest in celebrating. She, too, had lost both of her parents in a car crash. Brenda had heard Mandy telling Daddy about it, so they shared a common grief, without the need to even mention it. Marina had arranged for Brenda to help her in another class baking cookies. "You even get to take them home to share with your sisters," she promised her. This made her a hero in the eyes of Brenda.

Finally the bell went, and Brenda jumped excitedly out of her chair, pushing the offending books into her bag.

"The questions on the last two pages are your homework," reminded Miss Thomas, a small middle-aged woman, with mousy brown hair caught up in a bun. Brenda grimaced, maths was not her favourite subject, and she hadn't been listening, but she joined the others, all chatting excitedly as they left the room.

Most of the class would be boarding the yellow bus that dropped them off at various points. Greenview Elementary was a few miles away from the local towns, and Brenda and Kathy, who had just started school, usually came that way too, but now that Rosina had left, they had to come out early when daddy left for work. Not that Brenda really minded, she liked riding with Mandy and Marina. She found Marina particularly fascinating. Although she looked nothing like her mother, with her dark hair and eyes, she had the same English accent that Brenda had loved, and there was an air of fun about her that all the teachers lacked.

Marina was waiting in the playground with Kathy. Kathy was chewing on a candy bar, and when she saw that, Brenda remembered hers still in her bag. She had been so busy sampling her cookies that she'd made earlier, that she had forgotten about it.

"Hi guys," she said, smiling at Kathy. She did love both of her sisters, even though they argued a lot. Their bond was really close since their mother had died. They all needed each other, and were almost like a little gang; the Scotts against the world. That's how

42

it felt to Brenda sometimes, especially when no one seemed to understand.

"I made a poem for Grandma," said Kathy, frowning. She, too, hadn't liked being reminded of Mothering Sunday, but it would come round relentlessly every year. She knew she would have to get used to it. She had spent a year recovering from the physical effects of that accident, but being the closest of all three of them to her mother, the emotional effect would take much longer.

She was aware that Daddy had paid her much more attention since the accident, and Brenda had been quite jealous about it. She had heard Grandma tell him he must, and he had said he had a guilty conscience about that because he had been away flying for the first year of her life, and had hardly seen her. Kathy couldn't even remember her first year of life. All she could remember was her mother always being around; and then suddenly she wasn't, and she had been told she had gone to heaven, but Kathy didn't know where it was, and she couldn't understand why they couldn't have all gone with her.

"I did cooking with Miss Virdini," announced Brenda, as they were getting into the car. She couldn't help herself, being singled out to do something different made her feel privileged.

"That's not fair!" interjected Kathy, feeling jealous herself this time. Close as they were, there was rivalry between the elder two, and Brenda always showed her maternal side to Maria.

"Well guys, we've made plenty of cookies for you to eat when we get home," Marina reminded them, as they set on their way.

This seemed to pacify Kathy, and Marina quietly heaved a sigh of relief. She very much disliked brats when they argued, and these two often did.

"Well, next stop Grandma's; time to pick up Maria, and then home," she announced.

"Miss Virdini, are you good at maths?" asked Brenda, remembering the dreaded homework.

Marina sneered quietly to herself. She'd have to be some sort of cretin if she couldn't do the homework set for an eight-year-old!

"I'll have a look when we get home, and by the way, you can call me Marina, except in school," she said, smiling, noting that Brenda's face lit up. She was getting closer. She could think of better things than Maths homework; boring though it was, she had to appear interested. These kids were so demanding! Grandma looked after Maria at the moment, but it was her good self that had to do all the running about. Never mind, it was Mandy's petrol, not hers.

"You never even did your homework for Rosina!" said Kathy, remembering all the conflict there had been.

"Rosina wasn't a teacher," said Brenda defensively. She couldn't explain to Kathy how much she was beginning to trust Marina, or how much she looked up to her and admired her. Her feelings were very new and private, and she wasn't going to give Kathy any opportunity to make fun of her.

Caroline was pleased when she heard the sound of the car arriving. It wasn't that she objected to looking after any of her granddaughters, but sometimes it was just nice to go and visit a friend, or spend a relaxing afternoon with a good book. Since Ricky had lost his nanny in March that hadn't been possible. It was now May, and in June the summer term would end. She had taken care of Maria for five days a week, and then after school she had gone over to meet the other two off their bus, and taken care of them until their father came home.

But although she was still caring for Maria during the day, that nice teacher Marina from England was very kindly taking them all home each day, and relieving her a little. She wondered how long it would last. The agency only seemed to be able to offer live-in ones to Ricky. Personally Caroline thought that was the answer, and then it wouldn't matter if he had to work late, which Ricky frequently did, but would he listen to her? No, of course not! He insisted he wanted his own space. Well it was obvious to her that he wouldn't get that for years, not until the girls grew up and went.

"Ganma, Bema's here!" said Maria excitedly.

She ran to the window, adoration of her sister, who had virtually become her mother, apparent. She was only three, and could be excused for not pronouncing their names properly. Caroline felt a wave of pain for the situation course through her, and anger for the wicked waste of a young vibrant life.

She had been very fond of Amy; the bubbly, happy person who had always been such fun to be around. If she could have chosen a wife for her stubborn son, she couldn't have chosen better. Amy had been just like another of her daughters. Although Maria had inherited her father's long and narrow face, she had her mother's beautiful eyes, and her character was absolutely Amy. She was a very sunny child, always laughing, and although only three, cheeky and feisty in the most lovable way.

She was the least complicated of the three girls, and less affected by her mother's death. She didn't remember the car crash, after more than a year she didn't remember her mother either. She had been less than two, but for a week after she had cried 'Momma' all day long, and no one could pacify her. It had rent at Caroline's heart to hear her, but now, if her mother was mentioned, it meant nothing. Out of sight was out of mind. She had heard that her mother had gone away, and accepted it because she didn't even know who she was, and there didn't seem to be a sense of loss.

Caroline watched as the three sisters greeted each other, their closeness so apparent. They were great girls really. Hard work, like all children, and so close to their dad. Her mind pictured the last time she had seen Amy; she had Maria on her hip, and she was cooking dinner with her one free hand. She had handed Maria to her, laughing when Maria objected, saying, "She might have learned to walk now, but she still likes me to carry her around. Thank goodness for you, grandma!"

Maria had been born prematurely at thirty weeks, and it had been touch and go for the first two days whether she would make it. Her breathing was poor, she was a low birth weight, and she had bleeding in her brain. Ricky had sat by her cot in the special care baby unit for those nights, so scared they would lose her, whilst poor Amy was recovering from her traumatic birth, and feeling poorly herself. Luckily they had both survived, and although a little late in walking, everything else had been fine, and Maria had developed into a bright little girl. Poor Amy hadn't lived long enough to see this. She would have been so proud. Although she must never show it to him, Caroline's heart ached for Ricky. He had lost the love of his life, and all the joking and laughing that he did around the girls constantly didn't fool her. After all, she was his mother, and she knew he was a person who couldn't share grief. He was proud, his feelings were kept very firmly under control, but nevertheless, she knew they were there.

45

"Well, hi Marina, how are you today? Can I make you an English cup of tea?" she said, smiling widely at her. It was so good of her to help Ricky out like this, and by all accounts, she wouldn't even let him pay her any money. What it was to have good friends!"

"That would be lovely, Caroline. Brenda has made some cookies that we can all share." Marina smiled back at her. She had to win this old bag over. After all, she wanted her approval when she married her son.

Later, when they had gone, and the house was quiet again, Caroline reflected on the situation. If only, one day, Ricky could meet someone like Marina. She seemed such a nice young lady, and it was such a tragedy that she had lost her parents and had no one else in the world. Life seemed to be cruel to the nicest people. What had Ricky done to be widowed at thirty, with three young daughters to raise alone? Still, she comforted herself, he was a great father, he'd even got Maria potty trained on his own; he'd just taken over the reins when it all happened. He was definitely a son to be proud of.

Chapter Eight

Three months later:

"Daddy, why can't Marina live with us? She's hot. I like her!"

Ricky looked at Brenda's face, alight with excitement, and swallowed uncomfortably. He was aware that Brenda was very taken with her, but how could he explain to her that he didn't want another woman living with them? Their life was private, their good times and bad times should have been spent with Amy. No one could take her place. He only hired a nanny because he had to, but a live-in one, he felt, was a bridge too far.

"I don't want to talk about it right now!" he said firmly. He had to be firm with Brenda. If he showed any sign of weakening, she would cash in on it, and he didn't want to make promises he couldn't keep.

He ignored the mutinous set of her mouth. She knew he would, but it was worth trying anyway. Grandma was there, and she thought about bringing her into it, but then thought again. Daddy wouldn't like that. Brenda had found in her short life, involving other people, arguing, or throwing tempers didn't move him. She would have to work on him in a different way.

"I'm gonna check the emails," she announced, and left the room. Ricky knew why. Amy's mother from England visited every summer, and she had promised to email them when she had booked her ticket. She usually came in June, but this year it had to be August. She had taken another holiday on the continent in June, and the girls were looking forward to seeing her. Ricky had mixed feelings. He had always got on with

Coleen, but her accent reminded him so much of Amy, and she looked like her.

He thought briefly about last year. She had been due to come in June, when the baby was due, but Amy hadn't made it. She died in March, and Coleen had found herself attending her own daughter's funeral. He tried to swallow down the all too familiar pain. Coleen had been devastated to lose her beautiful daughter. She had made a supreme effort to be strong for the girls, just as they all had, but three months later fate had struck again, her second husband, George (who was not Amy's blood father, but had been the one to bring her up), collapsed, and died with a blood clot.

Ricky had been horrified when he heard this. It temporarily made him forget his own plight. He wondered how she was now. It was seventeen months since Amy's death, and fourteen since George's. If she was like him she'd be carrying on with life as normal, and no one would really know how much she was hurting, because that's what they had to do. But he knew, they shared a common bond.

Caroline interrupted his thoughts. "How's Coleen, have you heard?" she inquired sympathetically. Having lost her own husband in a similar way, seven years before had been tough, but she hadn't lost a child as well. "She's always bright on the phone, but seeing the girls without Amy may be hard for her. I may have to take some time off to take them all out and about, as she doesn't like to drive over here."

The one time that Coleen had tried her hand at driving had been a standing joke between Ricky and Amy. It was when Amy was in hospital resting before Kathy had been born, some five and a half years earlier. Amy had driven herself to hospital, he hadn't known until after because he'd been at work, and Ricky had brought Coleen there to pick up the car whilst he drove his back.

Coleen was driving behind him and he didn't think he was going that fast, but when he reached the freeway she wasn't behind him. It had been when he was stationed in San Diego, and she didn't have the address because they'd only just moved.

Amy had given him hell when she found out, particularly when Coleen had ended up downtown in a very seedy area, and she had knocked on a door to say she was lost. But fate had been with her, instead of drug dealers, rapists, or murderers, a young English woman, married to an American, had let her in, and made her welcome. They rang him, and he had gone down there with his neighbour, Jason, to collect her and the car.

Coleen had not driven in America since then, and when Amy had got over her anger with him, they had all seen the funny side of it, even Coleen. She had been a good sport, with the joke at her expense, but although she drove herself around everywhere in England, he knew that if Amy was here now she would say that he wasn't to expect her to do it here. She didn't like driving on the right, and it wasn't fair to expect her to take out his space wagon with the girls in. She was coming for a vacation, not to be stressed.

Caroline looked at him, knowing Ricky as she did, she would have to phrase her words carefully. If he thought she was trying to plan his life he would be pigheaded and stubborn. Tact was the answer.

"Did you think about asking Marina if she could come and stay just while Coleen is here? Now that school is out, if you let her use the space wagon she could take Coleen and the girls out, and you needn't have any time off work."

Ricky considered her words. His mother was also used to her own car, and would not drive the space wagon. They couldn't all fit in her car, and he didn't really want to take time off work. They were in the middle of a very important investigation, trying to bust a drug ring, and he wanted to be a part of it. His job had been his salvation since Amy died, he put a lot of effort into it, and he wanted to do well so he could climb the ladder to promotion.

Mother's idea was good, he could have Marina and mother-in-law at the same time, and then after, he could have his space back. There would be two extra people to look after the girls, and do the cooking. Ricky hated cooking. It was easier to eat out, and often they did.

He didn't want to get nostalgic again and think about when Amy had shown him some of her English dishes, but he couldn't help remembering when she had made shepherd's pie with baked beans. When he had teased her about it, she had told him it was her mother's recipe, and it had been a good one. The girls loved it. No doubt Coleen would make it when she came.

"I was thinking that myself," he said slowly. It wouldn't do to let mother think she had all the good ideas. "But I want Brenda to

49

understand it's only whilst Coleen is here on vacation, after that I want my house back."

Caroline exulted inwardly. He was seeing sense at last. Once he had someone there all the time, not only did it make her life easier, it would give the girls more stability, and Ricky could cope with the huge demands of his job, and the unsociable hours he had to work. She decided to ignore the fact that he only wanted it to be temporary.

"I'll probably go out with them a bit too. We can take the girls out shopping, you know how much they love that!"

Didn't he just! Ricky had gone out only once with them to the Mall, and that had been enough. He had pushed Maria in her buggy, and Brenda had wanted to go into every shop to choose, and try on, a new outfit with her birthday money. Kathy too, had been just as demanding. They had spent over two hours whilst she tried on everything, and bought nothing. To him it had been a totally wasted afternoon. He wondered, if she was like this at eight, what would some poor guy have to put up with when she was older. Shopping was definitely only for women.

The door burst open, and his three blonde princesses, as Ricky thought of them, came in excitedly.

"Nannie's coming next Monday, by British Airways. She's landing at five-thirty," said Brenda, sounding important.

"Great!" enthused Caroline, glancing at Ricky to see his reaction.

Maria had climbed onto his lap, chanting, "Nannie's coming, Nannie's coming." Kathy and Brenda were positioned one on either side of him, leaning against him, all intent to have a share of him.

"Enough girls, I can't breathe," he protested, laughing and tickling them to make them go.

Caroline watched them all collapsed in a heap on the floor, which the girls thought was great fun. It was good that he horsed around with them, instead of getting mad when they became clingy. The doctor had said they would grow out of it when life settled down. Somehow Caroline doubted this. Ricky was the centre of their world, the one person who had remained constant in it. Obviously they would want to cling onto him.

She joined in the laughter as they got up, and Ricky tried to brush his jeans down.

"Right girls," he said briskly. "We have a house to clean up before Nannie arrives, starting with your bedrooms."

He ignored their protests, and sent them off.

After they were out of earshot, he picked up the telephone to call Marina. "I'd better check that she's up for this before I tell the girls."

It had never crossed Caroline's mind that she might not be, and as she listened to Ricky explaining the situation to her on the telephone, it seemed that Marina was more than willing. She glowed inwardly at the kindness of her, the way she helped this family in their time of need. If only there were more people like her around.

"I'll only accept your help if you let me pay you this time!" said Ricky very firmly. "Don't argue!"

When he had finished, his face wore a look of relief. "She's coming on Sunday," he said simply, "I don't want to take advantage of her kindness, so she's a paid babysitter this time, much against her will, I might add."

"It's better that way," agreed Caroline, ". . .that way she gets something out of it, even if she doesn't want it. It just makes you feel a bit more independent."

At the other end of the telephone, Marina smirked with satisfaction as she replaced the handset. This was just what she wanted. Working subtly on Brenda she had put the idea in her head without the child even realising it, but Ricky's stubbornness was hard to crack. After she moved in she would be another step closer to her goal. She was going to have to play the part of her life and make herself so indispensable that he wouldn't even consider getting rid of her.

The thrill of it all charged up her adrenalin. This man was a member of the FBI, and he didn't even realise she had a fake ID. She'd have to work hard on mother-in-law from England. She'd be bound to resent another woman in her daughter's place. She'd ask her where she came from, so she'd have to think up something good. But this was all the fun of it, and her reward would be marriage to this man, as short as possible, closely followed by divorce, and then money, lots of lovely money.

She'd always wanted to play the Casinos at Las Vegas, and when she got her money she would. Well, after putting up with his kids, pretending to like his mother, and nurturing his mother-

51

in-law, she would have earned it. They all made her sick, and at times it was quite an effort hiding it!

Mandy wouldn't notice her absence. She was spending more and more time with Calum. On the occasions when he came round, Marina felt like a spare part. She was quite sure she could have stolen him from Mandy if she wanted to, but he had no money, and was of no use to her, except in bed maybe, but she wouldn't find out. She had to keep in with Mandy, just so she still had somewhere to go when the time came.

However, she could get away from the smelly dog that was allowed to jump on all the couches. What did she find worse, dogs or kids? Both were tiresome, but kids had their uses. Brenda had allowed her to step into Ricky's world, which as far as he was concerned, was kept as tight as a fortress. Whatever they had suffered as a family did not move her in the slightest, and it was definitely to her advantage. She knew she must carry on playing her part for as long as it was necessary.

She took the bull by the horns, and went to explain to Mandy how she needed to help out Ricky and the family for the next couple of weeks. She found her in the lounge, seated at the table, reading a magazine.

Mandy listened sympathetically, until she had finished. "Gee honey, they are so lucky to have you. It is so hard for that family, and you're like an answer to a prayer! Of course I don't mind you staying there."

"Did you ever know their mother?" asked Marina, vaguely curious.

"No," said Mandy, " . . .like you I've seen the photographs. She was real pretty. I did hear that she did a lot of sport, running, swimming and suchlike. But he moved into the house after she died, and everyone knows he's a widower. News like that travels fast."

Marina made sympathetic noises. She, too, had seen the photographs of the blonde smiling female all over the house. They were going to go when she took over, she couldn't be living in her shadow all the time. She was a bit too pretty for Marina's liking!

Mandy looked at Marina with warmth and affection. It had been a good day when she met her in the park. She was loved by all the children at Greenview, and now she was so kind, she was giving up her time to help this lovely family, who through no fault of their own, had lost their mother when the children were barely out of babyhood.

Maybe if it went well Ricky might ask Marina to stay, and although she would miss her company, she could think about asking Calum to move in. He was paying a huge rent for a tiny poky apartment, and he already spent a lot of time with her. They got on well and they shared the same interest in teaching children. Who knew? But it could work out very well for everyone.

Chapter Nine

Coleen Harris walked into the departure lounge at Atlanta. The long haul flight was now behind her. She had only the short flight to Greenview to cope with. She had always hated flying, it scared her, and now that George was gone, she had to face it alone.

She had been so happy for Amy when she met Ricky, they made such a great couple. The only thing that she'd been sad about was that she would be living in America. She hadn't told her that. It was Amy's life, she couldn't lead it for her, and only George had known just how much she had missed her daughter. No matter how hard she tried not to think about it, she couldn't help wondering if Amy would still be here now if she hadn't come to the States to try and further her sporting career.

But this wasn't fair of her; she knew that really. Amy could have died in a car crash in England too, and she had to accept that Amy wasn't destined to be long for this world. If only she'd known, she'd have given her more attention, not taken her happy bubbly nature for granted, but maybe it was better that she hadn't known. If Amy had wasted away with a terrible illness, how would she have coped with that?

It was all running through her head again, and this time she didn't have George to turn to. The man who had taken on her three children when her first marriage ended in divorce, and treated them like his own. She had been lost without him, but after more than a year now, she was trying to learn to cope. She was longing, and dreading, to see the girls again. The last time had been at the funeral, a time that they all desperately needed to put behind them and forget. She had George's strong arms to hold her at night during those first dark days, but then three months later he, too, had gone.

Oh how her heart had gone out to Ricky, bravely coping with his pain. Maria scarcely more than a baby, sobbing for her mother, Kathy having horrific memories of the crash, waking up at night and screaming, and poor Brenda, old enough to remember more of her mother, and missing her like crazy! The whole thing had been like a nightmare, but sadly, not one that you could wake up from and find that's all it was. This was for real!

She looked around her at the other passengers waiting to be called into their seats. They all looked calm, but she was terrified, longing to get the flight over and done with. She would never have started flying if Amy hadn't lived in America, and now she would have to do it as least once a year to see the girls. She just had to pluck up the courage. All her life she'd suffered from a fear of heights, but this was her family, and now that their mother was gone, it was even more important to keep up the contact with them.

She had put a blonde rinse on her hair to brighten herself up. Her hair was worn short in a bob, which would be easily manageable after the frequent trips to the swimming pool. At the age of fifty-four, she had to battle constantly with her weight. She managed to keep it at a size fourteen, but would have liked to be a twelve. A ten, as she had been when young, would have been even better, but it seemed impossible now. Her skin was still fair and soft, she knew she would have to cover herself totally with sunscreen to avoid burning. A light tan suited her, but she didn't want to end up looking like a dried prune.

She sat down, crossing her still slim legs over, and brushing an imaginary speck from her white cotton trousers. The kingfisher blue silk blouse she had on complemented her eyes and made them look even bluer. She was wearing only light make-up, and her white sandals with open toes meant that she was prepared for the heat when she arrived at Greenview.

The reception clerk picked up his microphone, and she studied her seat number, waiting with breathless anticipation for it to be announced. She was, by nature, a more reserved person than Amy had been. Amy would have been cracking jokes to cover her nerves, but Coleen kept it all in, glad that the other passengers couldn't see her agony.

55

Amy had resembled her in looks so much, as did the girls, and Coleen had been so proud of her bright confident daughter. But she hadn't got her confidence from her mother. Coleen wished she could have been more like that herself in the past, because now, without Amy, and without George, she was having to learn to be.

After what seemed like an eternity, but was only a couple of minutes, she was called to her seat. She picked up her hand luggage, with the shorts in that she would soon need, and forced a purposefulness into her step. In just over an hour she would see Ricky and her beloved granddaughters, and she was going to put the biggest smile on her face that she could possibly muster.

"Come on girls, let's get going." If Ricky's voice sounded impatient, it was no wonder. The girls had spent ages getting ready . They had absolutely no sense of time, and he knew he would have to step on it to get to the airport in time for Coleen's arrival.

Brenda was the first out into the car. It was a hot day, and she was dressed casually in shorts and T-shirt, as was Kathy, who followed not far behind, exclaiming, "Maria's got her new dress on, and she won't take it off!"

Maria then appeared in a pink lacy dress that she had chosen out of her birthday money.

"I said you could wear it when you go out," said Ricky, knowing he really didn't have time for this.

"But Daddy, we are going out," said Maria, her big blue eyes beseeching him. It was hard to say no to her, especially when she stood there looking so cute. But he must be strong.

Marina appeared at the door behind her. "If you wear your dress today, Maria, what will you wear tomorrow, when we take Nannie out for brunch?"

Maria, with the usual balkiness of a three-year-old didn't want to give in, but Marina had it all worked out. She held up a shorts and top set in the same colours as Brenda's. "We need you to get changed real quick, otherwise we'll be late to meet Nannie. You'll look trendy like Brenda!"

Ricky held his breath, wondering whether she would fling herself down, in typical three-year-old fashion, kicking and

56

screaming against authority. But, to his absolute amazement, Maria ran up to Marina, tugging at her dress, in an effort to take it off. Marina took her back inside the hall, and helped her off with it, and she was soon in her shorts and T-shirt, and strapped into her car seat.

"Thanks a million, Marina," he said gratefully, as she slid into the back of the car next to the girls.

As he was driving he allowed his thoughts to wander. Marina seemed to have such a way with the children. They looked up to her. Maria would never have changed her clothes like that for him without a fuss, and he didn't really have time to deal with these things. It was so nice to have the support from her. Already he was beginning to rely on her.

Maybe, after Coleen's visit, he ought to think of offering her a permanent position. The girls were so fond of her. He really ought to make an effort to keep her, because the girls would be devastated if she left. They were so insecure since the accident, and he owed it to them to give them some stability. In the beginning he hadn't wanted a live-in nanny, but it would definitely make life a lot easier.

He glanced at the clock on the dashboard, only fifteen minutes left until she landed. He hoped the flight was late, and it would take her a while to get through customs. Marina was playing I spy with the girls, and he increased his speed. He didn't want to go too mad, better be late than not get there at all. Not that Amy had been driving fast. Whatever had happened to her would remain one of life's mysteries. Nevertheless, he often thought about her when driving. For the umpteenth time he wished he had been with her that day. But it was done now, and he wished he could move on. Maybe one day the pain of her loss would dim.

When they arrived, he sent Marina ahead with the girls whilst he parked the car. He joined them at arrivals, but Coleen was not there yet. He scanned the passengers filing through, and then he spotted her. She always seemed to travel light, only one small suitcase and a cabin bag on her trolley. The girls shot forward, happy and excited, but then suddenly became shy and over-whelmed when they saw the person who looked so like their mother.

Coleen hugged them, exclaiming at how they had grown, and then she hugged him too, and he thought fleetingly of Amy, she had the same wide smile that Amy had, but he had to stop doing this to himself, Amy was gone!

"Coleen, this is Marina, she's been helping with the girls, and she's staying over with us whilst you're here."

Coleen shook hands with Marina. She could see what a pretty girl she was, and judging by the way the girls were standing with her, and Maria was clinging onto her hand, they were very taken with her. He hadn't called her his nanny, and Coleen's curiosity was roused. Could she be a girlfriend? It was only just over a year, and she felt a pang to think that Amy could be so easily forgotten in such a short time.

She wrestled silently with her conscience. Of course Ricky had to move on. Amy would never be forgotten, but in an ideal situation Ricky could marry again, and then the children would have a mother figure to look up to. No one could love them, or be as close to them as Amy had been, but sometimes life only offers second best, and that is better than nothing at all.

"It's lovely to meet you, Marina," she said warmly, and she meant it, having now resolved the conflict inside her.

Marina smiled back, knowing she must act well. This woman mustn't have any reason to cause trouble for her. "My, how fresh you look after travelling all day," she murmured, privately thinking that the old bat didn't look too scary. She'd recently been widowed, and would probably be very easy to manipulate. Well, she had to suffer her for two weeks, and Ricky's mother, too, would be coming out with them, so her main aim would be to show them just how well she got on with the girls. That was easy, the kids were so desperate for a mother figure. It was their weakness, and her strength.

"Oh, you're English!" said Coleen wonderingly. "Do you live out here now?"

Marina told the same story that she was getting used to now. She came from Walton-on-Thames, had met an American in London, come out here to marry him and settle, and then he had dumped her.

She also explained how she lived with Mandy, had become a classroom assistant, and loved children, so was helping Ricky out for the holidays. She watched Coleen's face change from a sympathetic look, to one of relief.

"How wonderful that you can help Ricky out," she said warmly.

58

Marina guessed that Ricky would tell Coleen that Marina, too, had lost her parents in a car crash, later that evening. She was almost beginning to believe it herself! It would be better coming from him, because they mustn't think she felt sorry for herself. They must think she was brave and independent, a suitable partner for Ricky when the time came.

When they arrived home, Ricky excused himself to go and check his answer machine. Marina made some tea for Coleen, and then to her annoyance, which she skilfully hid, all the girls wanted some too. She kept her smile pinned to her face whilst she was doing it. Waiting on people was quite new to her, she'd never had to. Her mother had cleaners and a housekeeper, and until she left home, she had been waited on hand and foot.

"They always drink tea with me when I come," explained Coleen, laughing ". . .Ricky says I bring out their English genes."

Marina continued to smile at her and share the joke. Then Ricky arrived, and the kettle was put on again to make him tea. Usually he came in and grabbed a can of Coke from the fridge, and hopefully, after Coleen went home, that's what they could all go back to. Marina very much resented being their servant, although she knew for the sake of her plan, it would stand her in good stead with Coleen.

When the tea was finished, Ricky carried Coleen's bags up to the room she would be sleeping in. She was in the guest room, which had its own en suite, was fairly large, with a big bed draped with pink furnishings and cream walls and carpet. There was also a TV in there, and it was quiet with a pleasant view over the garden towards the wooded area.

Brenda had been only too willing to give up her room to Marina, just so she could stay. Normally she would object to sleeping with her two sisters, so if Marina did move in later, she would obviously get the guest room. She liked the idea of that, her own space away from them all in a nice room. At the moment she had to make do with vivid striped wallpaper in red, very jazzy looking curtains, although she didn't mind the oatmeal coloured carpet. It was soft with a deep pile, and Brenda had been told to leave her portable TV in there, because it might be nice for Marina if she wanted to watch it. But the main reason really, Marina thought, was because it would keep the younger two awake in their room. If it had been for anyone else, Brenda would have argued, but not for Marina.

Whilst Coleen was unpacking, Ricky went to round up the girls. They were in Coleen's room with her, curious to see what she had in her luggage. Somewhere inside the case there would be presents. Coleen never came empty handed, and like elephants, they never forgot.

"Come on guys, Nannie's tired and she wants to take a shower," he said smiling. "If it's OK with you, Coleen, I'll order some pizza for dinner tonight."

"Pizza will be nice," said Coleen, snapping her now empty suitcase shut. By the end of this holiday she knew she could say goodbye to size fourteen, and hello to size sixteen. There would be burgers too, and other fattening things to eat, but she had no intention of saying anything. Ricky had a difficult life as it was, without her adding to his worries. She did love pizza, she loved all food, that was her downfall! She made up her mind that she was going to enjoy this holiday, not count the calories, and take herself in hand when she got home.

The girls were now arguing about which toppings they wanted, and Ricky winked at her as he chased them out into the hall. Amidst all the squealing and laughing they were pretending to fight him, not acting like girls at all, but was it any wonder, when their father was the main influence in their life?

Coleen got three parcels wrapped in pretty paper out of her zipped holdall. "Here you are girls, it's time for presents."

This made them all leap off the ground, and when they opened them, Brenda had a Disney packed lunch box, with sweets inside, for Kathy who had only just started school, a pencil case with everything she could need inside, and Maria also, just learning to colour, a book and a set of pencils of her own. She had also bought a large tin of English chocolates, which she knew would go down well, and for Ricky, some beer.

The girls wanted to run down to Marina to show her their presents, and Coleen had the presence of mind to find something for her. She might only be helping, but it wasn't nice to make her feel left out. She had bought a smaller box of chocolates for Caroline, so she gave it to Brenda to take to Marina. She could soon replace it with something else before she saw Caroline. She

60

felt generous towards this young woman who had made herself available to the family.

Marina received the chocolates graciously, saying to Brenda, "Tell Nannie she shouldn't." She took them to her room, saying she would sample them later. As far as she was concerned they were cheap and nasty. She only ate Thornton's, or expensive continental chocolates, but Coleen wouldn't know that. She was just an ordinary person, and Marina didn't do ordinary, nothing but the best for her. She would throw them in the garbage later when no one was looking.

Marina retired to bed early, at about nine o'clock, after the girls had been read to, and settled for the night. It was a strain pretending to like what she was doing, and her resentment that Ricky was stretched out on the sofa chatting to Coleen whilst she was reading stories had to be kept hidden. She congratulated herself on playing her part so well.

She accepted Coleen's offer to use her shower, and was glad when in the confines of her own room, she was able to switch on Brenda's TV, and watch what she wanted in peace. She'd been forced to chat about England to Coleen, and she didn't really want to, although she had wondered from time to time whether her flat and Nathan had gone up in smoke, and did her parents now think she was dead? But it was only a fleeting thought, and she didn't allow it to trouble her for long.

Ricky chatted to Coleen about the plans for the next day. "My mother is coming over, and she would like to take you, the girls, and Marina for brunch. Marina can drive the space wagon. I have to be at work, but we can do stuff together at the weekend," explained Ricky feeling a little guilty, but Coleen hastened to assure him that he needn't worry. The three women and the girls would do fine together, and even if he'd come, he would have been surrounded by women, and hopelessly outnumbered.

"Do you think that Marina will make her home here permanently, or is she just filling time here, and at the school?" Coleen asked. If that was the case, it would be yet another loss for the girls when she moved on.

Ricky hadn't thought about it before. She seemed to love America, and it had been an escape route when she lost her parents. The thought of the girls being without her was not one that sat well with him. He preferred to bury his head in the sand at this moment in time.

"I don't think she wants to return to England. She lost her parents in a car crash about a year ago, and she never speaks about having any other family."

"Poor girl! and then she fell in love with an American who got her to come over here to marry him, and then promptly dumped her. She's really been through the mill! No wonder she has such a lot of sympathy for you, and wants to help with the girls."

"I know, I'm very lucky, I've had a succession of nannies in the past year, but this time the girls chose her really. Brenda liked her so much, it was like an answer to a prayer."

Coleen wondered whether she should point out to him that it wasn't a good idea to let the girls think of her as a permanent fixture. She decided not to, otherwise she would be a typical meddling mother-in-law, and she had always tried so hard not to be that. She knew that Caroline had been in hot water in the past for venturing her opinions, but she could get away with it. She was Ricky's mother.

Surely Ricky had noticed what a lovely girl she was with her very dark eyes and raven black hair? She had breeding too. When she got over her jilting, there would be other boyfriends, and marriage one day. Would the girls be so important to her then? But her mind was flying ahead. Ricky had only said she was helping out for the holidays. There had been no talk of her having a permanent position. Well, all she could do was to stop worrying about it, and live for the moment, losing George so young had taught her that. Who knows what is around the corner? Certainly she hadn't expected all this! She would enjoy her time spent with Ricky and the girls, and then she would go back to England and get on with her life, and she would leave Ricky and the girls to get on with theirs. He was coping brilliantly! She must not interfere, he always put his girls first, and he was capable of making the right decision.

She stood up and stretched. Although only ten o'clock, for her it had been a twenty-nine hour day, and she felt tired. She needed to sleep. "I'm off to bed now, Ricky, I'll see you tomorrow evening."

"OK, night," said Ricky absently, the remote control in his hand. He was getting tuned in for the late movie. Now everyone had settled for the night this was his time. Watching movies was his habit, because since Amy had gone, he dreaded going to bed alone in that big bed they had shared. When he did go, he couldn't sleep that well, so late movies were a diversion he needed. He had a photograph of her, wide-eyed and smiling, looking so full of life it was painful, which greeted him every time he woke up. But he still had to keep it there, on the dressing table.

He found a nice fast moving movie, and settled back on the couch. Often he had woken at three in the morning, to find he had fallen asleep there, and then moved quietly up to bed so no one would know, and occasionally he'd even woken up there in the morning. Life was a little crazy right now.

If Marina was in the habit of going to her room early it might be an idea to let her stay. He could still have his space, do his own thing, and if he put a video and DVD player in her room for her, she would go in there even earlier. Maybe he could make it part of the deal. He would see how it worked out over the next two weeks, and make a decision then.

Chapter Ten

The next day was Tuesday, so Caroline reckoned it wouldn't be too busy to go out for brunch. They hadn't needed to book because it was only weekends when families went together normally. Greenview Hotel was a very nice place, with beautiful grounds, areas of parkland and trees, and had a thoroughly restful feeling about it. Coleen would like that after her tiring journey, she was sure, and with Marina to keep an eye on the girls when they got lively, as they always did, that would give them a chance to talk together.

She arrived at ten-thirty, having risen early, and been out already for a short walk before it got too hot. The weather was set to be around 33 degrees today, and Caroline always made sure she kept out of it at the hottest time. That would be around midday, and by then they would be sitting in an air-conditioned restaurant. That would obviously suit Coleen too, because coming from England, she wouldn't be used to those sort of temperatures.

The girls were as lively as ever; right now they were out playing on the swing set that Ricky had installed for them further down the garden, but they soon left it to run in and inquire if it was time to go when they saw her arrive.

"We'll let you know when it is," promised Caroline, and they ran off again outside.

"How are you today, Coleen? Feeling exhausted no doubt," commented Caroline, as she entered the room. Coleen was dressed in a pale peach shorts and matching top set, which suited her light skin and hair. "Your jet lag doesn't show," she added.

Coleen laughed, and pretended to prop her eyes open. "Not bad really, but I woke up at four o'clock and couldn't go back after that, not that it matters really, I am on holiday after all."

"Yes, in England it would be nine o'clock," said Caroline, remembering it had been the same for her when she had visited England. "You don't have to go to the pool later you know, with the girls, you can take a nap and Marina will drive them there."

Coleen knew this was true, but it was OK for Caroline, she saw the girls all year round. She wanted to share as many experiences as she could with them this holiday. She wouldn't see them again until next year. Ricky had said that Brenda and Kathy were in the local swimming team, and they were racing. She wanted to see that. Maria was having lessons to learn, and she wanted to encourage her, too. No matter how tired she felt, she was going to support them!

"I'm coming to watch them. I'm really looking forward to it," she said enthusiastically.

"I'm glad it's not until six o'clock, the sun's so hot today! I've told Ricky not to let them go out in that heat. He thinks that a little bit of sunblock means they're OK but look how fair their skin is," said Caroline anxiously.

"I'm sure Ricky's aware of that. He takes such good care of them." Coleen found herself defending him in his absence. Caroline was a worrier, and this was why Ricky felt she was interfering sometimes, when she thought she was helping.

At that moment Marina entered the room carrying a tube of high factor sun block. She had heard their conversation, and was determined to ingratiate herself in their eyes. She called the girls inside to put some on, and Brenda informed them that Daddy had already done it before he left for work. Marina said she thought it would be a good idea to have some more as it was going to be such a hot day, and she was rewarded with a grateful look from both the women.

Caroline once again thanked her lucky stars that Ricky had such a conscientious person to take care of the girls. Her granddaughters were so precious to her, and it wasn't that she didn't trust Ricky, it was just that the poor guy had so much on his mind all the time, it was a marvel that he found time to fit it all in.

"Can we go now? I'm starving!" grumbled Brenda.

"Yeah, we're ready now," said Caroline.

They drove for about ten minutes until they reached the hotel. Coleen sat with Caroline, Kathy, and Maria in the back. Brenda had been allowed to sit up front next to Marina as a special treat. When they went home it would be Kathy's turn. They had to treat them the same, but Maria had been told, on numerous occasions, that she couldn't have a turn until she was older, and tall enough to sit there. In the beginning it had caused ructions, but she was learning to accept it now.

"This is my treat!" said Caroline very firmly, ". . .choose whatever you want."

"How kind," murmured Marina, flashing her a friendly smile. It was the least the old biddy could do when she put up with her brats all day long!

"Well, thank you Caroline. It will be my turn next time," said Coleen, always prepared to be independent and pay her way. She decided that she, too, would treat Marina as well, just to show her appreciation that she was caring for the girls. Ricky had said he was paying her, but she hadn't been very keen to take the money; surely no one would expect her to give up two weeks of her holiday for nothing? She was truly a very nice person.

The dining room at Greenview Hotel was large and airy, with solid oak tables and very comfortable padded chairs to sit on. The light oak beams gave it an interesting character, although they were obviously fake, and the walls were cream, and the lush carpet was patterned green and cream.

The long tables were laden with food, just about everything from fruit, cereals, bread and rolls, cooked sausages, eggs, bacon, etc, and, Coleen noticed, even Chinese food; noodles, rice and cooked chicken and prawns were available. The Americans certainly liked their food!

The girls would be having doughnuts, but Coleen had never quite been able to get used to the idea of eating them for breakfast. She settled for some strawberries to start off with, with yogurt, and then after that, she chose scrambled egg, with mushrooms, tomatoes and a bagel. This was all washed down with coffee. The Americans knew how to make coffee all right, but not tea.

Marina ate doughnuts with the girls, and Coleen envied her,

66

keeping so slim, and eating what she liked. Just like she had been when young. Caroline had settled on an omelette, which was full of ham, cheese and mushrooms, and looked thoroughly delicious. Coleen resolved to try one later in the week.

When they had finished eating, Marina went off with the girls outside. There was a duck pond. They took some toast to feed the ducks, and there was also a playground, which would keep them amused for a while.

Caroline and Coleen sat, feeling very full, but still managing another cup of coffee each.

"Well, that was really delicious," said Coleen, patting her full stomach contentedly.

"Yes, we come here from time to time, but at weekends it is very busy," explained Caroline.

"I'm not surprised, the food's lovely!" commented Coleen.

Caroline took advantage of the girls' absence, to ask Coleen how she was coping with life. Coleen explained that she was keeping busy, going out with friends, gardening, and she'd also joined an evening class, learning Spanish. She'd met new friends there, and was contemplating taking a holiday next year with another lady from her class. Her son and daughter were good to her too, but she wanted to show them that she could cope.

Caroline admired her independence. She, too, had found it devastating when her husband had died suddenly, but poor Coleen had lost her daughter three months previously. It was the worst tragedy she'd heard of. Caroline missed Amy, her happy go lucky nature had been like a breath of spring, so goodness only knows how her own mother must feel. She hid her pain well, but Caroline knew it was there.

She didn't show her pity, that was no good. They had to carry on being bright for the girls. That was what Amy would have wanted, and maybe Amy was up there somewhere looking down on them, and smiling, because Marina was there too. Caroline had firm religious beliefs, and she had prayed so many times for Ricky and the family. Maybe, now, her prayers were being answered.

"You're doing great!" said Caroline enthusiastically, and at that moment Marina and the girls returned, forbidding any more intimate conversation.

The afternoon was spent quietly at Marina's insistence. Ricky had said that as they were swimming later, they were to rest. Only Maria actually rested on her bed. She would sleep for about two hours still, on hot days, but it was always a tussle to get Brenda and Kathy to rest.

They were allowed to watch TV, if they sat still in the room. This was called 'quiet time', so they watched children's programs. Coleen took advantage of the spare time, and went to her room to lay down and read a book. Caroline went home, after promising to meet them at the pool later to see them swim.

Marina was angry, but she couldn't show it! They had worn her out this morning. She'd had to push Maria on the swing, and they argued a lot, which got on her nerves. They might have just been doing normal children's things, but she wasn't used to it, and it was hard going.

She, too, would have liked to have a rest this afternoon, but as Coleen was resting, and Caroline was vanishing, she couldn't really disappear to her room and leave the little horrors to their own devices. Maria would sleep, but the other two argued too much. She had to make it look good for Coleen, but it was hard. She wasn't used to this heat, and she really felt shattered. She resolved that when they married, life was going to change. She was going to have help.

She sat with Brenda and Kathy, pretending interest in a Disney film, but allowing it to float over her whilst she cheered herself up by contemplating her future. It was a shame that it would take quite a few months to win Ricky over. She knew she had to be patient, but all her life, up until now, everything that she had wanted had been instant gratification. She didn't do patience well.

She wasn't looking forward to going to the swimming gala, but she had to. Ricky would be meeting them there, so she had to drive the wagon. The only compensation was that they were eating there, burgers and salad, then ice cream to follow. Although Ricky had said he didn't expect her to cook the evening meal, there were still always dirty dishes around to be put in the dishwasher, washing for the girls to put on, and plenty of other things to do. If she wasn't there this evening, she didn't have to do it. Why couldn't he have a cleaning woman like other people? Up until now he had done it himself; a complete house clean every Saturday morning, with the girls helping, as much as kids of that age can. Now she felt obliged to do it, but she hated it, and she made up her mind that it wouldn't be for long, only until she had got her feet very firmly under the table.

Maria woke up after her nap, and they all had cold drinks and cookies. She heard Coleen getting up, and she put the kettle on. Much to her relief, Coleen made her own tea, saying firmly, "It's the least I can do. You have your work cut out, caring for the girls."

Marina smiled her appreciation, and sat down. It was all right for Coleen, she'd spent the last two hours lying on her bed! Coleen sat sipping her tea, and Marina wished she could just stay there doing nothing. All day long there seemed so much to do.

She sent the girls off to get changed into their bathing suits, and also to find their towels. They usually seemed to get distracted on to something else, so she would have to go in and round them up like she'd seen Ricky do. She was learning their ways, and she didn't like it much.

Maria would only be watching, so she had changed into some lemon shorts with a cream coloured top. Even after six o'clock, it would still be hot.

"I can watch the girls if you want to use my shower to get ready," offered Coleen. The poor girl hadn't had any time to herself. She'd been with the girls all day.

Marina brightened. The old biddy was good for something then. She gave her a bright smile. "If you're sure you don't mind. That would be great!"

"It's the least I can do," said Coleen.

After showering and washing her hair, Marina felt much better. She put on some white shorts with a white top. She was pleased to see she was tanning up nicely, and she knew she looked good. The outfit contrasted so much with her dark eyes and hair. She looked very striking, and even if Ricky never noticed, she would get glances from other men; she had ever since she could remember. It was a shame she couldn't do anything about it. She hadn't had sex for quite a few months now and she was missing it!

When she returned downstairs, Coleen commented at how fresh and cool she looked. They rounded up the girls together, and then got in the car. It was time to go to the pool. Now she would have to sit through a couple of hours of children swimming.

Personally she couldn't care less whether they won their races or not, but she would join in with Coleen in giving words of encouragement. It was what was expected of her, and at this moment in time she had to play ball. Her time would come later.

Coleen, for her part, would be thrilled to watch them racing. She'd done it so many times with Amy, who had been a brilliant sportswoman. As far as the girls were concerned, she didn't care where they came, as long as they enjoyed it. That was all that mattered. She looked across at Kathy, sitting silent for a moment in the car, at side view with her blonde hair caught in a pony tail, it could have been Amy at that age. Then she heard the tinkling laugh of Maria on the other side of her, who could see the funny side of everything. She had mischief in her eyes, and she hugged the little girl quickly. She was as affectionate as her mother had been, and responded by nestling her head against Coleen's shoulder, saying, "I love you, Nannie."

Coleen hurriedly choked down her tears of emotion. That pain was sweeping through her heart again. It never went away; it just lay there inside her, ready to stab her at any time.

But there was another feeling inside her too, it was anger. Anger that she had been deprived of a beautiful daughter, that Ricky had been deprived of his lovely wife, and probably most tragic of all, that these three dear little girls had been deprived of their most loving mother! No matter how hard she tried to move on from it, it was always there.

Maybe if she hadn't lost George as well, so soon after, the pain wouldn't be so intense. During that three months after Amy he had been such a rock. He understood if she wanted to spend time in her room alone sometimes. He had arranged a memorial service in England for all Amy's friends, and she had many.

She had belonged both to a swimming club, and a running club, and George had even come up with the idea of buying a memorial cup for each club to be presented to a deserving athlete in Amy's memory each year. Coleen had liked that idea, but she knew that without George, her state of mind at that time had been such, that she would never have thought of it.

Oh how she longed to have George back, and Amy! But no matter how much she wished, it wasn't going to happen, and she knew she had to come to terms with it. She had to keep herself bright, and help the girls to enjoy the time spent with her, so that

70

when she went back to England, they would have happy memories. They deserved happy memories. Hadn't they suffered enough? and at such a young age!

They had arrived at the pool now, and Coleen's thoughts were interrupted as Maria sprang up, anxious to get out of the car as quickly as possible to be with her sisters. Coleen opened the door, and they all ran off, leaving Coleen and Marina to follow.

"Let's go and find some spectator seats," said Marina.

Coleen smiled at her and followed after them, round the edge of the pool. They had found Caroline, who had already sorted out somewhere to sit.

"You need to go and get ready to swim," reminded Marina, and they disappeared.

Coleen and Caroline settled in their chairs ready for another chat. Maria was sitting on Marina's lap, and Ricky turned up too, so she jumped down with a squeal of excitement when she saw him. After greeting them all, he sat down next to Marina with Maria on his lap.

"What have you been doing today, Daddy?" she asked him.

"Chasing all the bad guys!" exclaimed Ricky solemnly, winking at the others. It was a simple way of describing a very stressful day arresting criminals to a three-year-old.

Maria seemed to be content with that, which pleased Ricky. He liked to leave his work behind when he came home. The whistle blew for the end of the warm up, and the children lined up ready for their races.

"Come on Greenview," Ricky shouted encouragingly, and they all settled down to watch the gala.

Chapter Eleven

On Wednesday, the morning was spent quietly, and then after lunch Coleen accompanied the girls to Greenview Library, so that they could change their books. After that they went to the local supermarket. Marina helped Coleen to fill the trolley with all the things they were getting low on. Coleen also allowed the girls to choose some candy, as they called it, and then she paid the bill.

No doubt Ricky would tell her she shouldn't have worried when he found out, but Coleen could see how busy his life was. He went out early in the morning, didn't arrive until six o'clock or later each night, and the last thing he needed to worry about was food shopping.

She had bought the ingredients to make a shepherd's pie, which she knew was a firm favourite, and also a beef stew with mashed potato. She bought some broccoli to tempt the girls, because apart from peas and carrots, they didn't seem to eat many vegetables. However, she had noticed that Ricky gave them side salads with their meals, and was pleased to see that.

She could take the weight off him a little whilst she was here, and it would be really nice for him to come home from work and find his dinner ready for him. She had also helped Marina with washing the girls' clothes, and folding them when they came out of the tumble drier. It was nice for Coleen to feel useful, it gave her a sense of purpose.

Coleen told Marina that she didn't mind doing the food whilst she was there, explaining that she did a great job caring for the girls, and Coleen liked to keep busy too. It was her way of helping, and Marina accepted gratefully. She had never had to cook and wasn't a whiz in the kitchen. She had noticed that the girls were quite fussy, and they probably wouldn't like her attempts at cooking.

Brenda and Kathy had both won their races the previous night, and had small rosettes for their efforts. Brenda put hers on the shelf in her bedroom. She called Coleen in to see it, and she noticed there were more on display.

"My, you're getting quite a collection, well done!" enthused Coleen proudly, thinking to herself that although out of the three of them, Brenda might look the most like her father, she had certainly inherited her mother's sporting ability.

"This one's for freestyle, and this one's for breaststroke," explained Brenda.

"Yes, your mummy, too, was good at breaststroke," said Coleen, feeling nostalgic. She glanced at Brenda, her face didn't change, any emotion was kept hidden.

Coleen had noticed that nobody mentioned Amy much. She had found that her best way to cope was to talk about her, and remember her. Maybe her life was over, but the memories were there. She hadn't gone through nine months of pregnancy, a very long and difficult birth, and all those years of bringing Amy up, just to forget her, as if she had never existed!

She would love to talk about her to the girls, tell them some of the things she did when she was a little girl, but they didn't ask. Maybe their way of coping was not to speak about her. Maybe they had found that Ricky couldn't speak about her. Whatever the reason, she would have to accept it. She had no intention of causing them more pain. But she couldn't help hoping that one day, when they had all moved on, they would ask her things, especially Maria, who didn't seem to even remember Amy.

Later in the afternoon they went to the pool for a swim. The best time was after four o'clock, when the sun wasn't so intense. Coleen still found it very hot, and had to retreat into the shade when she came out of the water. She had enjoyed playing in the water with Maria, and judging by her determined efforts on her own, she would soon be swimming like her sisters.

She remembered how Amy had insisted on putting them all in the water right from birth so they didn't know fear. She had said she didn't care whether they swam competitively or not, she just

d

wanted to make sure they would never drown. Well it had done wonders for their confidence, and Ricky was carrying on the good work too, because they came here every day and had the time of their lives.

Marina had also played in the water with Maria, knowing that the other two were confident enough to go off and swim alone. They also liked the water chute, as did Maria, so she had to take her down a few times as well. When Coleen offered to take over Maria, she was glad. She could go and have a quiet sunbathe in peace. "It's only fair you have a turn with your grandchildren," she said, smiling sympathetically, knowing that Coleen would think that she was only taking a break from them for her sake.

Whilst she was sunbathing, Marina resolved to make a close friend of Coleen. She needed to learn how to cook, even if she was only going to do it for a short while. She could offer to help her, and see what she did. It couldn't be that difficult to pick up.

They went home at six o'clock. Ricky had said that he wouldn't be in until seven, so the plan was to have dinner ready at that time. The girls all wanted to bath, so Marina left Brenda in charge, just as Ricky had said she could, and went to help Coleen prepare the meal.

"Are they all right?" inquired Coleen. "I can manage if you want to supervise them."

"Normally I would," explained Marina, "but Ricky says that Brenda really likes to be in charge. She would call out if anything was wrong."

Coleen's face saddened. "Yes, I suppose she's had to be like a little mother to them, especially Maria. It's so sad!"

Marina pretended sympathy, it was expected of her. Quite frankly she was tired of Amy. No one mentioned her name, but the photographs annoyed her; Amy smiling, Amy in her wedding dress! Marina had always been the centre of attention before, but in this house, she could feel the ghostly presence of Amy.

It wasn't that she felt guilty about anything. She didn't imagine that Amy was looking down on her, berating her for using her husband and children for her own devious ends. After all, life is full of opportunities, and she felt it was up to her to take them. This guy might think that he was still in love with his dead wife, but what was love anyway? Love softened people up, and made them do stupid things. She had loved Daddy, but where had it got

74

her? Hating people was much more satisfying, causing mayhem and unrest was more her style. She got a real kick out of that!

She saw that Coleen was cooking minced meat, and draining off the fat. "Do you mind if I watch you cook the dinner? My mother would never allow me in the kitchen, and I want to get it right because Mandy, my flatmate, can't cook either."

"Yes, I've noticed that most people tend to eat out over here. Don't worry, I'll show you. I use baked beans on top, and it will taste different, because in America you can only buy beans in barbecue sauce, but the girls like it, and so does Ricky."

Coleen was surprised at Marina's admission. She usually came over as being very confident. Fancy her mother never letting her cook! She admired her honesty. If she showed her the ropes, who knows, it might be useful in the future.

Pleased to be able to exercise her cooking skills, not only did she show her how to make shepherd's pie, she also gave her a lesson in making pastry, and also how to make a tasty casserole. Marina was generous with her praise, and when they had finished, she went off to check that the girls were getting dressed ready for dinner. Coleen was left with a feeling of closeness and affinity towards Marina.

It enhanced her opinion of Marina even more; because she wasn't perfect, she didn't know everything. She had needed Coleen's help, by her own admission. Not only was she honest, but helping her had improved Coleen's own sense of self worth. She valued Marina's private confession to her. She almost felt like a daughter to her now, it had made them close.

The girls came bouncing down, all ready to lay up the table, and Marina busied herself getting the plates and napkins out. Ricky came in, and after the girls had fought for his attention as usual, they all sat down to eat their meal. As Marina sat next to Maria, helping her to cut her food up, Ricky felt like a huge weight had been taken off his shoulders. At this moment in time, life seemed much easier.

Coleen had done the shopping and cooked the dinner, and Marina was there for the girls. His mother had always helped when she could, but he didn't like asking her too much. She deserved her own life. Well, he was going to relax and enjoy this whilst it was on offer. This was great!

75

Chapter Twelve

There were two things that Marina liked at Greenview. One was the huge shopping mall, which was situated about ten miles away. Unfortunately, at the moment, she had no money to spend there, so all she could do was look longingly at all the clothes and shoes.

The other thing was the open air pool. It was a private pool, Ricky paid a monthly membership, and family and friends could come as his guests. Marina had been used to something similar when she had visited Daddy's country club. That all seemed such a long time ago. It was five months since she had left her flat, and Nathan, but it seemed so much longer.

The pool was situated near to the river, with many footpaths and interesting walks nearby. It had a small pool for little ones, with which Maria had now become bored; she wanted to be with her sisters. The bigger pool had a slide, which the children found great fun, and this led round to the main pool; this had swimming lanes for those that were serious swimmers, another area with a basketball net, which was where all the young men tended to be, and at the end of the pool the diving boards, and a springboard.

There was plenty of room for sunbathing, with loungers laid out both on the grass and also the vast paved area. There were tables and chairs with sunshades, and it also boasted a cafeteria upstairs, and a balcony to sit out on, too. This was all in a woodland setting with trees round the outside, and little borders where various shrubs grew, and paths made out of bark chippings.

If Marina had been on her own it would have been easy to find a man, but all these people were friends and neighbours of Ricky.

Unfortunately it was too close to home. She had to act the dutiful child carer; play with the girls, talk to Coleen and Caroline, and generally pretend she was having a wonderful time.

During Coleen's stay they visited the pool every day, either in the morning before it got too hot, or later in the afternoon. The girls had tanned up to a gentle golden brown, but Marina, with her darker complexion, was turning a bronze coloured brown. She liked the sun, it was a refreshing change to have day after day of continuous sunshine. She intended to enjoy America whilst she was there.

Caroline had joined them at the pool a couple of times, although she didn't swim, preferring to sit under a sunshade and watch. She had recently moved into a retirement complex, which had its own swimming pool and sauna, so she tended to swim there at her leisure.

On these occasions Coleen had sat talking with her, and Marina knew it was up to her to amuse Maria. Privately she thought it would be a good thing when Maria could swim unsupervised like the other two, but she pretended, to the others, to encourage her efforts, saying, "Well done, Maria, kick your legs harder, and use your arms more, and then you'll be swimming too."

She was getting more used to the daily routine now, but still resented that she had to work so hard. It would get worse when Coleen went home, because she would have to cook and clean. Maybe Ricky didn't know it yet, but Marina was staying. The sooner she could get him into bed, the sooner he would marry her, and then life would change. She had no intention of being anyone's skivvy!

She had managed to get Coleen onside, and now she had to make a good impression on Caroline. As her future mother-in-law, she would be a necessary tool when her plan unfolded, so she had to make sure that Caroline absolutely trusted her.

She knew that as long as she appeared devoted to the girls, as far as both of the grandmothers were concerned, this would stand her in good stead. She made a great play in front of them of being fond of the girls. Maria always settled on her lap when she could, and the girls had now taken to kissing her when they went to bed at night. Unwittingly, they were helping her to get even deeper into the family circle.

She drove everybody wherever they wanted to go, without complaining. She played computer games with the girls, did jigsaws, and spent her time amusing them. She even played on their karaoke machine with them. She'd always thought she didn't have a bad voice, so she liked impressing them. It fed her ego to hear them tell her she was good, and Brenda looked at her so admiringly, and then went and told the adults she was cool.

"Marina's such a good sport. Those girls need amusing twenty-four seven," laughed Caroline, and Coleen agreed with her.

"They need to be kept busy all day. When I see them, I wonder how I managed with mine."

"Well, we were all so much younger then," pointed out Caroline.

Marina would have loved to have said that at this rate she'd be old before her time, but it was all going well. She just kept a smile glued tightly to her face, and silently congratulated herself on her acting skills.

Caroline had suggested to Ricky that he let Marina have the weekend off. She had a small house near the beach, which was used for the family in the summer, and she wanted to take Coleen and Ricky and the girls there for the weekend. Not only was there not enough room in the space wagon for Marina, she also thought that she looked tired, and maybe needed a rest. She couldn't resist saying to him:

"It's a lot to do, you know how lively the girls are! Give her the weekend off, we don't really need her, and then she'll be refreshed for next week."

Ricky frowned. Mother was interfering again. If he hadn't been so busy with work, trying to bust this drugs-ring, he would have thought of that himself. It was going to be just family this weekend; nice as Marina was to the girls, he wanted to spend time with them. They hadn't been so clingy lately, and although it was a relief, he didn't want to share them with her. Without Amy there, they had become an even closer knit family unit.

"I'd already thought of that. I will still pay her, of course, it's only fair. She might be relying on the money."

"If she'll take it," said Caroline. She could tell Ricky was a little put out with her, but she had broad shoulders, and she didn't care. In her opinion he needed organising. She was doing it for the girls, and Amy, so she ignored the frostiness of his tone. She knew her son better than most, and please or offend, when she had to, she would make suggestions, whether he had thought of it

78

already or not, and knowing Ricky as well as she did, he had probably been wrapped up in other things and had needed a prod in the right direction.

"The only thing is the girls might make a fuss, especially Brenda," he reminded her.

"Well they've still got me and Coleen," pointed out Caroline, slightly put out. As pleased as she was that the girls liked Marina so much, she didn't like to think that their family were now only second best.

Ricky said nothing. He didn't want to point out that Marina was young and funny, closer to the girls in age, and that Brenda hero-worshipped her. Of course, they loved both their grandmothers, who spoiled them a little, but family tended to be taken for granted, and Marina was exciting to them. He understood, but the last thing he wanted to provoke was rivalry for the affections of the girls.

He had made up his mind, after only one week, that he was going to ask Marina to move in to take care of the girls. It was mainly for them, but it would make life so much easier. He told his mother of his intentions. Normally he would have kept it to himself, until it was arranged, but he didn't want her suggesting it. He wanted her to know that he had thought of it himself.

Caroline was delighted. She had been anxious about how the girls would be when Marina returned to Mandy's apartment. They were beginning to rely on her, and it was obvious that Brenda adored her.

"I've just had a raise at work, so to make it tempting I'm going to pay her a proper wage. She can still help out at the school, but here I want her to be nanny and housekeeper," said Ricky.

"What about Maria?" she asked. She had helped him before when he was stuck, and although she was a delightful little girl, Caroline didn't want to look after her every day. She wanted her freedom to go to golf and entertain friends. If she was selfish, she couldn't help it. She had finally reached a time in her life when she could please herself, and that's what she wanted to do.

"She's old enough for preschool now, and it's held in another wing at Greenview, so they could all go off together in the morning."

"But I didn't think you could afford it. You may be getting a raise, but by the time you've paid that, and Marina, you'll be no better off."

Ricky knew this was true, his wages would rise periodically, but because of his situation, that's how it had to be. However, the peace of mind it would give him would be immeasurable, and the stability for the girls would make the sacrifice worthwhile. He didn't go out, or smoke, or spend much on drink, his family were his world, so his money would be spent in that way, and he wouldn't resent it.

Caroline felt guilty now. It was her duty as a mother to help him too. Maria would be at school herself in a couple of years, so she squashed down her feelings of regret. Perhaps she could meet him halfway.

"I could take Maria for two days, that will save you some money," she suggested.

"No, that's OK, I'll manage," he said. "Thanks anyway."

"If you're sure."

He could see the relief in her eyes and was glad that he had refused her. In the past he knew he'd been a little selfish, his mother had the girls a lot, and they tired her. She had been there, and he'd been grateful. His sister Eliza had helped occasionally, but more often or not it had been his mother. Now that she was living at her new home, there seemed to be quite a social life and he mustn't stop her from enjoying that. She'd come on so much since his dad had died, it wasn't fair for her to give up her life.

"I'm going to ask her when I give her the weekend off. Then, assuming she agrees, I can tell Brenda that she's having the weekend off, but moving in on Monday. That will soften the blow."

It hadn't occurred to Caroline that Marina would refuse, so she put it out of her mind. Why should she? She loved the girls, and they adored her, it was a perfect situation. Maybe it wouldn't be for ever, but it might get them through the next few difficult years. The sad situation they had been put in had made Brenda appear to be much older than eight and a half years, she had to grow up quicker and watch out for her sisters. Having Marina to guide her along would be just what she needed for now, and the future would take care of itself.

She looked out of the window at Marina pushing Maria on the swing. The other two were with Coleen in the kitchen. Coleen had insisted on cooking a beef stew, and a wonderful aroma was floating from there. It looked like everything was in hand, so she could go home.

80

She went to say goodbye, reminding them all of their seaside trip the next day.

"What time shall I come round tomorrow?" she asked Ricky.

"About two o'clock. I'm working half a day tomorrow, and we can make it in two hours. There will still be time for dips in the sea."

"That's right. It's warm right up until sunset, and then we've got a full day on Saturday, and most of Sunday too."

Caroline was pleased. She liked the little holiday home to be used. It wasn't big, with only two bedrooms, but nobody minded that. Ricky would sleep on the pull-down bed in the lounge, she could share the smaller bedroom with Coleen with the two fold-up beds, and the girls could sleep in the larger room with the double bed, as they had done in the past. It would all be great fun, with lots of nice sea air to enjoy, dips in the lovely warm sea, and soft sand beneath their feet.

After she had gone home, Ricky took the opportunity to talk to Marina whilst the girls were having their baths. Coleen was taking a shower, after producing a very tasty meal, and Ricky helped Marina to load the dishwasher.

"Marina, how would you feel about working here and living in? I would offer you a realistic wage, of course."

Marina forced a note of surprise into her voice. "Ricky, you took me by surprise. I only thought I was needed whilst Coleen was here."

Ricky held his breath in anticipation. She couldn't say no! Normally he was a man of few words, but this time he would have to flatter her, to get the desired result.

"You're so good with the girls. They look up to you. And you seem fond of them, too. Am I right?"

"I'm very fond of them, yes." Even Marina herself was convinced by her words, and when she told him that she would take the job, the relief on his face filled her with glee.

She was even happier when he told her that she was going to have the weekend off and be paid for it. They were all off to the beach, but she didn't mind missing it. She had other plans. She could spend Saturday in the shopping mall. She needed some new clothes, and shoes, and then if she could get Mandy to lend her the car, she would have a night out, away from this area, and find herself a man. She'd been a good girl for a long time now, but she needed a screw, and there was always someone around to oblige.

81

Chapter Thirteen

Marina had forgotten what it was like to be free. It was so wonderful to go shopping without kids tagging along, wanting to buy everything they saw. She could concentrate totally on herself, and she did. She bought several new pairs of shorts, a slinky black dress with a low neck, that she had intentions of wearing later that night, and gold sandals with stiletto heels, which looked just perfect with the dress.

She also looked longingly at the gold earrings, but she needed enough money to take her out that night, so she would have to make do with what she already had. She had never been able to hang onto money, it was easy come, easy go, all her life, so by Monday she would be spent out and waiting for her next injection of cash. If she could find someone with a bit of money, she could relieve him of it. She'd always managed to before.

Mandy was still keen on Calum. They didn't go out much, they seemed like a boring married couple, and now that she had told Mandy that she was moving in with Ricky and family, she wouldn't mind betting that Calum would move in with Mandy.

She'd pretended to be so sad that she was leaving, and said she hoped that Mandy didn't mind. What a laugh! It was obvious Mandy believed every word. Marina had always done what was best for her in life, and always would, but she'd managed to fool Mandy, who held her in such high regard. Mandy must be cultivated, because she might be a base that she could retreat to when she started playing mind games with Ricky.

She felt jealous that Mandy had got Calum, whatever did he

see in that plain Jane? She'd been tempted to have him for herself yet again, but it was too close to home. It would spoil all her plans, so she must control herself until she went out. Not that she couldn't take him from Mandy. It would be dead easy!

Ricky had given her a key of her own, so on Saturday afternoon, she officially moved in. She only had a few belongings at the moment, but that would soon change she promised herself, as she unpacked them. One more week in Brenda's room, and then Coleen would go home and she could move into the other room.

She helped herself to a bath in Ricky's en suite. Of course, he had the biggest and best bedroom of all. It wasn't a feminine room, the walls were cream and he had a navy blue carpet, and his huge king size bed had a plain navy blue quilt. The curtains were also plain navy, and the whole room looked dark and morbid. It lacked a woman's touch, and obviously Ricky must have chosen the extras himself, probably after Amy had died. Once she was in this room, Marina decided, she would get him to redecorate, and they would have lighter furnishings.

Ricky kept his computer in here. He allowed Brenda and Kathy to use it sometimes. They had games they liked to play, and judging by the empty cases left on the computer table, they had been on it yesterday. Marina would have liked to use it, but she didn't know the password. But that would all change when she became a member of the Scott family, and she hoped it would be soon.

She'd washed her hair, and now she stood by the mirror, brushing it. The sun had added chestnut brown highlights to her normally black hair, and she liked it. She knew her looks could stun any man, there was no lack of confidence with Marina, there never had been.

Her glance shifted to Ricky's dressing table, and there was the face of Amy, smiling at her, looking straight at her face. Oh how she hated the memory of her! This was why it was taking so long to get him, the soft fool was still in love with his wife!

Her instinct was to smash that photograph into a thousand pieces, in any other situation she would have done. But she knew she couldn't, everyone would know it was her. All her life, up until now, Marina had given vent to her temper whenever she wanted, but for the first time ever, she had to learn self control.

She paused to ask herself why she was so jealous. It wasn't that she was in love with Ricky. She didn't really understand herself at all. Love had never touched her life, all her sexual encounters had just been sex, with men or women, nothing else, no emotion. All she knew was that she loved to cause unrest, she enjoyed hating people, it was exciting.

She had also felt the need, from ever since she could remember, to be the centre of attention, and if anyone stopped that, desperate measures were needed to get rid of them. That's why her brother Jeremy had to die. She hadn't felt remorse. Marina didn't do remorse.

Nathan had to go too. He knew she had changed her name. She wanted her parents to think she was dead, and then they wouldn't try to find her any more. As for the flat; Daddy hadn't bought it in her name as she had hoped, her vile mother had persuaded him only to rent it, so she was angry, and leaving Nathan to unwittingly destroy it as she had, had been perfect. That was what she thought of the flat!

She had so much anger inside her, she didn't know why. To her it was normal to feel angry. Ricky seemed such a wimp, pathetic, like her mother had been. Why waste your life pining for someone who's gone? Didn't he realise there were plenty more fish in the sea and she was one of them?

In this house, especially in this room, the presence of Amy presided; she was the centre of attention, even though he never mentioned her name. He didn't have to. She could tell that, so far, he hadn't even noticed her as a woman, and she felt piqued about it. She was just good old Marina, who loved the girls. If only he knew just how much they got on her nerves. What a clever actress she was!

She went back to her room, leaving the smiling face of Amy behind. Well, she didn't have anything to smile about now. Marina was going to make sure she did OK out of her husband! He wouldn't know what had hit him when she started getting nasty. She was really looking forward to that.

She dressed carefully. The sleek black dress made her feel good, with its clingy material, which accentuated the slim lines of her body. Her cleavage showed impudently at the top, and her legs, now nicely tanned, looked great in the gold sandals.

The dress still looked as if it needed some relief at the top, so she went into Coleen's room to see what she could find. Coleen had told her when she had seen them, that the gold earrings with a matching chain had been bought by George, and she only wore them on special occasions. As she guessed, she hadn't taken them to the beach, they were on the dressing table.

She tried them on and, as she thought, they set it off nicely. She would borrow them, Coleen would never know. They were about the only thing that Coleen had that was of any value. Her other earrings were cheap and trashy. Marina never wore anything less than pure gold.

She had managed to get Mandy's car. It was a laugh really, neither Mandy nor Ricky had asked if she had a driving licence, they just assumed. And him in the FBI too. She didn't have one, and the thought of her deception pleased her. She was now free to drive about twenty miles away. It was unlikely she would see anyone she knew then. She had looked on the map and seen the town of Burley. There would be bars and restaurants on the outskirts. She would find someone.

She still had some dollars left, enough to buy her a drink or two, and after that whoever he, or she was, she didn't rule out either possibility, they could then pay for her. It was quite easy really, being attracted to men and women had its own advantages. She would never go short of partners.

When the telephone rang she ignored it. Let the answer machine take it. She was off duty! She could hear it. Some guy that Ricky worked with wanting him to call back. He said it was urgent. Well tough, she wasn't about to ring his mobile and tell him. It could wait until he came home.

It was eight o'clock in the evening now, and getting a little cooler. In about an hour it would be twilight, so it was a good time to go. She got into Mandy's car and drove until she reached Burley. She had found that, unlike England, most of the small towns didn't actually have a town centre with shops and restaurants, they were in shopping malls, or on the outskirts of the town. She drove around for a while, and then, in the middle of nowhere, she found a bar.

When she looked through the window, it looked rough and bare with just a wooden floor, and tatty blinds at the window. The men were sitting on stools up at the bar, steadily drinking, some were even smoking, and a juke box was blaring out. This was nothing like the welcoming pubs and restaurants in England. For once, her confidence almost deserted her. She couldn't go in that smelly place. No man was worth that. She hated smoke, it would get in her clothes. Nathan had smoked, and she wasn't putting up with it again!

She returned to the car, and then drove towards an open air shopping complex. It was now closed, but there was a burger bar that was open. How the hell could you meet anyone in this country? Suddenly she missed home. She was in a huge country, didn't know the customs, and was out of her depth. Her last resort was tears. Tears of anger and frustration.

Donna Taylor came out of the burger bar. It was Saturday night, and she was going to enjoy a takeaway with large fries and a salad. She had worked hard all week at the drug store, and now this was her time. She had given up men for the time being, and was currently single and enjoying it.

She saw the young woman parked up in the old jalopy. She was a beauty all right, looked like a younger version of Catherine Zeta Jones. She guessed her age to be early twenties, and she was dressed to kill, as though she was going somewhere real special, not a takeaway burger bar.

She smiled in a friendly way at her, and that's when she saw her shoulders heave and shake, she was crying. Being a compassionate person by nature, Donna stopped, and tapped on the window.

"Say honey, I hate to see you like that! Anything I can do for you?"

Marina thought fast. Her usual line was a good one, so she sobbed out the story about a man who had let her down, this time on the anniversary of their meeting, two years ago. They had met for dinner, and he had callously dumped her after telling her he was married. All women had been dumped at least once in their life, and it was a good way to elicit sympathy.

Donna gave her a tissue to wipe her eyes, and she allowed her to take control. It was fun playing a helpless female. "My you're English," she said, wonderingly. ". . .Do you live here, or are you on vacation?"

"I was going to live here, but now I shall go home. England is my home," she said sadly.

Donna couldn't help herself. She was intrigued. This English beauty had been dumped by a jerk, who probably didn't recognise class when he saw it. She felt annoyed he had let down the side. She had met many English people, and liked them very much. This girl was heartbroken, she couldn't leave her sitting in her car. Her naturally friendly nature made it impossible for her to ignore this.

"Well, let's start again. Not all Americans are like him. I'm Donna, I only live one block away. Would you like to come back and talk about it, and I can make you some coffee?"

Things were not going quite how Marina had planned. She was looking for a night on the town. Nevertheless, Donna was tall and slim with red gold hair, and very green eyes. She had a friendliness and air of innocence, and she was very attractive. Marina guessed that she was straight, so she might not get her night of passion that she so desperately needed. But common-sense told her she couldn't sit out here in the parking lot, dressed like this, with nowhere to go.

She shook her outstretched hand. "I'm Marina." She gave a forced smile. "It would be nice to talk to someone, thank you very much," she said, keeping a downcast expression. What a laugh it all was really. As if she'd ever let a man get to her like that!

Donna slid in beside her, and directed her to her apartment, which turned out to be on the ground floor, set around a courtyard, surrounded by others the same. It was quite pleasant with palm trees and little paths between, and when they went inside, she could see how spacious it was, with a large well equipped kitchen, and a nice lounge overlooking the courtyard.

Donna busied herself with the coffee percolator, talking continuously. She made Marina sit down on the comfortable cream sofa in the lounge, and then returned to the kitchen to make the coffee. Marina sat there, feeling a bit ridiculous in her black cocktail dress. Donna was dressed casually in pale green shorts and T-shirt, so she realised she must be a sorry sight. She was the girl who had dressed up for a posh night out with her lover, and then been dumped.

She noticed there were photographs of Donna on the sideboard with a guy who looked sexy. She got up to have a closer look. He was tall, with hair as dark as her own, very sultry brown eyes, and a lean tanned body to match it. If only she had met him instead of Donna.

Donna entered with the tray. "That's my step-brother, Jason.

He'll be in soon. He's come to stay for a while. They're trying a case at the local courthouse, he's an attorney."

"I see."

Marina was quiet. So this hunk would be in soon. How could she get him? But Donna thought she was heartbroken. Nevertheless, the idea of this challenge was exciting. She would have to see what developed.

Donna produced the salad, cheeseburger, and fries from their wrappings. "Would you like some of this, there's enough for two?" she inquired hospitably.

"No thanks."

"Did you actually get to eat dinner."

"No, but I'm not hungry now."

Donna understood. If she'd been dumped by the love of her life, the last thing she would want was food. Obviously, if she had come all the way over here from England to marry him, the guy must have been special to her. Was it a bit unfair to sit eating in front of her? As sorry as she felt for her, she was starving, and wanted to do her cheeseburger justice.

But at that moment, she heard Jason. He would come in and open a bottle of wine to unwind, he always did. Perhaps she could introduce him, and then take her food out into the kitchen.

"Hi Jason, how was your day?" she said, as he entered the room, and then rushed on before he could answer. . . "This is Marina."

Jason shook Marina's hand, noting her eyes; although very beautiful, they still had traces of tears in them. Donna had brought home another lame duck, but this one was cute, no maybe cute didn't do her justice, she was sexy, beautiful, and there was a certain presence about her; he could sense it, even though she was obviously distressed, and he found it exciting. Being an attorney he was used to summing up people's characters, and this girl was deep, he could tell. It wasn't a question of what you see is what you get. Her complexity attracted him.

"Hi Marina, how are you?"

"I'm fine, thank you."

So she was English. That made her even more interesting. An English Rose, he thought to himself. The touch of her hand was exciting, and he was sure he didn't imagine it, her eyes showed

88

that she, too, liked him. Well didn't he know only too well how far those looks had got him with most women. He wasn't averse to the idea of cheering her up in his own inimitable way.

"Would you like a glass of wine, Marina?"

"Thank you very much."

Marina could feel her luck changing. She recognised the same wild streak of adventure in this very appealing young American as herself. He might have a high powered job as an attorney, but he'd been round the block a few times. He would give her a night to remember, she was sure. Judging by the cut of his suit, and the silk shirt he was wearing, he had money. She had always been turned on by a man in a suit, not that many wore them these days. It reminded her of when she was a child, and she had adored her father as if he was the only man in the world.

Jason strode determinedly out to the kitchen and returned with a bottle of French Wine, which he proceeded to open and pour out for the three of them. After offering him some of her takeaway, which he didn't want, Donna took the opportunity to take her food into the kitchen and eat it alone. As far as she was concerned, Jason had come in at just the right moment. She could eat her food, and then go back in and pour out the coffee.

When Jason came in to top up her glass she filled him in about Marina's predicament.

"Well, maybe I should take her out to dinner," he suggested whispering. "Poor little lady's all dressed up with nowhere to go."

"As long as you act properly with her. She's just had some guy break her heart, remember."

Donna looked severely at him. In spite of her close affection for Jason, who was her brother as far as she was concerned, she knew he was a hit with women. Bringing home Marina had been meant to be a kind gesture, and she had no wish to cause the girl even more havoc in her life.

Her mother, who had been widowed when Donna was only young, had married Jason's father after his wife had divorced him. He had been her mother's lover for years, and she had grown up knowing him as Uncle Dan. They went out together quite openly, and Jason, who was seven years older than her, had become her great friend.

Dan had died at only fifty; a heart attack, they were told, and her mother had never got over it. A year later she'd got cancer, and somehow she didn't have the will to live; she'd only lasted six months. This was five years ago, but Donna still missed her. Life had to go on, and she knew she was lucky to have the apartment that Dan had bought for them. As for Jason, he was always welcome here, they had suffered their losses together, and she almost felt that this was his home too.

Jason went back into the lounge to replenish Marina's glass, but this time she declined.

"I have my flatmate's car parked outside, as much as I like wine, I need to know that I'll be in a fit state to drive it back home."

Normally Marina wouldn't have cared tuppence about drinking and driving, but she had pretended to be upright and respectable, so she must carry it through. Donna mustn't get suspicious about her. She'd hardly drank at all since moving in with Ricky, and she missed it. If he had seen her drunk it would have blown everything. That was the only time when the real Marina came out, so she couldn't risk it.

When Donna returned from the kitchen, she took the opportunity to pour out some coffee for Marina and herself. Jason refused it, as she knew he would. He must be the only American who didn't like coffee. She noted that they were chatting together in a relaxed manner. Marina's eyes were sparkling now, no sign of any tears, and Jason was joking with her, cheering her up. Maybe it wasn't such a bad idea if he took her out for dinner, if she wanted to go. Then she could settle down without any conscience and enjoy the evening alone, just as she had promised herself.

Because she had a simplistic outlook on life, it never occurred to Donna that Marina was making a play for Jason. She believed Marina's story without question. She trusted her. After losing her mother at eighteen, and working at the local drugstore since then, she had never even left the county, and didn't have much experience of life. She carried this naivety into her relationships, and although now twenty-three, seemed much younger.

Jason, on the other hand, was now aged thirty, and so far had managed to avoid any serious entanglements with women. This was how he liked it. Donna didn't know the extent of his misdoings, and he didn't want her to. He loved Donna and her trusting nature, and he wanted her to stay that way. What she didn't know, couldn't harm her.

His voice became caressingly intimate as he spoke to Marina.

"I was wondering if I could be your dinner date? You look so beautiful all dressed up, it seems such a waste."

Marina could see how easy this could be. This guy was definitely giving her the come-on, but she mustn't succumb too quickly.

"Well, I'm not too sure. I've just broken up with my sweetheart and am not ready to try again yet." She exulted at the disappointment in his eyes, she had dangled the bait, and he was hooked. This was fun. Jason addressed Donna this time.

"Well sis, after sitting in these clothes at a meeting all afternoon, I need to take a shower and get changed." He had no intention of taking her refusal as an answer. He could see it in her eyes, she fancied him, and his excitement rose as he thought of it. He didn't want a commitment, and neither did she. She was a lot more of a woman of the world than Donna realised. She didn't fool him. "Put a good word in for me," he whispered to Donna, as she came into the hall to give him a clean towel.

When he returned some fifteen minutes later, after showering and changing into cream trousers and a chocolate brown shirt, he saw Marina's eyes on him, appraising him.

"There's a cool little restaurant, very quiet, where we can talk, just two blocks down, you can leave the car here. No strings, I promise!" His brown eyes begged her, and for the benefit of Donna, she looked shyly back.

"OK, I trust you," she said innocently. "Donna has vouched for your good character."

He looked just as sexy in this getup as he had in the suit. She tried to hide the lust in her eyes, but she knew he could read her, even though Donna couldn't. They were so different these two, one very naive, and one worldly wise. Most men were fooled by her, but he was only pretending to be. They both knew that after a meal and a lot to drink, they would end up in bed, and wasn't she looking forward to it! No strings attached, just how she liked it.

"All right, let's go," he said, sounding relaxed.

Marina thanked Donna for her hospitality, then got up, pulling at her skirt, conscious of the way it clung to her. Jason was watching her, and she enjoyed the look of admiration in his eyes. How long since that had happened? Too long, Ricky hadn't done

91

it. But tonight she was going to forget about all that, and enjoy herself with Jason.

She could see he was already a little merry, having drunk more of the wine than she had. She hadn't realised Mandy's car would be such a nuisance. But, she reasoned, if she left it here, it would be her escape route from him later, if she needed one.

They both said goodbye to Donna, and went out into the night air. It was still warm, and the darkness was just descending. There were street lamps on now, and the quietness of the neighbourhood was only broken by the echo of their feet as they took the path towards the restaurant.

After about five minutes walk they arrived there. It was by now nine o'clock, quite late for this sleepy little town, but although the restaurant was fairly empty, Jason explained that it wouldn't close yet. Luckily for him he knew the owner, he dined there a lot when he visited Donna.

It certainly looked welcoming, there was a small garden surrounding it, with a wishing well, and shrub borders. A small stream wound its way through the garden, and you had to cross a tiny wooden bridge to reach the restaurant.

As they entered, Marina noticed the delicate pink tablecloths, with crystal glasses and fine china on them. This was her style, it wouldn't be cheap. Even the waitresses were dressed in black and white with tiny aprons on, which was very unusual in a land where so far she had eaten out of cartons with her fingers.

"I knew you'd like this. It's an English restaurant," explained Jason.

Marina smiled back at him, now she was dining in a way she was accustomed to. Her evening was turning out very well indeed. The waitress came over to seat them, indicating a table by the window, which was set in an alcove. That meant they could talk and flirt privately. Marina liked that idea.

As they sat down, she noticed the waitress looked very friendly with Jason. How dare the bitch flirt with her date! She gave her a grim look. She didn't care how well he was known there, Marina wasn't about to put up with that, no second best for her!

That look didn't escape Jason. Mary Lou was a pretty little blonde girl, with very blue eyes, but only seventeen. He didn't date girls that young, or else he would have snapped her up before. Not only that, she lived right across the street from

Donna, so she would soon hear about it, and he'd be in trouble. He was aware that she carried a torch for him, and he was pleased that Marina was jealous. She didn't seem to be grieving over her boyfriend too much now. This date with her would kill two birds with one stone, it would let Mary Lou see he had someone, and he could enjoy a very fulfilling one night stand with someone who he would probably never see again.

He had every intention of getting her drunk, and then booking in at the motel opposite. Donna wouldn't know, she never woke before about ten on Sundays, and she would have driven off by then, and he could go back and slip in quietly.

He might be thirty years old, and free to do as he wanted, but for some reason that he didn't really understand, he never wanted Donna to think badly of him. She was a refreshing change from his time defending criminals and low life. Donna was so simplistic, and he didn't want her to know he'd been a naughty boy.

They spent a relaxed hour dining and drinking. As Marina drank, the wild side of her nature came out. Gone was the unhappy hard done by young woman, replaced by a tough and alluring female, who although pretending to hold him off, was really making herself available by looks and body language.

Jason didn't ask her any questions about her life, and Marina, in turn, didn't ask him either. They were not trying to get to know each other. They both knew what they wanted, they were perfectly tuned to each other's needs. They flirted outrageously, Marina especially enjoyed giving him tantalising glimpses of her cleavage by accidentally leaning forward. It wasn't hard to cross her legs and allow him to see the top of her thighs. She'd done it all a million times before, and it never failed.

Jason could see, by the time they left the restaurant to book into the motel, that he had been right about her. She might have fooled Donna, but she didn't fool him. She had been after a good time, and he was about to give her one. He couldn't have resisted this very sexy female if he tried, and he certainly didn't want to try. Tomorrow, when they were both sober, they could go their separate ways, and no one would have been hurt, but tonight was the night!

Chapter Fourteen

Marina returned home nursing a king-sized hangover the next morning. She couldn't remember much about the night before, although she had woken up at five in the morning in a motel room with Jason fast asleep beside her.

She made her getaway, picked up the car, and drove straight to Mandy's. After leaving it there, she posted the keys through the door, and took the short walk back to Ricky's house. Her head was pounding so badly, why did she do it to herself? Once at Ricky's she spent the rest of the day in bed, quiet and undisturbed, sleeping off her excesses.

By the time the family arrived in the early evening, she had got up, showered and dressed, and was feeling much better. She appeared to listen whilst the girls happily recounted their weekend. They had been in the water, made loads of sandcastles, and thoroughly enjoyed the beach. The more she heard, the more pleased Marina was that she hadn't gone. She'd always hated sand, it got everywhere. Now that her liver had settled down, and she had managed to eat something, she could look back on last night with pleasure.

She allowed Brenda's excited babbling to wash over her as she relived her night out. Jason had been very able in bed, she recalled. Now that her head was clearer, it all came back to her. It had been a great time, but the only disappointment was that she had come home empty handed. Her headache had been so bad that she hadn't stopped to search his clothes for money.

As for seeing him again, she had no plans, and as for him, he had said no strings, and she had agreed, but she was still a little piqued. Most men wanted to see her again, some even fell in love with her, but it was just as well that he hadn't. It wouldn't do for him to come looking for her, if he ever found out where she lived, that would mess up all her plans. He had simply been there when she needed him, they'd had great sex, but he was only a one night stand.

"How did you spend your time, Marina? Resting, I suppose."

Coleen's question took her by surprise, and she immediately resumed her interested pose.

"Yes, I have been resting. I suffered a really bad migraine, which kept me in bed for all of today. It was a good thing that I had moved all my things on Saturday."

"Poor you! My George used to suffer from migraines. He had to lie down in a darkened room for hours sometimes. Are you better now?"

"Yes, I'm fine now." Marina smiled, but Coleen was privately thinking that the poor girl did look tired. Ricky had said she had taken the live-in job, and Coleen and Caroline had already discussed it together whilst away. They both hoped it would work out. Ricky had said that she could have most weekends off whilst he did stuff with the girls, so maybe that was the answer, to let her have time to herself. They were three very lively little girls, enough to make anyone tired, and she marvelled once again, at Ricky's resilience since Amy had died.

Ricky had enjoyed his time at the beach. He was able to temporarily put the stresses of his job behind him. His mother and Coleen had joined in the beach games with the girls, and then they had enjoyed a steak barbecue whilst the sun was setting. It was good old fashioned family fun, Amy would have loved it. He could feel the pain stabbing at his heart again. Did Amy know how hard he was trying to get on with his life? He forced himself to focus on the present.

"Marina, if you feel up to it, the girls would like to go to the pottery tomorrow".

"Yes, of course," murmured Marina. She knew what that meant. It was a shop where various items of pottery were on sale. They would buy them, and then the girls would go into the studio at the back and decorate them. Boring stuff, as usual!

Coleen and Caroline had asked to come too, so she could turn it to her advantage. She would make sure that the girls chose a gift for both their grandmothers, and then decorated it 'with love'. Coleen would take hers back to England, and every time she looked at it, she would think of that day. Caroline would put hers proudly on display, and remember that it had been thanks to Marina they had gone there that day. She was burrowing even deeper into this family circle. The only person she needed to get closer to was Ricky, that was the hard part.

Most of the time he didn't seem to look at her much. Marina wasn't used to that; most men did, even if they shouldn't have done. She sighed inwardly. She was having to learn patience. Now she was installed here, she could go to her room in the evening, away from them all. She enjoyed having her own space. When the time came, she would make a move on him, because it didn't look as if he would ever make one on her. She wasn't giving him much longer, her patience was running out!

Jason had woken up to find Marina gone. He'd checked out quickly as the time was getting on, nearly nine o'clock. He felt very fragile after all the drink, and was relieved to find that the apartment was quiet when he arrived back. Donna was still asleep. He felt too liverish to eat, and he didn't like coffee, so he helped himself to some orange juice from the fridge. His throat felt dry and disgusting, but he knew it was his own fault. He'd drunk far too much last night.

He went back to bed, waking again about eleven. He could hear Donna moving about, and the smell of coffee drifted into his room. He still didn't feel that great, but it was about time he got up, so he showered and dressed. The weather was already hot, so he put on olive green shorts and a T-shirt. Maybe he could sit quietly out on the decking and read the paper.

He went into the kitchen to see Donna. She was eating doughnuts, and his stomach lurched at the sight of them.

"Would you like some?" she asked, pouring herself a large mug of coffee.

"No thanks. I've eaten earlier," he lied, it was better that way.

"Well tell me, how did it go? Are you dating her again?"

"No, she was real nice, but she needs space after her guy let her down."

He felt a little guilty for the lie, but how could he possibly tell Donna that they had been screwing all night. If she wanted to believe that he was a chivalrous guy who had cheered up a heartbroken girl, then he wasn't about to spoil it for her. He didn't think that he had done anything wrong because Marina had definitely been up for it. They had both enjoyed a good time, and he hadn't minded that she had disappeared. But Donna wouldn't have approved of his behaviour. Donna didn't really know life, she lived in her own little world, and he had no intention of shattering her ideals. That's what made her so special.

Donna noticed he was subdued. He probably had a hangover, but wouldn't admit to it. Maybe he liked Marina more than he had said, and was disappointed that he wasn't seeing her again. Her naturally kind heart felt sad for him. Jason never seemed to have a girl for long, though he was so good looking. He always said he didn't want to settle down, but he left his luxury apartment quite regularly to come and see her. Maybe he was lonely. She resolved to make a fuss of him today: "What would you like to do today? We could see a movie."

Going out was the last thing Jason felt like, but he knew how to get out of it without hurting her feelings.

"Do you know something sis, when I come to see you here it's real cool. After being at that courthouse all week, and then the meeting yesterday, it would be great just to sit on the decking and read and chat together, like a family should."

"That suits me, too."

Donna's eyes glowed with happiness. They only had each other left for family, that's what made them so close. Jason's mother lived in Colorado now, too far for him to visit that often. She was so happy to think that he thought of this as his second home.

"Later I'll order some pizza for us, my treat," he said smiling at her. He was starting to feel a little better, and hopefully in a few hours time he would be able to face pizza. He picked up the paper and headed out onto the decking, where the sun loungers were, and Donna followed with her mug of coffee in her hand.

Caroline drove home from Ricky's that Sunday evening thinking about how much she had enjoyed the weekend. It had been great

e

to see the girls enjoying the sun and the sea. If she had her way Ricky would take them to the holiday house more often, and for longer, but he didn't seem to take much leave for vacations, and she wasn't sure she could cope with them on her own. They had loads of energy, and she wasn't in the best of health. The doctor had told her that she mustn't get stressed, or overtire herself, and so she dutifully lay down every afternoon with her feet up and rested. It was out of the question with them. Maria would rest, but not the other two.

Maybe she should ask Ricky if she should spend a week there with Marina to help her. That would work. But then she remembered that after next week, when Coleen went home, it would be time for the girls to return to school. The summer had passed very quickly, this year, it seemed. Not like last year, but it had been so soon after the accident, and they had been all over the place emotionally. Thank goodness life was now settling back into a less crazy routine.

Ricky was very lucky, because Marina had said that she was going to give up working at the school so she could concentrate on looking after the family. What a dedicated person she was! Maria was going to preschool for two mornings, and Marina would care for her the other three days at home. Although it was very sad, fate had dealt her a cruel blow, it was so lucky for Ricky and the girls that she had been jilted, otherwise she wouldn't have been with them now. Life was funny really, how it panned out. Her loss had been their gain. Some good had come out of Marina's pain, and hopefully, one day she would look back on it and realise that man hadn't been right for her.

She didn't know how Marina felt about him because she never mentioned it now. Being kept busy with the girls was probably the best thing for her. Nobody could fail to be moved by their tragic circumstances; not that it was ever discussed, but it was there, deep inside them all, the feeling of loss and pain, and this was probably what had drawn Marina to them. She, too, had lost her parents in a car crash, and been jilted.

It was difficult for her to analyse Marina's character. She had obviously been very badly hurt, but she hid it well. She was always polite, a trait that Caroline admired; manners cost nothing. She had been brought up in a wealthy home, that was obvious. She only wore expensive clothes and jewellery. The girl must have money. If she was an only child, she would have inherited on her parents' death. She probably didn't need to work at all, and that's what endeared her to Caroline most of all; she loved the girls, her precious granddaughters, and was obviously drawn here because of her own circumstances.

She laughed with the girls a lot and kept them entertained, but Caroline sensed another side to her, a deep side, where all her pain was stored, a private side that she kept hidden from the world. It's what everyone had to do to survive pain. Caroline had done it herself when Theo had died. In the end you found that the play acting paid off, because you came to terms with it, you had to, there was no choice if you wanted to survive, you had to move on.

Chapter Fifteen

The second week of Coleen's holiday passed very quickly. As Marina had thought, the outing to the pottery proved a memorable event for both Coleen and Caroline. The girls chose a planter set for Coleen, who loved indoor plants, and a fruit bowl for Caroline, who always had one on her sideboard. These had painted flowers and hearts with messages of love on them, even Maria had added her row of coloured dots.

Coleen had packed hers very carefully in her suitcase, sandwiched between soft clothes. She was determined to get it home safely. She knew that every time she looked at it, she would think of that day, and the fun that they had together.

The weather was set fair, although there were one or two thunderstorms at night. Even after the rain it didn't take long for the sun to come out. They had put the pool to good use, and been to the shopping mall with Coleen, who allowed the girls to choose something new each, which she paid for. She had also bought Marina some earrings as a little present. To Coleen Marina seemed almost like the daughter she had lost; she was so devoted to the girls, and she wanted to express her appreciation.

Marina received them with good grace, dutifully hugging her, and saying "thank you". When she had gone, she intended to dispose of them post-haste. She could see that they weren't the sort of quality that she had been used to. Marina only wore the best, and these weren't it. As far as she was concerned, the silly cow need not have bothered. Nevertheless, she called Coleen "A very special person," which clearly impressed her, as it was meant to do. It was a term that she had heard lots of people say in America, maybe it was grovelling a bit, but then that's what they were here, in her opinion, a nation of grovellers.

Caroline invited the family round for dinner one evening. It was a chance for Coleen to see her new home. So Marina too, enthused about the open plan rooms with lots of space, the smart kitchen with pine units and wood laminate floor, and the lounge with the big picture window which looked out onto the private pool. Marina secretly envied all these people with their spacious homes. If only Daddy had bought the flat like he'd promised her, she wouldn't have had to go to these sort of lengths to make her way in the world. She made up her mind, that when she was finished with Ricky, she, too, would have a nice home with a swimming pool.

Ricky gave Marina the weekend off again, so she took the opportunity to go to a movie, and then out for a pizza afterwards. She was a little miffed that Mandy's car wasn't available. She had gone away in it for the weekend with Calum. This meant she had to stay in the immediate neighbourhood, so there was no chance of finding a man. That was the trouble with this country, everything was so far away, and if you didn't have a car, you couldn't go anywhere. She really needed a car of her own, but there wasn't much chance of that. She consoled herself with the thought that maybe, once she'd got control of him, Ricky would get her one.

She spent Sunday at home, just sunbathing and reading. She was glad that she wasn't going back to the school when the girls did on Tuesday. Looking after Maria was the perfect excuse. She had no intention of flogging herself to death, and looking after these three was quite enough for her. It was useful that they all thought it was her devotion to the family. How sweet that this family lived in cloud cuckoo land!

Ricky had managed to negotiate a couple of hours off on Monday afternoon to take Coleen to the airport. She had said her goodbyes to Caroline on Sunday, and now the girls were sitting in the back of the car, ready to give her a send off. He had left Marina behind this time and she was busy having a clean up, and cooking a shepherd's pie. He liked the idea of arriving back and sitting down to dinner almost immediately. It was more like the old days. Not that Marina could ever fill

Amy's shoes, no one could, but it was nice to have home cooked meals again.

He could see that Coleen very much approved of Marina. They seemed to have developed a close relationship in a short time. He was pleased that his mother and Coleen approved of what he'd done. It only served to reassure him even more, that having Marina as a live-in nanny and housekeeper, had been the best thing he could do for himself and the girls. Even the evenings weren't a problem. She went to her room, so he still had his own space.

Next week, when the girls returned to school, she would take care of Maria most of the time. He really appreciated her giving up the job at the school for the family. Of course, the other children at school would miss her, but she had said she wanted to spend time with Maria. He could understand that, Maria was a very sunny natured child, she had her mother's bubbly and funny character, although lately he had noticed she was becoming a bit of a madam, developing a mind of her own with a paddy if she didn't get her own way. His heart warmed even more to Marina. She seemed to know how to distract Maria, much better than he did, so he would leave her to carry on with her good work.

As they pulled into the airport at Greenview, he looked for a place to park, and once they were all out the car, he helped Coleen with her suitcase. The girls, now, were subdued. He guessed that they didn't want her to go. They went with her to book in, the queue was reasonable, that's why Coleen chose Mondays to travel. She didn't like flying, or crowds.

"Say hi to everyone in the UK," said Ricky, kissing her.

"Yes, I will," said Coleen. She had tears in her eyes when she hugged the girls. She knew she wouldn't see them for another year, so parting was difficult. The girls hugged her back, but without tears. If they were upset, it didn't show. They were used to pain, and had developed a resilience to life and what it threw up at them.

"Have a good flight," said Ricky, remembering her fear. Thank goodness it didn't stop her from visiting. They all waved at her as she went through the security area, and watched as she went along the corridor towards the gate. She turned round once more and blew them a kiss, and then she was gone.

"Come on guys, let's roll," said Ricky, and they all made their way back to the car.

Coleen continued along the corridor until she found gate number twenty-eight. She was nervous, but she never found it so bad flying back. Although she had the short flight first, her luggage would go straight through, no immigration or visa form to fill in, and when she landed, Jamie, her son, would be there to meet her. She had enjoyed her holiday, but now she wanted to get back to England.

It had been painful at first seeing the girls, and being reminded of Amy when she was a little girl, but often happiness and pain go hand in hand, and they had certainly shared two weeks of fun and happiness together. They were such an amazing family! Ricky showed no sign of the misery he must have suffered. He hid it so well from the girls.

The only thing Coleen would have liked was to talk about Amy sometimes, but maybe she was expecting too much. It was still only just over a year, but time was a great healer, and when the girls were older they might be curious to hear about their mother.

She sat down next to a family of Americans. They were chatting in an easy manner about the shopping they would do when they arrived in New York. It was funny really, in this large country, flights were used like taxis to get around. If she had lived out here, would her fears have been any less? Who knows, but she was greatly looking forward to seeing England again. In her opinion, even without George, there was still nowhere like it, England was her home. She rummaged in her flight bag and found the crossword, doing this would take her mind off things. In a few hours she would be home.

Caroline had enjoyed seeing Coleen, but now that she had gone back to England, she resolved to take things a bit easier. They had been out most days, and she hadn't found the time to take her afternoon rest. Last time that had happened she had ended up in hospital, and she didn't want a repeat of it. She was not so robust these days, and the relief that she felt that Ricky had Marina now was tremendous. She had done her best to support him at the worst time in his life, but now it seemed to be getting easier. He had a nanny who would stay.

Laying with her feet up in the afternoon resting, allowed her mind to focus on other things, and she re-lived the last two weeks again in her mind. The trip to the pottery had been great. She would treasure that fruit bowl forever. Brenda had painted 'I love Grandma' on it, Kathy had added some flowers and hearts, and Maria had done dots, lots of them in all different colours. It was thanks to Marina really, not only had she taken them there, but it had all been a surprise. Whilst Coleen and herself had been browsing in the shop, she had taken the girls into the studio, and helped them with their painting.

One day they had gone to Wet and Wild, a water park which was fairly close to them. She had opted out that day. At the age of sixty, with a neck that was a bit prone to injury at times, it wasn't a good idea to do those water rides. Coleen had gone, but by her own admission, she'd only tackled the easy ones, and then gone for a swim. She had needed to be there for Maria, because she was too young for all of the scary ones. But Marina, by all accounts, had taken the girls on everything, and they had loved it. Marina was fearless, and they really looked up to her.

She looked at the clock. It was four-thirty, and she'd been laying here for over two hours. It was now time to get up and have a cup of tea. That was one English habit that Caroline thoroughly approved of. After that she would take a walk for about twenty minutes, just to loosen up her stiff limbs. Later she would need to go to the grocery store to pick up some food, but there was no rush. They would be open this evening, too.

She swung her legs over the bed, wincing a little at the pain. Her neck was very stiff again, but she wouldn't have thought she'd overdone it. She put on her slippers and went into the kitchen to make herself some tea.

Marina was looking forward to about three hours of peace whilst they were at the airport. She would flash the vacuum over quickly, she wasn't going to dust, just puff a little bit of fresh air spray round when she heard the car in the drive. Ricky wouldn't notice. She had prepared the shepherd's pie. It was all ready to put in the oven. If her mother could see her now she'd never believe it! She hated all this really, but it was a means to an end. Her reward would come later, she promised herself.

Ricky had said he would be back about six, and although she wasn't used to conforming, she would have the meal ready for then, because the girls had to have their baths and get to bed early in readiness for school the next day.

She rejoiced that she didn't have to return to the school. She only had Maria during the day, and she slept after lunch for about two hours; she might even stretch her to three. Maria couldn't tell the time. This was definitely an easier option than being with loads of brats all day. Now that Coleen had gone home, life would be less hectic with them, and hopefully she'd only have to put up with Caroline about once a week.

She hadn't wasted any time after Coleen had left. All her belongings had been moved into the guest room. This was so much better than Brenda's room. Ricky had found a spare TV and DVD player, so he wouldn't see much of her at night. She now had her own shower, it was almost like her flat in England had been. She took a shower, changing into a clean pair of lemon shorts and T-shirt. She liked herself in lemon, it contrasted well with her hair, and her tan.

The time passed very quickly and as Ricky had predicted, he arrived home at six o'clock. After they had all eaten, and the girls were in the bath, Ricky came into the kitchen whilst she was loading the dishwasher. "Dinner was great, Marina, you did well!" he said enthusiastically. He noticed, for the first time, her dark eyes, they sparkled when she smiled. He'd never even noticed the colour before. She was wearing lemon, and it suited her well. Even in casual shorts, Marina always looked smart. She had class.

Marina smiled at his compliment, but her dark eyes hid her anger. She felt like a skivvy! "You're welcome," she murmured, and then for the first time she could remember, his eyes looked straight into hers. Ricky rarely looked into her eyes, but this time he did, and she saw admiration in them. Had he finally realised she was a woman? Thank the lord!

So all her 'loving care', was paying off at last. She had to move more slowly with him than she'd ever done before, or else she might blow it all. In fact, when she thought about it, she never had moved slowly with any man or woman in her life. If she fancied them, she made it clear, and then it was straight into bed. They always fancied her too, but she was choosy. Ricky wasn't bad looking, she could tolerate him for a while.

Later, when she was in bed, her bad mood now forgotten, she

felt pleased. Today they had taken a step forward, he was beginning to respond to her charms, she knew it even if he didn't. He had noticed her, and she promised herself, before the year was out, he would be hers. Marriage would have to be the answer, his family wouldn't tolerate an affair, it wouldn't be good for the girls. Once he made her his wife she could stay in this country. Her visa had run out months ago, not that she was worried about it. Flouting authority gave her a buzz. Ricky had never asked her about it, and no one had caught up with her. Even if they did, she'd beat them at their own game and be off again, but at the moment she was sitting pretty, and determined to stay that way.

Chapter Sixteen

After the girls returned to school, life settled down into an agreeable routine. Ricky found he had much more time to concentrate on his work, and if he was needed to stay late, it was no longer a problem. Just a quick call to Marina, telling her to carry on without him, and feed the girls whenever she liked.

He didn't work at weekends, he kept them free to spend time with the girls. It suited him to give Marina the time off because he was determined that his daughters were not going to grow up totally centred on her, with him as the distant father figure. During the weekend, even if she didn't go out, she kept to her room, but they didn't see her much, he was in and out with the girls all the time, either swimming, going to movies, visiting his mother, and always eating out. He knew how much the girls enjoyed the weekend treats, and so did he; his daughters were the most precious thing in the world to him.

When Halloween came, it was at the weekend, and he willingly gave Marina the time off. She had gone shopping with the girls to get pumpkins, and helped his mother to make them some cool costumes to dress up in. That was the hard part over with, so he was more than happy to accompany them round the local neighbourhood for 'trick or treat'. They came back very happy with a bag full of candy, which he helped them to eat, much to their indignation.

"Well, I helped you, and anyway, too much is bad for your teeth," he said, grinning. Brenda looked a little sulky, so he tickled her until she couldn't help but collapse with laughter. He enjoyed these little fun times with them, life was settling down, even the pain of life without Amy was not quite so acute; all the while he kept laughing, trying hard, for the sake of the girls.

Marina had offered to do the Christmas shopping for him, which he was very glad about. He hated shopping, that had always been Amy's department, and if it had been left to him, there wouldn't be any presents. His mother had done it for him last year, so she had gone out with Marina and helped her to choose the right things. Marina had put it all on her credit card, she said she didn't mind, so all he had to do was give her the cash for the whole amount. It was so easy and stress free. She had spent more than his mother had last year, but he wasn't going to complain about that. He'd got a bonus at work, so he could afford it. She'd got the girls all the presents they'd asked for, even down to the exact Barbie outfits and props, none of which were that cheap. Kathy had been smitten on a pink Barbie limousine, which in his opinion cost the earth, but he consoled himself with the thought that Christmas does only come once a year.

Maria, at the age of three and three quarters, had just learned to balance on Kathy's two wheeler. He was very proud of the fact that she had mastered a two wheeler before she was four, that was quite an achievement, so she had to have a new pink bicycle. She wanted to keep up with her sisters.

His mother had been easy, a gift certificate to spend in the fashion store at the mall, and on his mother's advice, because he didn't have a clue, it seemed that Marina wore Coco Chanel perfume. Mother had bought that for her, and the store had wrapped it beautifully. He grimaced to himself at the price, but said nothing. His mother was right, she wasn't just a nanny, she was a friend to the girls, and deserved to be appreciated.

Caroline had wondered what would happen to Marina at Christmas in a strange country. She had already told Ricky that he couldn't let her spend it alone. They were going to her on Christmas Day, and the invitation was extended to Marina if necessary. But when he asked her about it, it turned out that she had booked herself in at a house party. These were held at nice hotels, where they had log fires and parties with games and presents. She had said it reminded her of England. She explained that she had been brought up in a beautiful thatched cottage, loads of character and charm, and she was looking forward to meeting up with a friend from England who had come to spend the three days there with her. It all sounded very nice to Ricky, and it was a relief too, that he didn't have to worry about her. As nice as Marina was, he could enjoy his girls, and so could his mother, on their own, for Christmas Day.

On Christmas Eve he took the girls to midnight mass. His mother would expect it, and it was the way he had been brought up. If Marina had been there he would have left Maria with her, but as she wasn't, they all came. It was the tradition to open presents afterwards, but he could see that the girls were too tired. Not that they thought they were. He ignored all their protestations, and eventually marched them to bed. They were tired and so was he. Christmas wasn't starting too well. When he finally sat down, after they had settled, he promised himself he would have more patience with them tomorrow.

Marina sat watching Andy as he played with the steering wheel, his long sensitive fingers caressing it, those fingers that would soon be caressing her. She shivered with delight at the thought of it. He wasn't bad looking, his eyes were a greyish blue, he had a ruddy complexion, his nose was straight, and his chin square. His brown hair was cut fashionably short, well didn't the Americans invent the crew cut? He was twenty-seven, married with a young baby, and a wife who gave him hell by all accounts. Right now she was suffering from post natal depression, so he hadn't found it that difficult to engineer an argument to get out.

Andy was very well matched to Marina. Neither of them suffered from pangs of conscience. He wished he'd never got married, let alone had a baby. If they parted, he was resigned to paying her loads of alimony, so if he could keep out of her way when she was like this, and lead his own life, it would be more tolerable.

Marina had met him quite by chance. He lived in a small town called Milton, which was about ten miles away from Greenview, but because there was no cinema there, he had come to the local one at Greenview. He had been so angry that day; all she did was cry, and he'd stormed out of the house and gone to a movie. Marina had been there alone, all ready for his chat up line. She'd decided he would be more than a one night stand. He had a car, so that meant she could go further afield, he lived far enough away not to know Ricky and the family, so they started to meet on a regular basis at the weekends.

Marina had told him that she wanted to see him for Christmas. He was falling for her, and she found him easy to manipulate. He didn't relish the idea of Christmas with Clare and their screaming baby. Life was hell at home, but with Marina it was exciting. They laughed and had fun, had a great time in bed, and it was like being single again. Now maybe if he'd married Marina, life would be much more exciting.

It was easy to upset Clare, so after another one of her tearful outbursts, he made a quick exit on Christmas Eve, exactly as they had planned. He had already put his overnight bag in the car the day before, and to make it sound good in case any neighbours heard, he stood at the door as he went saying, "I can't take any more of your whining, Clare. I need to go away. You're doing my head in."

Now they were off together for three days in a motel. They could eat drink and be merry, he'd been let off the leash, or rather he'd slipped the leash. Whatever it was, it felt good, and it had been such a relief to walk out of that house and leave his boring wife behind.

Marina, too, was looking forward to these three days away. She was taking what she considered to be a well earned break from Ricky and the girls. The thought of spending Christmas Day with them at Caroline's had filled her with horror, but luckily she'd come up with the story about the house party, which Ricky had swallowed so easily. She had to be a bit vague about where it was, saying her friend had booked it, but it never ceased to amaze her that even though he was in the FBI, how easily fooled Ricky was. Obviously he trusted her.

It was thanks to her connection with Ricky that she'd managed to get a credit card. He had vouched for her good character, and so his bank had extended their credit facilities to her as well. Now she could spend, spend, spend, and not worry about paying it back yet. Not that she intended to over Christmas. Andy was lucky to have her company instead of his grizzling wife, so this was going to be his treat.

At the moment Andy was a very useful person to know. When the time came, he would go, as soon as he was no longer useful

to her, but right now she didn't want to look ahead, she just
wanted to relax and enjoy the next few days ahead of her.

Brenda missed having Marina around at Christmas. Sometimes
she just wanted someone older than her sisters to talk to. Marina
was fun, she wore nice clothes, and she knew lots of good
hairstyles. In Brenda's eyes, she was a fashion icon.

When she came back after her break, she allowed Brenda to
come in her room and see a new dress she'd bought. This was a
treat indeed, because Daddy had said that Marina's room was out
of bounds unless they were invited in. It was a long dress; cream
brocade with lacy embroidered flowers on it, fitted at the waist
and the bodice had thin straps. Brenda thought it was so lovely
that it took her breath away.

"Is it for the New Year's Eve Ball?" she asked breathlessly.

"Well, it was," said Marina holding it against her and looking
sad, "but I haven't got a partner."

She had really bought it to go to a party with Andy, he'd paid
a lot of money for it, but then tragedy had struck. Whilst they
were away, his wife had been taken to hospital, Andy said she'd
tried to top herself. This meant that Andy had to help her parents
with caring for the new baby, so he had put his plans to meet her
on hold. Marina was really annoyed about this. She had been
looking forward to that party.

But then she had hit on a plan. Greenview Elementary was
having a ball for the teachers, along with teachers from other
schools, for New Year's Eve. Mandy had invited Marina too.
Originally she had declined the offer. Maybe with a little help
from Brenda she could persuade Ricky to take her. It was now ten
months since she had known him, she had to make a move soon.
Not only that, it looked like Andy wouldn't be available for a
while.

"Can I see it on you?" asked Brenda, and by then Kathy and
Maria had arrived too, curious to see why Brenda was in Marina's
room.

They stood there, eyes wide, and Maria gently stroked the tiny
flowers, exclaiming, "Wow, it's a princess dress."

"Don't be silly, Maria, it's a grown up dress, not for one of
your Barbie dolls," said Brenda trying to sound very grown up

and important. Whatever must Marina think of her kid sister? But Marina just smiled.

Marina put the dress on. The nipped-in waist looked perfect, the bodice was quite demure for her; no boobs on show, a higher neck made a change, and full length, so no legs on show. She felt really good, the girls were gazing with rapt attention, which pleased her, with everyone, even children, Marina always liked to be the centre of attention.

Ricky wondered where everyone was. It was suddenly very quiet downstairs, except for the TV which was pounding out to an empty room. He came up the stairs to make sure that the girls were not up to mischief. He had heard voices coming from Marina's room, and he had expressly told them not to go in there.

As he approached, the door was open, they were all quietly standing there staring, his eyes followed them; Marina was dressed as he'd never seen her before. During the summer she had worn shorts and tops like everyone did, or jeans and shirts, but she was standing there in a cream dress, full length, and he couldn't help noticing how tiny her waist was. He'd never really looked at her properly before, but he could see she was very attractive. Maybe she had a boyfriend, because she surely wouldn't wear something like this unless she was going somewhere special. His heart lurched uncertainly, surely this wasn't going to be the beginning of the end, and she would leave them.

"Daddy, doesn't Marina look beautiful?" said Brenda, excitedly. "She wants to go to the Teachers' Ball, but she hasn't got a partner."

Ricky made sympathetic noises. This was women's stuff, and he didn't want to get involved. He had taken Amy to one or two balls, and he remembered how she had loved to dress up, and he'd worn his white Naval suit. He'd been so proud to have her on his arm. If Marina had bought a new dress especially for it, she must have had someone in mind. Maybe they had fallen out, poor Marina!

"Come on guys, give Marina some peace," he said, attempting to distract them. "You need to clear up your bedrooms."

They reluctantly left her, but Marina had seen Ricky look at her, and she decided to be bold later. Brenda had done her bit, and now she would take over. She was impatient for the time to pass until the girls went to bed, so that she could talk to Ricky on her own.

112

Ricky settled himself on the couch later, searching through the channels for a suitable movie to watch. He was surprised to see Marina come back into the room. He had got used to her going to her room with a cold drink just after the girls, and he felt a little disappointed at her invasion of his privacy.

Marina took the bull by the horns. Ricky would dither for ever, and it wasn't in her nature to be tactful. "Ricky, Mandy's asked me to go to the Teachers' Ball, and I really would love to, but I haven't got a partner."

Ricky didn't look too happy. Had she blown it?

"Well you've bought yourself a new dress. Who did you expect to go with?" He tried to sound kind. He had a feeling it might be himself, but he didn't want to feel trapped, and at this moment he did.

"No, this dress isn't new," lied Marina. "I wore it the evening when I was dumped." Her tone became angry. "It's been nothing but bad luck for me. I think I should rip it to shreds!"

Ricky saw the anger and passion in her eyes. She had suffered like himself. He was beginning to feel a bit of a jerk. This girl had been so good to his family, his mother adored her too, she sang her praises to everyone. But he didn't go on dates. He had wanted no one since Amy, she must understand that!

But then he weakened. He had been told by guys at work he should get out more, meet up for a beer, or go and play golf sometimes. He had tried so hard to give the girls stability, and be there when he wasn't at work, his own social life just didn't exist. Would it really do any harm to go to the ball tomorrow with Marina? His mother would have the girls and, after all, it was New Year's Eve.

"How about if I take you?" he said easily. "We don't want you ripping up your dress."

"I'd like that very much, Ricky." Marina smiled back at him, relieved. She sensed his reluctance. He was being a gentleman, doing it for her. She had succeeded in rousing his sympathy.

She went to bed happy, knowing that tomorrow could be the start of her new life. It wouldn't take much to capture him. He'd been celibate for nearly two years now, by the time she'd finished with him he'd be gagging for more. He was going to feel as if he'd been hit by a very large truck!

*　　*　　*　　*

Caroline was more than happy to have the girls on New Year's Eve. She had said they could stay up late to see the New Year in, just for once, and then in the morning Ricky would come over to pick them up, and stay for lunch. Ricky had explained why he was taking Marina to the ball. She had no one else, and he felt sorry for her. Caroline was pleased that he was finally making an effort to spend time with people of his own age. She had thought, for a long time, that he should have interests outside the home. She thoroughly approved of him partnering Marina to the ball. Inevitably people would talk, and speculate, but she was going to try not to go down that road. He had said he felt sorry for her, and maybe that's all it was.

Brenda was happy when she found out that her dad and Marina were going to the ball. She had never told anyone, not even her sisters, because it was too embarrassing, about her dream. She had dreamed so many times that Marina had married her dad, and become her stepmother. All her friends at school had a mother, she was the odd one out, and she hated it. She'd never understood why Mummy had to die. God punished you if you were wicked, but Brenda didn't think she had been that wicked, nor had anyone else. Maria had only been two. How could she have been wicked?

Marina was so nice, of course she wasn't Mummy. Even two years after her death, she was special, and no one could take her place. But Marina was someone she looked up to, and if she did marry her dad, then they could be more like a normal family.

She'd pretended she didn't care when other girls had tried to offer sympathy. They had been told to be nice to her by their parents, but Brenda didn't want sympathy, it gave her pains in her stomach, and made her think too much about Mummy. She had learned to be tough, and protect her two sisters. But how nice it would be to have someone as a mother figure, for no matter how hard he tried, Daddy couldn't cope with girls' things, like clothes, shoes, hairstyles, and make-up.

She didn't want to hope too much, it was such a lovely dream, but everyone else spoke as though Daddy was just being kind to Marina because he felt sorry for her. They said she was in a strange country without any family, and going to the ball would make her very happy. It was almost like Cinderella. But that was a fairy story, it wasn't true.

"Are you ready, Brenda. We need to go to Grandma's right now."

114

Ricky's voice interrupted her reverie. She closed her bedroom door, and ran quickly downstairs. He was in the hall with Kathy and Maria. Marina stood at the door to see them off.

"Daddy, can we pick up some movies from the hire shop to watch at Grandma's?" asked Kathy.

"Yea, if we get going now," said Ricky.

They all hugged Marina and said goodbye. Maria was grumbling because she wasn't coming in the car with them, but Ricky explained that she was taking a rest and a shower before getting ready to go out. He was now getting used to the idea of the ball, and although he would never have admitted it, was looking forward to having a drink and a natter with friends.

Marina lay on the bed. She planned to be on her best behaviour amongst all the teachers. She'd have a drink or two, but couldn't let her hair down and get really drunk. She had to move carefully, having waited for so long to get him, she mustn't blow it. The patience she'd shown was amazing, Ricky didn't know it yet, but after tonight they would be an item.

After a while she heard him return, so to avoid seeing him at that time, she took a long shower and washed her hair. She had recently had the ends trimmed, and a fringe cut to soften her face. It was still long, she liked it that way, it suited her small face, and when she looked in the mirror, she could see the fringe gave her a look of innocence, which was enhanced by the modesty of the dress.

She dressed carefully, choosing her gold sandals, which matched the dress beautifully. Andy had bought her some gold hooped earrings, so she added these to complement the outfit. When she looked in the mirror she was very pleased with the end result. Ricky couldn't fail to be impressed. She stayed in her room until he called up and told her it was time to go. She wanted to make a grand entrance, and judging by the look on his face when she came down the stairs, she had certainly succeeded.

Ricky was waiting nervously in the hall for Marina. It was so long since he'd been on a date, and it had been with Amy. They had known each other inside out, known what to talk about, and been able to share companionable silences. This was different. What could they talk about, the only thing in his life now was his work and the girls. He mustn't talk about the girls, Marina deserved a break from them. He couldn't talk about work, it was highly confidential. He'd have to think of something.

He looked up as she descended the stairs. He had already seen the dress on her, but now she looked as far away from being a nanny as she could. Her beautiful black hair was swept back on top of her head, with just a demure fringe brushed forward. The sun had given it tawny lights, which matched her brown eyes. She had make-up on, only light because her skin was like a flawless peach. Her eye shadow was green, and her lips were painted in pale peach. He felt a swell of pride inside him, that he would be accompanying this very beautiful and sophisticated young woman to the ball.

Marina noted the look in his eyes, and was pleased. When she looked at him, he didn't look bad either. He was dressed in a black suit with a crisp white shirt and bow tie. She had seen him in a suit lots of times when he went to work, but this was obviously a very well cut and expensive one, and his tall lean frame did it justice.

The cab had arrived, so he held the door open for her as she swept through, murmuring, "Wow Marina, you sure do scrub up well!"

When they got to the ball, there were many people to talk to. Marina knew all the teachers, and had to listen to so many of them telling her how much she was missed at school, but nevertheless what a fine job she was doing in the Scott family. Ricky, of course, endorsed this. After a while they drifted apart, Marina wasn't short of partners, even Calum danced with her. Mandy was talking to Ricky, but after that he was up at the bar talking to other men he knew. For once in her life, although she normally loved the attention, Marina wished all the other men would leave her alone, and then maybe Ricky might dance with her.

She hadn't had much to drink, just a couple of glasses of wine, but Ricky had sunk quite a few beers. He could see how popular she was, and he wasn't surprised. He wanted to get up the courage to ask her to dance, but there was a nagging voice inside him, chiding him for not being content with Amy's memory. He had promised himself when she died, that he would never look at another woman, he would always be true to the love of his life.

But for the first time in almost two years, he felt as if he wanted to move on. She was dancing with Calum again, Mandy didn't mind, she was her best friend, but Ricky suddenly found

116

that he did mind. It surprised him, but he told himself it was because of the girls. She was so beautiful, one of these days someone would come along and scoop her up, and they would be back where they started, and he didn't want that.

The dance came to an end, and to his surprise, the lead singer announced that it was the last waltz. Marina's eyes met his across the floor, and he decided right at that moment, that he, not Calum, was going to share the last waltz with her. It wasn't that he felt jealous, it's just that she had come with him, and therefore they should finish the evening together.

He felt a little light headed as he went across the floor, his legs were OK luckily, and she smiled encouragingly at him, whilst Calum still had his back to him. He was cheeky if he thought he could have the last dance with her, he was with Mandy.

"Hi everyone, Mandy's looking for you, it's the last dance," he said pointedly to Calum. Normally he wouldn't have been like this, but Calum was monopolising her, and Ricky was a little tipsy.

Calum looked guilty, he too was a little the worse for wear. He'd always thought Marina was a very attractive female, and what was the harm in a little flirt. Mandy knew he was her man. He had thought that Ricky and Marina were not a couple, but now he wasn't sure. Ricky did seem jealous, so the easiest thing for him to do was to dip out, and go and dance with Mandy, then everyone would be happy.

Calum slid away, and Marina turned her attention to Ricky. She could not believe it had taken him all night! She was planning to ask him, but she had enjoyed Calum's attention. Now, seducing Calum would be no problem, but as she might need Mandy's friendship later, she would have to contain herself. She wasn't sure if she could trust him not to tell her.

Ricky said nothing to her, just sliding his arms around her tiny waist as the music struck up. Her body seemed to melt into his, and he closed his eyes as they moved slowly together. It had been such a long time since he had held a woman, and it felt good. She was holding her arms round his back, he felt her fingers touch his neck, and he felt himself tingle, and move even closer to her.

Ricky didn't know how long that dance lasted, nor did he care if other people were watching them, all he cared about was the rapture of that moment. Maybe this was crazy, but all his sense of

117

reasoning had gone. He was very strongly attracted to her, and the thought of being alone with her tonight, without the girls, was driving his senses mad.

Suddenly the soft and slow music stopped abruptly. The New Year was being welcomed in. They counted the chimes together, and then everyone mingled, hugging each other, wishing one another a Happy New Year, his moment of passion had gone. He looked around for Marina. Of course all the men wanted to hug her, and now there was lively dancing, and such like. The romantic moment had passed.

Marina knew he was smitten, now was the time to get him home to bed. She managed to extricate herself from the other merry revellers, and she went over, putting her arm through his.

"Thank you so much for a wonderful evening," she said warmly.

Ricky responded immediately. "Does that mean you'd like to go now?"

"If you would," she murmured, her eyes gleamed. This guy had been such a challenge, and now she was almost there.

"I'll just go grab a cab," he said, and went off to the foyer, hoping that there would be one waiting. Marina went to fetch her coat. She had needed one to protect her dress because when they had left home it had been snowing.

Ricky came back triumphant and they quickly got in the cab, out of the biting wind. The snow had settled about four inches deep, but Ricky hardly noticed it. The only thing that was dominating his mind was Marina, and he hoped she felt the same as he did. Her body language had been warm and inviting, but it was a big step, and now his doubts set in.

Marina sat close to him in the cab, pretending to be cold. Ricky enjoyed the feel of her body next to him, and he put his arm protectively around her. They sat like this, not saying anything, until they reached home, and then he took her hand and walked her inside before he returned in the cold night air to pay off the driver.

His head was feeling clearer now, but he didn't want the night to end there with Marina going off to her room. "How do you fancy a nightcap? I've got some wine in the refrigerator," he suggested, and was pleased when she agreed.

"I'm just going to put something more comfortable on," said Marina, skipping up the stairs quickly.

Ricky, too, changed out of his suit into his towelling robe, and then went to get the wine. He took it into the lounge. By that time Marina had appeared; she too, was dressed in a white towelling robe, and her feet were bare. She had loosened her hair, which made her look very sexy. They shared the bottle of wine together, and suddenly he found himself talking to her, talking in a way he had never done to anyone before, all about Amy, the accident, and how the children had been affected. It was as if it had all been locked up inside his heart, and suddenly Marina had found the key.

Marina listened to him without saying much. This wasn't in her plans, but she would have to listen, and pretend to be the sympathetic shoulder to cry on. They were both getting a bit lightheaded again, and finally he stopped speaking, he'd said it all.

"Poor you," she murmured. "I'm so glad I've been able to help."

She couldn't help wondering about the sex part, all he wanted to do was whine.

Ricky grabbed her arm, excitedly, saying, "Help, more than that. You've saved us!"

She could see he was pissed, and now there was a look of adoration in his eyes, a puppy dog look, so she leaned over and kissed him gently on the cheek, allowing her dressing gown to part and reveal her luscious thighs.

Ricky was in out of his depth, but at this time he chose to ignore it. He had spent a wonderful evening with this very beautiful young woman, and he felt full of goodwill. He had confided his innermost thoughts to her. Things he'd never told anyone else. She had kissed him, and when her body was close to him, he found he wanted more. He kissed her back, on the lips, and then he knew that she wanted it too. They didn't even make it from the sofa. There, in the lounge, with such passion fuelled by a long abstinence, he made love to her, and then they fell asleep together.

Chapter Seventeen

Ricky and Marina set their wedding day in April. March was to be avoided because it was the month that Amy had died. As far as Ricky was concerned, everything happened at break neck speed, and he didn't seem to have time to collect his jumbled thoughts.

After that night, he just couldn't get enough of Marina. All his loneliness and feelings of emptiness vanished, he felt alive again, and loved by a woman, and he couldn't do without it. He craved a normal life, an affair with her was not possible, he couldn't risk it with the girls, so after only two weeks of sneaking around to be together secretly, he proposed, and to his great delight she accepted. She wasn't Amy, but she loved him and the girls, and he knew life had to go on.

He made a vow to himself from that moment that she would not have to live in the shadow of Amy. He really wanted this marriage to work with all his heart. The girls were allowed to keep a photograph of their mother in their bedrooms, but although it hurt him to do it, he removed the wedding photograph of them both, and also the big photograph of Amy on the dressing table in his bedroom.

He replaced it with a photograph of Marina taken with the girls when Coleen was there, telling her, "When we're married, our wedding photo will be in the lounge, for everyone to admire." And he was happy when he saw her smile. She was like an idol to Brenda, and the other two loved her too, so wherever Amy was, and he did believe her spirit was around them, she would understand what he had done. The last two years were the loneliest he'd ever known, even though he had been surrounded by his children and family. But now he felt alive again.

Marina was right. He had fallen so hard for her, that the rest was easy. He had agreed to a very expensive wedding. Her dress had cost a small fortune. It was made of cream silk, with long sleeves gathered around the wrist, a very fitted waist, and flaring out over lots of petticoats with a long train. Her headdress and veil were very ornate, and when she saw how she looked, she was very pleased. Ricky was like putty in her hands. She had pointed out that this was her first and last wedding, so she wanted it to be special, and he had understood. The reception was being held at Greenview Hotel, with about fifty guests attending, and they were having a sit down meal, followed by a live band for dancing. Not that they would be staying for long. Mandy and Calum had gallantly offered to stay at the house with the girls whilst Ricky and Marina spent two weeks in the Bahamas.

This had been Marina's idea again. She had arranged everything, and all he had to do was take time off work. She was enjoying all the attention. Caroline had been delighted to hear the news. Marina, herself, had written to tell Coleen, saying that she would be welcome to come to the wedding if she could, and making sure to refer to her as 'a very special person'. She knew, at this late stage, they couldn't afford to have any negative opinions from anyone, particularly the mother of Ricky's dead wife.

The girls were going to be her bridesmaids, and were so excited about it. They were driving her a little mad, but she hid her irritation. They were all wearing peach coloured long dresses with cream shoes. She hadn't wanted them dressed in cream as well. She was the bride and they were only the bridesmaids!

Caroline was the happiest she'd been in two years. What a turn up for the books! Ricky had come through all that misery, only to find a lovely wife, who would be committed to caring for both him and the children. Her faith remained unshaken. To think that out of such a tragedy, for both Ricky and Marina (because she had lost her parents in a car crash) could come such happiness.

Coleen wasn't that surprised when she read the letter from Marina. Deep down inside she had wondered if it would happen, so in a way she had prepared herself. Her loyalty to Amy caused a conflict inside her. She knew she must repress it, although the wound of her loss was still there, even after two years. But, she

f

reasoned with herself, Ricky had chosen such a lovely person. Marina felt like another daughter to her, not Amy of course, but a great friend to the girls, and wife for Ricky. Coleen felt she had a bond with Marina. The girl seemed so fond of her, always referring to her as 'a special person', which made her feel good. She resolved to ignore her feelings of regret that it wasn't Amy. Obviously Ricky would have remarried at some point, but two years seemed quite soon to her. But on the other hand, if he had waited, would she have liked someone else as much? And what about the girls? They adored Marina, and Amy would have wanted their happiness.

So, now that her inward conflict was resolved, she went shopping for a new outfit, choosing a long black dress with a border of pink and green flowers at the bottom and also around the neck. It had short sleeves, so she teamed it with a pink jacket and black patent shoes. Caroline was wearing lilac so they wouldn't clash. She was staying with Caroline this time. She preferred that because it was going to be pretty hectic at Ricky's house, and she was only there for three days.

She arrived the day before the wedding, and the weather was pleasant, about twenty-two degrees, very sunny, unlike the wet weather and cold wind she had left behind in England. Caroline met her and they drove to her house chatting avidly, both excited about the wedding and pleased that Ricky had found such happiness.

"I hope you don't mind staying with me, but it's real crazy over at Ricky's right now. You won't see the girls until we meet at the church, they've got all sorts of stuff going on there," explained Caroline, a little anxiously. She was aware that Ricky and the girls usually met Coleen from the plane, and that she had always stayed with them. She hadn't really expected Coleen to come, neither had Ricky, but she was glad to see her. She obviously approved.

"Well, Marina wrote me such a nice letter. I felt I wanted to be a part of it all. I can't tell you how relieved I feel about Ricky and the girls." She didn't add anything about Amy, or even mention her name, it was there in her heart, her love for Amy, and there it would remain. She was finding this best way to deal with her loss, to go with the flow. Life had to go on, and this is what George would have wanted. Her darling George, if only she could have been holding his arm tomorrow, it would have been so much easier. But she had her friend Caroline, who probably felt the same without her husband. They spent a quiet evening at Caroline's, which Coleen was glad of after her flight. She spoke later on the telephone to Ricky and the girls. She could see what Caroline meant, the girls were well over the top with excitement. Ricky kept threatening them with bed, and Marina wasn't there. She had been to the beauty parlour, having her nails done and the whole works, and then gone out for a final evening of freedom with Mandy and some other teachers from the school. Ricky was going out later, and the next door neighbour had agreed to baby-sit.

"Well, they're very lively!" she commented as she put the phone down. "I'm sure after all the excitement of the wedding, when life returns to normal, they'll be fine."

"Yes," said Caroline. She had no doubt with Marina back at the helm, her wedding behind her, she would have time to devote to the girls. Everything would be great. It had to be because Ricky had another chance, and life had to go on.

Ricky hadn't told anyone how he felt, because he didn't really know. His life seemed to be like a merry-go-round. His emotions were whirling all over the place, and it was hard to cope. He knew he wanted Marina, and so did the girls. He had done his best, but they needed a mother figure in their life. Deep down in his heart he felt guilty about Amy. She would always be the love of his life, the mother of his children, she had been unique, but Amy had gone forever.

Marina was very keen to get married, and he did love her, mainly because of the girls, and how she was with them, especially Brenda. He certainly fancied her, she was a very sexy young woman, and it was wonderful to have his sex life back again. He was grateful that she wanted to take on the girls. They were lively and time consuming, and they were someone else's children. That alone endeared her to him.

He had removed Amy's photographs, no one else would know the pain it had caused him, but he was going to work hard to make this marriage a success, he owed her that. In time, he hoped the pain would fade, but he had to get on with it. Marina would never have to feel she was second best. She had a completely different personality to Amy. She veered between quiet moods and vivacious moods. He suspected that was because of her pain. She was trying to hide it. She seemed fairly deep, unlike Amy, who had been like an open book; bubbly, friendly to everyone, and always laughing. He really didn't know that much about Marina, her air of mystery attracted him. She had no photographs of her parents with her, although she had said she had some in England, and now she knew that she was living here, they would be sent over, along with the money for the house that had recently been sold.

He was relieved to hear that she would be bringing some money into the marriage. He had taken out a loan to finance the wedding. He would have been happy with a modest one, but it wasn't fair on Marina. All women like to dress up on their special day, and she had booked a honeymoon in the Bahamas, but he knew she was right, they needed time on their own without the girls.

She had also told him that she had a credit card bill that she temporarily couldn't pay, so he had helped her with that. He was just a little worried that she seemed inclined to overspend, but she had assured him that when the money came through from England, not only could she pay him back, she would have quite a lot of money to put in their joint account.

He had never had to worry about Amy overspending. She had held the purse strings, paid all the bills, and although like all women she loved clothes, she always put the girls first. Marina had come from a wealthy family and a different lifestyle, so he must be fair on her; this was all quite a change for her, and they would be comfortably off when the proceeds of her house sale came through.

She had even said that maybe they could move to a bigger house with a pool in the garden. Of course, it wouldn't be immediately. Ricky liked this house. Quite a lot of it had been paid for out of the fund set up for the girls by well wishers when Amy died, so it was really the girls' house, but to show good faith, Marina, on paper, was the joint owner with himself. He had also put the space wagon in their joint names. She would be driving it most of the time, as he had his FBI car, and only used the space wagon at weekends.

After Marina had gone out he had found the girls very fidgety and excited. Brenda had wanted to go to the beauty parlour with her, but he had put his foot down. It wouldn't take long for the other two to want to go as well, and then his credit card would be paying for four lots of nails, hair, makeup, and all the other things that women seemed to spend their money on. The fact that they were far too young wouldn't make any difference. He wasn't mean, but enough money had been spent, so the girls were at home tonight, he had arranged for them to have a pizza delivery, and then he was off out with the guys for a few beers.

He hadn't expected Coleen to come, it had been Marina's idea to write to her, but he didn't need to feel guilty. She liked Marina, and she was here. The girls were pleased she was coming, so was his mother, and when he thought about it, so was he. He just hadn't had the courage to tell her, Marina had, and Coleen was cool about it.

He put on his jeans and check shirt to go out for the drink. His new suit hung up with a polythene skin to keep the dust off. He would have worn his other one, but Marina wanted him to wear an oatmeal coloured one to match her outfit, which was a light colour apparently, so she'd come with him to choose it, and it had been the most expensive one in the shop. This was a far cry from his white naval uniform when he married Amy, but that had been a military wedding.

He wasn't exactly having second thoughts, but he knew he would be glad when it was all over. The girls were hyper, and he told them very sternly that if Mrs Egan told him that they had been bad, he would find other bridesmaids, and they would stay at home. Hopefully that would do the trick, and when he went out, he was satisfied to see they were curled up quietly on the couch watching their favourite Disney movie.

Brenda was looking forward to the next day so much, and she wasn't about to let her two dumb head sisters spoil it for her. "Don't you guys dare be bad tonight!" she warned them. It was like a dream come true for her that her dad was marrying Marina. No more uncomfortable silences when her friends were trying to be 'nice' to her, no more feeling left out for being in a freak family. She had allowed herself to feel again, to be loved by Marina would be wonderful. Brenda felt she loved Marina. Her dad was happy again, and her sisters, they would be a complete

125

family again. She would always love Mummy, and treasure her photograph, but it had been necessary for Mummy to go. She had never understood why, but she had moved on. Now, with Marina to look up to, she could move on even further.

Marina drove to Mandy's after leaving the beauty parlour. She would have liked to stay there for the night, away from the hyper brats, but she would have to go back to Ricky's. He wouldn't know how to get the girls ready in their outfits, or how to do their hair. She could do all that, and then they would go over to Mandy's to wait whilst she got ready. She wouldn't have to see them again until they met at the church. She was glad. Their incessant babbling and arguing and screaming was getting on her nerves. Letting Mandy think she was her best friend had definitely been a good move.

Ricky was going off from his sister Eliza's house, that way he wouldn't have seen her wedding dress until they met at the church. Calum was the best man. Her wedding ring was white gold with a criss cross design on it. She hadn't gone overboard when choosing it, after all she wouldn't be wearing it for that long. Although it was becoming the tradition now for men to also have a ring, Ricky hadn't expressed a desire to have one, and she wasn't bothered whether he did or not. It wasn't as if it really would be 'until death us do part'.

She left the space wagon at Mandy's and they got a cab out in the evening. She would take it back home in the morning. Here she was, driving around in a car worth about twelve grand, it was a step up from Mandy's shabby old jalopy.

She played her part well that evening, dressed modestly in a black straight dress with a high neck and calf length skirt. She didn't get too drunk, talked about all the right things, and gracefully accepted all the praise and admiration given for what she was taking on. Her head swelled with pride at the knowledge that she was such a hero in everyone's eyes. These people were all so stupid! Who would want to take on someone else's noisy brats unless it was financially worthwhile. She had no feelings for them or their father. But, she corrected herself, that wasn't strictly true. She had feelings of lust for Ricky, he was good in bed, and in the absence of anyone else, he would certainly do for the present.

*　　　*　　　*　　　*

The wedding day dawned bright and clear. It was a beautiful April day, the blossoms were out in shades of pink and lemon, and the hedges were becoming green again. Greenview was looking clean and fresh, before the summer sun was at its strongest. A spring wedding, a new start, how apt, thought Caroline. If anyone had told her ten years ago, when Ricky married Amy, that he would lose his wife, and then marry again, two years later, she wouldn't have believed them, but it was happening now!

When she stood in the church with Coleen, they were both moved by the sight of the girls, flushed with excitement, looking lovely in their peach outfits, and their golden hair shining in the sunshine. Caroline spotted Ricky, as smart as always in an oatmeal suit, his hair recently cut, and a look of happiness on his face that she hadn't seen for a long time.

Everybody gave a murmur of excitement when Marina appeared on the arm of Jackson, Ricky's elder brother. She looked very beautiful, her dark hair was swept up on top of her head, and her ornate headdress nestled on it. The gown fitted her perfectly, and as she walked, Brenda supported it, with help from Kathy. Maria was a little overawed, but she did remember to follow them down the aisle.

It had been necessary to ask Jackson to give her away, even though he had never met Marina before, and he had willingly agreed. Caroline thought fleetingly that it was sad that Marina had none of her family to share her special day, but they were a big family. Ricky's brother and four sisters, complete with children had all come. She loved having her family all together, and what had pleased her even more; they all seemed to really like Marina.

As Coleen stood there she tried not to think about the day, ten years ago, when Amy had walked down the aisle at the Naval Academy. She always felt emotional at weddings, but this one affected her more than usual. She blinked away tears when she saw Marina walking towards Ricky; she was the complete opposite of Amy, as dark as she had been fair. Her eyes were dark brown, Amy's had been of deepest blue. Amy's gown had been as white as the snow, Marina's was cream.

She concentrated on looking at her granddaughters, the

solemness of the occasion was lightened by Maria, forgetting to hold the train, and then lagging behind down the aisle. There was a ripple of laughter as she ran to catch up, giggling herself, with shyness. Maria, once again reminded her of Amy, the way she could always entertain. She was just so natural. The service started and Coleen comforted herself with the knowledge that although Amy had gone, she certainly lived on in her children. By the time it was over she had squashed down her memories, she was as happy and ready to congratulate the newly married couple as everyone else.

Chapter Eighteen

Ricky very much enjoyed his honeymoon in the Bahamas. It was the first time he had been away from the girls for a holiday since Amy had died. They spent long relaxing days on sun beds round the pool, sipping drinks, and not caring how often they fell asleep. It didn't matter, there were no children to distract them, they just had each other.

In the evening, after the hotel dinner, they went for a stroll. It was still very warm and pleasant even at dusk. When they came back there were more drinks, and then they retired to their bed, and he made love to his beautiful new wife. She certainly knew how to turn him on, and now that he had a sex life again he felt liberated. He felt, every time he got close to her, as if he was moving further away from all the misery of the last two years.

Marina was getting tired of Ricky by the second week of their honeymoon. She had achieved what she wanted, lured him into marriage, but now it was all legal, it was boring. She had expected to have his complete attention, but every day he was on his mobile phone to them, his brats! Why couldn't they have some time to themselves without all that?

He'd screwed her silly the first week, but by the second, she needed a change. There was a very handsome coffee coloured waiter she'd noticed, and he had noticed her too, so one evening when Ricky wanted to go back early to their room, to sort out some postcards, she invented a headache, and said she would need to go for a stroll, to clear her vision.

"Will you be OK alone?" he asked anxiously. He never wrote

postcards normally, he had been hoping that Marina would do that, but he had promised Brenda he would send one.

"I'll be fine!" said Marina firmly. Her tone was such that it prohibited interference. He didn't pursue it any more. She sounded put out, which he wasn't used to, and he had no wish to offend her on their honeymoon, so he gave her a kiss, saying he hoped it would help to clear her head, and maybe he would see her in about an hour.

Marina was annoyed, and she barely managed to conceal it. She wasn't used to being timed! Her waiter took her off in his car, and she never got to even ask his name. He shagged her silly, and that was all she wanted, so when she finally got back to their room, she'd been gone for over two hours, and Ricky gave her a look of reproach.

Ricky tried hard not to sound possessive, but Marina was very important to him, and he had been worried about her on her own. "Did you have a nice walk?" was all he said.

"I suppose so, but I've still got my headache," said Marina evasively.

They went to bed and he held her close to him, stroking her brow. Maybe tomorrow she would feel better. She seemed edgy, he couldn't sense what was wrong as he had been able to with Amy. Marina was deep, but he was undeterred. He realised he had married a completely different person, and he would have to work at keeping her happy.

For the rest of their honeymoon Marina found herself bored. She took diversion from him whenever she could, with Ricky it was easy. He believed all her excuses. Perhaps he wanted to because his life had already been so complicated; now all he wanted was peace and happiness. But this was the last thing that Marina wanted, she thrived on misery and unrest; harmony was not for her, it was too boring.

When they returned home, they were greeted warmly by family and friends, but already Marina was planning her escape. She was angry because he thought more of his children than her, she was not the centre of attention! She continued to feign headaches, she stopped doing housework, saying she wasn't well enough, and stopped taking the same interest in the girls, so Ricky found himself getting more and more involved again.

Ricky felt absolutely desperate, he just didn't know what was

130

happening. Suddenly Marina had gone from being very capable to not having any interest in anything. He made the mistake of challenging her about it when he arrived home from work, only a few weeks after the honeymoon, to find the girls running wild out in the street, and Marina lying on their bed. She had quickly hidden the magazine she was reading when she heard his step on the stair. He was an hour earlier than usual and there was no dinner prepared.

"Marina, if you are still having headaches, then you need to see the doctor," he pointed out.

Cooking had soon become boring to Marina. Ricky had enough money coming in, so takeaways were becoming a habit now. She didn't feel the need to impress him any more, so her veil was slipping. However, she knew if she wanted to get a reasonable settlement from him when they divorced, she would need to get pregnant. She didn't have a maternal bone in her body, but it was a means to an end.

"I'll go tomorrow, after the girls have gone to school," she said. His face looked puzzled. She was leading him a merry dance, but he didn't realise why, thank goodness. She saw him glance around their bedroom, she had changed her clothes three times that day, and they were all just dumped on the floor. The carpet was covered in dust, and the bed hadn't been made. His best shirt lay amongst it. He hadn't put it in the washing basket this morning, so he bent down to pick it up.

He found the magazine under the bed, and in spite of his effort to control it, he was getting cross. He had come home to a dirty house, the girls were playing in the street unsupervised, and she was up here reading. Her headache hadn't stopped her from reading!

"Does this help a headache?" he asked sarcastically, flicking it towards her with contempt.

"No, but whilst I'm up here you can't get at me! I may not be the perfect wife, my name's Marina not Amy!"

Ricky felt in that moment so angry that he was speechless. This was so unfair. He'd never compared her to Amy, he wouldn't. He sidestepped her comment, reminding her.

"You know I don't like the girls playing in the street unsupervised, especially Maria. She rides her bike in the road."

"You're always telling me how good Brenda is with her," returned Marina defiantly.

"But the girls have got you now. Brenda doesn't need to be responsible, she can play like any other nine-year-old."

Marina lost control. She screamed at him, "Yes, they've got me, but I'm no good, am I? I can't measure up to Amy, no one can!" Then she flung herself down on the bed sobbing, loud enough for everyone to hear, and she couldn't resist a catty remark. "Amy was just so perfect, and I'm not!"

Suddenly all Ricky's self control snapped. Amy wasn't here to defend herself, and he wasn't going to allow anyone to slag her off. "How dare you mock at Amy! Leave her memory alone." And then he was instantly sorry, he'd done what he had tried to avoid, made her feel second best. He tried to put his arms around her to make it right, but Marina was having none of it, so he left the room in despair. He went downstairs to order a pizza takeaway, and as he passed Brenda's room, he saw her at the door. He knew by the look of fear on her face that she had heard every word.

Marina was as good as her word the next day. After Brenda and Kathy had gone on the school bus, she dropped Maria off with Caroline whilst she visited the doctor. She had a bruise on her knee where she had knocked herself on a door. It wasn't a life threatening injury, but it would be useful on this occasion.

Dr Brett was aware of the new family situation, and wondered idly if the new Mrs Scott was pregnant already, when she entered his consulting room. He dismissed that thought immediately when he saw her face. This very beautiful young lady was distressed, her huge dark eyes looked as if they were about to fill with tears. She sat down, and he watched helplessly as sobs racked her body. He hastened to offer her a tissue, waiting patiently for her to compose herself.

Marina guessed him to be about fifty, he seemed a very sober sort of man in his grey suit, and his hair had streaks of grey in it. His eyes matched the grey effect, but his face looked kind and sympathetic, and that was what she needed.

She sobbed out her story. They had only been married for a few weeks, but already she was finding it tough. Her new husband expected her to be as perfect as his first wife had been. She was trying hard, but last night she had lost her temper and shouted at him, and he had lost his temper and knocked her to the ground, causing this bruise on her leg. She blamed herself, she shouldn't have mentioned Amy's name, and now she felt so depressed, she wasn't sure what sort of life she'd let herself in for.

Dr Brett was staggered, but he knew he must remain professional about it all, no taking of sides, even though this lovely young girl looked so vulnerable. He had never met Amy because Ricky had moved here after the death of his wife, but Ricky had been treated by him for depression; not for long, a month maybe, but he had told him he didn't really like taking pills. He had pulled himself together so quickly, which showed his strength of character, and coped with his girls almost single handedly. Now he had a new wife and a new start, he was a fool if he was going to blow it.

He went through the usual procedure, talking slowly and calmly to her about how hard marriage was in the beginning. He suggested that he arrange marriage guidance for them both, but she shook her head, saying Ricky wouldn't go for that.

"Well in that case you'd better make an appointment for Ricky to see me, we can't have him being violent towards you no matter how angry he is," he said gently, refusing to be beaten.

"Ricky mustn't know I've told you. It was very disloyal of me, and I'm sure he's sorry now," she said, making her huge eyes even bigger with a look of fear, which won him over completely. Just for good measure she dabbed at her eyes again with the tissue, and reminded him how depressed she felt, and totally unable to cope.

So Dr Brett did the only thing he could. He gave her a prescription for antidepressants, and some advice on surviving marriage in the first year, from his own experience, making her smile for the first time; and after making her promise to come back if Ricky was violent again, he sent her on her way. He hoped Ricky's outburst had been a one-off, hopefully their life would settle down soon, the girl had proved herself more than capable during the last year, but he had to respect her confidence, and say nothing to Ricky.

Marina thought about the situation whilst driving to Caroline's. She didn't really want to get pregnant, she hated kids anyway, and her body would stretch out of shape. But if she had no children by Ricky, she couldn't expect much of a divorce settlement, certainly not half of the house. Any court would decide that Ricky and the girls needed it.

Her other plan had been to find a way of helping Ricky to have an unfortunate accident. He had altered his will, and she would inherit everything. But for sure she didn't want the girls cramping up her life, and Ricky's family would certainly fight for the house for the girls, on their behalf. She couldn't afford to have the police sniffing round her. They would find that Marina Virdini didn't exist, they might even run a check on her in England. Regretfully she would have to give birth, and if her body did get messed up, the money she would receive would pay for any surgery she needed.

Maria was pleased to see her when she arrived at Caroline's. She picked her up and cuddled her for Caroline's benefit. She guessed that Ricky wouldn't have said anything about their difficulties, especially to his mother. Caroline's beaming face endorsed the fact that she was still basking in the euphoria of her son's newly found happiness.

Caroline made her some coffee, and they sat in the kitchen talking whilst Maria was watching TV.

"Ricky and I are not getting on too well," said Marina, suddenly, allowing her voice to falter, as if it had been so hard to tell Caroline.

Caroline was hearing words she didn't want to hear. This couldn't be happening! The last year had proved how well Marina fitted into their family life. Whatever had gone wrong? She tried to keep her voice light, to minimise the seriousness of the situation, but it didn't stop a pang of fear rushing through her. "I know my son's the most stubborn man to live with, just like his father before him. You have to learn to stand up to him!" she didn't add that Amy had, and he had respected her for it. It wasn't fair to bring her into this.

Caroline had felt as if Amy was like one of her own daughters. At the beginning she had found Ricky inclined to be selfish and stubborn, and had missed her own mother and family in England. Caroline had taken her to one side and told her she had an ally in her, and they had been close. Eventually, like all newly married couples, they had learned to live together, although Amy had definitely got the measure of Ricky, and how to get the best out of him. He had adored her, but Caroline knew he was a bit old fashioned, he didn't want to be a modern man, he was a chauvinist.

Marina went on to explain falteringly, as if she shouldn't really be saying it, and after making Caroline promise not to tell Ricky, or anyone else about it, the same story she had told Dr Brett. She finished her tale with the visit to his surgery, and produced the bottle of antidepressants to back up her story.

Caroline was absolutely aghast. She couldn't make light of this. Whatever was happening to Ricky? When he was a boy his father had given him a slap if he needed it, but he had been brought up to respect women, and he had certainly never laid a finger on Amy. He shouldn't be so sensitive about Amy now, otherwise he was going to mess up. She was very tempted to tell him that, but Ricky didn't like her interfering in his life, and she had promised Marina she wouldn't.

She poured her more coffee, realising that none of them had thought Marina would find the adjustment from nanny to wife difficult. They had all assumed she would be all right. Ricky had a lot to lose here, and so did the girls. She didn't want to take sides against her own son, but he must learn to control his temper.

"I'm sure he'll be sorry when I see him tonight. I certainly am, for shouting at him," said Marina. She knew she mustn't go too far just yet. She still had to get pregnant. She just wanted Caroline to know that things weren't hunky dory between them. Hopefully she would remember this conversation at a later date.

After they had gone home, Caroline sat down in her comfortable armchair by the window overlooking the pool, with sadness inside her. She felt that Marina was very forgiving. Ricky was so lucky to have her, and he didn't appreciate it. Amy had found he needed someone with a will as strong as his own, and she had learned to cope. In fact, it had made their marriage even stronger. Marina would have to do the same, because as much as Caroline loved her son, she also knew all his failings, and that's where 'for better or worse' came in.

When Ricky came home that evening, very contrite, Marina put on a show of unity. She had cooked roast beef and all the trimmings and also helped both Brenda and Kathy with their homework. Their quarrel was forgotten, the girls were happy, and Ricky made himself believe that everything was all right again. All new marriages have their hiccups.

135

Marina told him that the doctor had given her some pills for her headaches. She was suffering from stress, caused probably by the change to her new married life, and all the responsibility that went with it. Ricky felt guilty again. Maybe he expected too much of her, so he arranged from that day onwards that she should have someone else to do the housework. Sometimes he needed two shirts a day for work, so instead of Marina doing all the ironing, he arranged to have a lady pick them up, and deliver them back, crisp and ready for him, later in the week.

He also said it would be nice to spend an evening out on their own once a week, and he would leave her to arrange something when she felt like it. Marina went along with it. She would have to suffer it for the time being. She hoped to get pregnant soon. She had stopped taking her pill, unbeknown to Ricky. He had said that a baby at the moment was not a good idea, because the girls kept them both very busy, but maybe when Maria was at school full time, next year, then they could think about it. Marina seethed at his attempt to dominate, but pretended to go along with it.

In early June, Coleen wrote to check that it was OK for her to visit. In the beginning Marina wasn't too pleased about it, but then she realised that she would have another ally for a short time if she played her cards right. She suspected she might be pregnant, but held off going to the doctor. She didn't want it known until after she left him, and as Coleen was coming the last two weeks in June, she could escape after that.

The arguments had started again, she found it easy to upset Ricky, just mention Amy disparagingly and he went off like a rocket. On one particular day he had blown his top because he had found her reading Amy's diary. He had kept it because it was her private thoughts, and he treasured them. It was just ordinary family things, like when Brenda had got her first tooth and took her first steps. He wouldn't have minded her reading it so much, it was what she said, and the way she tossed it at him! "How boring was Amy, all she talked about was her children. Didn't she have anything else in her life?" Her lips curled in a sneer.

Ricky tried very hard not to swallow the bait, but failed. "She had loads!" he said proudly. "She was well into sport. All her life she won races, and even after Maria was born, she did pentathlons and won them. She was fitter than you'll ever be, even though you're only twenty-two!"

He'd done it again. Marina found this great fun! He slammed out of the house, forgetting the girls for once, and Marina used the opportunity to use her tears on Brenda. "I can't live with your dad any more. He shouts at me, and he's rough. Look at my arm, where he bruised it."

Brenda was heartbroken. Her dad did shout sometimes, but he had never laid a finger on any of them. She didn't understand why he was so cruel to Marina. She was scared Marina would go away too, and they'd be on their own again. She felt really angry with Daddy. She wanted to be with Marina, and so would her sisters when she told them. Suddenly her life seemed to be falling apart again, her stomach pains returned, and there was a terrible fear inside her. Marina said she didn't want to stay with Daddy, and her fear fuelled her anger towards him. How could he do this to them?

Marina lost no time in taking the girls and herself round to Caroline. They were all crying and saying they couldn't live with Ricky any more. Caroline tried to keep her cool, but this time she waited until Ricky came home, and please or offend, she didn't care, gave him a real dressing down. He wasn't just making Marina's life a misery, it was affecting the girls, too. Whatever had come over him?

They stayed for two days before Ricky came to apologise and take them all back home. Caroline was relieved to get her house back to herself, and also praying that they could sort things out. Ricky didn't admit to anyone how hurt he was that his own girls could turn against him, because he was now beginning to suspect that Marina was mentally sick. Her behaviour was so erratic. One day she was everything she should be, happy, loving, and good with the girls, the next she was moody, morose, kept herself away from all of them, or was determined to pick a fight. During these fights, she always blamed Amy for their troubles. In his opinion, she was obsessed with Amy, and he couldn't help wondering if she was suffering from paranoia.

He wondered if he could go with her to the doctor. Maybe if she could have some treatment, she would get better. In spite of all that had happened, he still wanted the marriage to work. It wasn't just for the girls. When Marina was acting normally he still loved her, but when she changed he didn't recognise this stranger.

He wasn't too happy when Marina told him that Coleen was coming. She knew nothing of their difficulties. His mother did, but would probably say nothing. He knew his mother blamed him, but then she'd only seen the good side of Marina. It wasn't in his nature to redeem himself and put the blame on Marina. Ricky's best quality was his loyalty, and he felt, as his wife, especially if she was ill, she deserved that.

So on the third Monday in June, he found himself at the airport with Marina and the girls, waiting for Coleen's arrival, acting like a happy family. He planned to keep a low profile whilst Coleen was there. No matter what Marina said or did, he wouldn't be intimidated, and then when Coleen had returned to England, he planned to take Marina to the doctor whether she liked it or not.

Coleen didn't notice immediately that something was wrong, but, on the second day, she had a growing realisation that things were not right. The girls were behaving a little wildly, arguing more than usual, and Brenda seemed very moody. Usually when she came to stay they were happy and excited, but now they seemed out of control, and what was even worse, Ricky and Marina didn't seem to notice.

Ricky seemed a bit distracted by work, saying he was very busy, so she didn't expect to see that much of him. The change in Marina was more obvious. Instead of glowing with happiness as she had been at the wedding, she looked tired, her eyes had a glazed unnatural look about them, and she seemed to have lost her animation and interest in life.

Coleen was shocked. They had been married less than three months, whatever was going on here? She had seen Caroline yesterday, and she had said nothing, but when she thought about it, Caroline had been a little short with her. She hadn't wanted to stay for long, saying she was having problems with her air conditioning, and couldn't find someone to fix it, but maybe it was more than that. Coleen was a naturally sensitive person herself, and she could definitely sense an atmosphere that wasn't right.

Her sympathy went out to Marina. She didn't look well. Could she be pregnant? That would explain it. She wanted to feel relief, but she wasn't sure. It would be perfectly natural for them to want a child of their own, after all Marina was doing such a good job with the other three, but somehow she had imagined they wouldn't plunge into that immediately. Their life was already very busy.

It wasn't her business really. She couldn't ask her, so she would just have to act normally, but that would be hard; she was filled with apprehension and fear, and she felt it in her bones that this time she wasn't going to enjoy the visit.

On the third day of her visit Marina asked her if she wanted to go to the graveyard where Amy had been buried. Coleen was surprised, she hadn't mentioned it herself. Normally Caroline took her whilst the girls were otherwise occupied. She knew that Ricky took them once a year, but he felt that was enough in case it was distressing for them.

"Are you sure, Marina?" she asked doubtfully. She felt it was a lot to expect of her.

"Sure! The girls are out for a fun day. I thought we could get some silk flowers, and then after we could have lunch out."

It sounded really nice, and Coleen warmed towards her for such thoughtfulness. She always felt emotional when she visited Amy's grave with the little headstone in memory of Amy and baby Emma. Her heart lurched with horror, even now, when she thought of the loss of life, not only Amy's but also her baby almost ready to be born.

They dropped the girls off for their fun day, and Marina then drove to the local shops. Her idea had been great. Coleen would be really grateful for this, and later she could win over her sympathy when she told her tale of woe. She helped her to choose some silk flowers, and then drove over to the cemetery. She went for a walk whilst Coleen paid her homage. No doubt she would be blubbering!

Coleen was glad that Marina had remained at a respectful distance. Even after two years, every time she saw that slab of stone, and remembered that her beautiful daughter's body, as well as baby Emma's, lay beneath it, she felt sick inside. Her eyes filled with tears. It was such a waste of two precious lives!

She said a prayer, and stayed there, trying to feel at peace. Caroline's husband was also buried there, and on this hot June day, she found solitude on a wooden seat under the shade of the trees. She felt grateful to Marina for bringing her. She was so thoughtful.

When Marina returned they got into the car. There was a quiet restaurant on the other side of town, with alcoves around the tables so other people couldn't hear what was said. After they had sat down and ordered, she lost no time in capturing Coleen's attention.

"Did Amy ever complain about Ricky's temper?" she asked gently, making her face look as sober and downcast as she could.

Coleen looked up from the wine menu she had been studying, with horror. She felt like a glass to steady her nerves, after the sad but very necessary, visit to the cemetery. She didn't know what to say here. Her loyalty to Ricky was strong. Obviously Marina was going to unburden herself to her, but should she get involved? She had known of Amy's home sickness at the beginning, and that she had found Ricky stubborn, but she didn't think she should mention it. Sometimes things got misinterpreted. She decided to simply tell the truth.

"No, Amy never complained about Ricky's temper. She couldn't really, she had one of her own." She then added quickly, "Amy had a hot temper, she blew her top, and then she got over it. She never held grudges."

Marina smiled to herself. So even the great Amy had not been perfect! She had found a flaw, from the lips of her own mother, too. She felt pleased with herself.

"My problem is that I'm living in Amy's shadow. Our marriage won't work because Ricky is still obsessed with her. I only have to mention her name and he goes mad. Last week he pushed me away when he was angry, and I fell against a table, see the bruise."

She then proceeded to show Coleen a bruise on her shoulder which she had got when slightly the worse for wear, after too much wine mixed with her pills, when she had fallen against the dressing table. So far Ricky didn't know he was being blamed for her bruises, she had sworn Caroline to secrecy, and she would do the same with Coleen.

Coleen swallowed hard. She had never expected to hear this. It seemed so awful that after all she'd done for this family, and her willingness to take it all on, Marina still seemed to be suffering. Inwardly she felt so angry with Ricky, but she said nothing. Why had he married this poor girl if he still couldn't forget Amy? It wasn't fair on her. As her mother she had wanted to think he would never forget Amy, but this was too much. He was wrecking so many lives by hanging on like this. He had to let go of Amy! She leaned over impulsively, and touched Marina's hand.

140

"Give him time, Marina. Your marriage is very new still. I'm sure he will adjust. He's had to hide his grief from the girls to keep them going. He probably only talks about her to you because he feels close to you."

Marina was disappointed. She had expected Coleen to be the typical mother-in-law and list all the faults that Amy would have told her that Ricky had. She had been so certain she'd even slipped a small tape recorder into her handbag. But it hadn't worked. She hadn't said anything that could be used as evidence in her divorce case. She gave it one last shot, producing her antidepressants from her bag. "Dr Brett has given me these to help me to cope."

Coleen looked at the bottle, and then it fell into place. That explained why Marina's eyes looked glazed. She was on antidepressants. How sad that at the age of twenty-two, with her whole life ahead of her, she was so down. It wasn't Ricky's fault that she'd lost her parents, but he could have been a more sympathetic husband. Her heart went out to her. She remembered Amy saying once that Ricky scoffed at pills. He thought anyone on pills was weak. She did so hope he wasn't giving Marina a hard time about it. She couldn't say anything about it to Ricky, but she would speak to Caroline before she went home. There was a marriage at stake here. For the sake of Ricky and the girls, they must try and save it!

Chapter Nineteen

Ricky was at work as often as he could be whilst Coleen visited them. He could see that Marina was behaving oddly again, so it was best if he kept out of the way. To argue with her in the house would be unthinkable. She seemed to be trying to provoke him again, although in front of Coleen she was very subdued. In the confines of their room she was sullen, and although, in the past, he would have said something to Amy if she had stopped cooking, he said nothing to Marina, even when she went to the lengths of taking the girls and Coleen out for breakfast at eight o'clock one morning.

She seemed to spend his money quicker than he could earn it, but he gritted his teeth and ignored this, safe in the knowledge that soon he would be taking her to the doctor. After a few days Coleen stepped in and cooked some dinners, which he enjoyed. This in itself was not unusual, but he wondered if she had noticed Marina's unusual behaviour. If she had, there was no comment about it, but he felt as if he was treading on eggshells, and couldn't really enjoy her visit.

By the second week of her holiday, Coleen found herself longing for home and normality. Marina, most of the time, seemed to be in a world of her own. Apart from the visit to the cemetery, she didn't want to go anywhere much. When Ricky had found out that she had taken Coleen there he had been very happy, saying that it was a great thing that Marina had done, but even that had left Marina stony faced.

Coleen noticed that Marina lay on her bed for two hours every afternoon, and even though Maria had outgrown her nap, she insisted that she did too, and Brenda and Kathy were not allowed to leave the house during that time. She didn't seem loving towards the girls any more, they seemed bewildered by the whole thing, and several times she went off alone leaving them with Coleen, without any explanations as to where she was going, or when she was coming back.

Coleen was quite happy to look after them, she often had for Amy during her past visits, but she was confused by Marina's behaviour. Obviously she was ill and depressed, she couldn't cope, even with housework. Ricky had someone to do that, and the ironing, but in her opinion he still needed to address the problem. He hadn't discussed anything with her, so she had to remain silent.

He was hardly ever with Marina. They met at mealtimes, Marina went off after that to take a long bath every night, leaving Ricky to sort the girls out. Sometimes she was in bed before the girls, leaving Ricky to settle them and read bedtime stories. When he came downstairs again, about nine o'clock, to tune into his movie channel, Coleen, too, felt obliged to go off to her room and read her book.

She assumed that it was the pills making Marina so tired. When she saw Caroline just before her return to England, she took the bull by the horns. She couldn't go back home knowing how bad things were. Marina had got up from her midday rest and taken the girls to swimming practice, but was due back any minute.

"I'm a bit worried about Marina, she doesn't seem very well," she said mildly, as they sat sipping ice cold water on the swing seat in the garden.

Caroline stiffened. Her loyalty to Ricky had prevented her from saying anything, but in a way it was a relief that Coleen had noticed. She had time to think since the first indications of trouble, and now her sympathies were with Ricky too. She didn't want Coleen to think he was the villain of the piece.

"Yes, I'm sorry about that. She's having a tough time being a wife and stepmother. Ricky has tried to help by having someone to clean and to do the ironing. I really can't see what else he can do."

When Caroline realised that Marina was losing interest in the girls, her sympathy towards her had waned a little. It wasn't fair to put them through all this, they were only children. When she thought about Marina turning up at her house with the girls that day, initially she had been angry with Ricky, but on reflection she had decided that Marina had been wrong to take them away from Ricky. Did she have any idea how this family had suffered? It seemed that since she had married Ricky, instead of life for them improving, it was getting worse. In her opinion, depressed or not, Marina was acting like a spoiled child herself, and couldn't she spend the money! Ricky hadn't said anything, he wouldn't, but she had seen copies of huge credit card bills. If he wasn't careful, she'd bankrupt them!

Always a person to speak her mind, Caroline relayed all this to Coleen, who couldn't really help agreeing with her. It was obvious the girls were going through the mill again, and they both agreed it wasn't fair they should suffer any more.

"She knew what she was taking on when she married him!" pointed out Caroline grimly. "If she couldn't cope with it, she shouldn't have married him."

Coleen wanted to defend Marina and point out that she, too, had lost her parents, and her man, and suffered, but now she wasn't sure any more. Like Caroline, she had been hurt to see Marina virtually ignoring the girls. Brenda had been hit worst of all because she adored her. Her idol had fallen off her pedestal, and Brenda had retreated inside herself by being moody and morose with everyone. Regretfully she had to admit to Caroline that Marina seemed very selfish, and inconsiderate towards the girls. If Ricky didn't take her for some sort of help or counselling, they both thought the marriage couldn't last.

"I can't believe how she's changed in the last couple of months," said Caroline, shaking her head in disbelief. "She doesn't even want to do the girls' hair in the morning. Do you remember how cute she made Brenda's hair look for the wedding?"

"Yes," said Coleen. remembering how painful she had found that day. She would willingly suffer those pangs again just to know that Ricky and the girls would have a happy future. At the moment it wasn't happening, if only things would get better. They had all had such high hopes of Marina.

Their conversation had to end there, as they heard Marina

144

returning in the car. They both smiled a little guiltily as she came out into the garden to speak to them, knowing they had been bitching about her. Marina smiled back through gritted teeth, knowing she only had to suffer all this for a bit longer. She could sense their changing attitude towards her, there was less sympathy, but she didn't give a damn. Mandy was her next tool. She had sobbed her heart out about Ricky's 'treatment' of her, and Mandy had said she felt responsible for introducing them. Mandy had a sister who lived in Florida, so maybe she could go and live there whilst the divorce was sorted out.

"Well, I guess I need to go to the grocery store now," said Caroline, getting up with her empty glass in her hand. She walked into the kitchen, and Coleen followed her, wishing that she wouldn't go. She no longer felt comfortable in Marina's presence. She just seemed so unpredictable.

But it seemed she had nothing to worry about. Marina announced that she was going out, and would pick up the girls later, on the way back. She had to get away from these two with their miserable faces. She was going out for a bit of retail therapy, that always made her feel better. Anyway, she needed some new clothes for her next venture in Florida.

Ricky could feel himself getting more and more stressed with every day that passed. He realised that he had known very little about the woman he had married until now. He had trouble coping with her mood swings, and her addiction to shopping. She had so many clothes and shoes, but it didn't make any difference to her, she still wanted more. He realised he had made a huge mistake by having a joint credit card, in fact Marina shouldn't have a credit card at all!

He wished the days to pass until Coleen went home, there were only three left now, and he had already booked an appointment for Marina with Dr Brett. He was going too, and when he arranged her therapy, her spending was going to be the first thing that they would discuss. Her money from England showed no sign of coming through, and already doubts were forming inside him. Just suppose there was no money, but why would she lie to him? Once Coleen had gone, he would find out all the answers, but in the meantime, as stressed as he felt, he must act normally.

g

Marina feigned a headache on the day of Coleen's departure, so it was left to Ricky to take her to the airport with the girls. He would have gone anyway, but the absence of Marina was more noticeable now because of the enthusiastic way she had supported him before. She had seemed to really like Coleen, but in his opinion, since she'd been taking those damn antidepressants she seemed to have lost touch with everything. In his opinion, they needed to be thrown out of the window. She had tried to fool him that they were headache pills, but he knew differently. He planned to ask Dr Brett if they were really helping, because they certainly didn't seem to be.

After Coleen had gone he took the girls out to eat at a burger bar. He knew that if Marina had one of her headaches, she would be in bed for the rest of the day. He found her depression seemed to be rubbing off on him, and it certainly was affecting the girls. They had settled down for a time, and life had been good again, very briefly, but now they were all over the place, and he blamed himself. They deserved a treat.

When they arrived home, just as he suspected, the house was quiet. She would be up in their room with the curtains drawn. He wondered just how much more of this he could take. He settled the girls in front of the TV and nipped quickly up the stairs, just to check that she was OK. He opened the door quietly, in case she was asleep. The curtains were drawn, and the duvet was pushed right back. There was no sign of Marina.

He felt angry. So she wasn't really ill, she had gone out, but as he looked around him it was as if they had been burgled, all the drawers were hanging open, most of them empty, with fear clutching at his heart, he strode right into the room, and pulled back the curtains.

His eyes took in the scene. His drawers were intact, but these were the ones that had held all her underwear and small things. With a feeling of realisation growing inside him, he walked towards their dressing room, which had all their outer clothes hung on rails. Once again, his had not been touched, but most of Marina's were gone. Burglars didn't only steal women's clothes. He looked in the en suite, her hair brush and shampoo, and all the other little bottles that women have for their needs were gone. She had left him!

He looked around for a note, there was none. He could feel

146

panic building up inside him. He couldn't live with her, but he didn't want to live without her! My god, what had she done? It was his fault, he should have realised how bad she was. He blamed himself, and suddenly he felt as if his life had been a total failure. He had lost his wife because he should have been driving the car that day, and now he had lost Marina because she found him intolerable to live with. For the first time in his life, in the privacy of his room, he sat on the bed, covering his face with his hands and wept for the way he just kept on messing up his life.

Marina was impatient for them all to go to the airport. She went upstairs until she heard the car drive off. Her heart was beating with excitement. She'd been at this place now for over a year, and now she was off to pastures new. She quickly pulled open drawers, packing her things in her case. She collected all her bits from the en suite, and then put as many of her clothes and shoes as she could in the very large suitcase. Regrettably it wouldn't accommodate everything.

Ricky might only be gone for a couple of hours, so time was of the essence. After she packed as much as she could, she dragged the very heavy case by its wheels downstairs. She was sorry that she couldn't have taken the space wagon, that could have been her own car, but she just had to get away, and this was the first opportunity that had presented itself!

The cab she had ordered was waiting for her outside. She was going to Mandy's, and because Mandy was riddled with guilt, she would help her to escape to Florida, she had absolutely no doubt of that. She would also keep it from Ricky, because she was so highly implicated in Marina's escape, that she would never want him to know. Marina had power, it was a very satisfying feeling, and she would stop at nothing to use it.

Chapter Twenty

Seven months later:

Marina stirred when she felt the pain shoot through her, raising herself up awkwardly in the bed. Oh, how she hated being so cumbersome, like an elephant! She felt ugly and ungainly thanks to this parasite in her body. It was like a leech, sapping all the energy out of her, but not for much longer.

Another pain, even fiercer than the first one built up inside her, and she clenched her fists against it. It got more and more intense, and she found herself screaming in terror. She hadn't thought it would be like this! Then, just as she thought she could take no more, it died away, and she reached for a tissue beside the bed to mop her sweating forehead.

She picked up her mobile and switched it on. Her bedside clock showed the time as eight o'clock, it was still not that light on this grey February morning. Her baby was due next week, but judging by the agony she was in, it was either a very severe case of indigestion, or he was on the way now. She quickly dialled Babs' number. She couldn't face this alone. She needed her.

"Babs, I've got pains, terrible pains!" she wailed, as yet another one ripped through her body.

"Oh no, how far apart are they?" Babs immediately came to life, pulling her clothes on hastily, and picking up her car keys. "Hang on, I'll be right over to take you to maternity!"

"Right on top of each other," groaned Marina, determined to make her feel as guilty as possible. They were actually at least ten minutes apart, but Babs couldn't know that. Let her hurry over, full of remorse for going home in a huff last night, just because she'd asked her for a loan.

By the time she got there, Marina was lying on the couch with her dressing gown on, so she helped her into the car, thankful that as yet her waters hadn't broken. She drove as quickly as she could along the highway until she reached the hospital. Marina was groaning all the way, and Babs couldn't help feeling sorry for her. Marina was having this baby alone, there was no one else there for her, so she felt obliged to stay with her.

When Mandy had asked her if she would mind if Marina stayed with her for a while, Babs had willingly agreed. She had a large apartment, which she shared with Clio, her cat. She wasn't into men, but her family didn't know that, they just thought she liked being single. She had always liked women, such soft and sensitive creatures, but she'd never had the courage to come out and admit it.

Her affair with Marina had been passionate and all consuming, but when she had found out that she wasn't serious about her, it had broken her heart. Marina had left her husband, and was pregnant, but she had used Babs for her own convenience. She realised she had been a fool. She'd let her stay there rent free for over six months, and she'd even run up a huge amount of bills on Babs' credit card. She hadn't thought to hide it, and whilst she was at work, running the office, Marina was ordering anything and everything, over the phone, on her card. If she hadn't been so fond of her she would have reported it to the police.

As it was less than a month before her baby was due when Babs told her to go, there was only one thing for it. Babs found her an apartment, and helped her to move in, and even paid for the first month's rent. Marina's divorce would soon be through. Ricky had to maintain her and the baby, so she would be repaid then. Marina had money owing to her, but Babs wasn't so worried about the money. She recognised that Marina had a hold on her, and she felt as though she was dragging her down. It was pointless loving her, Marina was untrustworthy and heartless, but even knowing all that, she couldn't bring herself to turn her back on her now.

Marina was screaming by the time she was put in a wheelchair, and whisked up to the delivery room.

"Is anyone with her?" inquired the nurse briskly. She could see

149

this one was a bit dramatic. Even after her pain relief, she was still airing her lungs. Some bore it bravely, but some loved the drama and the attention.

"No, only me," said Babs awkwardly.

"Well, maybe you can talk to her and keep her mind off her pain, if you're staying."

Babs weakened. There was really no other choice. She would just do this last thing for her, and then after that, she would wash her hands of Marina Scott, and her new baby.

Ricky heard the news about his new son with mixed feelings. He had always wanted a boy to complete his family, but, until the DNA test, he couldn't be sure. Marina seemed to have turned so much against him; she had said, via her lawyer, that she would never allow him access to their son. This hurt him so much. She had done so many things to hurt them all. She had told lies about him, trying to sue him for divorce on the grounds of physical cruelty. As if he would have ever hit her, or any woman, come to that! She was ill, she must be, to say such dreadful lies.

He put down the letter with a sigh. Even Mandy had thought he had attacked her, and had felt obliged to arrange a safe place for Marina to stay. She seemed convinced now that it was a story, a ruse to get money out of him. Marina was doing her best to squeeze him dry, half of the house, the girls' house! half the value of the car, half of everything! How dare she after only three months of marriage. He felt so stupid for not seeing through her. He had been blinded by love, and now he was having to pay heavily.

In spite of all this, the thought that she might be carrying their child disturbed him. He wanted a part in his life; he had sisters, they should all be growing up together. He wondered whether Marina would be able to cope with him. She had proved she wasn't stable. But he realised, even if it was his son, no one would give him custody. All he could offer was the care of a nanny. He had to work to support his family, and if Marina got her way, they would have to sell this house and live in a very modest apartment. He should have hated her for what she had done to this family, but somehow he couldn't, although he didn't really know why.

*   *   *   *

150

Marina left hospital the day after her son was born. She felt nothing for him whatsoever. His wrinkled face and blond spiky hair, just the colour of Ricky's, did not endear him to her. From the moment they handed him to her when he was born, she saw Ricky, and she wanted to get away from Ricky.

She was relieved that he did look like Ricky, and didn't have coffee coloured skin. The DNA test would prove it, Ricky was his father, and this baby boy would enable her to get a lot of money. Once she had done that she would be away. She was off to Las Vegas to have some fun, and then she would see how she felt after that. Young Ricky would fetch a few thousand dollars, too. There was a married couple she had found, absolutely desperate for a child, and they would buy him.

She had to be careful, it was illegal, not that she cared about that; they wouldn't say, and she would be long gone. Babs mustn't know about it. Now that Babs had brought her home from hospital, they had both agreed it had to end there. She had found Babs so different from her plain and dumpy sister, with her long slim legs, her sensuous body and impish good looks. With her short hair, she reminded Marina of a young Audrey Hepburn, and the affair with her had been a pleasant diversion for Marina whilst there were no men around.

Hopefully she wouldn't have to put up with this baby for long. Thanks to him, her stomach was flabby, her boobs droopy, and she had only just had her twenty-third birthday. She definitely wasn't going to breastfeed, and make her boobs even worse! She would have to invest in some surgery to put her body back as it was, otherwise no one would ever fancy her again.

She settled into an uneasy way of life. Little Ricky was a model baby, hardly ever crying, feeding well on any formula; Marina wasn't that fussy with what she gave him. He slept well at night too, but she took it all for granted. She didn't want any hassle, and he didn't give her any. She showed him no love, she had none to give him, but he showed no signs of distress, and life went on in this way for six weeks.

One morning she received a letter from her attorney, and it wasn't good news. Owing to the complexity of the case, and the fact that they had only been married for three months, it seemed this case would take some time to resolve. Marina needed to provide some proof that her husband had physically abused her.

151

Her doctor would be called, and other people who saw her bruises, to give evidence. She would need to go to court, but Ricky would not.

Marina felt angry. This godforsaken small town was not a place she wanted to hang around! She was tired of young Ricky's demands. She always seemed to be feeding him. She could sell him right now, the couple were most anxious, but if it came out she would lose everything, and she didn't want to move on until she got her money.

She picked up the telephone to speak to her attorney but, to her annoyance, was only allowed to speak to his secretary. "I need to contact Mr Hilton right now!" she said imperiously.

"You'll have to make an appointment to come in and see him," said the girl, unconcernedly filing her nails whilst she was speaking to her.

Marina made an appointment for later that morning, banging the telephone down in annoyance. Who the hell did that little jerk think she was? But it was no good, she had to comply, just like everyone else. She would take little Ricky with her, that way she would look like a much more pathetic figure.

When she got there, she was kept waiting for twenty minutes, and as she paced up and down with little Ricky in her arms, she could feel her temper rising. This was all getting so stressful. She hadn't realised they would want so many forms and legal documents out of her. All she really had was her fake passport and her marriage certificate. The lack of a birth certificate, which she had pretended to send off for, to England, was holding things up.

"You can go into Mr Hilton's room now," said the girl. "It's right down the hallway there."

Marina didn't even bother to thank her. She just went, leaving the girl wondering why she was so surly. She saw all sorts in here, and this one might look nice but she was sadly lacking any manners.

"Good day, Mrs Scott, what can I do for you?" said Mr Hilton, pulling up a chair for her. "What a cute kid." Young Ricky smiled at him, his tiny fingers gripping his hand.

Marina pretended to be moved. "He's such a good baby," she murmured, "but I have no money to look after him. His father only sends a small amount, it's not enough, and now you've written to tell me that my divorce will take some time!"

John Hilton felt a wave of sympathy for this young woman. She'd come to America, got married, and then found out her husband wasn't how she thought he'd be. She had only stayed with him for three months, but now there was a child, which had been proved to be his. In his opinion, she seemed a little unstable but this could be because of how her husband had treated her, if, in fact, it was true. Maybe she wouldn't be able to take the stress of lengthy court proceedings.

"It's all going to take a long time, partly because all your important documentation needs to come from England, and also after such a short marriage, we have to prove that your husband made your life intolerable," he said kindly, seeing her eyes begin to fill with tears.

"I can't take much more," she sobbed. "First of all a miserable marriage, and now all this!"

John leaned forward and gave her a tissue, feeling awkward. She looked a pathetic figure, her big dark eyes brimming with tears, but her baby had fallen asleep, seemingly unaware of his mother's distress. He leaned back in his chair, brushing out an imaginary crease in his navy blue trousers. He was a smart man, with his dark hair neatly groomed. At forty-five, although married for twenty years, he was not immune to her charms. He stood up, pushing his chair back with determination, and addressed her.

"I think the best way to go with all this, if you want it to end quickly, is to agree to an out of court settlement. You will still get a substantial amount of money to help you to rebuild your life. It won't be half of everything, but even if we go to court, you may not get that anyway."

Marina's mind was working overtime. She knew she was on a knife edge with the whole thing. She couldn't produce the papers he wanted without admitting she had a false identity. It had seemed like such a good idea to marry Ricky, but she just hadn't thought it through properly. There was just so much red tape, and she'd had enough.

"Will we still have to wait for the papers from England?" she asked slowly, making sure her voice sounded nervous and uncertain. "Because my parents are now dead, it might be difficult for anyone to find them. She allowed her downcast eyes to fix on little Ricky, and just for good measure, planted a kiss on his downy head.

John was moved by the sad little scene. The more he heard about this young woman's life, the sadder it seemed. He must try to help her!

"Don't worry too much about the papers," he said, smiling confidently. "We know you married Mr Scott, and we will go after a settlement, if that's what you want, but not on physical cruelty."

Marina stood up smiling, her tears now forgotten. Little Ricky stirred in her arms but remained asleep.

"Thank you so much Mr Hilton. I will go for that, if you think you can sort it out quickly."

"I'll get right onto it," he promised, as he opened the door to let her through.

Marina caught a cab back to her apartment. On reflection, this was the answer. There was always a chance she could have lost in court, or her real identity become discovered. This way she could have her money and then go. Ricky could pay her a lump sum, and she would promise not to come after him for maintenance, either for little Ricky or herself. She would willingly sign forms, and then she would be away again. She could feel the urge to move on so strongly. She just had to go.

Caroline was so relieved when Ricky told her that he was settling out of court. It was a quickie divorce, both parties agreeing to irretrievable breakdown of marriage, and a smaller settlement. In her opinion, that little schemer didn't deserve anything, but the law said differently! She had been worried about Ricky's good name being dragged through the courts, he could have even lost his job, although she knew he wouldn't have hit Marina as she claimed.

If only Marina hadn't got pregnant. This was a grandson she would never know. She could live with that, because with Marina for a mother, she didn't expect to ever see him. She understood how sad Ricky was to be denied access to his son, but at least it got her out of his life for good. She felt so angry every time she thought about it! Once again, Ricky and the girls would have to rebuild their lives.

Caroline had been a Christian all her life, and always tried to treat others in a way that she would like to be treated herself, but for the first time ever, she felt real hatred for Marina for what she had done. There was no doubt in her mind that Ricky had been used by her to get money, and she didn't blame Ricky. It was a very clever trick, and they had all fallen for it. Marina had seemed perfect for him and the girls. How could she stoop so low?

Ricky still made excuses for her, but not Caroline! She wasn't sick in her mind. She'd worked out how to get a good few thousand dollars out of him. Caroline now had doubts about whether she really had lost her parents, or if there was a house back in England. Hopefully Ricky's son would come and find him one day, and then he could explain his side of the story, but in the meantime, he was back to trying to cope without a nanny, Mandy was helping after school because she felt responsible.

Coleen had written from England to say how sorry she was. All their hopes for Ricky's happy future were dashed. He was alone again, now saying he trusted no woman, and Brenda had become all tough again, which meant she was hurting badly.

All in all, it was a complete mess. The only good thing was that Ricky had been granted a second mortgage against the house to pay Marina off. They could stay there, but he would be quite a bit poorer for a few years. She cheered herself up with the thought that it could have been worse. At least they still had their home, but both Ricky and the girls had lost their faith in women. As far as the girls were concerned, firstly their mother had gone away, and then Marina had, so women were bad news. Hopefully, when they were older, they would understand more. They really did need to move on.

Chapter Twenty-one

Jill Hopkins got up with a new spring in her step today. This was the day! She glanced over at Simon, still huddled under the duvet. How could he sleep at such a time? In less than two hours, baby Ricky, or Billy, as they planned to call him, would be their own darling son for ever.

"Simon, are you awake? I'm going to take a shower. We have less than two hours left."

Simon stirred, forcing his tired eyes open. They had sat up talking until late last night. Jill was so on edge about this, so worried that it might not happen. He was philosophical, after years of trying, and three miscarriages, they were both close to forty years old, he was prepared for anything. He sat up, his eyes resting on her, noting the flushed cheeks and sense of purpose.

"I'll take a shower when you're done," he said, preparing to grab a few more minutes. It wouldn't take him long to get ready, but Jill yanked the duvet back, laughing.

"Get up now, you lazy slob!"

He hadn't seen her that happy for ages, and he felt a warm glow inside. They had a strong marriage, but it had been put to the test over the years without a baby. Jill had suffered from fits of depression, there had been endless tests, but there was no reason that could be explained for her inability to carry a baby full term.

"I'll go and make breakfast," he offered, getting out of bed. Her energy was beginning to rub off on him.

"I couldn't eat a thing," was her reply, as she went into the en suite to take her shower.

Simon took absolutely no notice of that, going into the kitchen and getting out cereal and yogurt. He was used to Jill, she was always the same when she was stressed or excited, and this morning she was probably both. He opened the refrigerator and took out a carton of orange juice, carefully pouring out two small glasses of it.

After a few minutes she joined him. Her red and gold hair was wet, and the curls sprang obstinately out, refusing to lie flat. She had wrapped a white bath sheet around herself, and when he looked at her, she had hardly changed from the slim twenty year old he had married almost twenty years ago.

"I'll just take a yogurt, and maybe a little juice, I need to style my hair," she said anxiously glancing at the time.

"You need some cereal too, and your hair looks fine, don't straighten it!" said Simon.

Jill sat down obediently and poured a small amount of cornflakes into the bowl. She knew how good Simon was for her with his laid back approach to life. If only she could be more like him. He was her rock, and she was only too pleased when he took control. If he hadn't, she knew she would have been all over the place.

Now that she wasn't straightening her hair, she had more time to spare. When she was a child she'd enjoyed having curly hair, and as a young woman, but now she was close to forty, she didn't want people thinking she looked too old to wear her hair curly. If Simon liked it, that's all that mattered. He had made her feel confident just at the time she needed to be.

She finished her cereal and got up from the table, planting a kiss on his brow. He gave her a wink, which made her laugh. He was great, she had married a wonderful man who understood her so well. She brushed her fingers lightly through his dark hair which showed the early signs of grey. Not that it mattered to her. He had the kindest brown eyes she'd ever seen, and he was a little rounder these days, which made him so cuddly.

"I've got some toast on the go, how about you?" he asked, pushing his empty bowl out of the way.

"No thanks. I'll put the coffee pot on, and get dressed whilst it's going," she said, leaving him to finish his breakfast and take a shower.

Jill dried her hair, and then brushed it until the tawny red lights in it shone. Anyone would think they were going to a ball, not to pick up their baby, but she wanted to look just right. Such a lot had happened since they had found Marina, who was pregnant, but couldn't keep her baby because she was divorcing her violent husband and returning to England. What a sad life this girl had! No wonder she wanted to go back to England, and her baby would serve as a constant reminder of her violent marriage.

She put on a cream sweater, and matched it with a chocolate brown skirt, which was mid-calf length and a loose style. It would be more comfortable when she nursed little Billy. She hoped Marina wouldn't be too upset when she parted with him, after all he was now six months old, quite late to be parted with really, but there had been no choice, her divorce had taken up until now to come through.

They had taken a huge risk; not only was what they were doing illegal, but also they had sold their house to finance the deal and moved into a flat locally, just so they could be near to Marina whilst she was pregnant. Then after he was born, they were on hand to get to know him, and babysit for her sometimes. It had been seven long months in all; no wonder she was stressed, but after today Marina would be gone, and so would they, right away from here. America was such a huge country, she was sure they could find somewhere safe to live.

First of all Simon had not agreed, but this was so important to her. She couldn't explain how being unable to have a baby of her own felt, but it was overwhelming, the feeling of being incomplete. He had understood in the end, and now they were taking this huge risk. They couldn't look back. Marina was still up for it. To stifle any feelings of guilt she reminded herself, that with Marina's husband being so violent, they were doing the best possible thing for baby Billy.

"Well honey, are you ready?" asked Simon in his lazy drawl when she went back into the kitchen.

"I am, but you're not!" she said pointedly.

"I'll soon fix that." He laughed, and she watched as he disappeared into the bedroom, with his towelling robe on.

She could feel the butterflies inside her, she didn't know whether to laugh with happiness or cry with fear. All these emotions raged away inside her until he emerged, dressed in his best suit with a blue shirt and tie.

He pulled awkwardly at his neck, he'd only done this to please her. In his opinion the office was the only place to wear a suit, but Jill seemed to think that when they went to pick up Billy, the more respectable they looked, the better.

"OK honey, let's roll," he said, taking her arm and steering her out into the car.

As they drove to Marina's apartment they were both silent, remembering what this baby had cost them. They had sold their big house, and would only have enough money left for a very modest one wherever they went. Jill had chosen a baby over a comfortable life. She just had to satisfy the maternal need in her. She didn't regret it, and if Simon did, he was keeping it quiet. All they both wished for now was a straightforward handover, and then they could vanish into the mist with baby Billy.

When they arrived Marina opened the door smiling. She thought she had a lot to smile about now. She had emptied her bank account of all the money that Ricky had settled on her, and now the brat was going, but the icing on the cake was that these two mugs had given her almost as much money as Ricky had, to buy the baby. These crawlers were that desperate. They were pathetic!

"Come in, all his things are ready, I've fed him, and now he's ready to go."

Simon handed her the big wad of notes, which she took eagerly, then remembering that this was her last bit of acting for their benefit, she took out a tissue and wiped her eyes.

"Take him away quickly, before I change my mind," she said, allowing her eyes to gaze at him once more. He was sitting in his baby seat, paid for by them; she hadn't had to buy anything. His eyes looked into hers and he smiled, but she felt nothing. He had been useful to her to get money, but now she could get back to normal, forget all those feeds, and all the hard work having him had given her, and all that excruciating pain when he was born! She could live again.

Jill's eyes widened with fear at her words, but Simon acted quickly, picking up the baby seat, and returning Billy's smile.

"Jill, honey, I'll sit in the car with him whilst you help Marina to check it all."

"Don't worry, I trust you," said Marina hurriedly, as she heard her cab hoot from outside. She couldn't afford to hang about. She hoped the bastards were honest, because she knew that if she was in their place, she wouldn't be. The driver was knocking on the door now, and she must go before any of her neighbours were watching. Ricky must not find out that she had gone, and so had his son. Once she had gone away, America was such a large country he would never find her, she was sure.

Jill heaved a sigh of relief inwardly. So Marina had been as good as her word, and obviously she wanted to go quickly to spare herself any more pain. She impulsively hugged her, taking her by surprise. "Good luck with your future life!" she said warmly, and it was sincere. No words could ever express the gratitude she felt for having her longed for son, as she now thought of him.

Marina released herself and shook Simon's hand. As they went out, past the driver, she gestured him to put her case into the car. He was taking her to the airport, and her flight for Las Vegas was booked. She had money once again, and now she could have a good time. She didn't even look at them as they got into their car and took her son away. Why should she? She was off to enjoy her life again, and meet someone new.

Chapter Twenty-two

Marina spent six months in Las Vegas. First of all she had her nips and tucks done in a clinic which had the reputation of being the very best by all the famous celebrities, and then she spent some time convalescing afterwards. She was very pleased with the end result. Her breasts were as pert as they had been before little Ricky, and there were no signs of her stretch marks any more. The skin on her abdomen was as smooth and flat as she wanted, so she was very happy.

She wasted no time in going out to get some new clothes and shoes. She had her hair cut a bit shorter and styled. It fell in loose waves level with her chin, and she grew out her fringe and just had it waving back at the side, which was the current fashion.

The next few months became a busy time for her. She gambled at the tables; sometimes winning and sometimes losing, but the bug bit her badly, and at the end of the time she had lost most of her newly acquired wealth. Not that it bothered Marina, there was always another man to finance her evening; so many one night stands, nothing memorable about any of them. They all just became a blur afterwards.

She now drank as freely as she wanted, there was no one to put on an act for, and she enjoyed just being herself. During one of these evenings she met Alice, and in their conversation, drunk as she was, she recognised a kindred spirit. She was quite clearly someone who felt bitter about life and envied other people, a little hard done by, and maybe an opportunist.

Alice had never met her before, but she had seen photographs.

Even though a few years had passed, she knew that this was Sadie Morton Brown. She might call herself Marina Scott now, but she would never forget that face, and the harm she had done. She had carried round this grudge against her for so many years, it had made her bitter and twisted. One day Sadie, or Marina, as she called herself, would find out, but not yet, the time wasn't right yet.

It had been easy to get her talking, she was the worse for wear, having been drinking without a man to share her time with. She was moaning about the hard time she had when she married an American, so Alice pretended sympathy. "Didn't you get some sort of compensation from him? After all, you're in a strange country without a home now. You can't live in a hotel for ever," she asked curiously.

Marina looked at her. She hadn't quite bared her soul yet. There had been no mention of a baby, you never knew who you could trust with a secret, but the way Alice spoke, she seemed to have the same flippant disregard for rules as Marina did.

"I did get a small sum from him, but it's all gone. I need to move on in my life and find a way of making money."

"Money disappears like water here. This is a playboy's paradise, but there's no future here for you in Las Vegas."

"Tell me about it," moaned Marina.

"Well, I'm only here for a holiday, which finishes soon. I'm off back to Spain," explained Alice. She then went on to say that she had been a twin, but her sister had died.

"We weren't identical, but we were close," she said, watching Marina's face for signs of emotion.

Marina studied her. She was probably no older than thirty, with her auburn brown long hair and very unusual green eyes. She was very striking, and somewhere in the dim recesses of her mind Alice reminded her of someone, but for the life of her, she couldn't remember who it was. Although her accent was English, she explained that she had lived in Spain for the last eight years, and trained to be a PA after leaving school.

"How did she die, was it an accident?" Marina asked. If necessary she could tell the tale about losing her parents in one too. The intensity of the conversation was sobering her up, she was listening properly now, so Alice lied. It was too early to tell the truth.

162

"Yes, she was killed in a car crash," she said sadly.

Marina then continued with her tale of woe. Alice pretended sympathy. Somehow she didn't believe her, although she couldn't refute it, having been in Spain for the last eight years. She could check later if Marina's parents still lived at the same address in England. Right now she wanted Marina to think they were friends.

"My experience of life so far, is where there's men there's money!" she said. "If you want to get some, you should come back to Spain with me. There's so many men out there, and they just love English women. This country's OK for a holiday, but the men here are fake."

She smiled grimly, wondering if Marina would buy it, but unbeknown to her, Marina had already been contemplating moving on. There was always the possibility that Ricky would track her down. After all, he was in the FBI, and if he found out she had sold his son, he would certainly cause a lot of trouble. She'd got away with it so far, but Spain sounded great.

Maybe now was the time to change back into Sadie Morton Brown again. Then there would be no trace of her leaving the US, and even if she was 'dead' in England, this was Spain. It sounded good, but she would have to admit to Alice that she'd changed her identity.

"Who do you work for in Spain as a PA?" she asked her, thinking that maybe Alice would have some useful contacts to help her meet someone.

Alice had deliberately saved her most important information until last.

"I was PA to Danny and Eleanor Foster."

"What? *THE* Danny and Eleanor Foster!"

Now Marina gave her all of her attention. She had been away from England for nearly three years now, but when she was there they were in every newspaper, they were the Royal family of all the celebrities. Danny Foster, young Essex footballer, made good by marrying Eleanor Hart, who already had a high profile as a model. The public loved them, their golden couple, and he was forgiven for being a mediocre footballer because his astute wife, who had all the money, took him in hand and made him into an idol for kids to look up to and emulate.

"I know everyone thinks he's so fantastic, but personally I

always thought he loved himself too much!" she said. When she'd seen him on the news it seemed that he had forgotten that it was his wife who had made him. So many women professed to fancy him, and it had gone to his head. Men like that just didn't interest Marina. He would be the centre of attention, and that wouldn't suit her.

Alice leaned forward and whispered like a conspirator. "I had an affair with him whilst she was away in England. He didn't deny it after, so I went to the newspapers, and the story made me a lot of money."

She was pleased to see the look of respect on Marina's face, but she didn't tell her how upset she'd been when Danny dumped her, or that her feelings for him were still very much there, and in control of her.

"I hope you weren't daft enough to let him get to you," said Marina. "Did all the scandal ruin him? After all, he's supposed to be a family man and a loving husband, not that I ever believed all that crap!"

"Come on, let's get out of here. There's two weirdos ogling us," said Alice getting up hurriedly. She had fed her enough to whet her appetite. Marina didn't know it yet, but she was going to help her get revenge on Danny, the untouchable Danny Foster had come unstuck! He might think he could get away with everything, but when he had met Alice Lorenzo, he had definitely met his match.

Marina hurriedly swallowed down her drink, and pushed the chair back. She couldn't see anyone leering, but quite honestly she'd had her fill of this place with its cheap looking red plastic padded chairs and gaudy curtains. It wasn't cheap, the rooms were pricey enough, but there was no class. She'd definitely had enough of America.

"Let's go to my room and you can tell me more about all this," she said, totally intrigued by the whole thing.

When they got there, she put on her towelling robe and Alice made the coffee. She listened whilst Alice explained how she had threatened to reveal their affair to his wife unless he paid her off, but Danny had laughed, and said that Eleanor wouldn't believe her anyway. He had also said he didn't care if she did. His wife had been very useful to him in the past, and she couldn't leave him, they had too many lucrative sponsorship deals which relied

164

on them acting like a happy family to the public, who were stupid enough to believe it.

"That man thinks he's God!" she said, banging her coffee cup down angrily. "I became a celebrity for a short time, everybody wanted to interview me, but now I'm forgotten. He's never denied it, the public know what he's like, but because he's a footballer, he gets away with it, and his lily livered wife puts up with it. He's still at it even now, last time it was with her agent, but once again everyone chooses to think it's not true!"

An idea was forming in Marina's mind. This man was a challenge. She had no doubt she could make him fall in love with her, every other man did, but this time she would bleed him dry. She would succeed where Alice had failed.

"What about his football manager? Does he give him stick about it? The scandal could cost him his place in the team," she asked, wondering why this very average footballer, whose only claim to fame as far as she could see, was his brown spiky hair, which he alternated in wearing in a pony tail, or having cut very short, and his very expressive hazel eyes. He was good looking, and obviously had a body to die for, but whenever she'd heard him being interviewed she'd almost thought he might be a bit slow because he couldn't pronounce his words properly. He had no intelligence, but loads of money. She could soon relieve him of some of that.

"His manager, you must be joking! He looks the other way when he does a deliberate foul. They're as thick as thieves, and just as dishonest! I hate him!" said Alice passionately, trying to convince herself it was true. "Anyone's welcome to him. It's not as if I wanted to marry him. I'm still married to Pablo; he gave me some money, but I never saw him again after we got married."

Marina grinned. Alice was a girl after her own heart; do anything for money. She felt she knew enough about her to tell her a bit more.

"Well, my name is not Marina, I'm really Sadie Morton Brown. I faked my own death when I left England to spread my wings. The only problem with a false passport is you don't have any other papers, so I'm reverting back when we go to Spain."

"Wow!" said Alice, pretending amazement. As if she didn't already know!

Marina became even bolder. "My parents aren't really dead,

but they must think I am." She then went on to explain about Nathan, and what she had done, telling Alice how angry she had been that her father had only rented the flat for her.

Alice listened, pretending to care. This woman was barking mad and very dangerous. She had always suspected it, and now she had proof. She needed to get back to her room now. If Marina, or Sadie, found out her words were on tape, who knows what she might do?

She got up and yawned convincingly. "I'm off to bed, but we'll get our flight and check out tomorrow then."

"Yes," said Marina, "that suits me fine."

Later, when Marina lay in bed, she marvelled that once again she had fallen on her feet. Alice was a PA, and she had connections. She would find a way to track down Danny Foster. He was going to be her latest meal ticket. This was her new challenge, and she was certainly up for it.

She awoke the next morning and wasted no time in packing and joining Alice in the breakfast lounge. Whilst they were eating they discussed their plans for the day. Their flight was taking off early in the evening, and flying overnight to Spain. Marina had no need to worry about looking for a hotel in Spain, she was going to share Alice's apartment. As her money was now getting low again, this was a blessing for her.

They went out shopping to pass the time, and Alice found herself paying for Marina. She did this for her own reasons, not because she believed any of her sob stories. She had to make Marina, or Sadie as she would now be, and in fact was really, feel as if she could trust and depend on her. If only Sadie, who thought she was the bees knees, her head was so inflated, realised that Alice would always be one step ahead of her.

Chapter Twenty-three

Danny Foster put on a light pair of trousers this very hot August evening to go to the bar. It was still very close, after an extremely hot day, but he consoled himself with the knowledge that the bar would be nice and cool with the air conditioning .

After a day spent training, followed by a nice long shower, he reckoned he deserved a night out. If Eleanor were here, she would be reminding him not to drink too much with the game against Milan coming up next week, but she wasn't. He enjoyed the freedom of not having her breathing down his neck all the time. She might be a world famous model, but she was so boring to live with.

It had been different when they got married. He had picked the most famous model in the world because football was all he knew, and he didn't ever expect to get rich on it. His parents had found that their son wasn't going to be very bright, he always lagged behind at school, but he did like sport, so they encouraged him to play football and he progressed enough to join the local team.

But after his marriage to Eleanor, everyone wanted him. Money really did talk, and before he knew it, not only was he in the English team, he also played for Spain. Again, it was thanks to someone else, namely his English manager, that he was in the Spanish team. His profile as a celebrity had become so high, he was always in the spotlight, and it made the game of football pale into insignificance, so it had been his idea to send him off to Spain. Not that Danny minded that, Eleanor and the boys were in

England, and he saw them only briefly when he returned to England. They visited Spain, but only occasionally, because Eleanor didn't like it there, and that suited him perfectly. When he only saw her briefly, they didn't fight, she was still nuts about him, and when he was on his own he could lead his own life.

He put on a short sleeved shirt, and admired his tan in the mirror. No need to sunbathe out here, just walking about in it did the trick. He was anxious for the company of a woman, but he had been through most of the available senoritas, and also some of the unavailable ones too.

He didn't have to worry about irate husbands out here, he was too respected, he could do as he liked. Everyone looked the other way at what he did; unlike England, where he couldn't go anywhere without a bunch of minders following behind, and didn't he hate that!

He ran a comb through his hair, which had blond lights amongst the brown, due to the Spanish sun. He liked the effect, and since he'd been here his pony tail had to go again, it was just too hot for anything other than very short hair.

His hazel eyes gleamed back at him in the mirror. He knew those eyes were his fortune. As long as he didn't open his mouth too often to speak, he just looked at women and they were lost. It was amazing what you could get away with if you were an icon; just do a bit of charity work every so often, make sure it gets in the papers, and the public, being so gullible, will believe in you.

Even Alice, his recent fling, had come unstuck. She'd been assigned as his PA when he arrived in Spain, and it hadn't taken him long to seduce her. He liked her fiery spirit, her very blatant sexuality, and her company. She had been there just at the right time, and with Eleanor off the scene it had been so easy to have an affair with her.

But he hadn't liked it when she started to get serious. She wanted him to leave Eleanor, which was laughable. That would be like cutting his own throat; without Eleanor he would be nothing, he knew that. In the beginning she held the balance of power, but now, because of his iconic status, he did; but he wasn't so sure how it would be if they split up.

The bar was within walking distance from the villa, so he went through the iron security gates, making sure to press the button and close them. This villa, tucked away in a secluded spot in the ancient walled city of Girona, was more modest than his English home, but even so it could attract thieves or nutcases if they could get in. He felt only a little safer here than in England, where his home had been broken into several times. Afterwards he had made sure it was safe, and installed much tighter security.

He could actually walk down the street here without being mobbed. Spanish people just seemed to accept him, and although it was a relief, his vain side missed the idolatry and attention. Here he was just another member of the team. He had ditched most of his minders, in the bars he might sign the occasional autograph, but mostly he was accepted as a regular bloke. His regular fix of attractive women appeared to go unnoticed, and wasn't commented on, so he had no worries about intrusion from the press, just how he liked it.

Well, thanks to Alice, he now had to be more careful. When he refused her blackmail demands after he had dumped her, she had been a typical example of a woman scorned. She had gone to the English newspapers and sold her story, gone on television and given interviews, and for about six months, had been quite a celebrity. He'd kept a low profile for a while because suddenly they had descended on him from England, watching his every move.

He'd never denied or admitted to the affair. Even Eleanor didn't know for sure. She didn't want to know the truth, and she had stuck by him with all the loyalty of a wife who didn't want to lose her man, no matter how much humiliation she had to put up with. It was through knowing that, he realised he could do anything to her, and she would never leave him, she couldn't. He couldn't love someone like that, but she was useful as a doormat.

There was a part of him that admired the feisty Alice for trying to engineer his downfall. But as she hadn't succeeded, he now believed what a powerful man he was, no one could touch him, and he could carry on living the way he wanted, and the public would still continue to adore him.

He could hear the music blaring out from the bar now. There would be the usual array of senoritas waiting for someone to buy them a drink. Maybe he should re-acquaint himself with Carla, she had been nice. He couldn't expect to have a different one every time. Luckily he didn't have to impress her too much with chat, her English wasn't good, but her sex was, and that was a way they could communicate without saying a word.

169

h

He saw the young woman sitting outside, slowly sipping a glass of wine. She was alone, but hadn't gone unnoticed by the local Spanish males, who sat nearby, eying her up and down and whispering amongst themselves. She seemed oblivious to their admiration, but her eyes met his as he passed near to the bench she was sitting on.

Danny put on the smile he was famous for, but she stared back at him haughtily. He might be the great Danny Foster, but she wasn't in awe of him, and she didn't seem to melt when he smiled. His need to conquer her rose inside him; after all, no woman could resist him. Why should this one be any different?

He had chosen this bar because most of his team mates went to another, so it was fairly private. It was in a side street, with cobblestones and narrow lanes winding their way upwards, with shops on either sides. He had been here with Alice, and now that the press interest in her had died down, he could return. The young woman, he guessed, was in her early twenties, he liked her sleek dark hair with auburn lights in it. He could see she had a fabulous body; the white very short skirt exposed her beautiful legs and thighs, and the casual lemon top clung to her, exposing just enough of her shapely boobs to rouse his lust.

He wondered how he could get to know her; conversation wasn't his strong point. Maybe Eleanor had been right when she suggested elocution lessons, but he didn't want to end up like a snob, although he did want to impress this girl. She was drinking white wine, so he took the plunge, and went up to the bar and ordered a carafe of it.

He carried it over to where she was sitting, and tried very hard not to sound like a typical Essex twit. "May I top your glass up?"

Sadie grinned inwardly. She was going to play hard to get, this guy wasn't used to that, women usually dropped at his feet. She could have had her pick of any bloke in here tonight, virtually, but this one was loaded, and not only that, he needed taking down a peg or two, even Alice thought that, and Sadie had told her she would do it, she would help her with her revenge on him.

"It will save me from fighting my way up to the bar," she said lightly, and this time she allowed herself to smile, showing him her straight white teeth. She knew she would have to do most of the talking. Alice had told her he wasn't the brightest of people, there would be no scintillating conversation, but he was good in bed.

She watched him as he poured the wine into her glass. She could see why women went for him. Those eyes made up for his lack of personality. His skin was a golden tan, she liked his straight nose, and for a man, he had quite a small mouth. The golden lights in his spiky brown hair were very attractive, and when he smiled the whole of his face lit up. Standing there, waiting for permission to join her, he didn't seem like the cocky footballer she had imagined he would be, and she was pleasantly surprised. "Sit with me, I can't drink all of that myself," she said, watching with amusement how eagerly he sat down, as if he was scared she might change her mind.

Danny was delighted to find she was English. She looked a bit Spanish with her hair, but her accent was definitely a very middle class one. It was ironical really. She probably came from a rich family, but he didn't. He had lived in a council house in Essex, but because of his marriage to Eleanor, he probably had more money than she would ever see in her life, even if he lacked the posh accent. It had been a good day when Eleanor had seen him playing football and fallen for him.

They sat drinking together, and as the wine did its work, he forgot about his Essex roots, listening to her telling him about her life so far. She had gone to the States as a nanny, married her employer, who had turned out to be a violent psychopath, and then left him to come to Spain.

"Wow!" was his response, but to his amazement she asked about his life. She actually didn't know who he was! "I'm Danny Foster," he said proudly, adding, "If you're English you must know me."

Danny was used to seeing reverence on people's faces when the penny dropped, but there was none.

"I'm not really into football. Aren't you married to Eleanor Hart," said Sadie, sounding as disinterested as she could. This was the way to play it with him. She wasn't going to be just another adoring woman, dropping at his feet like a groupie just because of who he was. He was the male equivalent of her, marrying into money, and hadn't it furthered his career? Everyone knew that he wasn't the best footballer around, but he was a celebrity, so he didn't have to be good at anything.

Danny was a little piqued at her lack of interest, he wasn't used to it, but it made him even keener on her. Because she was a woman, she was more interested in Eleanor, that was understand-able, or was the fact that he was married enough to put her off? He couldn't believe that. She was dressed in a very provocative way, and as the English papers had carried endless stories about his supposed liaison with Alice, and then other women had come out of the woodwork to try and cash in on it too, she must know that he was available for her. He had seen her eyes appraising him, but her manner was cool. She was giving off mixed signals.

They had finished the wine between them, and he had the intention of ordering some more. Her eyes fascinated him, like dark pools, hiding her thoughts, but he sensed a wildness in her that he liked, tame women were boring, but trying to tame a wild one was exciting.

He clicked his fingers at the Spanish girl behind the bar, but Sadie used that moment to rise from the bench, making sure that he had a good glimpse of her legs. "Well, thanks for the drinks, and listening to my tale of woe," she said, adding primly, "I need to go home now. I have things to do."

Danny looked at her in amazement. She'd started off like an ice maiden, then he had thawed her and she'd confided in him about her life. Then she had given off signals of being available, her sexuality had shone through, and then she had gone all prim on him. This woman totally confused him. He was at a loss to know what to do next, and before he knew it she had left the bar and gone without even giving him her mobile number. He'd been so busy trying to work her out, that she had disappeared amongst the crowd of merry revellers outside the bar, and he hadn't a clue which way she had gone. Whatever was the matter with him? Was he losing his touch?

He left the bar a very disappointed man. He didn't feel like drinking any more, and he didn't fancy any of the women there either. He only wanted Sadie. She was exciting and different. He didn't know where to find her, the only thing he could hope for was that she would return to the bar again, and he would have better luck next time.

When he returned to the villa it seemed lonelier than ever. He was missing his boys, they were growing up in England away from him, and he didn't like that. He had plans to turn them all into mini Danny Fosters, footballers like himself, but Eleanor didn't want to live in Spain, and that was the bugbear. He felt angry with her when he thought about it; she travelled all over the world, her career kept them apart a lot. He couldn't see why the boys and their nanny couldn't come to Spain with him. She could still visit. At least the boys would be with one of their parents. As he removed his clothes and slipped into the huge, but lonely bed, with its cool silk sheets, he gazed around the elegant bedroom with the cool marble floor, and the ceiling fans. He vowed to talk to Eleanor on her next visit, use every bit of charm he possessed to get the boys out here. After all, they were the sons of the great Danny Foster, and he was proud of them.

Sadie made her way back to the street where Alice was waiting for her in the car. She could see that he really fancied her, so she was determined to hold out for a while before she slept with him. She wanted to control the situation, not to be like Alice had been, clinging on like a limpet. Danny knew he was a heart-throb, but secretly, she had to admit, she had enjoyed the past hour or so spent in his company. He wasn't a great conversationalist, but she didn't care. His hypnotic eyes had been enough to turn her on, and when the sex did happen, she was sure that she wouldn't be disappointed. Holding out was the best thing at the moment, she would get him absolutely hooked, and after that, if she played her part carefully, she would be in line for a bucket load of money.

Chapter Twenty-four

The rest of August passed, and gradually, as September progressed, the pleasant mellow weather of early autumn came in. The trees were still quite green, and the nights were cooler. It was a very nice time to be in Barcelona. The only hint that winter would soon appear was that the evenings were getting darker. Winters here were not harsh, unlike England, but it didn't stop Alice wistfully thinking of England, and what remained of her family, her beloved parents.

She had made up her mind that once she had her revenge on Danny, and Sadie, she was going back. Spain held nothing for her any more. She had rented an apartment some twenty miles away from Danny after all the fuss of their affair. That way they should never bump into one another, but now that Sadie was with him, although she had encouraged her to do it, the jealousy it caused inside her, was crucifying her. She struggled to hide it from Sadie, the thought of them in bed together just did her head in, and she loathed them both with all the passion of a woman who has lost the man she loved, the man she wanted to spend her life with.

She had never felt complete again since her beloved twin had gone. How many times had she agonised about the suicide? If only she'd been there with her at the time, she was certain she could have talked her out of it. They were as different as chalk and cheese. Alice had been the lively and outrageous one, with a spirit and a temper, to match her red hair. Her twin had been of a quieter disposition, with blonde hair, but the one thing they shared was the vivid green eyes. Alice had been born second, and there had been difficulties, she was a much lower birth weight, and her lungs weren't developed properly.

She had survived all that, and her sister had always been so protective of her. Their parents had told them of the trauma of the birth, which made them both so special, and Alice had felt so safe with her sister around. Life had gone along so happily like this until circumstances had forced her twin to go abroad. She felt the rage inside her towards Sadie. It was her doing! This evil bitch just went around ruining people's lives. She left a trail of devastation wherever she went. But not for much longer, she promised herself grimly, and then, after the deed was done, she could return to England.

The door opened, and Sadie, the object of her thoughts, stood there. How she hated that smug smile of satisfaction she always wore.

"Tonight's the night. My first shag with Danny. How do I look?" she asked, twirling around in a very short mini dress. Her hair looked as sleek as ever, her skin was flawless, and the cream coloured dress showed off her legs and shapely boobs in all their perfection. Alice hated her even more. She always looked fabulous, and she knew it. Pretending to like her was beginning to be a strain. She composed her expression into one of calmness, thankful that Sadie couldn't see the hate which was threatening to consume her.

"It's a bit creased at the back," she said, "gratified to see Sadie anxiously trying to peer in the mirror that went from floor to ceiling on her built-in wardrobe door. "But he won't notice that."

"No, in fact if everything goes to plan, I won't be wearing it for long," remarked Sadie, who was so busy admiring her reflection that she didn't notice the malevolent look that Alice threw at her.

"Has he invited you to the villa?" asked Alice, remembering her own visits.

"Yes, we're having dinner by the swimming pool, and drinks, of course," laughed Sadie.

"He can't swim you know, don't know why he's got a pool," said Alice. Sadie was surprised. She had assumed that because he played football, he'd be good at all sports. Fancy being a footballer in the English team, and he couldn't swim! "I swam when I went there, but he just paddled around up the shallow part.

175

He said he'd got the pool for his boys when they came. He wanted them to learn to swim, and Eleanor likes to swim."

Sadie's face darkened a little at the mention of Eleanor. She was coming on a visit soon, for a month, and that meant her plan would have to be put on hold. This knowledge had made her decide that tonight she would give him a time to remember. They had both waited long enough.

"I'm not going to swim. I'll be too busy seducing him," she laughed, and then she left the room. Alice had lent her the car, it was too far to take a cab, and she didn't like buses. She just had to park it nearby and then pick it up later. Danny must not find out she lived with Alice. He had been led to believe she lived in a complex about half a mile from his villa, and because this area was not safe at night, he had walked her back there every time, and she had waited until he had gone before picking up the car and returning to Alice's apartment.

She picked up the car keys and made her exit, leaving Alice to her own devices. She had noticed a change in Alice lately. Although she had encouraged her to hook up with Danny, now that she had, she didn't seem to like it. Not that she cared at all about Alice's feelings, she was another useful person to have in her life, and when the time came, Sadie would leave her and move on without a backward glance.

Alice watched her get into the car and drive off. She was fed up with sharing her apartment with Sadie. She'd never met anyone so self centred. She never had any money, spent it like water when she did have some, and all on herself. Then there was her crazy side. She had admitted a lot of things when she was drunk. Not only had she tried to set her flat on fire and kill Nathan, but also, as Alice had always suspected, she had killed her own brother, and for no other reason than jealousy, because he had come along and she was no longer the centre of attention. She couldn't stand it, so she had pushed him in the swimming pool. Anyone who could do that was a very dangerous person, and Alice knew she was playing a dangerous game, but she still had to do it.

She had recorded their conversations with Sadie boasting about how easy it was to kill. She didn't keep the tapes at the apartment, just in case Sadie found them. They were in a lock-up at the airport, in safe keeping until she needed them. Alice had absolutely no doubt that if Sadie realised she was trying to set her up, she wouldn't hesitate to kill her as well.

She went to bed early that night, trying not to think about Danny and Sadie in bed together, just like she had been this time last year. The difference this time was that Sadie felt nothing for him, whereas she had loved him with all her heart, and still did, and this is what drove her on, this feeling of love and hate towards him; she had to make him pay, and as for Sadie, she loathed her just as much, so she must pay too, she was such an evil woman!

Sadie lay contentedly in Danny's arms, her body spent after a memorable night of passion. She had expected him to be a good lay, but she hadn't expected this warm feeling of peace that engulfed her, making her feel so safe in his arms. She had only used men for sex before, and quickly tired of them, she had never felt anything for them other than lust, so this was a new experience for her.

Whatever was happening to her? She was going soft and losing control of herself, and that would never do! The only person who had ever evoked these sort of feelings in her was her father; ever since she had been a little girl, she had worshipped him, and wanted him to love her, but he had only ever shown her the father daughter love, and that wasn't what she wanted.

Her sexual feelings for him had been present since about the age of eight, but always her mother had been there, standing between them. That's why she hated her so much! To Sadie it wasn't wrong to want to sleep with her father. She believed in doing whatever she wanted, but in the end she had seen that her father had never picked up the signs. He had only loved her in a fatherly way, and that wasn't enough for Sadie. Her love for him, and as she saw it, his rejection of her, had caused her so much anger and pain. That's why she had to kill Jeremy.

But even after that she had still failed with Daddy, so her love had turned to indifference, Sadie didn't do rejection, and then he had angered her when he had promised to buy her the flat, but her hateful mother had persuaded him just to rent it. When she looked back at things, they had only got what they deserved; Daddy had caused her a lot of pain, and when she was in pain, she did impulsive things.

177

She told herself firmly that no matter how good the sex was, she didn't want to get close to Danny. Being tough kept her head clear, and she was on a mission of revenge. Danny was nothing more than a good shag. After she'd got him to part with a good sum of money, she would move on. She was getting tired of Alice and her moody silences.

She looked across at him sleeping, he looked handsome, like a Greek god, and she felt a rush of jealousy when she thought of Eleanor. What a lucky cow she was! But then she chided herself, being tied to one man would be so boring, there were so many more around, and women, if one took her fancy. She was only twenty-three, and had much more living to do.

She turned away from him, and plumped up her pillow. It was too late to go home now, being after three. She would stay the night and then drive back in the morning. She could get up early and go, but deep down she knew she wouldn't. She wouldn't go until he asked her to, because like it or not, she could feel herself getting hooked on Danny Foster, the golden boy.

When Danny woke up the next morning, he couldn't remember much about the end of the evening. He did remember having a good bout of sex with Sadie. He had waited patiently for over six weeks to get her into bed, and it had been great. But she was still there, so he must have asked her to stay the night.

"Sorry if I was too drunk to walk you back last night," he said, and as his hand brushed against her side, he realised that underneath that sheet, she was completely naked. Danny had never been one to look a gift horse in the mouth, and as he felt her hands touching him, he groaned. His weakness was women, he knew it, he lived his life through his trousers, and this little lady was a very sexy lay.

Even though his head was throbbing after the amount he had drunk the night before, he could feel his lust rising, her hands were all over him, and then her mouth, and he gave himself up to her. This was the pleasantest way that he had ever dealt with a hangover. Her lovemaking was frenzied and passionate, and he was carried along with her, she was in control and Danny liked that. This woman was bold and assertive, and such fun to be with.

After it was over Sadie rolled out of bed, and went into the

178

bathroom. She took a shower, and then helped herself to a large towel, which she wrapped around her. The coolness of the marble floor against her feet was pleasant as she walked back to the bedroom. She sat on the rumpled bed to dry herself. She felt very hungry now, and was looking forward to eating her breakfast with Danny.

Suddenly he appeared, with a glass of juice in his hand, but her smile of pleasure died on her lips when she heard his words.

"Sadie, I'm sorry, but you'll have to go. My daily is due any minute, and if she sees you it'll be all over town again!"

"But, I thought you said you weren't hounded out here!"

"Not like England, they used to camp outside the door, but my daily knows a lot of people, and she's a gossip. I can't take the chance!" he said, unceremoniously thrusting her clothes at her. "Listen babe, we had a great night, but now you must go!"

Sadie was most put out, for the first time in her life she was being thrown out by a man. How dare he! She dressed, then giving him a haughty look, she swept from the room. It was no good him asking when he could see her, she was so angry with him! But to her amazement he didn't, his only thought was not getting found out. When she pressed the button to exit the villa, she saw her, a young Spanish woman. She was very dark and attractive, with a voluptuous figure. Their eyes met, and Sadie gazed right through her without acknowledging her smile of greeting. She didn't care whether the woman talked or not. She was still getting over the shock of being flung out.

Whilst she was walking back to her car, a terrible thought struck her. Could the reason why Danny had panicked be because he was having it off with her as well? He seemed to be surrounded by very young and attractive women; after all, Alice had been his PA at first. She could feel a raging feeling inside her, so intense it took her breath away, and threatened to consume her. She could have quite easily plunged a knife right through that bitch's heart! But why did it matter to her so much? What was this man doing to her? She was here to get money out of him, no other reason, she told herself, but her heart wasn't listening. Sadie didn't do love, didn't even know what it was, all she knew was that she had an intense longing to be with Danny, and she couldn't share him with other women. This one would have to go!

She took a chance. Jealousy and anger lent speed to her legs, as she ran through the narrow little streets, to where her car was parked. All ideas of caution were gone now, her mind was totally dominated by her need to remove this girl from Danny's life. She got in the car and drove round to the outside of the villa. She sat there waiting, all thoughts of her hunger gone now. It was a quiet street with no other houses, that's why Danny had chosen to live there, and she was going to turn this privacy to her advantage.

After some time the gates opened again to allow the young woman through, and Sadie called her through the car window, asking for directions.

"Excuse me, I need the city centre. Can you help me?"

The girl stopped, shaking her head, her English was obviously not that good. Sadie noticed her raven black hair, and flawless skin, and she felt it again, a raging anger coursing through her, but she hid it and smiled, patting the seat beside her and pointing at her map.

Petra Gomez had finished early today. She hadn't really wanted to come to work this morning, after her blazing row with Carlos the night before. She was pregnant, and she knew her parents would be horrified. She had told him, but Carlos didn't want to get married yet, he favoured the idea of an abortion, but Petra knew that she couldn't do that. She had stormed off, after saying a lot of things she didn't mean, her hot temper got the better of her, and later when she had gone home she hoped he might call her, but no, not even a text on her mobile. And when she woke up, she kept her mobile on, even at work, hoping to hear from him, but it was obstinately silent.

They often argued, but they'd always made up before and she couldn't believe he would walk out on her when she was pregnant. Maybe he would be waiting outside for her, sometimes he sent a cab for her, and when she saw the woman in the car, her hopes were raised.

She spoke to Sadie in Spanish, without realising she had seen her earlier, nodding her head to confirm that she would help her, and got in the car and opened the map. Whilst she was looking at it, Sadie took the opportunity to drive off, knowing there was an area in Girona, a quiet spot overlooking the River Onyar, a few miles away .

The girl was babbling at her in Spanish, pointing at various places on the map, but Sadie allowed it all to float over her. This little bitch was just too provocative for Danny to ignore, she knew it, so she had to go. Those long legs, so slim, and boobs bursting out of her low blouse. She wasn't even dressed to do housework. What sort of an idiot did he take her for?

She drove at high speed, her car tyres squealing, and then the girl seemed to know that something was wrong. But Sadie was like someone possessed. She didn't stop to think about her actions, or whether any one would see her. She had reached the top of the hill now, and she skidded to a halt. As luck would have it, there were no other cars around.

She jumped out of the car, and wrenched open the passenger side where the girl was. She exulted at the fear in her eyes, it was very satisfying. She was cowering, and Sadie dragged her out. She was crying, begging for her life probably, if she could understand her. The last thing Sadie saw was the terror in her eyes as she pushed her hard, and her screams rent the air as she went over, and Sadie watched her body fall. She watched as it bounced off boulders and rocks, and finally entered the river below, just to make sure she was dead, then she got back in her car and returned to Alice's apartment.

Chapter Twenty-five

Sadie was relieved that Alice wasn't around when she got home. She was probably not that far away, and she'd be wanting the car back. The local buses were notoriously slow, and when they did come you had to push your way on, along with all the local Spanish women who didn't know what queuing was. They were like savages in Sadie's opinion, so she never used the bus.

She sensed a change in their relationship now. She could no longer confide in Alice as she had done. Alice mustn't know that she was keen on Danny, she must still think that Sadie was helping her with revenge. Neither must Alice know she had got rid of that little tart. The more she thought about it, the more she realised, Alice might have to go, too. She knew too much about Sadie.

She couldn't understand herself over Danny. All she knew was, that after just one night with him, she had to have Danny, and she would stop at nothing to get him! For some reason she couldn't explain, he got to her more than any drug she'd ever tried, or drink. She was absolutely hooked on him, and anyone who stood in her way, including Eleanor, would have to be removed.

She had to see him again, she was desperate! But this was all new to her. She'd never run after a man before, but Danny was different, he was childlike, yet sexy, he didn't have much to say, but those eyes! She just had to have him in her life.

He'd be out training now, so she'd have to wait until later in the day. She sent him a text telling him that she would be round about six o'clock. Maybe they could eat together, and sit by the pool. She liked it at his villa, all nice and private in a little world of their own. In the meantime she had to pass the afternoon, so she found a magazine and sat out on the balcony, enjoying the mellow autumn sun.

Alice arrived after a while, putting on a smile for Sadie's benefit. She was squashing down her jealousy, and although Sadie didn't know it, her time with Danny was numbered as far as Alice was concerned. She asked if she'd had a good time, hoping that Sadie would spare her the details.

Sadie didn't tell her much; suddenly it all felt very private, and she didn't want Alice to know. She never mentioned that Danny had virtually flung her out either, there must be no mention of the cleaner, so when her body was found, there would be no connection with Sadie. She had to be one step ahead of everyone, only this time she couldn't move on, or at least if she did, she wanted Danny to be with her.

It never occurred to her that he might not feel the same way. All her life Sadie had always got what she wanted. If he divorced Eleanor that would be better than Sadie having to kill her. She didn't want to be landed with someone else's kids again. She just wanted it to be her and Danny, so if he wasn't in love with her yet, Sadie was damn sure he would be by the time she had finished with him!

Alice noticed that Sadie had very little to say about the previous night. Had she, too, fallen under Danny's spell? she knew, only too well, how easy that was, although Sadie was the hardest person she'd ever met, totally lacking any emotion, Alice had thought. This meant that she would have to move fast with her plan.

"Are you seeing Danny tonight?" she inquired.

"Yes, of course!" said Sadie defensively. She was sure he would be there; after all, she had sent him a text, hadn't she? With all these feelings raging around inside her, and the agony she felt at being parted from him, she didn't feel as if she could eat anything, and as for taking a rest, that was out of the question. This need to be with him was so strong, she'd do just anything to be with him!

She suddenly remembered that she needed the car again. She had no money for a cab. The journey was about half an hour's ride, so it would be expensive.

"I'm off out in the car now. Is there any petrol left?" asked Alice, guessing what the answer would be.

"I didn't notice," said Sadie, her mind too full of Danny to worry about mundane things like that, adding, "I'll need it again tonight, if that's OK with you." Oh how she hated asking for the car!

Alice could feel her bitterness well up inside her. Of course there wouldn't be petrol; she filled the car up, and Sadie used it! How she hated this selfish, lazy, self centred person. How long could she keep up this charade of liking her? It was such a strain! Those faults were only the tip of the iceberg. She was mad, a murderer, in fact, a totally evil woman. Evil rubs off, and Alice had felt herself change. She, too, was becoming evil, she had an evil act to perform, but after that she would be at peace, having exacted revenge for her twin, and then she could return to England, and settle down near to her parents. They would have one of their daughters back at least.

When Danny received Sadie's text he felt a little irritated. He didn't like being tied to times, and he had a meeting with his manager. They were great mates, Kurt Jansen, a big blond German, who was happy to operate on the fringe of what was acceptable, not exactly breaking the FA rules, but not sticking to them either, had saved Danny from many an awkward situation.

Eleanor had been right when she said that money talked, and who you knew. Part of Danny's power was his closeness to Kurt and all his dealings, so he had taken her advice and cultivated his friendship. If truth was known, if he hadn't been so useful to him, Danny wouldn't have counted the big bluff German amongst his group of friends. He was all imposing, and loved to take centre stage, which made Danny feel less important. The one thing they both shared was a weakness for women, but in Kurt's case, he had a broken marriage to prove it. He just couldn't stay faithful to anyone, whereas Danny had the perfect wife; she just looked the other way and pretended it wasn't happening.

He wasn't particularly bothered whether he saw Sadie or not tonight, she was one of many women who were attracted to him. He was so used to the idolatry that he found he could just pick them up and drop them when he wanted to. If he was home by six she'd be lucky, but if something else cropped up, then she would miss him. He didn't bother to text her back, he had too many other things to think of.

When Sadie turned up at six o'clock, having gone to a lot of trouble with her appearance, she was annoyed to find that he wasn't in and she couldn't even get inside the gates. She wouldn't have waited for anyone else, but she made excuses for him. Maybe he hadn't got her text, and he didn't know she was coming. She just had to see him! It was less than a week before the well publicised visit from his wife and children would take place. Sadie wouldn't be able to see him for a month then, and she just didn't know how she would survive!

There was nowhere to sit, so she walked despondently up and down for what seemed like an eternity. It was past eight o'clock now, and getting dark. She was only wearing a flimsy peach coloured mini dress, and although it wasn't cold, she felt the first drops of rain falling on her. There was nowhere for her to shelter; she tried to brave it out, but after a very short time she was soaked, her hair hung lank and wet, with drops running down her neck, and her wet dress clung to her body like a T-shirt.

She was angry now! She couldn't let him see her like this. She ran back to the car, and drove quickly back to Alice's apartment. She put the car heater on to help her dry off, but then she got too hot. She arrived back feeling a total wreck, slamming the door in her frustration, as she entered the flat.

Alice heard her, and as it was only just after nine o'clock, her curiosity got the better of her, so she came out of her room to see why Sadie had returned so early. The sight of her soaking wet was funny, knowing how long she'd spent getting ready to go out, but Alice contained her mirth. She wasn't sure that Sadie would appreciate the joke.

"Whatever happened to you? Surely Danny didn't throw you out in the rain."

"Don't be silly!" Sadie said quickly. She didn't want Alice to know she'd been stood up. "I popped round on the off-chance to see Danny, but he wasn't in, so I waited, and then it rained."

"Danny goes all over the place, and he has no sense of time. If he arranges to meet you, there's no guarantee he'll make it on time."

185

"I'm sure he would have been there if he'd known I was coming," said Sadie, trying to hide her annoyance from Alice, and sound confident. She was trying to sound only mildly put out, and as for Alice constantly reminding her how much she knew about Danny, she was sick of it!

"Well, there's always tomorrow," said Alice, inwardly exulting at Sadie's obvious discomfiture. She suspected that behind the mask that hid her true feelings, Sadie was feeling most put out, and she was pleased.

"I'm off to take a long hot shower," remarked Sadie. She wanted to get away from Alice, she was tired and fed up, but one thing she had said made sense. Tomorrow was another day, and maybe on that day, she would see Danny.

Danny was annoyed that Petra had not turned up for work this morning. He had never been a tidy person, but since being with Eleanor they had maids and housekeepers everywhere they went, to tidy up after them.

He picked up the phone to contact the agency, pushing the empty cans of beer out of the way. The empty carrier bag, which had contained last night's takeaway, was screwed up on the table, and the towel he had used when taking his morning shower lay despondently on the marble floor. Whilst he was speaking, he walked through to his bedroom, which was littered with clothes all over the place, and the bed was in its usual rumpled disarray.

He was relieved to find that the agency was run by an English woman, who expressed her surprise that Petra had not come. She hadn't phoned in to say she was unwell, and was always very reliable. Her tone of voice was such that she knew she was dealing with a very important client, and she promised to try very hard to find someone else to fill the gap until they heard from Petra.

This wasn't good enough for Danny. Sadie would do. He would ring her, she would help him out, and there might be a shag in it for him later. He would act all helpless and ask her round for the day. Better than that, he decided to text her, he didn't like all this mess, but he didn't want to clear it up either. It was a job for a woman.

He sent her a text, and although it was early, he received one back within about a minute. She must have put her phone on early. He made no reference to her text yesterday, that was best forgotten, and neither did she. If she mentioned it when she came, he would say he hadn't received it. Danny was used to being evasive with the truth, it was often necessary for him.

Sadie reached his house within the hour. He had wanted her quicker than that, after all, she only lived less than a mile away. He wasn't sure which flat, he'd never asked, it wasn't a very nice part of the town; in fact, a notorious spot for pick pockets and low lives, that's why he'd always either walked her back, or called a cab to take her. He wondered idly why she lived in such a shabby area when she wore such expensive clothes, but he didn't ponder it for long, there were too many other things occupying his mind.

Sadie arrived in a blaze of excitement. So he had missed her, and wanted to see her. She felt absolutely radiant with happiness. It seemed, that no matter how much she told herself he was just another guy, her mind thought differently. He was dominating her mind in a way she'd never experienced before, and her moods veered between extreme depression when she was away from him, and total elation when she was with him. It was all a bit scary, and she didn't know what had happened to her.

One glance at the mess reminded her about the cleaner; she'd almost forgotten in all the excitement. As much as she disliked work of any sort, she would do anything to get in Danny's good books, so she set to, first of all cooking him some breakfast, and then bustling round afterwards clearing up and making the bed, whilst he was eating it.

When they sat drinking their coffee afterwards, she marvelled at the warm feeling she had watching him eating the eggs and bacon she had cooked. If this is what domestic bliss was like, then bring it on! Whatever was happening to her, she liked it, and when everything was back in order again, they jumped into bed for another frenzied bout of passion.

Sadie remade the bed whilst he was taking yet another shower. She could feel herself changing. Never in her life had she made her bed and done household tasks. Her parents had kept a housekeeper to do all that. It had been a shock during the short time with Ricky to have to act willing and pretend she was used to it. Now she was doing it again, but this time, truly willingly. Of course, looking ahead, to when she was with Danny all the time, he was a wealthy footballer in his own right, even without Eleanor, they would have help, but this was an emergency.

Danny would have been quite happy to chuck her out now that she had fulfilled her purpose, he mused as he took his shower. That bout of sex with her had made him all sweaty! But Eleanor and her entourage were not due for another five days, so Sadie might be useful again. Perhaps he ought to take her out for lunch as a thank you. There was a nice quiet restaurant by the river. He could get rid of her after that. It would be easy just to invent another meeting that he had to go to.

He stepped out of the shower, picked up a towel to dry himself, and walked through to the bedroom, where she had just finished remaking the bed. "Thanks for your help," he said, and she positively glowed, her dark eyes shining with happiness. She was obviously besotted with him, like they all were. "Would you like to go out for lunch? My treat, I know a quiet place by the river."

The towel slipped off, showing his naked bronzed body, and Sadie stared transfixed. These emotions that tumbled around inside her had given her an appetite, but not for food. "That would be lovely, but come here first," she said provocatively, peeling off her flimsy dress, and pressing her body up close to him.

Danny weakened once again. My this woman was sex mad; he had finally met his match! His last conscious thought was that she was very attractive, who could blame him? This would certainly work up an appetite, but whether they would make it to the restaurant, who knew, or even cared?

Chapter Twenty-six

Alice kept reading the letter over and over again. She had just been offered a part in a film. It was unbelievable! Ever since she was a little girl she had wanted to go into show business, but her parents had encouraged her into a career as a PA. Her lively personality, and ability to get on with almost anyone, seemed suited to that job, and she had always done well until she had met Danny and allowed her personal life to creep into her job.

Her mother had told her that if they had been more comfortably off, they would have encouraged her talents at performing by sending her to stage school, but it was not possible, so she had to be content with performing in all the school plays, and even for a while, before she left England, joining an amateur dramatic society. She also had a good singing voice, and she had taken part in musicals, too.

She was aware that some people frowned on her; the way she had found the limelight was because she had slept with such a famous footballer, but she hardened her heart to all that. Her five minutes of fame hadn't even given her enough money to buy a nice home, but maybe this film role would give her some extra money to help improve her parents' life. She wanted to make them happy, as happy as they could be after the loss of their daughter. She still missed her so much! The all too familiar pain of her loss stabbed at her heart, and she pursed her lips with determination. Let other people judge her, she didn't care, her parents never had!

Going away was a good idea. She was veering between terror

that Sadie would find out who she was, and the fear that she might fail to hide the anger and hatred she felt towards Sadie. It was all very stressful, and she welcomed the break. Sadie could keep an eye on her apartment whilst she was gone. It meant she had to put her plans for revenge against Danny on hold, but with Eleanor coming soon they would have to wait anyway.

Sadie wouldn't see much of Danny when Eleanor and her entourage arrived; maybe she didn't know that, but Alice did. All the press from England would arrive; they would be stalked everywhere, so Danny would have to behave himself and play the happily married man. He was such a phony! She felt her hate of him engulf her so strongly it could make her choke. He had ruined her life, together with that evil woman who lay asleep in the next bedroom!

She put the letter carefully into the drawer. Now she would find herself an agent. This could be the start of good things to come. The film was to be shot in London, so it would be a chance to visit her parents, and whilst she was there, she could look around for a new base. After she had tied up all the loose ends, she would not be returning to this country, so her apartment would have to go. In the meantime Sadie could stay here, only because it suited Alice's plans at this time.

She heard the toilet flushing. So Sadie had finally risen from her pit! She would go and make some coffee and have breakfast. No doubt Sadie would appear before she had finished and then she could tell her the news.

Sadie showered and dressed. She wasn't happy. Today was the last time she would see Danny for a month, he had said, but she was having none of it! So what if Eleanor was arriving tomorrow. He would have to try and get away from her. Sadie's obsession about him grew as each day passed. She just didn't understand what was happening to her. This need to be with him, to be physically possessed by him, overwhelmed her. Never had anyone else come close to that. She had used men all her life, for her own gratification, but not Danny. She needed him like a drug, and the withdrawal symptoms of not being with him were so devastating, they ruled her totally, and nothing else mattered.

She was tired of playing best mates with Alice, she wanted to leave her and move in with Danny. Alice was no longer useful to her, but she needed to work out a plan. The idea of Danny being away from her was just awful. He was so attractive, every woman's dream, and now his wife was coming too. The thought of him making love to his wife was too much to bear, her jealousy was threatening to choke her! He said he didn't love Eleanor, they had a businesslike marriage, but Sadie didn't really believe that he didn't sleep with her. They had children.

She didn't fancy any breakfast, so she just sat sipping coffee whilst Alice delivered her news. At one time she would have envied Alice's good fortune, but the news hardly caused a ripple inside her, her mind was too full of Danny.

"I should be away for about six weeks, so the apartment is yours." Alice said smiling. She felt like smiling, at this moment in time life felt good, and even the sight of Sadie taking over her kitchen, hogging the coffee pot, didn't bother her today.

Sadie dragged her mind away from Danny. Having the apartment to herself for six weeks would be great. No more pretending to be Alice's best mate. As soon as she could, she would destroy Danny's marriage, and then he would be glad to turn to her for support. She had six weeks to do it in. She had no desire to see Alice on her return. She forced a smile, and then put on an enthusiastic tone of voice.

"Well done Alice. A film part is great. Yes, I can take care of things here."

"Well, I think I'll go and pack right now. I'm flying off this evening, and I've got so many things to sort out," said Alice, happily humming to herself as she left the room.

Sadie found that Alice's happy mood grated on her. Like herself, Alice had made her fortune out of men, although in her case, only Danny and Pablo, the man she had married so that he could collect his inheritance. Evidently his father's will had stipulated that he could only be paid when he settled down. He had paid off Alice too, and she had never seen him again since her wedding day. The one difference between Sadie and Alice was that Alice managed to hang onto her money, but Sadie always managed to spend all of hers.

She thought of the huge amount of money she had spent since leaving Ricky. First of all his settlement had been enough to set her up for life, but she had been lured to the gambling tables and lost most of it there. Then there had been the money from the Hopkins, who had bought baby Ricky. But then, she reminded herself, she had needed some cosmetic surgery, her boobs had needed lifting up again, there was her Botox, her teeth were whitened, the list was endless, all in the name of Sadie's vanity. The truth was that ever since she was a child, she'd had money showered on her, and she had no idea how to save it.

She sat there and drank the coffee pot dry, but with her stomach in this uncertain state, she still didn't fancy eating. It was all the anguish over Danny that was causing this, and although she didn't like admitting it to herself, for the first time in her life, she was with a man who could live without her. Her feelings for him were much stronger than his were for her.

She forced herself to block out thoughts of him again. It was ridiculous! She needed to get on with her life. What the hell was happening to her? She felt like a sinking ship. No man had ever got to her like this and, she warned herself sternly, it had got to stop. She had plans and schemes to put into action.

There was still a bit of petrol in the car that Alice had put in, but as usual, Sadie was broke. She didn't want to, but she had to ask Danny for some money, he was her only hope. Normally she would have had no qualms about asking a man for money, but Danny was different, she wanted him to admire her as a free spirit, an independent woman, not a broke, desperate, hanger on, but she had no choice. With Alice gone, she needed to run the house, put fuel in the car, and generally live.

She picked up the car keys and called out to Alice as she went. "I'll say goodbye and wish you well now. I'm off to see Danny, but keep in touch, or text me with your news."

Alice would have preferred to have just shouted back, but she left her packing and came out into the hall. She gave her best performance yet, as she hugged Sadie and air kissed her, pretending that she would miss her so much. "Take care, and see you when I get back."

She watched through the window as Sadie got into the car. She most certainly would see her in six weeks time. By that time Eleanor would have come and gone, everything would be back to normal here, and Alice would have found herself a base in England to return to after her job here was done.

She squashed down her feelings of pain at the sight of Sadie looking as gorgeous and immaculately dressed as ever, going out with Danny. Why should she care? He had ruined her life, and by the look of it, even though Sadie hadn't said so in so many words, her behaviour was that of a woman in love. He had smashed her hard exterior. Sadie actually had feelings, and it wouldn't do her any good at all, he would walk all over her, just as he had done with Alice. It was knowing this that allowed her a certain satisfaction to take away with her. If she only knew, Sadie needed to live for the moment, because it would soon pass.

Sadie parked the car and walked to Danny's house through the narrow cobbled streets. Girona was a beautiful city with outstanding medieval architecture, but it was all wasted on Sadie. Danny was the only beautiful sight that she was interested in.

She pressed the buzzer when she arrived, and stood there expectantly waiting for him to let her in. After what appeared to be an eternity to her, but was probably less than a minute, his voice came over the intercom. "Yes, who is it?"

Sadie was impatient to see him, and replied quickly, "It's me, Sadie, let me in."

Danny's voice became firm and emotionless. "Sadie, I'm sorry, I can't see you. I'm being watched, it's too dangerous at the moment. You must lie low until after Eleanor has been."

Something snapped inside Sadie, and she had no control over her next actions. Her longing for him had eclipsed any commonsense she might have had. She didn't care who was watching him. What did she have to lose even if she was exposed as his lover?

She screamed and ranted out her feelings for him, kicking viciously at the big iron gate that was keeping her from him. "Danny, I must see you. I have something to tell you! This is our last free time!" And when he didn't appear to respond she became vicious, she couldn't help herself. "If you don't let me in, then you'll be sorry!" she screamed, like a woman possessed, and Danny realised with a sinking heart, getting rid of her wouldn't be easy. He made up his mind that he'd had enough of Sadie. She was too intense for him. There was a wildness about her that had initially attracted him, but he wasn't sure any more. He would spend today with her, and then he would tell her it was over. He wasn't worried about anything she said to the papers, or Eleanor's reaction, he had proved before he could ride that out. He wanted

j

Sadie out of his life, and if she proved to be a pest he would do what he should have done before, enlist the help of Mike Parker, his publicity agent, who not only helped him to get good press, but also stopped any bad press about him from reaching the papers.

He pressed the button to open the gates, and then came to the door to let her in. Sadie flung herself into his arms, distraught, trying to explain why she had flipped. "Danny, you mustn't tease me, you know how much I wanted to see you today!"

Danny, as usual, could feel his physical senses stirring. He had a great day ahead of him. This woman was a good lay. "OK," he said soothingly, trying to calm her. "I was nervous. The Spanish police were here earlier. My maid's body has been found floating in the river Onyar, and it appears I was the last person to see her alive. I just thought they might still be around."

Sadie felt her blood drain from her face. She'd forgotten all about that little tart! Of course they had to find her sometime, but what she had to hope for was that all the valeting she'd had done inside the car had been enough to remove any evidence of the girl being in it.

"Oh how dreadful, so she drowned then!" she said, feigning sympathy.

"Yes, it looks that way. They said her body had been in the water for some days before it was found."

"So they just asked you if you knew where she was going when she left I suppose," she said casually.

Danny frowned. "Well, she didn't speak English, so I just left her to do things," he said simply. They had a good look round, and took samples from my cars, but I told them I don't drive them, they're only used by my chauffeur to take me around. Not that I'm worried; they won't find anything, 'cos I've done nothing."

"Of course they won't," said Sadie soothingly. That was the longest speech she'd ever heard Danny make. It was amazing how fear could encourage speech! No doubt the Spanish police were happy with what he had said. With his stilted way of making conversation, it was obvious that Danny was not bright, but he did have an air of innocence about him; as if he could ever kill anyone, it was laughable!

Danny had felt shocked when he heard about Petra's death.

She might only be a maid, but she had been young, and it was so unexpected. It had been the visit from the police that had prompted him to call on Mike for help. It wouldn't help his image if it got into the papers that the police had been to see him, even though he had done nothing wrong. Mike had promised to keep it out, but had told him to lay low and keep quiet until Eleanor arrived the next day.

Danny had intended to do just that, but Sadie was here now. One more day with little miss sex on legs, and then she had to go, but right now he was going to make the most of it, and blot the thought of that young maid's death right out of his mind. You just never knew when your time was up!

After a day spent mostly in bed, Danny sent Sadie on her way. He had softened the blow by giving her some cash. She had told him how she was still awaiting part of her divorce settlement, and had a temporary cash flow problem. Danny didn't mind, he wasn't short of money, and although she had insisted it could only be a loan, he wasn't bothered if he didn't get it back.

He had chickened out of telling Sadie it was over. They had spent a great day together, and he didn't want to be subjected to one of her rages. If Danny could avoid trouble he would, not having the strength of character to assert himself, nor the courage of his convictions to see a difficult situation through. Anything for an easy life. He just hoped that during Eleanor's stay, Sadie would lose interest in him and find herself another man. If she didn't, then Mike would have to rescue him from this situation, after all, that's what he was paying him for.

Chapter Twenty-seven

Sadie sat glued to the TV, listening to the evening news. Just as she thought, a picture of Petra, the maid, flashed up; her body had been found. Evidently, Carlos Fernandos, her boyfriend, was helping with their inquiries. Relief flooded through her. That kept the trail away from her, thank goodness! This time she had acted a little rashly, but once again she had got through. She was beginning to think she was invincible!

She should have enjoyed having the place to herself, no Alice around, but she was tormenting herself again, thinking how Danny would now be spending time with Eleanor and his two boys. This was the next item on the news. Eleanor stepping off the plane looking chic, slim and always well dressed, as only a model can be. Her face, in Sadie's opinion was not beautiful, she was too thin, but she did have beautiful chestnut coloured hair, which she wore long and wavy, and it always shone with vitality. Her eyes, too, were a good feature; deep brown, and she kept her tan topped up all the year round. I'm much better looking than she ever could be! Sadie thought angrily, but it didn't matter what she thought, the simple truth of the matter was, Eleanor was married to Danny, and had borne him his children. The sooner she could mess that up the better! Sadie thought viciously.

She kicked the TV viciously, in her anger, and it responded by going off. Not that she wanted to watch it now, to see Eleanor's monkey-like face smiling at her, gloating that she had got her man. Oh how she hated her!

She went to the fridge and got out a bottle of white wine. She was going to drink herself into oblivion on her first of many evenings without him. She knew what she should be doing; going out to find another male meal ticket, but she didn't want to. For the first time in her life Sadie wanted to remain faithful, she wasn't interested in sexual gratification. She didn't understand herself any more, all she knew was she must have Danny, no matter what she had to do to get him, and she would do anything!

When she woke up the next morning with a very thick head, she reached for the headache pills, and made herself a pot of coffee. She'd been so stupid last night, getting drunk like that, and now she was paying for it! She hadn't even made it into her bedroom, and her body felt all stiff from being huddled on the sofa. She stretched out her legs to try and get rid of the cramp in them, wincing with pain as it shot through her calf. Then she tried to turn the TV on, and it wouldn't work.

She remembered why. She had lost her rag and kicked it when her jealousy of Eleanor had got the better of her. Never mind, Alice had a small one in her bedroom, and come to think of it, now she could take that over whilst she was away, it was bigger and more comfortable, with a nice en suite.

She went in there. It looked bare and empty without Alice's usual array of makeup and jewellery set out on the dressing table. She kept the blinds closed because her head was still hurting. She switched on the TV, and then peeled off the clothes that she had slept in, picked up a towel from the cupboard, the biggest she could find, and went to take a shower.

She felt better after showering and washing her hair, more human, and she walked through into the bedroom, and lay on top of the bed. She could see that Alice was obsessed by green. She lay on the silky apple green cover, she couldn't be bothered to turn it back. The walls were painted a very pale green, even the floor had a soft green rug on top of the marble floor, and the tiles in the en suite were a deeper shade of green. The overall effect was of restfulness, which helped to calm her mood, when thoughts of Danny threatened to engulf her once more.

To her annoyance, a picture of Eleanor flashed up on the news again. That woman really was the limit! Once she arrived, all the limelight was on her, and as far as the local news was concerned, it didn't matter how well or badly Danny was playing for the team, Eleanor seemed to be the main topic of conversation.

The English reporter was standing outside the villa, close to the iron gates that Sadie knew so well, the gates that kept her away from him. "Eleanor Foster arrived only yesterday with the couples' two sons, after a very successful world tour promoting her exclusive brand of fashion and perfume. Today, the couple have announced she is over three months pregnant with their third child, and it is believed to be a girl. They describe themselves as 'over the moon,' and Eleanor is now taking a much deserved rest for the next month to spend time with her husband and children."

Sadie felt her jealousy rise like a cancer inside her, blocking off everything, suffocating her, threatening to destroy her senses. Eleanor couldn't be pregnant! How long had the papers speculated over Eleanor's longing for a daughter? but Danny had kept out of it. His boys would be footballers one day, Sadie had no choice but to accept them, they were already in his life, but a girl to spoil, and the chance that she might make him mend his marriage. No, she couldn't take that!

She paced up and down, thinking, totally oblivious of the fact that the towel had slipped off and she was naked. She would have to keep an eye on Danny for the next month, and Eleanor too, and when the time was right she was going to make sure that Eleanor did not have this baby. Even she realised that this time she couldn't act in a fit of pique, she must plan her move carefully, and it mustn't fail!

It felt good to Danny to have his family around him. He loved his boys, and now that she was pregnant again, hopefully with a daughter, his relationship with Eleanor had taken on a new meaning. He could almost imagine himself in love with her when he only saw her occasionally. The only thing that was tiresome, and had caused friction between them in the past, was the entourage that she seemed to need to take with her everywhere. Even in the villa there were hairdressers, makeup artists, PR people, minders and bodyguards, not to mention three different nannies, and other people bustling about, full of their own importance. It was like Piccadilly circus, and it got on his nerves.

He had managed to persuade her to thin it down a little. They were only at home, after all, and she had agreed, but only temporarily. Evidently she would be going to some of the big stores to promote her new perfume, and she needed them all then.

Danny wasn't sure he would be joining her. He always felt a little out of things, and then of course there was his training, and matches. They were already half way through the season. His biggest ambition was to be made captain of the UK team, but so far he'd been unlucky. He reckoned he deserved it, all the travelling backwards and forwards he did between the UK and Spain. No one appreciated how much he put himself out, and he was a little bitter that the English captain was in fact five years younger than him. Danny realised that soon he would be too old, and it rankled him. He didn't like admitting it to himself, but most of his fame was due to Eleanor. She was his most influential, although unofficial, PA, when she was around.

Eleanor knew that her pregnancy had given her a bloom, a radiance she had lacked before, but most of all, it gave her the knowledge, that no matter how many other women fancied him, she was the one he had chosen to marry, and she was the one who was now bearing him a daughter. It was common knowledge how much Danny loved his children, they were a source of great personal pride to him, and with a daughter to complete the picture, it was just perfect.

She consoled herself by blocking thoughts of other women, especially the money grabbing Alice Lorenzo, right out of her head. She had still got her man, and she would keep him. Her career was very successful; enough money to live in style for the rest of their lives. She steered Danny in the right direction. He was like a puppet, but she forgave him his lack of intelligence and weakness of character. He needed her, they both knew it. The only thing she couldn't seem to engineer, because it was up to Danny and so far he'd failed, was to make his work on the football field so outstanding that he was a man to look up to, and he might be made team captain. Even Eleanor's influence couldn't stretch that far!

Sadie spent the next month following Danny to every football match he played. It had been easy to get on the internet and find out his schedule. She sent him texts, but didn't receive any replies, and was very tempted to send him emails. She had nothing to lose. But sadly for her, it appeared that he had changed his email address, or else she had remembered it wrongly, because one night, in desperation, she had tried it, but it came right back. She tried several times more, working herself up into a frenzy, but it was no good, Danny couldn't be contacted.

She watched him like a hawk, making sure that she followed him afterwards towards his changing rooms. He saw her, but she couldn't get close enough through the throng of fans to speak to him. She hated football really, but this was the only way to see him.

The only glimmer of hope for her was that Eleanor wasn't there. It had been reported that her pregnancy had made her tired, she was resting a lot, and making just a few personal appearances at the big stores to promote her new products. She, too, had a web site, so Sadie was able to monitor Eleanor's movements as well.

She had originally thought of trying to get into the villa whilst she was resting. Unbeknown to Danny, Sadie had a spare key. She had taken it, knowing that one day it might come in handy. Danny was notorious for his carelessness, and would probably not even notice he had lost it. She had gone there one day in the early afternoon, but was horrified when she saw the minders at the gate, and then realised the children were there too, with their nannies. Eleanor, it seemed, liked to surround herself with other people.

She agonised how she could get past the tight security that surrounded Eleanor. She needed an ally, but Alice couldn't help her, she was away. Then, on the evening news one night, it was announced that the Fosters had dismissed one of their nannies. Evidently Eleanor had been incensed to find out that just before they had left for Spain, Eva, who had been friendly with Alice when she was their PA, had bumped into Alice in England, and then spent the entire evening with her, drinking and catching up on old times.

Eleanor felt that she couldn't stay after that, and she had been released from her contract with them. Sadie took her opportunity to text Alice about it, and ask her if she should invite Eva to stay hidden away from all the reporters. She pretended a great sympathy for her, but really she was rubbing her hands with glee. Here was another embittered woman, feeling she had lost her job for no good reason, so she would be easy to manipulate.

200

Alice felt guilty for causing Eva to lose her job, but secretly she was glad she was in England and away from all the fuss. She wondered fleetingly what Sadie was up to, and decided she was probably short of money, so with Eva staying at the apartment, she could wheedle some more out of her. Why should she really care? She was enjoying her acting role and life was going well for her in England right now, so she agreed to Sadie's idea, and then sent a text to Eva's mobile.

Eva arrived the same evening. Sadie's first impression of her wasn't a good one. She was big, at least a size 18, invariably wore trousers, her face wasn't pretty, and she had long straggly blonde hair, that looked as if it needed to be washed and brushed. Her skin wasn't great either, with crops of spots and blemishes below her skin. In spite of her long hair, there was something masculine about her; and she was bossy, and seemed to want to control everything.

One thing that relieved Sadie was that after seeing her, she was positive that Danny wouldn't have had an affair with Eva. Maybe her plain looks had helped Eleanor to choose her as a nanny. She had not posed a threat to her. Eleanor's big mistake was to fire Eva. She obviously nursed a grievance about this and Sadie would use it to her advantage.

"Have you eaten tonight?" she inquired hospitably, noting how Eva's face lit up when she opened a bottle of wine.

"I had some fish and salad at lunchtime. But with all this stress, I must confess I'm not that hungry," said Eva, taking the glass of wine and settling her ample frame on the sofa.

Sadie was pleased. Now she didn't have to cook, so to make it look good, she put out a few crisps and nuts, and then she found a bowl of fruit. She had used some of the money that Danny had given her earlier to buy a large steak with all the trimmings, so nibbles were enough to satisfy her now.

It wasn't long before they were both drunk, so Sadie asked her about her life with the Fosters.

"I loved the boys, but Eleanor acts like a spoiled diva, and she's so moody. I only put up with her because of the boys. I tried to keep them normal and grounded, but it's so difficult with parents like that," she volunteered.

"What did you think of Danny?" asked Sadie curiously.

"He was always very nice to me, but he's such a womaniser. I told Alice he was vain and weak, and he'd never leave Eleanor. She's too much of a power freak; she virtually owns Danny, but would Alice listen to me, no!" said Eva, banging her glass down on the coffee table to accentuate her point.

"Well, you could always do as Alice has, sell your story to the newspapers, and make some money out of your misfortune," pointed out Sadie.

"No, I can't. I signed an agreement when I went to work for them that prohibits me from telling anything intimate about them to anyone in the press, or writing a book," she said gloomily. "They aren't silly, they don't want anyone else to know what goes on behind closed doors!"

"I bet they don't!" said Sadie, deliberately encouraging her anger.

"I know what I'm going to do. They've paid me off very generously, and I'm going to find myself a good lawyer, and I'm going to sue them for unfair dismissal. All I did was meet a friend for a drink. I was not disloyal, but I will be now!" said Eva fiercely, and Sadie made up her mind that she was going to keep on the right side of her. Eva, with her bulk, would be one hell of a woman to tangle with.

When Sadie got up the next morning, silence greeted her. She guessed that Eva had done as she had promised, and gone out to find a lawyer. She sat out on the balcony enjoying the sun. It was just warm enough with a light sweater on. In England she remembered November as being a damp and cold month, but here in Spain it was fresh and mellow.

She heard Eva putting her key in the lock, and turned round with a welcoming smile on her face, noting the disappointment on Eva's.

"Well, that was a waste of time," she said gloomily. "He doesn't think I have much of a case, and I'm sure I'm gonna waste my pay off money to fight them and then lose. Oh, how I hate Eleanor!"

"It's hard to beat people like that with their high profile. Money talks, after all, look at what Danny gets away with!" said Sadie, enjoying her discomfiture. It was dead easy to wind Eva up.

Eva was used to winning battles. She was big and bold, and still smarting from her dismissal. As a nanny, she knew she was competent. Her references were impeccable, even the Fosters had given her an outstanding one in spite of their differences. She would get another position without any trouble, and they had paid her enough money to keep her for the next year. Maybe most people would be happy with that, but not Eva! She always took pride in her work. Children were her main focus in life. She lived for their company. She didn't particularly like other women, and she despised men, particularly weak ones like Danny.

The more she thought about what she considered was the injustice of it, the more she hated Eleanor. She had everything; looks, fame and money. She deserved to be taken down a peg or two.

"Eleanor Foster thinks she's God! She controls everyone, but not me. No one tells me who I can meet in my leisure time!" she said defiantly, still full of anger.

"Well, she doesn't like Danny's indiscretions being discussed," pointed out Sadie.

"Whose side are you on!" flashed Eva, and Sadie decided now that the time was right.

"Yours of course, I hate her too! Danny and I are an item, and with your help I am going to tell her so."

"You as well. So many women!" sighed Eva.

Sadie ignored the jealousy inside her. She didn't like hearing about the others. It was different with her, that's why Eleanor had to be stopped. Danny would find how much he needed her.

"You want to pay her back, and I want to tell her about Danny and I; and I've got a plan if you listen up," said Sadie.

"He won't stay with you. It will hardly cause more than a ripple in their marriage," said Eva doubtfully.

"I'm not so sure," murmured Sadie, refusing to let Eva's words get to her. "We'll see!"

Chapter Twenty-eight

Eleanor was glad that this was the last of her visits to promote her new fashion range. She had called it Hart's Delight, because on this venture, she didn't want to be known as Eleanor Foster, she was an independent woman in her own right when it suited her.

Mostly the press referred to her as Eleanor Foster, and she didn't mind at other times. It reminded all the female fans of Danny out there, of which there were many, that she was married to him. She knew she fought a constant battle to keep his affection, and having his children had been her saving grace.

She was also aware of the fact that although they were referred to as 'The golden couple', she was hated generally by most women. Eleanor didn't care, she had tough shoulders, she had found she had to have them in this business, just to survive.

Her bump was just beginning to show, as she had now passed the four months stage of her pregnancy. She only had a week of her stay left, and then she was going back to England with the boys to prepare for Christmas. Danny, as usual, would be floating between Spain and England, according to which team he was playing for. It wasn't an ideal situation, but it was one they both had to accept, all in the name of football.

Deep down Eleanor resented Danny's obsession with football, even though it had been the reason they had met in the first place. After eight years of it, she could now invent excuses not to go to the matches, and her latest excuse was her pregnancy. She had a good PR man to squash any ideas that it was anything other than the need to rest that kept her away. Danny and herself had this unspoken agreement that he should pursue his career, and she should pursue hers, and when it kept them apart, so be it.

She always found their reunions very special, and hoped that he missed her as much as she missed him. He had been very attentive when she first arrived, but now she could sense his restlessness. She wanted to get back to England with all her friends and familiar faces around her again. Eleanor didn't really like Spain, and she certainly didn't want to spend Christmas out there. Christmas for her was being with her husband and children with a big Christmas tree and a roaring fire. She would even put up with Danny's mother, and that was saying something, just to spend it in England with the whole family.

She dressed in a lime green dress from her new range. The colour suited her chestnut coloured hair, and the style was simple, a round neck, with a silk scarf to give detail to her upper body rather than her stomach. Not that she wasn't proud of her bump, it was the fruits of her love for Danny. She added some gold hooped earrings, which complemented the dress perfectly, and then looked in her wardrobe at the array of shoes she had to choose from.

Her long slim legs were her assets, and because of this they were heavily insured. She ignored the little voice of commonsense inside her, trying to convince her that she needed to buy a low heel whilst she was pregnant. She never walked far, chauffeurs took her everywhere, and she only possessed elegant shoes with stiletto heels, which showed off her legs to their advantage.

She chose a pair of beige open toed court shoes. The heel was a little lower than most that she had, but she grimaced a little as she crammed her feet into them. Unfortunately, her pregnancy had caused her feet to swell a little, and they were tight, but on looking in the mirror, she could see they looked great with the dress, so she would suffer in silence.

Sadie had managed to get a position right near to the escalator. Most people came to see Eleanor in the Fashion department, so that part of the store was full of women, curious to see the woman who had launched her own products. She always looked band box neat; so many wanted to emulate her style, even if they couldn't afford her products.

After she had finished introducing her lines, which usually took about half an hour, she would go down the escalator, complete with her entourage, and that was where Eva would come in useful. She was the decoy who, unwittingly, would help Sadie with her plan.

Sadie could hear the sound of applause, so she nodded over to Eva, it was now the time to get things moving. Eva believed that she was only helping Sadie to get near to Eleanor to speak to her. It would hurt Eleanor, with this embarrassing incident being reported in all the papers, both in England and Spain, and in some measure it would make Eva feel better about losing her job.

Eleanor was coming past now, bodyguards in tow, and Eva gave a groan and pretended to faint just behind her, thus causing chaos. When Eleanor looked back she recognised Eva immediately; cameras were flashing, and to her annoyance, no one seemed interested in her at that moment. Even her bodyguards had temporarily deserted her.

She approached the escalator, intending to make a graceful exit down it to the red carpet below and then out to her waiting car, but then events occurred so quickly, that when she came to look back on it, she couldn't remember what had happened.

Maybe the crowd were jostling to get one last look at her. Spanish women were noted for their impatience, but all she knew was that now her feet in the tight shoes were beginning to ache, and she wanted to get them off as soon as she could.

As she stepped onto the first step she stumbled, there were so many people thronging about, and then she screamed as she realised that she couldn't stop herself. The crowd watched with fascinated horror as Eleanor desperately tried to hang onto the moving rail as she was taken down the moving stair. Her feet buckled beneath her, she lost her hold and her body flipped over, bouncing down to the bottom with a sickening thud. The crowd held their breath, then she stirred, she was alive!

Sadie watched gleefully. Luckily, even if it was picked up by security cameras, it would look like an accident. Several women had run over to see her get on the escalator, and in their impatience they had jostled Sadie nearer, so it had been easy just to trip her up. Most of Eleanor's security team had been distracted by Eva's fainting display. The only thing left was to hope that the shock of it all would make her miscarry.

Later that evening Sadie was positioned close to the TV, waiting for news about Eleanor. She had broken a rib, damaged her back, and was also suffering from concussion. She was also suffering from severe shock, and the doctors had gravely announced that it wasn't yet known if the trauma of the accident had affected her unborn baby in any way.

Eva was now feeling very guilty about her involvement. She was not malicious by nature, and she wouldn't have wanted to cause Eleanor to have such a nasty accident. Maybe if she hadn't distracted their attention, someone could have prevented her fall.

"I wish I hadn't done it now. She's lucky to be alive, and I feel responsible, don't you?" she asked Sadie.

"Don't bottle out now," laughed Sadie scornfully. "Eleanor's a bitch, and she deserves all she gets!"

"But not this!" protested Eva, scarcely believing what she was hearing.

She looked at Sadie, but could see no sign of compassion on her face, she looked hard and unfeeling. When she studied her, there was an unnatural glint in those dark, almost satanic looking eyes that she hadn't noticed before. She shivered. She didn't want to think it was anything more than a terrible accident, but doubts were creeping into her mind. She wished heartily that she had never gone along with Sadie's idea.

"I do hope she doesn't lose the baby," she said anxiously.

"Well, even if she doesn't, it'll be born crazy with all that bashing about it's had," said Sadie gleefully, and at that moment, Eva knew, without asking any more, that she had become involved with a dangerous woman. A skinny little thing she might be, but she was pure evil, and for the first time in her life, she felt in fear of a woman.

Sadie was deliberately goading Eva, and making her feel guilty. Now the silly fat cow had done what she wanted, she could be rid of her. She could see fear in her eyes, and it gave Sadie a wonderful feeling of power. She might be twice my size, but she can't wait to get away from me, and she won't dare say anything because she's involved in it right up to her armpits, she thought with great satisfaction.

Eva, herself, was full of remorse, but she knew it was too late now. Unwittingly or not, she had contributed towards Eleanor's accident, and if she could have turned the clock back, she would have just taken her payoff from the Fosters and gone.

She had no desire to stay with Sadie any more, so that very evening she packed her bags and set off for England. She prayed that she wouldn't be besieged by the press, or the police; but no one had suspected any foul play, it was just a nasty accident. Not that she believed that, one look at Sadie's face was enough for her, and she was glad to be out of it all.

Danny was sick with worry when he got the call to go to the hospital. Eleanor was alive, but she was in a lot of pain, and there was the worry that the baby could be affected too. At that moment he realised how important his wife was to him. Maybe he wasn't madly in love with her, but she was his rock, and he couldn't contemplate life without her.

He got to the hospital as quickly as he could. When the chauffeur drew up round the back, hoping to give him some privacy, some reporters had even found their way there. He pushed his way through the throng, ashen faced, and was taken to her private room.

Eleanor was asleep. Her face looked pale and even beneath her tan there was a pallor. She looked fragile, and he tried to touch her hands lying limply on the sheet.

"My god, Eleanor, please wake up!" he begged, wiping his own tears away. "I can't bear to see you like this!"

"She's had an operation to make her more comfortable, and she's under sedation for the pain," said the doctor gently. "She's tough, and I'm sure she'll pull through."

"And the baby?" asked Danny. He wanted this daughter, but to his horror the doctor's face was grave.

"We're not sure. Let's see what happens tomorrow. She has suffered a trauma, so has the baby, and now we can only wait and see."

After he had been left with her alone, Danny sat quietly for about an hour, waiting for Eleanor to wake up. When she did, she smiled at him. She could feel herself floating in a bubble, but in the midst of it all, there was Danny, the love of her life, and now she felt content. She was a little confused, where was she? But she didn't really care, as long as he was there. She couldn't remember anything except laying here in this blissful haze with Danny holding her hand. With this lovely thought in her mind, she drifted off to sleep again, and Danny took the opportunity to slip away.

Back at the villa he was besieged by press and telephone calls, and for once he was grateful for Eleanor's staff. Decisions were made for him, and matters he didn't want to deal with were taken out of his hands. He even had help from the nanny to tell the boys about their mother's accident. It was just awful, and he felt as if he was falling apart. All of a sudden his prop was gone, the children were crying for their mother, and he was so wrapped up in his own grief it needed the nanny to comfort the children whilst Danny went to his room, away from the chaos, to try and come to terms with what had happened.

Sadie was glad to see the back of Eva. Like everyone else in her life, once their usefulness was over, she wanted rid of them. She celebrated having her space back by opening a bottle of wine, but for some unknown reason, she found she couldn't drink much of it. She felt nauseous, which was unusual for her, having always been rudely healthy all her life. She put the bottle regretfully back in the fridge, it must be a bug she'd picked up. If it didn't improve, a trip to the doctor might be necessary.

Eleanor's accident continued to dominate the news for the next three days, and then on the fourth day her miscarriage was confirmed. Sadie was so elated, but to her dismay she still couldn't shake off her bug, so she visited the doctor. When she got the news that her 'bug' was in fact a pregnancy, her initial reaction was horror. After what her body had gone through with baby Ricky, she had vowed never to have another child, she didn't even like children!

But this was Danny's child, and to her amazement she actually felt pleased about it. She didn't understand her own mind any more. Being with Danny had softened her up. The more she thought about it, the more she thought that this child could be just what they both needed. It would be instrumental in binding Danny to her, especially now that Eleanor had miscarried. If it was a girl it would be even better, but even if it was a boy, it would be a miniature version of Danny, so she would go through it all again, getting fat and shapeless, because the end result would be so worth it.

Chapter Twenty-nine

Danny was in a deep depression. Football had always been his life, and now he had temporarily been dropped by both of his teams. The sadness he had felt at Eleanor's miscarriage was nothing in comparison to the feeling of utter dejection at being left out of the squad.

Kurt had said he just wasn't playing his best because of all his family problems. Everyone understood that he needed a rest, but Danny didn't want a rest, he wanted to throw himself into his game to help to overcome all his sorrow. However, it seemed there were other players, he had been usurped, and he found it very hard to take.

Eleanor had gone away to recuperate, and the boys had gone back to England. This made it even worse for him. The loneliness was unbearable; shut away in the villa, he felt very sorry for himself, and then, to make matters worse, he came in to find Sadie waiting for him after one of his rare visits out.

She greeted him with flushed cheeks, and a great note of excitement in her voice.

"Danny, I've got the most exciting news to tell you."

"How did you get in here?" he asked, totally amazed at her effrontery, and deliberately ignoring her last words.

Sadie smiled like the cat who had got the cream. "You gave me a key, remember?" she said. ". . .Now never mind that, I know something that's going to make your day!"

Danny looked wearily at her. He didn't remember giving her a key, and now he wished he hadn't. He was tired of Sadie. There

211

was something about her that made him feel uncomfortable. He couldn't quite put a finger on what it was, and he was deeply regretting their fling. Lately she had turned up everywhere he went to play, her dark eyes piercing into his. She seemed obsessed with him, and there was something unnatural about her. Why did she think she could tell him anything to make his day? The only one who could do that was Kurt by reinstating him in the team.

Sadie went over to him, grabbing his hand in her enthusiasm, she so wanted to share her news with him.

"I'm pregnant!" she announced dramatically, waiting to see his eyes light up with excitement and happiness. Surely he would leave Eleanor now, they had their own child to think about.

"You can't be!" said Danny in disbelief, horror flooding through him. An affair was one thing, but a child, evidence of his indiscretion. His only thought was that he was now finished when the papers got hold of this. He buried his face in his hands; he didn't want a baby with this woman, he didn't even want to continue his affair with her, but he couldn't see a way out.

And then she was there, her arms suffocating him, telling him it was so wonderful, it would bring them closer together. She was totally mad, and she thought he loved her too. What on earth had he got himself into? He could see his life with Eleanor coming to an abrupt end. Even Eleanor wouldn't be able to take a love child. Well, it wasn't even that, it was a fling, and he had been caught out. Anger and desperation took over.

"You told me you were on the pill, you deliberately trapped me!"

Sadie had been hoping for a better response than this, but he would need time to get used to it. She had been shocked initially, but she had convinced herself that Danny would love this child when he realised that they could make a life together. She excused his words, he didn't know what he was saying, it was the shock.

"I didn't do it deliberately, sometimes even the pill doesn't work," she said mildly. She wouldn't have allowed anyone else to talk to her like that, but she knew the truth was she hadn't always remembered to take it, although Danny would probably never know that.

Danny looked at her shining eyes and knew that he was going to take the coward's way out. He didn't really know how to be tactful, but he had to try.

212

"Sadie, I can't face this at the moment, so soon after Eleanor's miscarriage. I think you don't want to have a baby on your own really. Let me pay for a termination." His voice was practically begging. "I can't take any more at the moment!"

Sadie's face darkened. This wasn't what she was expecting! Didn't Danny realise how good they were together? He brought a softness out in her that she didn't even know she'd got. Fancy him even talking about an abortion!

He was fumbling in the drawer now and out came a cheque book. She watched him fill in a cheque with very shaky hands. She felt that anger coursing through her that she'd never been able to hold back when she was threatened by life. He handed the cheque to her.

"This is more than enough to pay for it. Please let me get on with my life Sadie, and you get on with yours!"

Sadie's voice became unnaturally quiet and controlled. She wanted to unleash the anger, but this was the man who was her world, and she still couldn't believe he didn't want her. She took the cheque, promising herself that the money would pay for their baby to have the best of everything. There would not be an abortion, and later Danny would thank her for it.

"Thank you," she said softly, noting his pale and dejected face.

"I need to go to bed," said Danny, leading her to the door, and making a mental note to have the locks changed soon.

"I'll be back tomorrow," announced Sadie, undeterred by him. She knew him better than he knew himself, and by tomorrow he would be as thrilled as she was. It was no good Danny fighting it, they were destined to be together.

But Danny had come to the quickest decision he had ever made. Tonight he was going to join Eleanor on an extended holiday, as far away from Sadie as he could get. His only hope was that she would have an abortion, but he knew he couldn't trust her. She was a woman scorned, but he couldn't cope with it, he was running away from all the turmoil. His life was in tatters; no football, and maybe the end of his marriage, Danny had just about had enough! Women had caused him nothing but trouble, and this time he had messed up big time. He could only hope that Eleanor would stand by him when the truth came out. He needed his football and his marriage, in that order, so he had to woo Eleanor and convince her that he cared.

*   *   *   *

Sadie was as good as her word the next day, but when she turned up to see Danny, he had gone. Her first thoughts were anger, a deadly anger that knows no reason, but then panic set in. How would she function without Danny? He was her world.

She sank into a deep depression, and returned to Alice's house, shutting herself away from the world, trying to get her head round his abrupt departure. She visited the doctor to try and get some antidepressants, but no luck there. She was reminded that she was carrying a child now, and must stay positive and eat a healthy diet. She was offered support and counselling, but Sadie allowed it all to wash over her. It was so clear in her own mind, she simply wanted Danny.

Alice returned home a few days after, and was amazed to find Sadie falling apart. She had always believed her to be incapable of any emotions other than hate and jealousy, certainly no warm emotions. It was true she had an unhealthy obsession about Danny, but ideas of them being together were laughable, she could only put it down to Sadie being pregnant. After the baby was born, she'd go back to being her usual cold and heartless self, Alice was sure.

She had wondered whether she should suggest an abortion to Sadie. Part of her felt jealous that she was carrying his child, but she realised that now she could pay Danny back for what he had done to both of them. He would be finished, both with his wife, and with the public, once the press got hold of it, and a DNA test proved he was the father. After that Alice could go back to England and pick up her life again, and Danny would have got his comeuppance.

But, she argued with herself, Sadie needed to suffer too, and the memory of her twin sister flashed through her mind, and she felt the pain of her loss which never seemed to diminish. She liked to see Sadie suffering as she was right now, hadn't she inflicted so much misery on everyone else she'd used during her life? Alice vowed to call a truce and help her through this pregnancy. She knew Danny better than Sadie. He was running away, just like he always did, running back to Eleanor, the true power in the relationship; but he would come back, and when the time was right, Alice would make sure that her plan would be put

214

into operation so she could sort both of them out and get on with her life. She needed one evil act to rid herself of Sadie. Sadie had had a lifetime of them, so she had no need to feel guilty, she told herself. After all, if she hadn't met Sadie, she wouldn't know how to be evil!

Sadie was too wrapped up in her own misery to take that much notice of Alice. Always self absorbed, she became worse, and allowed Alice to take charge of her, encouraging her to get up each day, to eat and dress, and focus on her baby.

Alice gave her hope. She talked about when Danny would return. The newspapers were full of stories about him being dropped by both of his teams. He was depressed, and had been photographed on holiday with Eleanor, although he was trying to hang onto some privacy.

But holidays have to end eventually, and after two months, Eleanor was pronounced fit and well, and let it be known she was ready to get back to work. Danny was offered a place in the English team for the rest of the season, so now, instead of the papers carrying stories that he was a 'has been', he was once again the golden boy of English football. The only problem with this was that he had now gone back to live in England at the moment, and would obviously stay there if he didn't regain his place in the Spanish team.

Christmas came and went. Alice's only regret was that she couldn't visit her parents. Sadie had turned into a hermit, and she totally relied on Alice to care for her. She was getting bigger now, quite a baby bump was appearing, so when spring heralded the return of mild weather, Alice encouraged her to sit out on the balcony and enjoy some fresh air.

Privately she was sick and tired of Sadie, but as the baby was due in June, she would encourage her to let Danny know about it, and after that, all hell would be let loose. Alice did spare a feeling of regret for the child that would be the tool used in all this. She had a feeling of guilt, but she hoped to find a way to let it be brought up by someone who would be more fit to look after it than Sadie.

The only thing that was keeping Sadie going was the thought that after her baby was born, she would find Danny, wherever he was, and then she was convinced they would be reunited. She didn't care about the pain of childbirth, in her mind it was nothing in comparison to the pain of being separated from Danny. Even the fear of returning to England in case the police were looking for her in connection with the fire and Nathan, wasn't there any more. All she knew was that she had to have Danny to make her life right again, it was nothing without him, they were good together.

She was due at the end of June but, to her surprise, she started her pains two weeks before the expected date. Alice wasted no time in taking her to the local hospital. If this was a warning, then she could be kept in. It wouldn't do for her to get this far and lose the baby. But when the doctor examined her he said that was it, the head was engaged, and the baby was big enough to be born.

Sadie's labour only lasted two hours. She was given drugs for the pain, and her mind was so fixed on Danny, and their child, she made very little fuss. The midwife praised her for her courage, and when her lusty eight pound daughter was born, to her immense surprise, Sadie could feel a protectiveness, and feeling of warmth that had been missing when baby Ricky had been born, less than two years earlier.

"She's just so beautiful!" she exclaimed, cradling the warm soft bundle in her arms. She had something of Danny, it was wonderful, and she vowed at that moment, that no matter what happened, this was her baby daughter, and they would never be parted!

"She is! Can I hold her?" gushed Alice. Sadie gently handed her over, and Alice noted how her eyes shone with pride. She actually seemed to love this little girl.

When Alice studied the child she saw nothing of Danny there. She had Sadie's very dark hair and eyes, she was a sturdy strong looking baby, in fact she was a miniature version of Sadie. Alice hoped she hadn't inherited her mother's evil nature. Her father could have been Spanish by the look of her, but Sadie had been adamant, Danny was her father, she hadn't slept with anyone else, and this time, Alice was inclined to believe her.

"Give her back to me now," ordered Sadie, and Alice obeyed. She noted how possessive Sadie was with her daughter. She had been jolted out of her nomadic existence. Now that her baby was born, she couldn't wait to leave hospital and pick up her life again.

Sadie gathered her daughter to her. Other than Danny, she was the only other human being that she had feelings for, and the strength of her maternal love surprised even her.

"I'm going to call her Danielle," she announced proudly. "A female version of Danny."

"Great!" said Alice, privately thinking scornfully that there was no surprise there. She was obviously still obsessed with him, the passing of the last seven months had done nothing to dampen her ardour.

"As soon as I'm fit enough to travel I want to go to England! Danny needs to see his daughter. The only problem is, I can't go back as Marina Virdini in case Ricky tracks me down. After all, he is in the FBI."

"Well, you can travel back as yourself," announced Alice. "Whilst I was in England I made inquiries. The flat didn't burn down, and Nathan is still alive. You got away with that one!"

"Really!" Sadie's dark eyes flashed, and a strange expression crept over her face. "How could you find out something like that without contacting my parents? What game are you playing Alice?" she asked in a chillingly quiet voice, and her eyes stared right into Alice's.

But Alice had her story ready. She had spent the last few months preparing for this revelation and the effect it would have on Sadie.

"I visited the block of flats, they are all still there, and then I went to the local pub for a drink with my publicity agent. He got talking to the barman, who apparently knows Nathan. Nathan is sunning himself in Portugal right now, and will be away for about a month. So you see, he's fit and well."

"Huh, I know where he got the money for that; drug dealing!" said Sadie contemptuously.

As far as she was concerned, she didn't care whether Nathan was dead or not, he had been a waste of space, but if he was off on holiday he must have cleaned up his act a bit. He knew she had gone away because he'd supplied the fake passport, but he hadn't known she was trying to burn him with the flat because surely he would have done something about it, and the police would have caught up with her. Well, she had got away with it, and didn't she feel pleased! Now she could return to England without looking over her shoulder to see if she was safe. She could find Danny and show him his daughter.

k

She cradled her little mite even closer to her, marvelling at her perfect skin and beautiful dark eyes. When Danny saw Danielle, he wouldn't be able to resist her, no one could, and then they could start enjoying their life together.

"Have you still got a key to Danny's English pad?" she asked thoughtfully.

"Foster's Hall, you mean. I most certainly have!" said Alice triumphantly.

"That's good, because Danielle and I are going to pay him a visit," said Sadie slowly. "The sooner I get out of this place the better. I need to go home."

"Well you're going tomorrow morning," Alice reminded her.

She felt sorry for the staff at this hospital. There would be no thanks from Sadie when she left. They had all served their purpose, brought her daughter into the world, and now she would discard them like an old pair of socks.

The nurse came in to settle Sadie for the night, and she very reluctantly relinquished her hold on the baby, watching like a hawk while the tiny infant was tucked into the cot at the end of her bed.

"Get some sleep, and I'll be back tomorrow," said Alice.

"Sleep, what's that?" retorted Sadie. How could Alice possibly understand how churned up inside she was at the prospect of seeing Danny again soon. Suddenly she felt as though she was getting her life back again, and there was no way she would even consider the possibility that Danny might not want her.

Chapter Thirty

When the plane touched down at Gatwick airport, Sadie felt the exhilaration of knowing she was in the same country as Danny once more. Foster's Hall was less than fifty miles from the airport, so they planned to drive near to it, in the hire car, rent a motel for a few days, and then Sadie would pay him a visit.

Alice, once again, found herself paying for everything because Sadie had run out of money. This time she didn't mind, because she could see the end in sight. All scores would be settled, and then she could go back to living in her nice flat near to her parents, carry on with her career, and put Sadie Morton Brown right out of her life and her thoughts.

They stood up to exit the plane, and Sadie gathered Danielle to her and strode down the aisle, leaving Alice to struggle with the hand luggage. Even though they were travelling first class, Alice felt like her maid, dutifully following on behind. She comforted herself with the thought that Sadie wouldn't be able to use her for much longer, as she tagged on behind. Everyone had let Sadie go first when they saw the baby, but Alice had to queue with the others.

Danielle was crying when they finally left the airport. "She's tired, and she needs feeding," said Sadie, her face showing concern.

"Let's stop somewhere to eat. That food on the plane wasn't much, and then you can feed her," suggested Alice.

They found a country pub, called The Fox and Hounds, and Sadie disappeared into the ladies room to breast feed Danielle.

Alice had now got used to her devotion to the baby, and it didn't surprise her any more. After more than a month, this child was still her main focus, she wasn't just a pawn to attract Danny back, Sadie actually cared about her baby.

In fact, she was unnaturally possessive about her. She did everything for her, Alice was only allowed to hold her occasionally. She seemed as obsessed with Danielle as she was with Danny, it was unnatural, and Alice didn't feel comfortable with it.

Sadie found it pleasant being in an English pub after so long. It was in the heart of the country, overlooking green fields, and suddenly England seemed a wonderful place. American bars had been bland and boring, and even Spain had become boring to Sadie once Danny had left. The oak beams and inglenook fireplace, with hops hanging down, gave it a character all of its own. They sat in the dining room on the old fashioned oak chairs, eating the roast of the day, and because it was only just midday, they had it all to themselves.

Danielle, unlike little Ricky, was a fussy baby. She had let Sadie know she had her, but even getting up in the night to her hadn't made any difference. If there was any good at all in Sadie, then having Danielle had brought it out. She was a good mother to her, with endless patience, never allowing her to cry it out, always cradling her off to sleep when she cried, and never showing any signs of losing her temper with her.

Alice's private opinion was that Sadie spoiled Danielle. She picked her up every time she cried, and she was making a rod for her own back. But the more she could see how much Danielle meant to Sadie, the more she realised how much Sadie would suffer for her sins. She stifled her conscience about Danielle by reminding herself that the baby would never remember her mother, and she would be brought up by someone who was not unnaturally possessive. Alice had no doubt in her mind that getting her away from Sadie's evil clutches would be the very best start in life for her.

Danielle started her fretting, and Sadie sprang up from her chair, leaving her half eaten dinner. Alice watched as she took her out of her baby chair, and walked up and down with her, exclaiming, "She must have wind, she can't be hungry!"

Alice continued with her meal. It was pointless asking if she wanted some help whilst she finished her dinner. Sadie would never let go of her, and thought no one else could comfort her, so she finished off her meal, enjoying every mouthful, and then sat back in contentment, whilst Sadie continued to walk up and down.

By now other people were starting to come into the restaurant, much to Sadie's annoyance.

"Come on, let's get out of here. She'll never get to sleep with all this noise!" she said angrily, as a couple came in laughing. She stalked out to the car, leaving Alice to settle the bill, and to reassure the happy couple that they hadn't woken the baby up. Alice explained that her friend was tired because she'd been up all night with her little one.

"Rather her than me!" said the woman feelingly. "When my son cut his teeth, he used to wake up every night!"

"Yes, we've got all that to come too," laughed Alice.

Luckily the motion of the car sent Danielle off to sleep, so they drove until they reached Foster's Hall. Sadie looked down the long sweeping drive that led to the elegant modern house, well known for its beautiful gardens, and impressive indoor swimming pool. Her heart quickened at the thought that Danny was in that house, and later she would call on him to show off Danielle. She planned to take her after her next feed, when she should be tired and settled, and then they could talk.

They found a motel within a mile. It was reasonable enough with a bathroom, and they both took the opportunity to lie down and have a rest. When Sadie woke up, Danielle was ready for her six o'clock feed, so she nursed her and then took great care winding her afterwards.

To her immense relief, Danielle settled back to sleep, so Sadie took a shower, and washed her hair. She dressed carefully in a lemon shift dress, simple in style with a high neck, but perfect for a warm summer's evening. She wore sandals without tights, and put her hair back in a pony tail, which made her look very young. Sadie had changed, she was a mother, gone was the sophisticated look, replaced by a simple mode of dress. Her dark eyes were even more noticeable, and her cheeks shone with natural colour. She still had the glow of motherhood, and needed very little make-up to enhance herself.

The time now was seven-thirty, so she picked up the car keys, then gently lifted the little seat with baby Danielle strapped carefully in.

"She looks lovely in that little pink dress," said Alice warmly. Sadie had changed her and she was wearing a pink lacy dress with a frill round the bottom.

"Of course, she's going to meet her dad!" said Sadie excitedly, her dark eyes glistening.

Alice saw them both into the car, handing Sadie the keys that she needed. "You can get yourself in if he's not there, but I hope you don't have to wait for too long. At least we know that Eleanor is in Australia."

"I'll wait as long as I have to, Eleanor or not!" said Sadie very determinedly, and after looking at her set face, Alice was absolutely sure that she meant it.

Danny had just finished a workout in his private gym, and was now taking a shower. His personal trainer had gone home, and he was once again alone. Life was better now he was back in the team, but he was most anxious to keep fit so he could play his best. Now that he had reached thirty he was well aware there would be up and coming new players, and he didn't want to be dropped again, it was humiliating. Eleanor had said he must retire before he was replaced. They were words he didn't want to hear. He didn't want to retire yet, so although a little voice was telling him she always seemed to be right, he worked even harder to keep fit.

He reflected that life had been very quiet in the last few months. After his holiday with Eleanor he had thrown himself into playing the best football he could for the rest of the season. Now the season was over for the summer he had even given up drinking much in an effort to keep his weight stable. What a sacrifice for football, giving up beer! but Danny thought it was worth it. His move to England had made his fling with Sadie seem a long way away, and as the months had passed without any incident, he had started to relax more, and convince himself that the little scrubber had taken the money and had an abortion. This was what he hoped, because he had never found the courage to tell Eleanor about it all.

He heard nothing except the sound of the water running in the

222

shower, and he prolonged it, enjoying the feel of it on his skin, as he vigorously soaped away the sweat from his hard workout. When he was satisfied that he was clean, he grabbed his towelling robe, and stepped out of the shower.

He put it on and then went downstairs, intending to put on the TV and lie on the couch, drinking a diet coke. But he never made it to the kitchen. As he passed the TV room, which was more like a cinema because the TV had such a huge screen, he glanced casually inside.

"Danny, I've found you at last, if you could know how much I've missed you!"

The blood drained from Danny's face, and her words bounced off him. He couldn't believe what he was seeing! She had crossed the room now, and he felt her arms, stifling him, he felt like he was choking, and almost wished at that moment, that he was.

The reality of the situation hit him. She had found him, he hadn't escaped, it seemed that even in his own home, he wasn't safe from her! She was an evil bitch, and she was never going to give him peace! His eyes took in the horror of it all, because there, lying on his couch, was a baby, and he didn't need to guess whose it might be. He couldn't bear to look at it, the one proof that could finish him!

"Danny, look at her, our baby! Danielle, the little girl you so badly wanted!"

Danny felt physically sick, and he couldn't find the words to say anything! His worst nightmare had been realised. She had found him again. He felt as if she had super powers, and she scared him! This was a woman who couldn't take no for an answer, and he wished he had the courage to kill her, to rid himself of her forever, but he knew he was too weak. He wasn't a bad person either, but desperation seemed to have temporarily robbed him of all reason.

What could he say? Never that good with words, he swallowed uncomfortably, his mouth and lips were dry, and he felt just like a rat caught in a trap. He tried to calm his beating heart by taking a deep breath. This woman was obsessed with him, and the only thing he could think of doing was to be as nasty as possible to her, to make her dislike him. Not dislike him, hate him, maybe then she would go away and take her baby with her, because Danny didn't feel at all fatherly towards it. This was his only hope. He stepped right back from her, refusing to look across at Danielle.

"I don't know why you're here! I felt sorry for you and gave you the money for an abortion, but I will never be a father to your child! Get this into your head! I don't love you, I don't even like you! Just leave me alone!"

Sadie couldn't believe his words! After missing Danny for all these months, she had so longed for this reunion. He wasn't looking at Danielle, but if he saw how beautiful she was, surely that would bind them forever.

"Look at her, for God's sake, look at her!" she screamed, her dark eyes gleaming with anger and frustration, and Danielle responded by wailing at the top of her voice from the couch.

"How many more times! I don't want you, you're just another scrubber, the world is full of them, I know! Take your brat and go!"

When Danny saw the livid rage on her face, even he thought he had gone too far. She came towards him, and the thought of hell hath no fury like a woman scorned, flashed through his brain. This time she knew he meant it, and she had nothing to lose. She looked as if she could kill him with her bare hands.

Sadie felt like a time bomb had gone off in her brain. She didn't care that he had called her names, she was not a sensitive person, but Danny had called his own daughter a brat, and refused to acknowledge her! Sadie could never forgive that! Danielle was her life, the proof of their love, in her eyes. At that moment, her love for Danny turned to a hate which threatened to consume her, and she sprang at him, using her long nails to draw blood on his face.

Danny used his strength to try and push her away as he felt the blood on his face, but she was surprisingly strong for her size. She brought her knee up with the intention of doing severe damage to his groin, but Danny was saved from further injury by the child that he had spurned.

Danielle had been put on the couch with cushions around her when Sadie had attempted to greet Danny, and when her first wail of protest had failed to alert her mother, she had decided to use stronger measures. She held her breath, and unleashed her rage in a spectacular temper tantrum that was surprising for a baby of one month old, but it was enough to stop Sadie right in her tracks.

224

Sadie's first thought was for Danielle, and her temper evaporated into tears of frustration. She put her in the baby chair, and then picked it up to carry her out, and the baby stopped crying. Suddenly Sadie realised how much they needed each other, it was her and Danielle against the world. She spat in contempt at Danny, and left, leaving him to nurse his wounds and reflect that now it seemed she had finally got the message.

Danny was glad to see the back of Sadie. He realised that she could still ruin him by trying to prove he was Danielle's father, so he made up his mind to go on denying it, and refuse to take a DNA test. In his reasoning, if he didn't take a test it couldn't be proved. Doubts might be there, but he'd lied to Eleanor before to save his skin, so he'd do it again. He didn't want to know if Danielle was his daughter, because he didn't want to feel responsible, or guilty. The thought of having mad Sadie as his baby's mother was horrifying.

He looked at the scratches she'd left on his face. She was a vile bitch. Danny's looks were so important to him. They didn't make him play football any better, but they did help him to pull. Hopefully by the time Eleanor returned from Australia, they would have healed, and he wouldn't have to explain how he got them.

He poured himself a drink to help calm his nerves. That bitch had certainly unnerved him, so his previous resolution was forgotten, he needed this brandy. He changed his mind about watching the TV because he couldn't seem to concentrate on anything, right now he felt he needed peace and quiet.

He took his drink, and the brandy bottle, in case he fancied another, and went to sit in the large tiled room which housed the big round swimming pool which was only used when Eleanor and the boys were there. He felt lonely again, knowing that his boys were away on holiday, complete with nanny entourage, but not with him or Eleanor. Why did she put her career above her family, he wondered, forgetting that he, too, was guilty of that.

It was a pleasant room, the water shimmered invitingly, and he once again regretted that he had never learned to swim. He had posed many times coming out of the sea in scanty swimming trunks, or at the side of an open air pool when on holiday, but it was a well kept secret from the public, no one knew he couldn't swim.

He sat in the lounger in his towelling robe, and so deep in thought was he, that he didn't notice how many times he'd refilled his glass until, after hearing a rustle, he tried to stand up. He swayed unsteadily, and then he saw the figure standing there, her face full of hate.

Sensing that danger was imminent, he tried to back away, but his legs were defying him, and he slumped down by the edge of the pool. His last conscious thought was the gleam of triumph in her eyes as she pushed him into the water and then held his semi conscious body down until the comforting blackness enveloped him.

Sadie was so full of anger and hate when she left Danny that she didn't even remember getting in the car and driving back to the motel. Her one thought was that he had spurned her and insulted Danielle, her innocent baby . She had been no different than Alice it seemed, just a bit on the side to help him cope with a boring marriage, and her pain fuelled her hate for him. This went a lot deeper than using him as a meal ticket! This was her life ruined, the only man who had got to her, had rejected her. She realised now that Danielle was all she had, Alice was a mere convenience as most people in her life had been, she was on her own now, with Danielle. All the good that loving Danny had made her feel, was gone, she felt so vicious she was capable of anything.

She had now reached the motel, and came to a quick decision. She was going to go from there, because she didn't want Alice to have the satisfaction of knowing that Danny didn't want her. She'd had enough of Alice, and felt no gratitude for her support during her pregnancy. Once again it was time to move on, but now she was responsible for another human being, so she had even more purpose in her life, to make sure her little girl was all right.

To her immense relief, Alice was not there. That meant she didn't have to explain anything. She didn't waste time wondering where she was, realising that without the car it couldn't be that far. She packed quickly, knowing that she could be back at any time, and also although mercifully asleep at this time, Danielle could wake up and cry for attention.

She left some of her clothes behind, but that didn't worry Sadie. She could soon get new ones when she had money again. There was almost a full tank of petrol in the car, so she planned to use it and then dump it before Alice realised it was missing. Alice had left £50 in the drawer beside her bed, having drawn it out yesterday after complaining she had no cash, so she pocketed that, and Alice's new bottle of perfume, which was as yet unopened. When she opened the door, there was still no sign of her, so she put Danielle's chair into the car and took off.

After she had distanced herself from the motel by about ten miles, she pulled over into a lay-by. It was by now nine o'clock, and still light, but Sadie realised it would be dark within an hour, and had no wish to be driving around all night. There was only one person who knew everything about her, and accepted it. Only one person she could pick up and drop whenever she wanted, as she had all her life. Even after five years, Sunita would stick by her because she was obsessed by Sadie, always had been and always would be. She took out her mobile and hoped that after all this time, Sunita still had the same number. If not, she would have to drive straight to her scruffy little council flat without telling her that she was coming.

Alice had been waiting impatiently for Sadie to go. She was keyed up, but very determined to put her plan into action. She had decided against getting a taxi to Danny's, instead she took advantage of the warm balmy July evening, dressing only in a pair of micro shorts and a flimsy top. She jogged the short distance, knowing that on a summer evening like this, she wouldn't look unusual to anyone who happened to be out.

One or two cars passed her, but she didn't look up, just kept going. Her visits to the gym had paid off, she was fit, and jogging this short distance was no problem to her. When she reached the area where Danny lived, she slowed down; mustn't arrive too early, let them argue first. Foster's Hall had its own private road leading to it, no other houses were around, so the chances of anyone else being around were slim.

She was relieved to find the main gate open, otherwise she would have to scale the very high wall, and it might have set off the alarm. She went up the main drive, making sure she followed the line of trees to hide her just in case anyone was looking from the house. The hire car was parked right in the middle, close to the front door, so Sadie was in there. For one moment a fleeting doubt crept into her mind. Danny had wanted a daughter, maybe he would accept Danielle and start a new life with Sadie.

She couldn't hear any shouting, Sadie would shout if she didn't get her own way. Alice couldn't bear the thought of them together! Alice blamed Danny for ruining her own life, and she would always blame Sadie for the loss of her twin. Her hatred was so strong it had driven her to this. In her mind, this one evil act would end up doing good, whereas all the evil acts that Sadie had performed had left so many people's lives in tatters.

She was hidden behind a big oak tree, and so she stayed for what seemed an eternity, but was probably only a few minutes. Just as she was thinking that she didn't know what to do next, the front door flew open, Sadie stood there with rage written all over her face. Danielle was airing her lungs, and she watched as Sadie too dissolved into tears, screaming. "I hate you! I wish you were dead!"

She slammed the door hard behind her, and Alice watched her put Danielle into the car and go. She knew exactly where Danny would be now, sitting by the pool, having a drink. Danny couldn't take stress, and Eleanor wasn't there to lean on. He really was a pathetic wimp, and she couldn't understand herself, why did she love him so much?

But he had poisoned her love, and now she hated him! She used the key to the kitchen door that she still had. The beautiful designer kitchen, which would be any woman's dream, was in the usual disarray that Danny created. The maid wouldn't be there until the morning, and Danny didn't know what the dishwasher looked like, or the washing machine. She picked her way quietly through the mess, along the hall, and stealthily made her way to the swimming pool.

Alice saw him sitting there in the lounger, and he kept refilling his brandy glass. Good! Let him get really drunk, that would make her job much easier. All the butterflies that had been chasing around inside her were now gone, and she watched from behind a pillar with a deadly calm, as he drank himself into oblivion. Without Eleanor there to stop him, this was Danny's way of seeking solace.

Her hatred towards him rose inside her, threatening to choke her, and as she made her move, he noticed her, and attempted to rise from his chair, failing miserably, and slumping on the ground. This was perfect for her, because when sober, Danny was much stronger than her. She used all her strength to push his semi-conscious body into the water, and then jumped in after. It was easy to hold him down until he was dead, he offered no resistance.

She left his lifeless body floating there, ripped off the rubber gloves she had worn, and escaped.

Chapter Thirty-one

Sunita Flynn, as she was now called since marrying Peter, looked out of the window on this balmy July evening, enjoying the sight of the small but very pretty garden with its shrub trees and flower borders, all lovingly tended by Peter. She thanked her lucky stars that she had found a good man to spend her life with. He had proved to be a good father to Jacob, who was now six years old, and they also had a daughter of their own, Jasmine, aged two, who lay sleeping upstairs in the next room to her brother.

Sunita knew exactly how long it had been since she had last seen Sadie; five years! She had just vanished without trace, and she'd never really known whether she was alive or dead. She had given up ringing her mobile, she'd even phoned her mother to try to find where her flat was, but she wouldn't tell her anything, only that Sadie had left home for good, and she didn't know where she was. Sunita had always known that Sadie and Isabel didn't get on, but she wasn't surprised that Isabel told her nothing, because in the eyes of her parents, Sunita was the one that had influenced Sadie to behave the way she did.

Only Sunita knew how ridiculous that was. Sadie did as she wanted, and wasn't influenced by anyone else. She'd always known that Sadie was bad news. She'd boasted that she'd killed her own brother, but Sunita hadn't wanted to believe that, it was just too awful! Ever since they were children together, Sadie had always had a very fanciful imagination, and told many lies, so Sunita had never known what to believe. Sunita, too, had a past, she had stolen from shops, not a great crime, and told many lies to get herself out of trouble. She had also managed to get another girl expelled from the boarding school where she was with Sadie, by putting the blame on her for stealing money from another pupil.

Sadie had known all this, and the knowledge of each other's faults had bound them together. Sunita had been scared, at the age of fourteen, to discover just how much she loved Sadie. She was obsessed by her, and so she decided she must be a lesbian. It was a secret that her parents must never know, and Sadie kept quiet. In the end she had tried to have a relationship with Jacob's father, but it was no good, she still loved and wanted Sadie.

She had tried to put Sadie out of her mind, because the pain of her loss constantly gnawed at her. If she was dead, no body had ever been found. It was more likely that something had happened at home, and maybe she'd gone to live abroad. There was bound to be a man in there somewhere. Sadie could always get herself a meal ticket, but even if she was alive, she wasn't bothered about Sunita.

Bringing up Jacob on her own had kept her busy, and then when he was three, she had met Peter. She was shopping, and Jacob was being difficult, throwing things out of the trolley as fast as she was putting them in. She had been tired and fed up, and when the presentable looking young man with the twinkling blue eyes and very black hair made light of it, and helped her, she was so grateful.

Peter was Irish and very happy go lucky, and he loved her with a devotion that had been missing from her life before. He wanted to marry her, and in her own way she did love him. Maybe it wasn't with the same passion that she had felt for Sadie, but he was true and loyal, and as time passed, Sunita became very grateful for how her life had turned out.

She had tried to be a better person, feeling ashamed of her past, but realising that it had been an act of defiance towards the parents who always seemed to be too busy to care about her, and had put her in a boarding school. Once Jasmine was born she was determined that she would have the close relationship that she hadn't enjoyed with her own parents.

Thanks to Peter, she had been reconciled with her parents. It was an uneasy truce, but they had grandchildren now, and they had mellowed. No mention was made of the fact that she hadn't married someone of her own race. Even Sunita's parents had come to realise that after spending so long in England, they would have to forget their Indian tradition of an arranged marriage. In their eyes, Peter was a good man, and they welcomed him as their son-in-law.

This was her favourite time, it was peaceful when the children were in bed. Peter was outside, watering the garden, in that short period of time when the sun sets but it is not yet dark. She loved this house, small though it was, with three bedrooms and a small garden. It was their own, not a council house, and they had both worked hard to get it. Peter was an electrician, and he worked long hours doing overtime when he needed to, and Sunita also worked every Monday, all night at a local factory to make ends meet. If Peter wasn't in when it was time to go, her mother would come and bridge the gap until he was, and Sunita was grateful for that. It wasn't an ideal situation, but they managed, and had even got enough money together to furnish their home nicely, with good curtains and fitted carpets.

Having started off with Jacob in a very small flat, made her appreciate the comfortable home they had now, and they had both worked hard to get it. Peter had given her stability and a purpose, and she trusted him totally. In fact, she had bared her soul to him when they first met, admitting that she was in love with Sadie, and that she well might be a lesbian.

None of this had put Peter off. They had started off as just friends, and by the time they had become lovers, she realised that the love for him was born out of mutual respect. He treated her so well, and obviously adored her, and she liked the feeling of security it gave her. The love she had felt for Sadie had been all consuming, and had ripped her apart emotionally. Now she felt ready to settle for a different kind of love, a love that could last a lifetime, and Peter could give her that sort of love.

She had plugged her mobile in the kitchen to charge up the battery. She didn't usually get calls when at home, but it was useful to have when she was out with the children. It was an old one, six years old in fact, but her birthday was soon, and she was hoping for a new one then. Peter had offered to get her a new one before then, but she had declined, after all, it worked OK, and right now the money could go towards a dishwasher.

She was surprised to hear it ringing. Her parents always rang the land line. Who could it be? She went into the kitchen to answer it, and at that moment Peter came in. "I thought I heard your mobile, who is it?"

"I'll just see," said Sunita, smiling, but as soon as she heard the voice, even after five years she knew who it was, the smile died on her lips. It was Sadie, from out of the blue, wreaking havoc in her life again!

"Sunita, how are you? I've missed you. Long time no see, but I need to tell you what's been going on in my life."

Sunita made her voice sound cold. She might have known this would happen one day. Of course she wasn't dead, and just like a bad penny, Sadie would turn up!

"Why bother, you've managed to keep it from me for five years."

"Don't be like that. I need a bed for the night, and my baby too. Danielle is only four weeks old. Her father doesn't want to know!"

Sunita felt sorry for the little one. Sadie would never give it a stable life. Now she found herself getting curious about what had happened, and she could feel the excitement that came with Sadie stirring her once again. But she had Peter now, and a settled life. What should she do?

She turned towards him, anguish in her eyes. She was dreading this.

"It's Sadie. She has nowhere to stay tonight, and she has a small baby. You don't want her to come, do you?"

Her look was pleading him to get her out of this, but Peter didn't think he could. He had guessed that one day Sadie would seek out Sunita, they had so much history. But Sunita had been loyal to Sadie, so all he knew was that they were childhood friends, and they'd had some sort of affair. In his opinion, Sunita wasn't a lesbian, she had just needed someone to love her, and he had tried to do that. Well, commonsense told him that sending Sadie away was not the answer. She would have to come for the night. It was a gamble he would have to take, because he risked losing Sunita either way.

"I don't mind," he said calmly, although his stomach was in knots. "We'll give Sadie and her baby a bed for the night. We've only got the lounge sofa, but if she's nowhere else to go, it's better than nothing."

233

Sunita didn't think Sadie would put up with it. She wasn't used to that. Maybe she would change her mind. "We've only got the sofa in the lounge for you. Our house is small," she said tentatively, expecting a sarcastic remark back.

"So you moved out of the flat then," said Sadie curiously. Sunita obviously had a man now. She didn't like the idea of a sofa, but right now she needed Sunita, so she feigned politeness.

"Yes, I'll put my husband Peter on now. He's better than me at finding his way. He can give you directions."

Peter took the mobile and introduced himself. He had seen photographs of Sadie, and knew she looked like Catherine Zeta Jones. He wasn't looking forward to this, but it was kill or cure for Sunita when she saw Sadie again. He hoped so strongly that Sunita would still love him afterwards.

"Have another glass of wine, Sadie."

"Thank you, I feel better now." Sadie smiled graciously, tilting her glass towards Peter. She was impressed with Sunita's husband. He smiled and joked a lot, but she had seen sympathy in his blue eyes when she had told him her tale of woe. Sunita, on the other hand, had looked dubious, not much sympathy there, and this made her angry. She was all right, she had Peter!

"So now that we've heard it all, the first thing we must do to stop you getting in trouble is to take the car back to the nearest branch of the rental company. Sunita, could you look in the Yellow Pages?"

Sunita felt a little resentful as she fetched the book. Peter didn't know Sadie like she did. The chances of Danielle being Danny Foster's child were remote, she probably hadn't even slept with him. Most of what she said was lies. She probably didn't even know who the father was. However, Peter was right. They didn't want the police coming round to charge her with stealing the car, so first thing tomorrow, he would return it.

She hadn't really wanted Sadie to come tonight, but she hadn't reckoned on this feeling of jealousy she had felt when Peter had got himself involved. Was it Sadie or Peter she was jealous of? She really wasn't sure, but Sadie had always messed up her mind. If only she hadn't phoned her.

"Here it is, there's a branch in Burton, not even five miles away," Peter said triumphantly stabbing at the page as if he'd found buried treasure.

"That's good, if you get there early, you can go straight on to work," Sunita remarked pointedly. She didn't like the idea of them together, without her. How could she ever trust Sadie? In her opinion, Peter had been totally taken in by her.

"Well, after I've run Sadie back here." Peter smiled, hiding his misgivings. He felt lumbered. Sadie had no money, a new born baby, and nowhere to go. Now that he had seen her the mystery about her had gone. She was just another woman, dumped by a man. She said he was the love of her life but now she hated him.

Although money was tight, he debated whether he should give her enough to find somewhere to stay. He could see Sunita was uncomfortable with her there, and he now wished they hadn't got involved. He had no argument with Sadie. She obviously wasn't a lesbian, she had a baby, but was she bisexual, and did she still yearn for Sunita? Her man had let her down, and as sorry as he was, he couldn't have her around for much longer. He couldn't risk his marriage to Sunita. If she swung both ways, she was a confused person, and she had a look in her eyes he couldn't quite work out; not madness, but definitely confused. He had to avoid her getting in trouble with the police, but with such a young baby, and no transport, whatever would she do? This worrying thought haunted him in bed that night, but he said nothing to Sunita.

The next morning he set off early, with Sadie following behind in the hire car. When it was returned he explained briefly that the young lady had suffered a family tragedy, and had to drive off very quickly. Her friend had been out at the time, so she couldn't explain.

The man behind the desk looked bored and disinterested. On such a beautiful morning he actually wished he wasn't at work. The car had been returned with a full tank of petrol, courtesy of Peter, it was undamaged, so why should he care what had happened? The only nuisance about this was he would have to ring the branch it came from and do some extra paperwork. What a pain!

"Do you think that now you have their granddaughter, your parents would take you back?" Peter asked hopefully, as they were driving back.

Sadie grimaced quietly to herself. Thanks to the flat business and Nathan, it wasn't an option. Even though there was no fire, he might have smelt the petrol. How much did her parents know? She wasn't sure, and anyway, she never wanted to see them again, not even Daddy. He had let her down!

"My parents were so badly affected when my brother died, I can't do anything right. This is why I had to leave home," she said sadly, and Peter's conscience pricked. The poor girl had been through a lot.

"Well, perhaps you'd better stay a few more days whilst we try to help you to get sorted," he said gently. He was rewarded by her smile of relief, but it didn't stop his feelings of misgiving deep inside him.

He dropped her at the house, and went to say goodbye to Sunita whilst Sadie was feeding Danielle in the lounge. The children were both up and eating breakfast. Jasmine smiled at him, flicking her cornflakes all over the chair. Her brown eyes were brimming with mischief, and her very dark hair framed the oval face which so reminded him of her mother.

"Careful miss," he admonished her, and he saw that Jacob was not eating his breakfast. "Come on, young man, it's time for school soon. Haven't you got football today?"

"Yes Dad, but I'm not hungry." Jacob had only known Peter as Dad, and he had always made sure to treat the children equally. If he did love Jasmine more, he never let it show.

"OK, go and get your bag, we're leaving soon," announced Sunita, and knowing what a pandemonium it was in the morning, trying to get out, he kissed Sunita hurriedly and left, explaining briefly.

"We need to talk about Sadie later, and see if we can help her, but she can't go today, she has no car and no money."

"All right," sighed Sunita. She had a conscience too. She had known Sadie for years, and the thought of hearing about her life after Jacob had gone to school and Jasmine was at nursery, was appealing.

The school was within walking distance, which made life easier. They were not in a position to be a two car family. Sunita left with the children after explaining to Sadie that she would be back within half an hour. This was the last week before the summer holidays, so she would have to find things to do with them, but at least today she could concentrate on Sadie and her problems.

236

When she returned she moved Jasmine's night things into their room with a made up bed on the floor, Sadie could have her room, she really needed a room of her own with a young baby to care for. It wasn't ideal having Jasmine sleeping in their room, their sex life would be put on hold; but somehow sex didn't seem right with Sadie in the house, she felt really conscious of her. Peter wouldn't know. He would think it was because of Jasmine.

She made some coffee, and brought it into the lounge where Sadie had now finished feeding and changing Danielle. "Have this, I've managed to find a room for you, Jasmine's."

"What the box room! Don't worry, by the time I've finished with Danny Foster, I'll have enough money to start up again, and then I can get out of your nice comfy little life!"

Sunita looked at her face, it was set and angry, and here was the Sadie she remembered, rude, selfish and ungrateful, so no change there! Maybe she was telling the truth about Danny. "How did you meet him then?"

"It was through Alice. I told you about her last night."

"Alice is the one you left yesterday. But it wasn't her fault that he dumped you."

"No, but she would have gloated!"

"Some friendship!" said Sunita scornfully. Sadie was always running away, when would she settle down? Maybe never. There was a restlessness in her nature that would never change. Now that she had heard it all, to her surprise, it didn't mean that much any more. She had always found Sadie's life different and exciting, but not now. What she had with Peter was so much more, and her children kept her grounded. She realised she had finally outgrown her passion for Sadie, and the relief this knowledge gave her was immense. Now she spoke her mind. After all, Sadie was the one in need.

"You can't go through life using men as meal tickets. You owe it to Danielle to give her a settled life. She's the innocent one in all this."

Sadie felt very bitter. She was jealous of the way Sunita had landed on her feet. She had a house, even if it was a modest one, and a husband, and it was everything Sadie had wanted with Danny. Sunita had been on the receiving end of her spite before, and Peter wasn't there to hear her.

"Just because you've become Mother Teresa!" she spat out. "What's Peter if he isn't your meal ticket!"

"Peter and I love each other, and my life has never been happier," said Sunita firmly but quietly. "It's only because we go back a long way Sadie, that you are here now. Don't expect to be here for long. You will have to put in for some maintenance from Danny, and then you must get on with your own life, and leave us to get on with ours."

Sadie looked at her with contempt. Sunita had gone all pious on her, and she could tell she had lost her hold over her. What did she care anyway! As soon as she could get out of this poky little house, and move on somewhere more in keeping with what she was used to, the better, but in the meantime, she would just have to suffer it.

Sunita went out into the hall, she was trembling slightly with suppressed rage at Sadie's rudeness, so she picked up the daily paper, which was lying on the mat, intending to read it with her coffee, lest she say anything and rise to the bait that Sadie always dangled. It would cause an atmosphere to argue whilst she was staying here, but it made her even more determined that with Peter's help later, they would sort out a solution.

As she opened it, the headlines screamed out at her from the front page. 'GOLDEN BOY FOUND DEAD IN POOL'; and there was a photograph of Danny Foster in his swimming trunks, smiling.

Chapter Thirty-two

Alice was very glad it was almost dark when she left Foster's Hall. Her body was dripping wet, and the micro shorts clung to her as she jogged her way back. Luckily her hair had remained dry, and on such a warm evening, by the time she arrived at the motel, she just looked hot and sweaty, which could be remedied by jumping in the shower.

She had expected Sadie to be there, and in a real rage, but when she found both her money and perfume missing, she realised that she had probably gone. She didn't care about that this time. Sadie never settled anywhere for long. She pitied Danielle, but she wouldn't be living like a nomad for long, that was for sure.

Alice was glad that Danny was finally dead. He couldn't hurt her any more, but she knew she would never forget him. The thought of him with Sadie had gnawed at her until she just had to punish them both. Even though he had used Sadie too, she couldn't let her get away with murdering her own brother!

She felt calm now it was over, and took a leisurely shower. Danny would be found in the morning by the maid, and it would probably make the midday news, and then all of the evening papers. Well, firstly they wouldn't know whether it was an accident or not, especially as he had been drinking, but Alice had a taped confession from Sadie, admitting to killing her own brother, so it wouldn't be that difficult to steer the police in her direction as a suspect for murder. After all, she was rejected by Danny, and she had his child. The fact that she had disappeared suddenly was against her, too. So, unwittingly, Sadie had done Alice a big favour.

She dried herself, knowing she could go to bed and sleep well in the knowledge that the tangled web of emotions that had dominated her life for a long time now, would finally be at peace.

Kurt had debated about calling on Danny at ten o'clock at night, but he had news that couldn't wait. The Football Association had got wind of some of the dubious deals that he had carried out, some were not quite legal, and for quite a few years he'd managed to get away with it. Tomorrow's newspapers were going to be full of the fact that he was going; asked to resign before he was sacked, and because they were so close, Danny would go with him.

Kurt had managed to keep Danny in the team, even though he wasn't that great a player, because he had power, but now that power was at an end, which also meant the end of Danny too. They had been as thick as thieves for years, Danny managing to look the other way when Kurt pulled a few strings and broke a few rules. There were younger and better players, and with a new manager, Kurt knew that Danny would definitely be out.

He was surprised to see the big wrought iron gates open, but there again, Danny was known for being careless. It was only when Eleanor was there that they had security with a man on the gate to direct visitors in. Danny was so wrapped up in himself. No wonder they had been broken into in the past. He drove up the long drive with its impressive avenue of trees. There weren't any cars outside the house, so Danny must be alone. He hoped he wasn't consoling himself with a woman, he had tried ringing the mobile, but knowing Danny, it wasn't on.

He rang the doorbell but there was no answer. Danny never went to bed early unless he had a woman, but no lights were on, and it seemed eerily quiet. Maybe Danny was in the swimming pool area, so he went round the side of the house to check. It was dark by now, but the door was not locked, so he pushed it open and went in, calling Danny's name so that he didn't startle him.

He could make out the figure floating on the top of the water, in a crab like fashion, and he spoke to him at first, not realising anything was wrong. But then he remembered, Danny couldn't swim, and the body he was speaking to was a corpse!

Sadie kept reading it over and over again, because her mind couldn't register it. 'The body of Danny Foster had been found floating in his own swimming pool by his manager Kurt Jansen. It was too early to know yet whether it was suicide or an accident, as it appeared he had been drinking heavily.'

All the feelings of hate and rejection had gone now. She felt numb and sick inside. She sobbed because only Danny had the power to rouse emotions in Sadie, and the loss of him was so immense. She forgot all her plans of revenge, there was only a nausea inside her, and an unreal feeling. She wanted to shout and scream because she'd lost the one man she could have settled down with, but she couldn't, she just felt dead inside, somehow money didn't seem important any more, and she just wanted to curl up and die.

Danielle let out a lusty cry, which reminded her that this wasn't an option. She had a baby now who needed her, her very last link with Danny, so she automatically stretched out her arms, picked her up out of her little seat, and cradled her to herself.

Sunita looked at her with sympathy. For once in her life she could tell Sadie was telling the truth. The grief she was showing was not faked. She definitely did care for Danny Foster, and probably Danielle was his daughter. This was not the Sadie of old, cold and emotionless, there was a heart under all that anger and spite.

It was ironical that the only man she had cared for had died, because now, when she got over it, she would probably go back to being just as hard again.

"I know it's dreadful for you Sadie, and I'm sorry, but at least you have Danielle to remind you of him."

Sadie said nothing, she felt too weary to speak. She left the room with Danielle in her arms, and went upstairs to the little box room so she could shut herself away from the world and mourn.

Sunita watched her go. As sorry as she was, she couldn't help thinking that this would make it even harder to ask her to go. Here was Sadie, back in her life again, and causing havoc as usual. She did so hope it wouldn't cause friction between herself and Peter,

l

because she had come to realise he was the most important person in her life and she didn't want to ever be without him.

Alice was surprised to read about Danny in the morning paper. Eleanor had been informed, and was on her way back from Australia. Apparently she was distraught and under sedation. Alice wasn't surprised by that. Eleanor adored Danny. He had been her weakness, and he had wiped the floor with her emotionally, but not any more!

She decided to get it all moving, so she went to the local police station, explaining about Sadie's disappearance after going to visit Danny to show him his baby daughter. The police didn't appear to be that interested until she gave them Sadie's taped confession about killing her brother Jeremy. The big burly detective looked at her with renewed interest, and knowing that her own DNA would be found at the house too, she explained.

"I am Alice Lorenzo, his ex PA. I met Sadie last year, and she asked me to help her get to know him."

Detective Inspector Miles Wilkins looked at this very attractive young woman whose face was familiar to him, and then he remembered. She was the one who had also had an alleged fling with Danny and sold her story to the tabloids. He'd also seen her make a career out of it. It was amazing really how you could make a career out of sleeping with someone. She should try doing a day's work like he had to!

"I know it was wrong, but I had a spare key to the house, I had been in it many times, and I lent it to Sadie so she could go and see him."

Miles looked at her steadily. She didn't seem that nervous, and there was obviously no love lost between her and Sadie because she had lost no time in coming in to shop her, if she had done it.

"When did you tape this confession?"

"Why, only yesterday," said Alice innocently. She had been expecting this question, so the lie came easily to her lips. "To be honest, I didn't know whether to believe her or not, but now that Danny has drowned in his swimming pool, it seems to be such a coincidence."

"But you taped it."

"Yes, but I didn't know the tape was running. I'd been using it to practise my lines for a play, that is what I intended, but I forgot it was on. When Sadie told me that, I forgot everything else because it was just too horrible!"

Miles stared hard at her, trying to decide whether she was telling the truth. It was a flimsy excuse. Taping a conversation was usually done for a reason, and she certainly hadn't let the grass grow under her feet before she came in. Well, it looked as if they'd have to track down this Sadie and see what she had to say, but with what she'd said on tape, it wasn't looking good for her.

"You're free to leave now, but we may want you back again," he said calmly. Turning to the officer busy scribbling notes, he added, "We need to track down Sadie Morton Brown, so if necessary we'll have to make an announcement through the news desks."

Alice hid a smile. It was going perfectly. Sadie would soon be found, and then her revenge would be complete and she could move on with her life and try to put the past behind her.

Time seemed to have stopped still for Sadie. But later that same day she felt the need to get as close to Danny as she could. She had to return to Foster's Hall, lay some flowers outside, and say farewell to her darling Danny.

She reluctantly left Danielle with Sunita because she had no choice really. The journey would take an hour each way, and there was nowhere she could feed her. She used the fifty pounds to buy a huge bouquet of flowers, and Sunita lent her some more money for the train fare.

Normally she wouldn't have travelled in this way. Public transport had not been for her, but this time she was desperate to spend some time as close to Danny as she could, knowing that this would be her farewell because she wouldn't be able to go to his funeral. She might be the mother of his child, but she had no rights, so this would be the last time she could visit Foster's Hall.

She sat on the train, clutching the flowers to her, trying to keep the bouquet from touching the other passengers. This was the first time in her life that Sadie had ever bought flowers for anyone, having always been a taker and not a giver. But this was all she could do for him, just a few flowers to remember the man who had been her life, and her future, as she had hoped. Her mind had allowed her to block out his rejection yesterday. He would have come round, and they should have been together with Danielle. Life had cheated her. Her one chance of happiness was gone for ever, and the pain was just so agonising. For once in her life Sadie couldn't have what she wanted because money couldn't buy it.

Sunita heard the police message on the radio, and saw the photograph of Sadie. They were appealing to her to come forward to help them with their inquiries. For one wild moment the thought flashed through her mind, had Sadie killed Danny in a rage after being rejected? But would she have been talking about getting child support off him? And that grief this morning had been real. She couldn't have done it, Sunita was sure, and felt ashamed of herself for even thinking that way.

The problem was that Sadie told so many lies, and she hadn't ever wanted to believe she'd killed her own brother. Now that her infatuation for Sadie had cooled, and she now recognised that is what it had been, she could see the bigger picture. She had been bound to Sadie because she had been lonely and had parents that were too busy to spend time with her. Now that she had her own life with a husband and children, much of Sunita's anger against the world had gone. She just wanted a normal life, but that would never be true of Sadie. She finally admitted to herself there was something about Sadie that wasn't quite normal, there were hidden depths there that no one knew. As sorry as she felt for her, she would tell Sadie she must go to the police, co-operate, and then she could be eliminated from their inquiries. She would tell her this when she returned.

The telephone rang. It was Peter, he had also heard it on the news. Sunita explained where Sadie had gone.

"I hope she hasn't done a bunk!" he said.

"No, never! She wouldn't leave Danielle!" said Sunita firmly. "I've got to go and meet Jacob from school now," she added, after glancing at the clock. Where had the day gone?

She put Jasmin in the front of the double buggy that was rarely used now, and picked up Danielle to nestle her in the back part. It wasn't ideal because she was so young and couldn't sit up yet, but she managed to pad her out with a baby blanket.

However, this didn't stop Danielle from waking up and protesting furiously.

Sunita pushed the buggy quickly up the road. She hadn't found looking after Danielle that easy this afternoon. She had screamed through her bottle because she was normally breast fed, and now she was awake again, but hopefully the motion of the buggy would calm her down. Sadie wouldn't be back until this evening, so she really hoped that Danielle would stop crying soon.

Kurt poured himself a glass of whisky and sat down in the comfortable and familiar penthouse that he called home. The shock of finding Danny drowned had knocked him for six. He had even forgotten that the papers were about to have a field day at his expense. None of that seemed to matter now because death was so final. What did it matter if Danny had been out of the team now? This time yesterday he still had his life. Whatever had happened?

The police had questioned him since last night. He had found the body and raised the alarm, he'd come with bad tidings for Danny. Had he killed him? Had they quarrelled?

He'd been asked all these questions and more. It was all chasing around in his head, and the shock of finding the body like that had left a huge impression on him. Danny, his friend, so fit and full of life, was gone, and that body floating face down was all that remained of him. It haunted him, it was just so awful! However would Eleanor and the boys cope?

Eventually they'd let him go. Nobody really knew whether it was suicide or an accident. Well, it couldn't be murder, who would want to kill Danny? They were both the more likely answers. He hadn't told Danny he would be out of the team, so chances are, it was just a dreadful accident. Anyway, Danny wasn't the suicidal type. He may have loved football, but he also loved women, and was used to consoling himself with them when things went wrong for him.

Kurt swallowed the whisky in one determined gulp. It warmed the inside of his throat, and he began to feel a bit calmer. It was good to be back home in his own space. The one thing that had surprised him, was that as he was leaving the police station, he had almost bumped into Alice Lorenzo. She had a nerve showing

245

up there after all the trouble she'd caused Danny when news of their affair got out. Kurt hadn't forgiven her for selling her story to the tabloids. Some PA she'd been!

He wondered what possible information she could give them, because as far as he was aware, Danny hadn't seen her now for well over a year. That little tart had made herself a nice little nest egg out of Danny, and then even got a part in a film. Famous for sleeping with Danny Foster; no real talent, just another hanger-on!

Well he shouldn't be too critical of that because women had also been Kurt's downfall. His various infidelities had ruined his marriage. The power of being the Manager of the English football team had gone to his head. Women still chased after him, but soon they wouldn't, when he was out of a job, no longer with a high profile; because he knew that it wasn't him they really wanted, it was the knowledge that they had slept with someone important, the England manager. Soon he would be a nobody, but at least he was still alive.

Chapter Thirty-three

Foster's Hall was situated very much on its own, up an unmade, and long, winding road with no other houses around. This road was only used by people visiting the house, so it was rare to see anyone going along there. That is, until now.

The sight that greeted Sadie, as she turned into the road, was like something from a movie. She hesitated, thinking she had taken a wrong turn somewhere when she saw that cars were parked all the way along, and several policemen were doing their best to keep a clear path.

But then she saw other people with flowers and children clutching cards with messages on, and it hit home hard, they had come to pay their last respects to Danny, just like her. She felt her resentment rising, she had wanted this to be a private moment, but it seemed that Danny Foster belonged to the people, as well as her.

She made progress through the throng. Women were sobbing, and as she got closer to the gates, she stopped, it was like everyone in the world was there. The screaming and sobbing was completely overwhelming, the crowd thicker than any at a football match, and the sea of flowers that greeted her made a colourful carpet which spread along the outside of the gates and also in the street.

Danny Foster, in life had become a bit of a joke lately, the press reviled him because he had been dropped from the team, and his amorous exploits were something the public forgave because he was a very attractive man. He was supposed to be a role model

247

for family life, and when people saw him making a show of unity with Eleanor, or buying her some new diamonds, they believed they were happy, because everyone likes a tale of happy ever after.

Now that he had died, he was suddenly an icon. The outpouring of grief was extraordinary. All his faults were now forgotten, and women of all ages, as well as children, came together to mourn him, to weep and wail because maybe weak, manipulated Danny had been a symbol of what was wrong in their own lives.

Sadie's big bunch of flowers was insignificant amongst this mass, and she felt usurped by every other woman in the country. In her mind he had been her man, and hers alone, as well as being Danielle's father. Suddenly she missed her little girl like crazy, and she didn't want to stay here with this surging mass of mad people! It wasn't as if she could even find a spot on its own to lay the flowers. To her intense anger she had to lay them with all the others, so she tried to prop up the card with her message, which was very simple, 'I will never forget you. All my love from Sadie.'

The young policeman, who was doing his best to cope with all the hysterical women, watched her lay the flowers. There was something familiar about her. He had never had much time for Danny Foster, a crap player in his opinion, but it would seem that all the women in the world would disagree with him, because right at this moment, it felt to him as if the whole world was here.

"Move along please, when you've laid your flowers, there's a queue behind." He tried to sound pleasant. God, this was a rough job today, watching women have histrionics! This one was pale and calm, not showing any emotion, and as she walked away, he glanced idly at her message. Sadie, that was the woman they were appealing for! No wonder she was familiar, her face had been on the TV today. Not only should he keep an eye on her, he also needed to report this siting. He walked to the side, and spoke into his radio. "I think I've just seen Sadie Morton Brown."

Later, in the police station, Sadie was being questioned by Miles. She was not being co-operative because all she wanted was to go back to Sunita's and be reunited with Danielle. She couldn't see why they were asking her so many questions even if she was the last person to see Danny alive. If he had fallen in the water accidentally, and that is what she believed, then all this talking wasn't going to bring him back.

"When you saw Mr Foster, how did he seem?" asked Miles.

"He was OK, no different from usual." Sadie's tone was sullen. "Look, I need to get home to feed my baby."

Miles looked at her closely. "This is the baby you say that Danny Foster fathered."

"He most certainly did, and if he was alive now we would be together!"

Miles just didn't know what to make of her. He had held off telling her about the tape at the moment, wanting to take one thing at a time. Was she a habitual liar? In which case she probably hadn't murdered her own brother. And had she been rejected by Danny? According to her, no, but her friend had said otherwise.

She was a beautiful young woman, even looking pale and without much make-up he could see it. She was like a younger version of Catherine Zeta Jones. But there was a hardness he could sense about her, and she seemed very streetwise. She could be capable of anything, who knows?

Sadie stared right back at him defiantly. She had forgotten Danny's rejection of her, and really believed that his untimely death had ruined their future together.

"Did you know that Danny couldn't swim?"

"Yes, Alice had told me earlier," said Sadie without thinking.

"I am suggesting to you, that you went to see Danny with your child, and he refused to believe he was the father. You lost your temper, and in a fit of pique, you pushed him in the water, but you didn't know he was going to drown, it backfired on you."

Sadie sprang up, very angry. This guy was getting on her nerves!

"That is absolute rubbish! Danny and I had plans to start a life together, now I want to go!"

"Well, we only have your word on that. I wish to question you about the death of your brother, too. Was that a nasty accident?"

Sadie was not expecting this. It came as a complete shock, but she quickly composed herself.

"Inspector, my brother died over twelve years ago, and yes, it was a tragic accident."

"Is that why you go around boasting that you've killed him then?"

Sadie looked at the impassive face of Miles, wracking her brains trying to think where he could have got that from. She couldn't remember telling anyone other than Sunita about that, but she was sure Sunita wouldn't tell.

"If I did say it, I was only joking. Who told you this?"

Miles ignored the question. "It's a bit of a sick joke, isn't it?"

"Sometimes I say things I don't mean."

"You mean you lie."

Sadie was close to losing her temper, but the reference to Jeremy's death after all these years made her uneasy. "I suppose so," she said sullenly.

Miles got up and pushed his seat back.

"Interview with Sadie Morton Brown terminated at seventeen-thirty." And turning to her he said curtly. "You are being held here pending further inquiries, and to answer further questions."

Sadie snapped. All the emotion of the day had built up inside her. Losing Danny, being parted from her baby, and now being held here against her will. Her mind had not yet registered how serious it might be for her. She just wanted out!

"Let go of me!" she screamed, as two policemen went to lead her away to her cell.

But no one took any notice as Sadie was taken, kicking and screaming, fighting all the way, down to the cells. After the door had closed on her with a bang, she sat sobbing quietly at the injustice of it all. She had lost Danny, and now it appeared that the world had gone mad!

Miles decided to speak to Alice again. She seemed to know a lot. It appeared that Danny Foster was the bone of contention between these two women. It was extraordinary what an effect this man had on people. Women had travelled from miles away to lay flowers at his home. There was a feeling of shocked disbelief at his passing, even the television programs had been rescheduled to show a documentary of his life. It was obvious that these two women had been rivals for his affection. Although from what he'd heard, Danny had a nice comfortable marriage with an adoring wife, so it was up to Miles to find out if it had been suicide, an accident, or murder.

*   *   *   *

250

Later, when she had calmed down, after realising that her behaviour was fruitless, Sadie was allowed one telephone call. She tried to think of who she could trust. She had walked out on Alice, so Sunita was the only one left, and she had Danielle. It had to be Sunita. She must have told someone else about killing Jeremy, because Sunita had known for years, so why would she suddenly tell now? Had she told Alice when she was drunk? She couldn't remember. She had told Alice about trying to burn the flat with Nathan in, but that hadn't been mentioned, yet! What a fool she'd been. For the first time in her life she felt scared. It all seemed to be catching up with her. But, she comforted herself, at least Nathan hadn't died. Alice had said he was around when she went to find out, and the flat was still standing. She had to keep her cool, and just tell them all that she couldn't help imagining things and making up stories; they'd never be able to prove it after all these years.

They had confiscated her mobile phone, much to her annoyance, but she was allowed to use the public phone on the wall in the corridor. It was eight o'clock in the evening, and she knew that by now Sunita would be very worried about her. When Sunita answered she could hear by her voice how fed up she was, and Danielle could be clearly heard screaming in the background. Her heart lurched at the loss of her baby.

"Sunita, I'm being held at the police station. They are questioning me about Danny's death."

Sunita gasped. "They don't think you did it, surely?"

"I haven't got time to talk much, but Sunita, you must help me. Please can you go and see my father, and see if he can pull a few strings to help me? If I'm charged I need a good solicitor, and also money for bail."

Sunita couldn't believe what she was hearing. Sadie had vanished into nowhere five years ago, and now she expected her father to help her just like that! Would he buy it, and did she want to get involved in it all? Most of Sadie's troubles were of her own making, and Sunita didn't want to get involved anymore.

"I can't go and see your father after all this time!"

Sadie could feel desperation creeping over her. This was the only way to go, and Sunita must see that. "You remember when I used to joke about killing my brother to you. You knew it was a made up story."

"Yes, I didn't take it seriously."

Sunita ignored the doubt inside her because if it had been true, it was just too awful to think about!

"Well, the police know about it, and they think I killed Jeremy, and my parents need to know that I made it up. If my father knows I'm being victimised like this he will want to help me."

Sunita sighed to herself. Sadie thought she was being victimised, but what did she expect after lying her way through life? Now was not the time for recriminations, but once again she seemed to be knee deep in Sadie's troubles. The last thing she wanted to do was to visit Sadie's parents; they didn't like Sunita, but this was a desperate situation. Maybe if she told them, and gave them Danielle, after all she was their granddaughter, the ball would be in their court.

"I'll do what I can, but I can't promise anything," she said reluctantly.

Sadie was ready to make a sarcastic remark, but then thought better of it. She must shut her mouth this time because Sunita was all she had left now.

"Please take good care of Danielle for me. I'm going crazy without her. You're the only person in the world I trust with her!" she said emotionally, and Sunita felt that pity for her engulf her once again. Sadie did love her baby, she was her life now Danny had gone. She couldn't just dump her on unwilling grandparents. She weakened.

"OK Sadie, I'll take good care of her."

She hoped it wouldn't cause trouble with Peter, because he must realise that she had no other choice. Sadie was still her friend, and although she had got herself into this trouble, Sunita still didn't believe she had killed Danny, or her brother, she was just a compulsive liar. Maybe if she got help she would stop doing it.

She looked across at Danielle. Peter was giving her a bottle. They had found that she seemed to like him, and didn't protest loudly when he fed her, even though she'd very abruptly been weaned off breast milk in Sadie's absence. Maybe he wouldn't mind too much.

"That was Sadie. She wants me to contact her father, he has plenty of money, and she needs a solicitor."

"That's a bit cheeky. Why you?" said Peter mildly. If the truth was known he was quite enjoying the fact that baby Danielle was quiet when he handled her. He had not done that much when Jasmine was young because Sunita had proved herself to be a very capable mother. That is why it had been a surprise that Danielle, who was only a few weeks old, had given her merry hell today. He had expected to go in the other room to feed her whilst Sunita spoke on the phone, but Danielle had stared straight into his eyes, and held his gaze, and he was convinced he saw her smile.

Sunita saw him sitting with the baby nestling comfortably on his lap, obediently sucking her bottle. She had felt very unsure with Danielle, but here was Peter, making it all look so easy. Well she would certainly need his help when he was around, for the next few days. She did so hope that Philip would help Sadie to get bail, and then she could come and collect her daughter and life could go back to normal again.

Chapter Thirty-four

Philip Morton Brown was thinking about booking a surprise holiday for Isabel. He was debating whether to book a nice quiet hotel somewhere, or a cruise. Isabel was very precious to him because they had been through so much together. They had lost their only son, then Sadie had vanished into thin air so they never knew whether she was alive or dead.

He had long since ceased to fret for Sadie. The day he had decided to pay her a visit had been quite an eye-opener for him as to her character, and hurtful though it had been, he had finally admitted to himself that his daughter was a bad person.

He had arrived at the flat, and as soon as he stepped through the door, he smelt the fire. Luckily it had only just started, and he had managed to put it out with a bowl of cold water, but not before he smelt the petrol, and realised just what Sadie had tried to do.

The shock of it had sobered up Nathan, and the truth came out. He had been using this flat as a base, and in return he had got Sadie a forged passport and a new identity. He was very angry that Sadie had attempted to kill him, and wanted to go to the police. The only thing that stopped him was his past life. He had dabbled in drugs and petty crime, and was known to the police.

Philip saw a way of helping him financially. It wasn't blackmail, in Philip's eyes it was compensation for what Sadie had done. As evil as she was, he still felt the need to stop the police from being involved. Deep down inside him he still loved his daughter, but he hated what she had become, and wondered if he had spoiled her too much as a child.

So Nathan stayed on at the flat, and Philip encouraged him to go and get counselling for his drug and drink addiction. His plan was for Nathan to get clean, and then he would send him on his way with some money to help him get started in life. What neither Philip nor Isabel had reckoned on, was how fond they would get of Nathan, and how proud they would feel of him after two years of trying to get clean and succeeding. Nathan was the son they had lost. He went to college and learned new computer skills, then found himself a very well paid job and a nice respectable girlfriend. He turned away from the sleazy life he had led, and they trusted and respected him. Nathan was now very much a part of their life.

Philip couldn't help comparing Nathan with Sadie. He had suffered a terrible start in life, and it was no wonder he had gone off the rails. His mother had been a drug addict who died when he was two, and he didn't know who his father was. He had spent most of his young life being pushed from one children's home to another, and grew up feeling tough enough to survive in his own way, but without any family bonds at all. Philip and Isabel had supported Nathan, financially and emotionally, and emotion was something he had never experienced before. But knowing that someone cared and believed in him had brought out the good determined character that lay buried deep inside Nathan. The young man who had nothing now felt as if he had everything because they cared about him.

Sadie, on the other hand, had been showered with love and advantages ever since she had been born. But Philip realised there was something inside Sadie's character that made her bad. She didn't want him now, and she had never wanted her mother, so it was for the best that she had gone. He knew he had to get on with life, so it had been good for both Philip and Isabel to have Nathan to fill it. They had even gone as far as to make Nathan the beneficiary to their estate when they died. As far as they were concerned, Sadie was dead. She had gone away and they never expected her to return.

Philip picked up the telephone in the office. He would book the cruise, that is what Isabel would prefer. If he did it now whilst she was out shopping with Tracy, helping her choose a dress for the dinner dance that Nathan's company had arranged, it would be a nice surprise for her when she returned.

He turned to switch the radio off so he could hear, but not before he heard the police appeal.

"We are appealing for Sadie Morton Brown to come forward to help us with the investigations into the death of Danny Foster."

Philip stood transfixed, fear and revulsion coursed through his insides. They weren't free of her. She was still their daughter! Whatever had Sadie done now?

Sunita rang as she had promised Sadie she would, but didn't feel very hopeful on her behalf. To her relief, it was Philip who answered. He was easier to talk to than Isabel.

"It's Sunita here, Mr Morton Brown. I wonder if I can come and talk to you about Sadie. I'm sure you've heard about Danny Foster's death, but she didn't do it!"

She had spoken quickly, hoping he wouldn't put the phone down on her. She really wanted to help Sadie if she could. Philip digested her words.

"Sunita, have you seen Sadie? I hear the police are looking for her," he said grimly, trying to ignore the emotional pain that ripped at his insides. Sadie, his child, could still affect him after five years.

"She was with me yesterday, but she gave herself up to the police today." Sunita knew that wasn't quite right, but she hoped it might get Philip onside.

"Well, I don't really want to discuss this on the phone. You'd better come over and speak with myself and my wife."

After arranging to come the next day, Sunita rang off. Philip had told her to come by taxi and he would pay. That meant Peter could stay with the children as he was not at work, but should she take Danielle? After all, she was their granddaughter. The only problem with that was whether, because she was such a demanding and fussy baby, she would be able to talk to them properly? She decided to take the easy way out and leave her with Peter. She didn't scream when he held her. She would tell them about the baby, and if they agreed to raise bail for Sadie, then she would probably stay there with Danielle when she was released. It all sounded quite easy, but nevertheless, Sunita had misgivings.

Philip also had misgivings. Isabel was not happy that Sunita was coming to see them. She had found it easier to switch off her feelings for Sadie when she disappeared. She had tried to love her daughter, but Sadie had rebuffed her so many times. She acted as if she hated her mother, and Isabel's hurt had turned to indifference, and when she finally vanished, relief. Now she was back, and not content with trying to kill Nathan, she had turned her sights to the biggest celebrity ever, Danny Foster. Isabel couldn't help thinking the worst about her, Sadie was bad through and through, and she couldn't see why Philip would even contemplate helping her.

Sunita duly arrived by taxi at eleven o'clock the next day, which was Saturday. She had been dreading this visit, and was not surprised to be greeted by a hostile Isabel, and an uneasy but polite, Philip. She sat in the grand drawing room, with its pink velvet brocade curtains and lush fitted carpet, nothing but the best here, she thought wistfully. The housekeeper served them coffee and biscuits, and Sunita tried to sit regally on her chair and sip it elegantly. The cups were white bone china with a gold edging, no mugs to be seen. This was how the rich lived.

"How did Sadie come to be involved with Danny Foster?" asked Philip, his curiosity getting the better of him.

"She went to Spain and met him there. They had an affair, and a few weeks ago she had his baby."

"There's a baby?" asked Isabel in disbelief.

"Yes, according to Sadie they were going to make a life together, so why would she kill him? She was absolutely heartbroken when she heard that he was dead."

"Sadie heartbroken?" questioned Isabel. Sadie didn't do feelings, well only for Philip.

Philip was weakening, and he knew it. "Well, the least we can do is get her a good lawyer, then the law will take its course. What about the baby?"

"She's with me at the moment. Her name is Danielle. She is missing Sadie. She cries a lot, so it will be good when they're reunited."

"You should have brought her this morning," said Philip. Memories of Sadie's childhood came flooding back to him, even though he hadn't meant them to.

"Well, she is unsettled at the moment, and I thought it might be difficult to talk to you," Sunita explained apologetically. "My husband is looking after her. She seems to like him and doesn't cry when he holds her."

m

This was all sounding very familiar to Isabel, and she didn't like what she heard. It sounded like history was repeating itself. Maybe they should fix up a good defence for Sadie, and then when her innocence was proved, if indeed she was innocent, she could take off again with her baby. Isabel had long given up trying to understand her, but she knew that Sadie would only use them for her own convenience, and then go without a backward glance, and this time she could take it, because she now expected nothing less from her. Sadie was lucky they had kept quiet about her attempt to kill Nathan, and he, too, had laid his feelings of anger aside because he was a decent man. She'd got away with that one, and sometimes fate pays you back in other ways. Well, if she was innocent this time, they would help her to prove it, not that she deserved it! She damned herself for these feelings of weakness, because that's what Isabel believed they were. But no matter how she tried to harden her heart, she couldn't forget that she had once given birth to Sadie, she was her mother, and so she had to help.

"OK, you can tell Sadie we'll arrange a good lawyer, and you, Philip, need to get the wheels in motion!"

"Yes, I will." Philip looked at her gratefully. Underneath all that tough exterior, Isabel did have a heart. He knew it, but Sadie had almost destroyed her mother's feelings. She was a very lucky girl that her mother still showed her loyalty, because she certainly didn't deserve it!

Miles decided after lengthy questioning of both Alice and Sadie, that Sadie probably had killed Danny Foster. She hadn't helped herself whilst in custody, having frequent displays of temper. She didn't like being told what to do, and she raged around in her cell, then she wept tears of frustration at being parted from her baby. He could see how unstable she was, and thought it more than likely she had killed Danny in one of her rages.

The evidence was mainly based on the fact that she admitted seeing him that night, and appeared to be the last person to do so. In view of that he decided to charge her. Although the evidence was flimsy he'd done his bit, and it was up to a jury to prove whether she had done it or not.

The public were still going crazy, and all the newspapers were full of stories. No one knew much about Danny's affair with

Sadie, it had been a well kept secret, but the fact there was a love child had leaked out, so there were lots of speculative stories going about. No one actually believed that Danny would have left Eleanor and his glamorous life to be with this nobody. The public hated Sadie. Some stories suggested she had lied about her affair, it had never happened. She had killed Danny because he wouldn't succumb to her. If she ever left prison she would probably face a lynch mob of women, feeling was that strong. They were not going to allow Danny's memory to be smeared with this. He was revered, an icon and a god, to them.

Her hearing at the local court was set for the next week. He wasn't convinced when she was charged, that she had taken it in fully. She seemed to have retreated within herself, and he actually wondered if she was sane. Well, there would be plenty of doctors and psychiatrists checking her before the trial.

Alice was pleased that Sadie had finally been charged. She had now been moved to another prison, pending the court hearing for next week. No doubt she would get out on bail, so before that happened, she would visit her. Alice had one last score to settle.

Sadie had been plunged into a deep depression after the loss of her baby. She had shut herself off from what was happening, she didn't care any more. Being shut in a cell was the worst thing that could happen to her. She had always enjoyed her freedom and liked moving from place to place. As far as she was concerned they could do what they liked. She had lost Danny and Danielle in quick succession, and there wasn't really anything left for her any more.

She heard the key in the cell door, and the burly figure of her female warden entered. What did they want her for now? She curled up dejectedly on her bed. She hoped it wasn't food again, she didn't want to eat.

"Visitor for you Morton Brown, Alice Lorenzo."

She had hoped it might be her father. Sunita had written to say that she had visited her parents, and they were going to help. If only she could get out of this place. The whole world had gone mad, she was the only sane one left. They all thought she had killed Danny. As if she would kill the father of her child, the man she loved! They were all crazy!

Alice's name registered in her mind. Alice had been a link with Danny. She allowed herself to respond to the warden's terse tones. "Yes, I will see her."

She was escorted out of her cell, and into the large room where all the prisoners saw their visitors. Alice was seated by a small table, and Sadie sat on the chair which had been put the other side. She gave Alice a glimmer of a smile, and asked. "Have you heard from my parents? They are getting me a solicitor."

So prison hadn't changed Sadie, thought Alice scornfully. No thanks for coming, all about herself as usual. But when she heard what Alice had to say, she wouldn't be thanking her. She ignored the fact that Sadie looked very pale and had obviously lost weight. She was being as hard as Sadie had been.

"Your parents now know that you said you killed your brother, so don't rely on them to help you any more."

Sadie came back to reality. Alice was gloating, she felt her hatred of her rise. Her spirit was not totally broken. "So I've got you to thank for that, no doubt!" she spat at her.

Alice was pleased. This was going well, so now for the bombshell.

"Oh yes, you've got me to thank. You Sadie, will be convicted of killing Danny, and it's no more than you deserve!"

"But I didn't do it!" Sadie's voice was getting louder, and the duty warden gave her a warning glance. She tried desperately to compose herself.

"It doesn't matter whether you did it or not, because you have killed, and at last it's all caught up with you. Sadie, you killed my twin sister, as surely as if you'd plunged a knife into her!"

Sadie looked at her pityingly. Here was another person gone crazy. Where could she go to escape it all? "I don't even know your sister."

"Yes you do!" Alice's eyes glittered with rage, but she kept her voice low and quiet so only Sadie could hear. "My twin sister Sarah was Jeremy's nanny, the nanny you testified against, the one you said was neglecting him. He didn't fall in the water, by your own admission, you pushed him in!"

Now it all made sense to Sadie; why Alice had seemed to be familiar. They were not identical twins, only similar, but why had Sarah died? She didn't understand. She tried to be bold.

"She was neglecting him, she was on her phone."

"She was a few yards away, and Jeremy never went near the water. He was frightened of it. How dare you criticise her when you were so evil that you killed your own brother!"

Sadie brushed her words away. All this was old news. "Why is Sarah dead?"

"Well, Sadie, that's down to you. She never recovered from the humiliation. She committed suicide. You killed her as well as your brother. You aren't fit to live. I hope they lock you away for ever, and throw away the key!"

Alice threw her a look of contempt, having said her piece, and got up to walk away. But as she did, it hit Sadie in a blinding flash. She had been duped. Alice had never been her friend. She had thought she was using Alice to further her own ends, but Alice had planned it all, particularly the affair with Danny, and now she was in it right up to her neck, and this bitch was just going to walk away and leave her!

The rage that swept through her was just impossible to control, she could feel the heat of it coursing through her veins, and there was nothing she could do to stop her hands from gripping Alice by the throat. Sadie had finally snapped. She snarled, "I'll kill you, you bitch!" and Alice gasped as her iron grip threatened to squeeze the last breath out of her.

But Sadie didn't get away with it this time. Within seconds there were people pulling her away, and Alice watched with satisfaction as she was taken kicking and screaming, back to her cell.

"Are you OK? Do you want to make a complaint?" asked the burly, but sympathetic warden.

"Maybe," said Alice. "But as you can see, she's barking mad and very dangerous."

She dusted herself down and rubbed her neck. It had been a bit scary for a minute, but her work was done now. She left the prison without looking back. Now she could get on with the rest of her life.

Chapter Thirty-five

One year later:

After various tests and examinations by three different psychiatrists, Sadie was found to be clinically depressed and also insane. She could have treatment for the depression, but her insanity was another matter. She was deemed not fit to stand trial, so a question mark hung over Danny's death. This was very interesting to the media, and various stories were banded around as to whether Danny had finished it all because his career was ending, or whether in fact it had been a dreadful accident. The third possibility was that Sadie could have done it, but no one knew for sure, so the death of Danny Foster, football icon, would go down in history as one of the most fascinating unsolved mysteries.

Sadie had been moved to a secure unit, and initially, because of her volatile temper, was in solitary confinement. She seemed to be in a world of her own, rarely speaking to her wardens, and even the various doctors and psychiatrists were convinced that she had now totally lost her mind. She didn't seem to know what day it was, or even who she was. She never asked about her family, or her baby. She was wrapped up in her innermost thoughts, but she still had to be handled with care because the slightest thing could trigger her temper, which was terrifying to see.

Philip and Isabel felt a small measure of relief that Sadie had been pronounced insane. She was not accountable for her actions, she was not responsible, so in their eyes she couldn't help it. It was something to cling to, she had been evil and bad because she was ill, but she couldn't be cured, so she would have to spend her life locked away. It was no different really than when she had gone abroad, only the knowledge that they would never see her again.

Philip had tried to pluck up the courage to visit her. He intended to ask her if she really had killed Jeremy, but in the end he decided not to. He didn't really want to know. It might have been one of her outrageous imaginings, and that is really what he wanted to believe. He didn't talk about her to Isabel any more, it was all too painful, so they did their best to get on with life, knowing that Sadie was in the best place possible for her problems.

As far as Danielle was concerned, Philip and Isabel had stepped in to stop her being taken into care. Nothing could alter the fact that she was their granddaughter, and being so suddenly deprived of her mother had been most traumatic for her. Sadie had no say in the matter because she had lost her mind, but although they wanted to keep Danielle and bring her up themselves, they were both well aware of the fact that being over fifty, it would be a hard thing to do.

Philip came up with the idea of a live-in nanny. Danielle could grow up in their home with a young and lively person to care for her, there was no shortage of money, and she would lead a full and happy life. That was the only thing left that they could do for Sadie, and in some measure, it made them feel a little better about the whole distressing situation. They had written to her to tell her about this idea, but had not received a reply, so it just seemed like Sadie didn't really care any more.

Alice had found that her career was failing miserably now. It seemed that the public were getting tired of her. She had made her name by sleeping with Danny, and telling her story, but since his untimely death, the public were more interested in the circumstances of his death.

She had not been offered work for over six months now. Magazines no longer wanted to do spreads on her, and she was in debt. She couldn't really afford her flat any more, as she had got it when her acting career had seemed to take off. It was very expensive to live there, and she'd never got as far as buying. It was ridiculous, at the age of thirty, to go back and live with her parents, but if she couldn't come up with an idea soon, then that is what would have to happen.

She was glad to finally be free of Sadie, and felt no compassion for her, but Danielle was another matter. Alice had loved Danielle in her own way. She was Danny's child. She chose to ignore that she was also Sadie's child too. On the few occasions that Sadie had allowed her to hold the baby, Alice had felt a bond, which surprised her, because until then she had never thought of herself as maternal. She had toyed with the idea of visiting Sunita to see if she would hand over Danielle, but she had forgotten about Philip and Isabel. They wanted their grand-daughter. So she resigned herself to the fact that they were decent people and would give her a good life. Well, she thought she had, until she saw they were advertising for a nanny to live in.

The more she thought it over, the more she liked the idea. They would know her face because of being in the paper so much, and the name Alice Lorenzo was infamous now. They would know she was Sadie's friend, but they wouldn't know that Sarah had been her twin. All she needed to do was to convince them that she loved Danielle, and only had her best interests at heart, then the job would be hers, but she needed to act quickly, before anyone else got in first.

She rang up, without mentioning the nanny position, and spoke to Isabel.

"Mrs Morton Brown, it's Alice Lorenzo here, Sadie's close friend. I just telephoned to ask how little Danielle is. I became very fond of her. As you probably know, Sadie was staying with me during her pregnancy, and I took her to hospital when she went into labour."

This was all new to Isabel. She only knew about Sunita.

"No, we never spoke to Sadie before she was arrested, only Sunita, but you are her friend from Spain?"

She did remember some of it. Alice Lorenzo was Danny's previous alleged lover, and his ex PA. She was a bit of a character, but if she cared about Danielle she wasn't that bad maybe.

"Well, she's obviously missing her mother, but we hope that time will heal. That's all I can say."

"If it's any help to you, I used to find when she cried a lot, if I sang to her she was much better. Not that I can sing, but Danielle seemed to like it."

Isabel laughed politely with Alice, and she found herself warming to her. The last two weeks had been hell. Like her mother, only Philip could soothe Danielle, and the sooner they could find a nanny, the better. Both her and Philip were getting too old for all this stress!

"Would you like to come over and visit Danielle?" she suddenly found herself saying. It was nice that someone cared. Most families wouldn't have survived what herself and Philip had been through in the last eleven years or more. Her heart still lurched when she thought of her baby Jeremy, and now Sadie was mad. Whatever had they done to deserve all this? But then she reminded herself of what kept them going. There was Nathan, and they had another chance with Danielle, a chance to right the wrongs her mother had done. Isabel no longer felt bitter towards Sadie, only sad that her daughter was mad.

"Yes, I'd love to come and see her!" said Alice. The words came straight from her heart. She was determined to prove to them that even without a previous job caring for children, she could cope with Danielle. Danielle had Danny inside her, and glad as she was that he couldn't hurt her any more, his child was special. Alice intended to be around while Danielle was growing up. She would make herself indispensable, they wouldn't be able to manage without her. Sadie's parents wouldn't live for ever, and in her mind, she would be the obvious choice to bring up Danielle. Maybe she could carry on living in the house with Danielle after they'd gone. In fact, if she played her cards right, they might even leave it to her, because who else was there? Sadie would never need it. She smiled confidently to herself as she put the phone down, because, as yet, she knew nothing about their closeness to Nathan.

Ricky Scott walked nervously into the secure unit, hoping and praying that Sadie would see him. It was over four years since Sadie had left him, and his life had never been the same. Because of the huge payout he'd been obliged to give her, money became tight, and he had to choose between getting a second mortgage, and working all hours to cover it, or moving into a smaller house.

265

He had opted for the second mortgage, knowing that this house was just right for the girls, and their welfare and stability was always his main concern. Today he tried to put behind him his feelings of regret that he had ever met Marina, or Sadie as he had now found out she was. Being hostile to her would not achieve anything. She had turned their lives upside down, and the girls, especially Brenda, still bore the scars. But he was proud of his girls. They had experienced things in their short lives that no children should have to, and they had learned that life could be very tough, but they had coped.

It had taken him all this time to track her down. He had never seen baby Ricky, only a photograph when he was a tiny baby, but he would be over three years old now, and he wanted custody of him. Sadie was proved to be unfit, so if he could find out who was taking care of him, he would go and see them. If he could bring up all his children together, at least some good would have come out of this mess.

He was shown into a room which looked like a padded cell. There were two minders in there, and when Sadie entered, she was flanked by two more. He was shocked when he saw her. Although only about twenty-five now, her once beautiful skin looked leathery; she had lost a lot of weight, and was thin and gaunt. Only her eyes remained the same, huge and staring like a woman possessed. He felt a shudder go through him.

"How ya doing?" he asked politely, but she stared blankly at him, not appearing to know him at all.

He drew a deep breath. He couldn't help pitying her. This broken woman had no resemblance to the person he remembered.

"Sadie, I'm Ricky, we were married, do you remember? Who's got baby Ricky? Please tell me," he begged. Surely if there was any good in this woman she would tell him that. He had been deprived of his son for such a long time, and his heart ached at the thought of it.

Sadie looked back at him without any emotion. Baby Ricky was a distant memory, a child she had never loved, and couldn't wait to get rid of. Danielle was the baby she had loved, and they had taken her away. She had lost her baby, why should she care about him? She used her perceived madness to escape from the situation. It was so easy because they were all mad, and she was the only sane one. Turning to one of her companions she said,

266

"I don't know this man, or the baby he's talking about. I want to go back to my cell."

Denise felt a glimmer of sympathy for her. The last thing this poor cow needed was someone to come in talking about babies. Losing hers had contributed to Sadie losing her mind, so the best thing was to get her back to her room before she started throwing a wobbly.

After Sadie had gone she tried to explain to him how Sadie had withdrawn inside herself after losing her baby. "She's given up on life. We have to watch her all the time. She has a baby daughter, now a year old, that lives with her parents."

"Well that's her second child, she had a boy after she split up with me in America," said Ricky, fear now creeping over him. What had happened to baby Ricky? After all, his mother was completely mad!

"I can't help you with that. She's never mentioned it," said Denise dismissively. This was getting more complicated by the minute. Sadie Morton Brown had led quite a life.

Ricky could see he was not making progress here, so he left, but his driving force was to track down his son. He would carry on searching until he found him. He would never rest until his family was complete. His heart lurched as he thought of the worst thing possible. If she had murdered him, he needed to know, because until he did, he could not move on.

Sadie sat in her room. Tonight she would eat to celebrate her victory. Denise, her burly blonde gaoler, was falling for her, she could tell, and once she had got her onside she would be laughing. Sadie's power had not diminished. She was invincible! Denise didn't know it yet, but she would help her to escape. Sadie needed to escape because everyone in here was mad. She needed to get back in the real world.

At the moment it suited her to pretend she was mad, but she knew exactly what she was doing. When she got out of here the first thing she would do would be to hunt down that evil Alice who had made a fool of her. By all accounts she lived with her parents now, and had taken over the care of Danielle. Sadie gleefully pictured her own hands choking that bitch to death, and if her parents tried to interfere, they would die too, they were nothing to her.

267

Then she would take Danielle and start a new life. She would find another Danny. She was over him now, and by all accounts, so was Eleanor, she had taken her children to live in America, and now had a new husband. Sadie had read the newspapers, because there wasn't much else to do in here. She had thought that Danny was the love of her life, but when she looked back now, she realised just what trouble he had caused. He had turned Alice's mind, so she had tricked her, and she wouldn't mind betting that Alice had killed him. She'd tried to tell them that Alice was mad, that she was dangerous to have the care of her child, but no one took any notice. Well, once she got out of here, they'd all take notice. It just seemed to Sadie, that she was needed to put things right.

Denise entered with a tray of chicken and rice. "Thanks so much. I do feel hungry," said Sadie flashing her a smile.

"Good, well eat up," said Denise in a motherly fashion. They were making progress at last. She was starting to eat. If the girl put some weight on, her gauntness would go, and she would regain her looks. Denise remembered how attractive she'd been when she first arrived, very much like Catherine Zeta Jones. The poor soul might be mad, but at least she might have some sort of life in here. She smiled back at her, and then left the room so she could eat her supper in peace.

Sadie decided her food protest was now at an end. After all, she needed to be strong to escape. She could feel her power returning, and it wouldn't be long before Denise was putty in her hands. She finished eating and then stretched out on her narrow bed, and went peacefully off to sleep.